DARKENERGY

Origins
of Myth

STEEL CITY SERIES: BOOK 2

N.J. COLESAR

entanglement
interactive.

ISBN-13: 978-0-9989280-2-9
Hardcover: 978-0-9989280-7-4
eBook: 978-0-9989280-3-6

This book is a work of fiction. Names, characters, businesses, organizations, places, events and incidents either are the product of the author's imagination or are used fictitiously. Any resemblance to actual persons, living or dead, events, or locales is entirely coincidental. Some locations described within the story are real places. Certain details may have been altered to better support the story.

Author: N. J. Colesar
Cover Art: Vanette Kosman

Publisher: Entanglement Interactive LLC

For information visit:
www.ENTANGLEMENT-INTERACTIVE.com

10   9   8   7   6   5   4   3   2   1

STEEL CITY SERIES

THE SHEARING
ORIGINS OF MYTH
BIRTH OF LEGENDS

To my beautiful wife, Cate:
For enduring countless hours of listening to my stupid ideas
and still supporting me every step of the way.

CONTENTS

PROLOGUE

Dr. Francis Burkhalter couldn't tell how much time had passed. Had it been hours? Days? Weeks?

The elderly physicist coughed and stumbled down the crumbling, smoke filled passage of the upgraded Large Hadron Collider as eerie lights pulsed in the distance until he came to a wall covered with a myriad of computer screens.

Most of the displays were either broken or showed nothing but static, however, there were a few that still operated. One such screen displayed the security feed from the front gate of the facility, nearly 175 meters above him on the surface.

At first glance, everything looked normal. But as he watched, Francis noticed that something was strange about the image. It was as if everything was... vibrating?

Francis leaned closer to get a better look. Yes. Everything did appear to be vibrating, and not just that, he realized suddenly, but the clouds were moving remarkably fast.

The sun unexpectedly appeared at the top of the screen and began a rapid descent. Within minutes, the sun had set, the screen grew dark and night fell outside.

Francis stared at the screen in disbelief and an abrupt, nauseous feeling welled up inside him as realization hit. It had only taken minutes for what appeared to be a full day to pass outside! Time must be distorted here in the remains of the Large Hadron Collider. Francis had already witnessed what he believed to be tears in the fabric of reality, and now time itself was being distorted! He must find a way to shut down the collider before there was a catastrophic meltdown that may, at the very least, destroy nearly 30 kilometers of countryside, or at the worst, create a black hole that would rip the Earth apart.

There was a secondary control room a little further down the tunnel. Francis hoped that he would be able to reach it and that it was still intact. The ruptures in reality (or whatever they were; Francis would need more data before he could accurately quantify the anomaly) were growing rapidly with new ones forming at an alarming rate.

The old physicist watched for another moment as a second day flashed by before he finally abandoned the displays and stumbled down the quaking tunnel.

Rubble rained down with every tremor, littering the cracked floor with even more debris. Smoke filled the air as sirens rang in the distance, but Francis didn't see another living soul and suddenly felt terribly alone.

Halfway to the control room, he spied a white shape amidst a pile of rubble. He rushed over and discovered the body of Dr. Matthew Jones. The promising physicist's head was cracked open like an egg from a large section of concrete that had broken off the ceiling. His quick wit would be sorely missed.

Francis was filled with grief, but he roughly pushed the feelings away. There would be time enough for sadness if he managed to avert the coming catastrophe. He stood and strode through the smoke and noise, more determined than ever.

When he finally reached the second control room, his heart sank. The doorway had partially collapsed and the heavy doors were pinned shut by the debris.

Dr. Francis may be old, but he was not about to let a few lumps of inorganic matter keep him from saving the world. He rolled up his dirty white sleeves and began dragging chunks of concrete and stone out of his way.

It was quite possibly the most physical work that Francis had done in the past several decades, but he threw himself into it with stubborn determination.

Sweat poured off the elderly physicist as he struggled to move the heavy debris away from the doors.

It seemed to take an eternity, but eventually Francis managed to create just enough space for him to pry one of the doors open and worm his way through.

Francis collapsed, breathless, inside the control room.

"Dr. Burkhalter?" a nervous voice squeaked.

Francis's eyes popped open and he scrambled to his feet as quickly as his old bones would let him. "Who's there?" he asked, as he scanned the room for the speaker.

This control room wasn't nearly as large as the first and it didn't take long to spot the figure huddled behind a pile of rubble in the far corner.

"Ms. Worland, is that you?" Francis asked in astonishment.

"Yes, Doctor," a terrified and filthy Alicia Worland answered.

"Thank goodness you're alive!" Francis beamed, overjoyed to have discovered another survivor. "Come out here and let me have a look at you. Are you hurt?" the old physicist asked gently.

"No… I'm fine," Alicia answered as she slowly extracted herself from the concrete pile and carefully picked her way through the control room.

"Wonderful!" Francis was relieved to find the young woman alive and well. The loss of such a promising mind would be a true tragedy. "But what were you doing in here, my dear?" Francis asked.

"When the main control panel exploded, I knew there was another emergency off switch in here," Alicia answered. "So, I came to try and turn it off."

Dr. Francis looked confused. "Why didn't you? The collider is still drawing power."

"I tried," Alicia moaned, "but it won't work."

Francis's heart sank at the grave news as Alicia sobbed. "And then the doorway collapsed and I was trapped in here."

"Don't worry my dear." Francis tried to sound positive, but he wasn't sure it came off that way. "We will get it shut down together."

"But the switch doesn't work," Alicia despaired. "I tried everything."

Then Francis had an idea. "Not everything." His eyes twinkled. "There is a secondary override command that requires two people to access simultaneously," Francis explained excitedly. "We can do it together!"

Alicia's sniffling stopped and she stood a little straighter. "Tell me what I need to do."

"Sign-in to one of these functioning work stations," Dr. Francis ordered as he found one for himself. The screen flickered to life at his touch and what he saw unnerved him.

"Oh dear…" he breathed, as streams of data flew by.

"Dr. Burkhalter?" Alicia asked nervously, as she activated her own station. Her screen flicked to life and the same data were displayed before her. "Oh my!" she gasped. "Dr. Burkhalter, are you seeing this?"

"Indeed I am," Francis breathed in awe.

Most of the collider's particle detectors had overloaded and stopped functioning altogether due to the massive spike in power, but miraculously one of them was still working. ATLAS was the Large Hadron Collider's largest particle detector and it was not just working, but exceeding their highest expectations.

The data flowing out of ATLAS was staggering. The detector always logged mass quantities of information, but due to its programming, it only showed those small pieces that would be of interest to scientists. Even so, ATLAS was displaying a fountain of data on its primary objective, the detection of dark matter.

The old physicist couldn't believe what he was seeing. The light from the monitor reflected off his glasses as he stared in wonder at the information on the display before him.

His whole life, Francis had dreamed of making a world-changing scientific discovery, and now he had done it. With the newly upgraded Large Hadron Collider breaking apart around him and nearly all the other scientists either dead or missing, Dr. Francis Burkhalter made the discovery of a lifetime.

If what ATLAS was displaying was correct, and Francis had no reason to doubt the machine that had been built for this very purpose, then he was looking at the first actual proof that the theoretical material known as dark matter actually existed. And if the data could be believed, that wasn't the only thing ATLAS was picking up.

The old physicist's heart nearly stopped.

"We found it..." he whispered in awe. "We actually found dark energy."

"Um... Doctor?" Alicia said nervously from her front console. "The levels are still climbing... we need to do something!"

"What?" Francis asked distractedly. "Oh, yes! Goodness gravy!" The elderly physicist briefly typed away on his keyboard and a new window appeared. "Here we are." The screen displayed a complicated-looking shutdown sequence. "Follow the instructions and at the end we must do the final sequence together."

Alicia nodded her understanding and began working. Francis did likewise and a few minutes later Alicia turned around. "Ready when you are," she announced.

"Very good," Francis said. "Now, on my mark, confirm."

Francis took a deep breath. This program was a total shutdown, only to be used in the direst emergency. But if this didn't count as an emergency, then he didn't know what would.

"3...2..." Francis counted down. "1...Mark!"

Together, Dr. Francis and Alicia confirmed the shutdown protocol.

Nothing happened.

"It didn't work!" Alicia cried with despair.

"Not to worry." Francis began rapidly typing. "There must be a system blocking the order..."

The ground heaved violently and sent Francis, Alicia, and several computers crashing to the ground. The doorway collapsed further, effectively trapping them inside. The compound shook for several more moments, but eventually the quakes subsided. When they did, Francis and Alicia slowly climbed to their feet.

Alicia gasped and pointed to the corner of the room.

There, twisting in the air and crackling with power, was a churning vortex that expanded to reach from floor to ceiling. Francis noticed that this anomaly was different from the others he had seen. Where the first ones appeared with fraying edges, this one was a more uniform oval with a clearly defined edge.

The surface of the anomaly quivered like ripples over water. Suddenly, three dark figures stepped out of the shimmering anomaly and into the control room.

They were each covered in dark green robes with their cowls pulled up. Elaborate masks depicting various reptiles hid their faces and ornate gloves concealed their hands.

Francis was rooted in place, frozen in shock at the sudden arrival through what he now knew to be some kind of portal. That seemed to confirm his earlier suspicions that the other anomalies were tears in space-time.

The portal abruptly collapsed in on itself and winked out.

One of the robed figures spoke from behind his dragon mask with a surprisingly deep voice and a strange accent. "We come to repair the Veil and return Order to this world."

Francis didn't understand what "Veil" they were talking about, or how restoring order would benefit them right now, but he knew that whatever was happening here was beyond his realm of experience. These new arrivals seemed to know what was going on, and if they could keep the collider from going critical then he was willing to take their aid.

"My name is Dr. Francis Burkhalter," he replied, "and I would love some help."

The dragon-masked figure, whom Francis took for the leader, stepped forward. "Greetings, Dr. Francis Burkhalter. I am Kadir el Ular of the Zahhāfa, Chief Priest of Ma'at and Protector of the Barzakh."

"Well, that's quite a mouthful," Francis noted, "and I have no idea what any of that means, but I don't really care either. All I know is that this compound is being torn apart and we can't stop it," Francis admitted desperately. "We don't have much time."

"Then we must make haste," Kadir hissed. "The Veil frays more every moment, so we have no time to waste. Both of our worlds are in peril."

"Both worlds?" Alicia looked confused, but Francis was not really surprised. The possibility of discovering alternate worlds was one of the main reasons he had joined the collider program in the first place.

"I would love to show you the way," Francis said as he pointed to the crushed doorway, "but as you can see, our only way out is blocked."

Kadir and his two followers glided across the room and stopped before the blocked door. Kadir raised a gloved hand and spoke a word that Francis didn't recognize.

A wave of force erupted from Kadir's outstretched hand and blasted the rubble-covered door. The power of the explosion flung the rubble and the door down the hallway.

Now, that was something the elderly physicist had not expected. He couldn't explain it, but Francis knew there was a perfectly logical explanation for what he had just seen.

Kadir, in his dragon mask, turned back and motioned down the hall. "After you."

PART I

CHAPTER 1

IT WAS A BEAUTIFUL DAY IN PENNSYLVANIA. Birds sang as a warm summer breeze blew through the rolling hills and rustled the bright, green leaves on the trees. Nestled into those hills, next to a slow-moving river, sat the small town of Clearfield.

A gleaming new wall, made of large, heavy stones expertly cut and placed seamlessly together ringed the town; but, the pristine view was marred by countless burned and damaged buildings.

A few short months ago, the town had been attacked by hordes of monsters. Orcs, goblins and other horrible creatures had swarmed the streets. But enemies had not been the only things to appear.

Dwarves had come to their aid, and together they had repelled the monsters and secured the town. Some people even discovered they had amazing powers and could actually use magic. Those powerful people, along with the Army and the desperate citizens, were barely able to stem the tide of monsters.

Since that first battle with the orcs, Clearfield had become a beehive of activity. The dwarves took it upon themselves to fortify the town and they began doing what dwarves do best - mine and build… and drink. Veins of ore and stone were discovered in the hills around the town where no such deposits had existed previously. Not questioning their good fortune, the humans and dwarves began mining as fast as they could. In no time, they had tunnels wormed all through the hills and piles of ore and stone ready for use.

But a month after the victory, the first new crisis appeared – food!

With no supplies reaching the town anymore, the people were forced to find their own. There were many farms around, but not enough to feed the whole population. So, as the dwarves built their walls and towers, the humans cleared away ruined buildings.

This land, once cleared of lumber, was then plowed and converted into farmland. The farms, while operating, would not produce any crops for some time, but luckily hunting was plentiful and there was no shortage of meat.

The dwarves' construction of the wall surrounding the majority of town on the east side of the river was progressing remarkably quickly. Large gatehouses arose from the thick walls to protect the bridges, while even larger gatehouses guarded the roads north, south, and east. Most of the walls were completed with just the finishing touches still being done.

What was taking far longer were the protective runes that the dwarves insisted be placed on each gatehouse and along the entire length of the wall. The dwarves only had a few journeymen Runesmiths with them since they had believed they would only be needed to repair armor and weapons while on campaign; but since being pulled to Earth, they were forced to do far more.

An immense foundation for some kind of building was being laid on the top of the hill in the center of town, but the dwarves were being very secretive about the project and nobody knew exactly what they were building up there.

Clearfield was not the only place being fortified, though.

The Shawville Generating Station was also experiencing renovations. A strong wall now ringed the entire facility and the dwarves were converting part of the plant into a massive forge to better build and repair their tools and weapons.

Solar panels that were discovered in an abandoned tractor-trailer were hastily installed on the most important structures. Windmills and waterwheels were also constructed and installed all over Clearfield to supply power should the power plant be attacked yet again.

After the battle, the remaining monsters had been driven out and hunted down. The small, single-runway airport was reclaimed and the few pilots in town flew scouting missions from their small propeller aircraft looking for survivors and patrolling for threats. It was discovered that most creatures were afraid of the planes, so the braver pilots began diving at any large clusters of monsters, scattering them.

The abandoned ethanol plant was recaptured and converted into an immense brewery by the dwarves. Soon, fine dwarven ale began to flow.

****

Standing at the bar of Denny's Beer Barrel Pub, a beautiful young woman waited as five large mugs of the heady brew were poured. Elizabeth McAllister adjusted her thick brown hair as she watched the mugs slowly fill up.

Liz wore a bulletproof vest over a long-sleeved shirt with holes for her thumbs. Looted black orc armor covered her shoulders and legs. Her jeans were tucked into her heavy hunting boots. A slender sword hung from her belt and a pistol was strapped to her thigh.

When the mugs were full, the bartender placed them in front of her. Liz thanked her and carried the mugs to a table in the back corner of the room.

Seated at the table were two dwarves and four humans. The dwarves were both short and incredibly muscular, with arms thicker than most men's legs. But besides their short stature, the dwarves couldn't be more different.

Jarl Baldor Deathkettle was considered tall for a dwarf. His head was bald and covered in an intricate pattern of blue tattoos that ran down his exposed right arm. A thick, red beard knotted in a complex design and held with metal clasps dominated his wide face. He wore a long chainmail shirt with steel plates running down his left arm. Plain bearded axes hung from his wide belt, while his horned helm and round shield rested next to his chair.

Lord Aurvang Twinpeaks on the other hand was shorter but even broader than the jarl. He had short, black hair and a full, bushy beard. Blue eyes peered out from thick eyebrows set above a wide, flat nose. He was encased in heavy plate armor inscribed with glittering runes of blue and gold. The armor rose up around the back of his head in a way that reminded Liz of a neck brace. A large, eight-pointed symbol dominated his chest plate, but was mostly hidden by his beard. Three interlocking triangles were embossed into his right shoulder guard and a stylized tower stood out on the left. A massive double bladed rune axe rested within easy reach.

Large mugs of ale already sat in front of the dwarves as Liz placed her new mugs on the table. She slid the first one over to a handsome and muscular young man with short-cropped brown hair and a goatee.

"Thanks." Mike's dark brown eyes sparkled as he took the mug.

He wore simple plate armor that he had scavenged from the dwarves and hammered out himself. An ancient and ornate mace hung from his belt, a gift from Lord Aurvang after Mike saved his life, and a circular dwarven shield leaned against his chair.

Across from Mike was a pretty, young woman with pale skin and long, black hair that fell in tight ringlets down her back. A small, black fedora was perched on her head, and a compound bow and quiver of arrows hung from the back of her chair. She wore a black and red corset, and a skimpy mini skirt that left little to the imagination. Liz must have made a face because Emily's green eyes twinkled mischievously as she flashed a wicked little grin.

Liz sighed and passed her a mug.

Seated next to Emily was a tanned, scruffy-but-handsome man in a combination of digital camo and glossy black orc armor. Jack had weapons strapped all over himself, including a wicked-looking katana that he had taken from an orc and that he never went anywhere without. He took his mug without a word.

The last man at the table towered over the others. He had dirty blond hair, a full beard, and a devilish cunning behind his eyes. Ted wore a simple breastplate with a modified white lab coat that had armor plates sewn into it. A tall, bladed staff was propped against the wall behind him.

Ted's armored-plated coat clattered around as he reached for his mug.

"Why do you wear that silly lab coat anyways? Emily asked.

"Because lab coats are cool," Ted replied simply.

Even the dwarves made a face at that but nobody argued with him. There was no point.

"Isn't Darrell coming?" Liz asked, as she sat down with her own mug.

"No," Mike answered. "He's out hunting."

"Of course," Liz laughed. "What else would he be doing?"

"Drinking" Ted added helpfully.

"Sleeping" Emily chuckled.

"Muddin'" Jack said, imitating Darrell's accent.

Everyone got a good chuckle out of that.

A sudden tremor shook the pub and everyone grabbed hold of their mugs and gear so that nothing fell. The quake was small and only lasted a few seconds.

"I'm glad we don't get those as much anymore," Emily said, as she let go of her arrows.

"Agreed," Liz said and took a deep breath. It was true the earthquakes had been getting less frequent, but they were usually stronger and lasted longer. Maybe they were finally going away.

"So, is there any news to report?" Ted asked. It had been several days since they had all found the time to get together.

"We have secured the last o'those *manhole* covers with new locks." Baldor said with an emphasis on manhole. "The ratmen will no be sneakin' out o' them again."

"That be good," Aurvang rumbled. "One less problem ter deal with."

"Oh!" Emily said excitedly. "I forgot to tell you, my dad was in town the other day!"

"That's great Em!" Liz replied. "How is he?"

"Good. He and his hunting buddies are still living out at Big Jim's camp," Emily laughed. "Klaige is loving the woods, too."

"I bet he is." Liz chuckled at the thought of the happy German shepherd, but then grew serious. "I still haven't heard anything from my family. I hope they are all alright."

Mike reassuringly placed his hand on Liz's. "I'm sure they're fine."

Liz smiled bravely, but was less confident.

"Eherm." Baldor cleared his throat. "So, how be yer Guardian trainin' progressin'?"

A pained look crossed Mike's face before answering. "It could be better," he admitted.

"Bwhahaha," Aurvang laughed. "Ye dun thinkin' it be easy ter master the thunderous powers o' Thor, did ye?"

"Mike has always been good at pulling crap out of thin air," Liz teased.

Mike shrugged helplessly.

"At least you guys can do *things*," Jack growled. "I don't have any cool powe-guh!"

Emily elbowed Jack hard in the ribs. "Quit your bellyaching, ya big baby."

"Hey!" Jack complained. "It's true though! I can't make things grow like you, or throw fire like Ted, or heal anything like Liz."

"Maybe not," Mike said, "but you are the best swordsman in town. And if it wasn't for you and that ridiculous machine gun of yours we would all be dead by now."

That seemed to brighten him up. "Ha, yeah. Ol' Bertha and I did save all yall's butts a few times."

A debate quickly broke out on who saved whom and how many times, but Liz was distracted when a guardsman came through the pub's door and hurried up to the bar. After a quick word, the bartender pointed to Liz's table.

"Oh, no," Liz sighed. That was never a good sign.

"What is it?" Mike asked.

Liz didn't reply as she watched the guardsman work his way through the room and come up to their table.

She didn't recognize the guardsman. He must have been one of the refugees that recently arrived. He looked nervous as he stopped in front of their table.

"Are you the Heroes of Awesome?" he asked.

Everyone at the table groaned.

Ted grinned and puffed up his chest. "Why, yes. Yes, we are. What can we do for you?"

Mike shook his head ruefully. "Ted, why do you keep telling people that?"

"Every group of heroes needs a name," Ted replied simply.

"But 'Heroes of Awesome'?" Emily groaned. "Really?"

Ted looked hurt. "It's a good name."

"*Anyways*," Liz interrupted and looked up at the guardsman who was standing there looking uncomfortable. "What do you need us for?" she asked nicely.

"Well…um," the guardsman stammered. "Cap- er… Mayor-Captain DiSantos requests your presence at the courthouse."

"What fer?" Aurvang rumbled.

The poor guardsman paled at the dwarf lord's tone. "Well…sir…" he swallowed nervously, "word has come back from Pittsburgh."

"Pittsburgh!" Ted exclaimed excitedly. "Does the city still stand? Are there survivors?"

"I don't know," the guardsman replied quickly. "I was just ordered to come find you."

"Well, we better get going then," Ted said as he gathered his gear and stood up. The others shared a look before joining.

A short time later, the Heroes of Awesome strode into the courthouse through several winding corridors and finally came into a large room that had become known as the Command Center. Inside they found Mayor-Captain DiSantos with several of his commanders, both human and dwarf, standing around a large map of Pennsylvania. Pins of varying colors were positioned across the map in a dizzying pattern. Liz noticed there were far more red pins than any other.

Mayor-Captain DiSantos was a large man in his middle years. He was dressed similar to Jack, with a combination of US military and black, samurai-like orc armor. DiSantos had a large, barrel chest and dark hair cut short in the military style with grey at the temples.

Lord Aurvang strode forward. "What news?"

Liz was anxious to hear the answer. So far, every town nearby was either destroyed or abandoned. DuBois was controlled by the orcs, Curwensville was a breeding ground for ratmen, and Houtzdale and Philipsburg were both overrun with goblins. It was rumored that there was resistance in State College, but they had so far been unable to establish contact. She hoped the news here was better.

DiSantos rested his hands on the table and didn't take his eyes off the map. "We received a message from Pittsburgh over the radio. The connection was poor and only lasted for a minute before cutting out." DiSantos paused as he continued to study the map before him.

"Well?" Ted asked impatiently.

DiSantos looked up. "Pittsburgh is secure."

Liz let out a breath she didn't know she had been holding. Relief flooded her. Pittsburgh still stood! They were not alone!

DiSantos continued. "- and they are offering a safe haven for any survivors."

"We should go," Ted said immediately.

The Mayor-Captain held up a hand. "Hold on. That wasn't all." He looked at Lord Aurvang. "There is also a dwarf Clan helping build their defenses."

"What Clan?" Aurvang asked with an excited glint in his eyes.

"We don't know," DiSantos replied. "The message cut out before they said."

"Odin's Breath," the dwarf lord cursed.

"But that wasn't all," DiSantos said. "Dwarves aren't the only allies

Pittsburgh has made."

Mike looked confused. "Who else could there be?"

Mayor-Captain DiSantos rubbed his temples wearily.

"Elves."

CHAPTER 2

"Elves?" Baldor scoffed. "There be no such thing as elves."

Mike laughed. "You said the same thing about humans." It wasn't that long ago that Mike had to convince the stubborn dwarf jarl that he was in fact a human.

"And we said the same of dwarves," Ted added.

Baldor scowled at the two of them. "This be different. We have legends o' our interactions with humans. Elves be nothin' but fairy tales told ter children."

"Really?" Emily chuckled. "After all the things you have seen, you still don't believe elves could exist?"

"I will believe it when I see it," Baldor replied defiantly.

Typical dwarf stubbornness, Mike thought.

"Regardless of if elves are real or not, we have more pressing concerns," Lt. Bowman said

"Precisely," DiSantos replied sharply. "Now, what are we going to do?"

"We go, of course," Ted answered.

Mike looked at him. "Everyone?"

"Why not?" Ted replied. "There are plenty of abandoned vehicles around and lots of fuel just sitting in the gas stations. We pack everyone up today and get to Pittsburgh in a few hours."

Emily shook her head. "That would never work. There are *waaay* too many people here. Do you really think that you are going to get thousands of people, and dwarves, all into cars and drive over 120 miles to Pittsburgh with who-knows-what in between? Besides, even if you could load them all up, I am willing to bet most won't even want to go."

"She's right," Liz added. "This is our home. People aren't just going to up and leave because there are more people in Pittsburgh."

"Then what do we do?" DiSantos asked again.

"Well..." Mike began, "we need some supplies, tools and things we can't make here. So, at least some people will need to go. We also don't know what is between here and there." Mike looked around the table. "I would say you get a small party of soldiers together and a few transport trucks to go see if they can make it. If they can, that's great. They can load up on supplies and bring them back to us."

"That is a good plan," DiSantos said. "We had come up with much the same idea." He glanced around at his commanders. "Our problem is that we don't know who to send. We can't spare too many soldiers and the dwarves are all needed to build the fortifications." DiSantos looked at Mike. "We were hoping you and your friends would volunteer to go."

"And why would we go?" Jack butted in.

"Well," DiSantos said with a shrug, "you are the Heroes of Awesome."

"Ouch!" Ted yelped when Emily suddenly punched him in the arm. "What was that for?"

"For being so smart, you sure are an idiot sometimes," Emily replied hotly.

"That was unnecessary," Ted complained, as he rubbed his sore arm.

Mike tried to hide a smile, but failed. "What's the real reason you want us to go?"

One of the commanders answered, "Because you five are the most powerful individuals here and most of you know Pittsburgh. If anyone can get there and back it will be you."

"I'll go," Jack suddenly said. When everyone looked at him with surprise he continued. "Look, we are secure here for the time being and I, for one, would like to get out and see what the rest of the world looks like."

"I'll go too," Ted quickly added with a nervous glance down at Emily as if he were afraid of getting hit again.

"Me, too," Mike said with an inward sigh. He wasn't too keen on the idea, but somebody needed to go. It might as well be him.

Liz looked between the three guys and shook her head. "*Men,*" she muttered to herself then spoke up. "If you clowns are going then I'm going, too. I can't believe I'm saying this but somebody needs to keep you goons alive."

"Thanks mom," Jack said with a sly grin.

Liz's glare could have frozen the sun.

"Settle down children," Mike teased, then looked at Emily. "You coming?"

Emily made a face. "Do I have to?"

"No."

"Then, no. I will stay here."

"Alrighty." Mike turned back to DiSantos. "Looks li-"

"Of course I'm going with you, you great oaf," Emily suddenly cut in. "You guys can't have all the fun."

"Good," DiSantos smiled. "It's settled then." He turned to the dwarves. "What about you two?"

"I will remain here," Aurvang rumbled. "I must oversee the defenses."

"I will go," Baldor said. "I want ter see these *elves* fer meself."

"Very well." DiSantos turned to his commanders. "Prepare a convoy from Iron Division. Spread the word that if anyone wants to join, we will leave at first light."

****

The sky was beginning to lighten as dawn approached. Mike heaved a heavy wooden crate into the back of Jack's heavily modified truck. It looked more like something you would see in a zombie movie. It had a machine gun bolted to the bed with razor wire and armor plates welded to the sides, and it came complete with a spiked plow mounted to the front.

Jack's truck was parked in the front of a line of military trucks that would make up the convoy. Five transport trucks sat in a line with a Humvee on either end. Soldiers moved about getting things ready as civilians gathered together awaiting orders.

Mike cracked a yawn as he hauled another crate into the truck bed. He hated getting up early. He wore a full suit of armor in the style of the mountain dwarves, complete with heavy collar. It was hot and heavy. Mike was not looking forward to riding in the back of the truck for the next several hours wearing it, but he wasn't about to go unarmored into the unknown.

Whose brilliant idea was it to leave at first light? Mike resolved to have a word with the Mayor-Captain when next he saw him. "This is for the birds…" he muttered under his breath. "Making us get up at the butt-crack of dawn…"

"What's that?" Jack asked as he walked up to the truck carrying an ammo crate. Jack was wearing his full set of black orc armor with weapons strapped all over, including his oversized orcish katana.

"Oh, nothing," Mike replied. "Just enjoying the morning."

"Uh, huh," Jack smiled knowingly.

Mike dusted his hands off and admired his handy work. Satisfied that the crates wouldn't move during the trip, Mike hopped up on the open tailgate. "Have you seen Ted yet?"

Jack shook his head. "Nope. Hopefully he isn't making a last-minute batch of that awful drink of his."

Mike was forced to agree. Ted's first attempt at his so-called "chemically perfect beverage" had been nothing less than a disaster. A mixture of gasoline, manure, and plastic would have tasted better than his chemical brew. Mike shivered at the thought. "We can only hope."

"Have you seen either of the girls?" Mike asked.

"Emily was still sleeping when I got up," Jack grinned. "She was up late."

Somehow Mike was not surprised. "So, are you two a couple now?"

"Oh, hell no," Jack quickly replied. "Not my type. That and she's kinda crazy."

"So why…?" Mike left the question hanging.

Jack chuckled. "Obviously, you have never been with a crazy girl."

"And why would I want to do that?"

"Because crazy girls are more fun," Emily said, as she suddenly appeared from behind one of the transport trucks.

"Speak of the Devil," Jack grinned wolfishly.

Emily was dressed in full woodland camouflage now. She had her bow in hand and a bulging backpack slung over one slender shoulder. Once she reached the truck, she opened the passenger door and tossed the backpack in. "Shotgun," she chirped happily, then bounced back and hopped up next to Mike on the tailgate while Jack hooked the ammo box to the machine gun.

"Hopefully, we don't need this," Jack muttered. "This is the last box. I was lucky to find it wedged in the back of Grice's a few days ago."

"Don't worry," Emily said. "If you run out, we can let Ted use his *firening*… or whatever he is calling it."

That made Mike smile. Ted had been experimenting with combining electricity and fire into one spell. Now, he was trying to name it.

"Personally, I liked *electrifier*," Mike chuckled.

"Ooo, that's a good one," Emily laughed back.

"Here comes Liz and Ted," Jack announced, "and he doesn't seem to have any of that blasted drink either!"

"Thank the gods," Emily breathed.

"Greetings!" Ted shouted, as they weaved their way through the throng of people. He was dressed in his patchwork armor and white armored lab coat. In his hand, he walked with a long-bladed staff that he had taken from an orc sorcerer. A large sack was thrown over his shoulder and it looked ready to burst at the seams.

Liz walked next to him in her bulletproof vest and armor pieces with a small backpack and rifle on her shoulder.

Jack finished preparing his weapons and sat down on a crate to wait.

Liz and Ted threw their bags into the back and then joined Mike, Emily, and Jack watching the rest of the preparations.

There were many tearful goodbyes as people left their friends and families to join the convoy. Mike had said his goodbyes to his family the day before. He was confident they would be safe here. He wondered how everyone else was feeling about them leaving.

He looked over at Liz. She hadn't heard anything from her family up in New York since the monsters appeared a few months ago. Jack's parents and Emily's dad were safe here in Clearfield. Ted's only family was a few cousins out near Pittsburgh. *Perhaps that's why he was so eager to go there,* Mike mused.

Mike's thoughts were interrupted with the arrival of Darrell through the crowd. Darrell was wearing his usual bib overalls, flannel shirt, and old ball cap. He had a double-barreled shotgun resting on one shoulder and a beer can in his other hand.

"Hey, ya'll! Weren't ya gonna say 'bye?" Darrel drawled.

"Isn't it a bit early for a beer?" Mike asked with a grin.

"Never too early fer a cold en'," Darrell replied in all seriousness. He looked at them and the gear in the bed. He seemed to notice the flurry of activity around him for the first time and looked confused. "Where ya'll headed?"

"Pittsburgh," Jack answered. "They say there are survivors there. We are going to find out if it's true, and if it is, hopefully we'll bring some supplies back."

"Want to come?" Emily asked him.

Ted groaned and scowled at Emily. He and Darrell had a history of not getting along. Ted thought Darrell was an uneducated idiot, while Darrell considered Ted a know-it-all.

"Naw," Darrell answered. "I dun like the city. Too many people."

"You sure?" Jack asked. "You can drive the truck."

Darrell's eyes lit up for a moment at that, but he shook his head. "Temptin,' but naw. Me home is herr."

"My," Ted muttered. "*My* home is *here*."

Either Darrell didn't hear Ted or he was just ignoring him, and drained the last of his beer. He looked sadly at the empty can and then suddenly smashed it into his head. The can crumpled and sprayed a mist of beer all over. Darrell looked at the flattened can then held it out to Emily. "Somin' ta remember me by."

Emily delicately took the flat can and forced a smile. "Gee, thanks."

"Yer welcome," Darrell replied happily. He looked up at the brightening sky and frowned. "Whelp, I best be off before I miss the coons."

"Good luck," he said, and with that he waved and disappeared back into the crowd.

"Are raccoons in season?" Liz asked.

Mike chuckled. "No. No they aren't."

Suddenly, a dwarf horn blast split the air.

"Well, that was unnecessary," Liz complained, as she tried to clear the ringing from her ears.

"Agreed," Emily said, as she lowered her hands from her ears.

At the sound of the horn, the loitering soldiers climbed into the waiting trucks and Humvees. The civilians followed and piled into the backs of the transport trucks. Mike was surprised to see several dwarves among those getting into the transports. Besides Baldor, Mike didn't think any would be coming.

There were a few more tearful goodbyes, but soon all the trucks were full and ready to depart.

"I guess that's our cue," Liz said, and hopped out of the truck bed. She got in the driver's seat and Emily joined her in the cab. Jack took his place behind the machine gun while Mike and Ted positioned themselves in the corners of the bed.

Mayor-Captain DiSantos strode over and greeted them. "The convoy is ready to go. The men have been informed that you are the lead. They will follow your orders."

"The trucks are slow so don't go too fast. I estimate it will take you close to four hours to reach Pittsburgh. You are still planning on taking the interstate, yes?"

"Affirmative," Jack answered.

"Good. I doubt there will be any traffic," he said with a straight face.

"No," Ted sighed, "but this is Pennsylvania, so there is probably going to be road construction."

DiSantos laughed. "You are probably right."

"Mayor-Captain," Jack began. "What should we do if we run across any survivors?"

"Direct them here," DiSantos replied, "unless you are closer to Pittsburgh, then bring them with you."

"Yes, sir," Jack said.

The Mayor-Captain snapped to attention and gave them a sharp salute. "Good luck and God speed."

"Thank you, sir." Jack returned his salute.

Liz slowly pulled out and the convoy began moving.

CHAPTER 3

The convoy moved slowly along the empty interstate. It was eerie driving for miles and miles and not seeing a soul on the road. There was the occasional abandoned vehicle, but no other sign of life. It was as if they were the last people in the world.

They moved slowly and stopped at every town they came across, and did a quick sweep searching for survivors. The first few towns were completely burned down but after the first hour, they came across a few battered people hiding inside an old farmhouse. The news from the survivors was grim.

A week ago, hordes of orcs and other monsters had ransacked their town and had taken many captive before they left. The survivors had been in hiding ever since. They did not know where the monsters had gone.

It was decided that the convoy could not go searching for the captives and would continue on to Pittsburgh. They would inform whoever was in charge of Pittsburgh to send someone to look for them and if they couldn't then they would form a search party themselves after they made it back to Clearfield with the supplies. The survivors were packed into one of the trucks and the convoy moved on.

"Are we there yet?" Emily moaned.

"No," Liz replied, for what must have been the hundredth time.

"I hate driving," Emily sighed.

"You aren't driving," Liz pointed out.

"Maybe not, but I still have to sit here," Emily grumbled, as she stared out the open window.

Emily watched the trees slowly pass by. *How had I been talked into this?* She hated traveling. It was even worse when they were going so slow. She took a deep breath and resigned herself to a long and boring ride.

She suddenly caught movement between some trees back in the woods.

"Um, Liz…" Emily began to point out the window when a horrible shriek suddenly split the air. It sounded almost like the cry of an eagle, only much more deep and powerful. The shriek had gotten everyone's attention.

"What the…?" Liz came to a stop and the convoy halted behind her.

Emily could make out more movement between the trees but it was hard to see anything with all the underbrush in the way. Another shriek issued from the woods followed by growls, hisses, and thrashing. Tree limbs snapped followed by thuds and cries of pain.

"I'm going to go look," Emily announced suddenly as she grabbed her bow and opened the door.

"Wait!" Liz cried, but Emily slammed the door closed and headed for the tree line.

Mike and Ted jumped out of the truck and hurried to catch up to Emily as Jack manned his machine gun. Liz got out of the truck and grabbed her rifle before she raced after them, angrily muttering to herself.

From the first transport truck, Baldor looked out and saw them headed for the tree line. "Wait fer me!" he cried, as he jumped out and charged over to them, his short legs pumping hard to catch up.

Before Emily, Mike, and Ted reached the trees, there was an explosion of leaves and sticks as an enormous shape burst through the treetops. Everyone stared up in awe as the creature flapped its huge, leathery wings to keep itself airborne.

The creature was covered in greenish-brown scales with two long, clawed arms protruding from a long, serpentine body. It had a large, reptilian snout filled with long, curved fangs and a wicked looking barb at the end of its tail.

The creature growled and spun in the air before diving back into the trees. More shrieks and thrashing followed the creature's descent.

Emily stared in amazement. "What was that?" she breathed.

"That," Baldor said as he finally caught up to them, "be a wyvern."

Liz peered into the trees. "What is it doing in there?"

Baldor scratched his beard. "That be a good question. Sounds like there be several o' them in there though. Fightin' I'd say."

"How do you know there are more than one?" Mike asked.

"I been on several wyvern hunts," Baldor replied, "and one no be makin' that much noise."

Another deep shriek split the air and suddenly two wyverns burst through the treetops. They hissed at each other as if they were arguing before they dived back in.

"It can no be... " Baldor muttered.

"What is it?" Ted asked.

Baldor shook his head. "That cry… it be soundin' like… nah, it can no be." He suddenly charged into the brush, using his axes to clear a path as he headed toward the sounds of battle.

Liz looked at Mike and he just shrugged before following the dwarf. Everyone else joined in and soon they were surrounded by forest.

Baldor abruptly stopped before entering a small clearing. He gasped as he stared into the glade. The others quickly caught up and stared at the titanic battle unfolding before them.

Spread around the clearing were four serpentine wyverns that had another creature surrounded. Two dead wyverns laid at the feet of this other beast.

This creature had the head of an eagle that was covered in brilliant, white feathers and a wickedly curved gold beak. Its body resembled an immense lion with deep golden fur, but its two forelegs did not end in paws but rather huge talons and marvelous feathered wings sprouted from its broad back.

The surrounded creature shrieked at the wyverns as it tried to keep them from getting behind it.

"I knew it," Baldor breathed. "A griffin."

Emily watched in awe as the majestic griffin tried to keep the four wyverns at bay.

A wyvern suddenly spun around and whipped its barbed tail at the griffin. The griffin dodged away, barely avoiding the wicked-looking barb.

It was then that Emily noticed the griffin's wounds. Bright red blood ran downs its white feathers and several large cuts marred its golden fur. When it moved one wing didn't bend like the other, which caused the griffin to struggle to stay balanced.

Emily watched as the wyverns struck again and the griffin barely avoided being skewered.

"We have to do something!" Emily cried.

"Aye," Baldor agreed. "We must help the griffin."

"And how do you plan to do that?" Liz asked, not taking her eyes off the enormous creatures smashing through the trees. "We'll be crushed."

"We have to try," Emily pleaded.

One of the wyverns suddenly lunged forward. The griffin screeched in pain as the wyvern's jaws bit down on one of its talons. The griffin tried to dislodge the wyvern but the serpentine creature wouldn't budge and clamped on to the talon even harder. Another wyvern roared and dove in, claws flashing at the griffin's exposed back.

A sudden twist and the griffin knocked the diving wyvern away with a mighty swipe of its uninjured wing. Another wyvern reared and quickly took its place.

A fireball grew in Ted's hand and he looked to Mike questioningly.

Mike unslung his shield. "Let's do this!"

Ted grinned back, thrust his arm out, and the ball of fire shot out toward one of the wyverns. It exploded on the wyvern's chest and the beast flew backwards from the force of the blast. A stream of arrows followed the fireball as Emily unleashed a volley at the wyvern that was still attached to the griffin's talon.

"Beware their bite," Baldor shouted. "They be poisonous."

Mike charged out into the clearing with Baldor close behind.

The fireball and arrows had drawn the monsters notice. Two of the wyverns turned their attention to this new threat as the wyvern Ted had hit was picking itself up, smoke rising from charred scales.

A few of the arrows found their mark on the beast's side, but most bounced off its armored scales. Emily cursed and set the bow down, and drew the scepter she had taken from a goblin shaman. The scepter looked like nothing more than a knotted stick with bits of bone and feathers hanging from the end. A skull from some unknown animal capped the scepter and when Emily drew it, the eye sockets began to glow green.

The wyvern was still clamped onto the griffin's talon and was thrashing wildly, trying to strike with its barbed tail. So far, the griffin had fended off the attacks, but Emily could see it wouldn't last much longer.

"Let's see how you like this," Emily growled, and pointed the scepter at the wyvern.

A bolt of crackling green energy erupted from the scepter. The wyvern lost its grip on the griffin as the energy coursed over it and caused its massive body to spasm momentarily.

The griffin seized the opportunity and launched itself at the stricken wyvern. The two beasts crashed to the ground, locked in a furious battle of claws and fangs.

Ted threw more fireballs as fast as he could, keeping two of the wyverns at bay. The spells were small and didn't do that much harm to the large beasts, but it kept them distracted. Liz joined him as she fired her rifle at the monsters as well.

The wyverns took cover from the bombardment by diving behind some trees. Using the trees as cover, they began weaving their way toward Liz and Ted.

The wyvern Ted had hit first was back up and using its two clawed legs to half crawl, half slither toward Mike and Baldor, who were charging directly for it. The beast roared and suddenly sprang at Mike like a coiled snake. Mike pulled his shield up, but just then a spinning axe sailed through the air and slammed into the wyvern's snout.

The wyvern recoiled and howled in pain. It reared up and shook its scaly head, trying to dislodge the axe that was still embedded there. Mike charged in and swung his ancient dwarfen mace. The enchantments on the mace increased the force of each blow and it struck with an immense impact. The force of the strike pulverized the monster's shoulder and it crashed to the ground, writhing and howling in pain.

"A little help over here?!" Ted suddenly shouted.

Emily looked over her shoulder and saw the two wyverns were dangerously close to Liz and Ted. He still rapidly threw small fireballs, but the wyverns were just shrugging them off now. Liz was having a little more luck; most of her shots tore into the monster's flesh, but must not have penetrated too far, for the wyverns didn't slow.

Ted paused in his casting and was doing something that Emily couldn't see. The sudden respite allowed the wyverns to lunge forward. Emily shouted a warning and sent a barrage of small emerald bolts at them. The beasts recoiled from the bolts as they crackled over their scaly hides.

Whatever Ted was doing he had better hurry it up! Emily thought, as she fired more bolts as rapidly as she could. Emily noticed that Liz had tossed her rifle to the ground and was now armed with a sword and pistol. *Wonderful,* she thought. *She is out of ammo already.*

Ted finished what he was doing and a ball of crackling fire erupted from his outstretched hand. The ball grew as it flew, snaking veins of electricity arching around a liquid fire center. The spell shot forward and detonated in the face of one of the wyverns. The concussion from the explosion knocked Emily backwards. She quickly pulled herself up and saw the wyvern lying on the ground; its head a charred ruin.

Liz slowly picked herself up as Ted fell to his knees, looking exhausted.

The other wyvern pulled itself up nearby and hissed in rage as it darted forward.

****

Mike rolled away as the wyvern with the broken arm stabbed the ground where he had just been standing with its barbed tail.

Baldor bellowed a battle cry and swung his axe at the monster's back. The beast spun around and fanned its large wings. Air buffeted Baldor, but he charged on unhindered, and drove his axe into the wyvern's side. The beast shrieked and pulled away before Baldor could swing again.

Mike ran at the monster's back and raised his mace. The wyvern suddenly spun around and cracked Mike with its thick tail. He sailed through the air, crashed into a tree, and landed in a heap.

****

More bolts shot from Emily's scepter and the wyvern dodged away from them. Liz fired her pistol, but the bullets had no effect on the monster. Ted used his bladed staff to slowly pull himself to his feet. Seeing his slow movements, the wyvern roared and lunged at Ted.

The beast's roar changed to a cry of pain as it bore Ted to the ground. It reared back with Ted's blade buried deep in its serpentine body. The wyvern growled and bright blood spilled forth as it drew the spear out and tossed it to the side. The beast had Ted pinned beneath it and looked at him with rage.

It opened its large mouth, fangs dripping venom. Suddenly, one of the wyvern's eyes exploded in a shower of gore. The beast howled and reeled backwards, as Liz fired at its thrashing head. Emily showered the monster with more small bolts, but then she heard the griffin shriek in pain.

Emily spun around and saw the griffin on top of the wyvern. The monster drove its barb into the griffin's side, again and again.

"NO!" Emily cried, but she was too far away.

The griffin groaned and the wyvern heaved the battered beast off. The griffin collapsed and the bloody wyvern rose above in victory. It roared as it moved in for the kill.

Suddenly, Mike was there standing between the monstrous wyvern and the wounded griffin. The wyvern didn't hesitate and dove at him, but Mike stood his ground.

Just before reaching him, the wyvern's head snapped back as it collided with an invisible wall. The stunned beast crumpled at Mike's feet.

Mike raised his ancient mace and with all the strength he could summon, brought it down on the monster's dragon-like head. There was a sickening crunch as the wyvern's skull collapsed under the force of the enchanted weapon. The beast quivered once and then laid still.

Emily turned back and looked at Ted and Liz. They were walking toward her.

"Where did it go?" she asked.

"Cowardly beast flew off after Liz took its eye," Ted grumbled.

Across the clearing, Baldor was straddling the corpse of another wyvern, trying in vain to pull his axe out from the base of the beast's skull.

Emily breathed a sigh of relief and smiled. *They had actually won! And they were all alive,* she thought happily, until she suddenly remembered the griffin. Emily dashed over to the fallen creature and knelt down beside it. Blood pooled around her feet as it seeped from numerous wounds all over the magnificent creature's battered body. The others gathered around her as she knelt beside the griffin.

Thank you.

Emily jumped as the voice whispered clearly in her head. She looked around but didn't see anything. "Did you hear that?" she asked.

The others all shook their heads no. "Hear what?" Liz asked.

Emily ignored the question and looked at the griffin. The beast slowly raised its massive beaked head and looked at her with one huge eye.

Thank you.

"Um... you're welcome?" Emily whispered back.

"Who are you talking to?" Mike asked.

"The griffin, I think," Emily replied.

The griffin nodded its great head before laying it back down and closing its eyes.

This was incredible! Emily couldn't believe it. She could understand this amazing creature and it understood her!

"You have to heal it!" Emily suddenly pleaded.

Liz looked at the dying griffin sadly. "I don't know if I can..."

"Please, just try," Emily begged.

Liz took a deep breath then knelt down next to Emily. She laid her hands on the beast's glistening coat and closed her eyes.

Emily could see Liz's mouth moving silently as she said something too quiet for her to hear. Liz's brow furrowed as she concentrated harder.

Emily watched anxiously. So far there had been no change. Would it work? Could Liz heal a creature such as this? Emily didn't know, but she prayed that it was possible.

Moments passed and nothing happened. Healing had never taken this long as far as Emily had seen. Usually it was almost instantaneous. *This was taking far too long. It wasn't going to work.* Emily was about to give up hope when the telltale golden glow appeared under Liz's hands.

At first nothing happened.

Emily held her breath.

The griffin's wounds slowly stopped bleeding and closed back up until they disappeared completely.

Emily let out a sigh of relief as the griffin shifted and opened its eyes. Emily and Liz quickly moved away as the massive creature heaved itself up and stretched its marvelous wings.

The griffin turned its enormous head toward Emily and her friends. It almost seemed to smile as it regarded its saviors. Or maybe it was just Emily's imagination.

My name is Eagle Feather. The griffin bent its front legs and inclined its head and bowed to them. *I owe you my life.*

Emily was surprised to discover that the griffin was female!

"She says her name is Eagle Feather," Emily told the others. "She says thanks and that she owes us one."

"Well, you are very welcome," Liz smiled at the magnificent beast.

The griffin looked at each one of them in turn; it eyed Mike longer than the others as if it were inspecting him for some reason with its too-intelligent eyes.

It must have been satisfied with whatever it saw for it suddenly leapt into the air and flapped its huge wings. After a few thunderous beats, it cleared the treetops and just like that it was gone.

"Well, that be interestin'," Baldor said.

"Yes." Mike looked around at the wyvern corpses that littered the small clearing. "Interesting."

CHAPTER 4

"It be a shame we had ter leave 'em," Baldor grumbled as they continued down the interstate once again. He had joined Mike, Jack, and Ted in the bed of their truck. "Wyvern-skin cloaks be highly sought after in the Empire. They fetch a small fortune, don't ye know."

The convoy wound its way down the empty highway at a steady clip. They had not seen any more creatures or any survivors. The few towns they passed were all abandoned, including one that had been completely destroyed. It became apparent they were getting closer to whatever was causing the destruction; smoke could be seen rising from several locations in the distance. Strangely, there were no bodies.

A fierce argument ensued over whether they should further investigate the distant smoke or continue to Pittsburgh. Eventually it was decided that it was more important to reach their destination and secure the needed supplies. They couldn't afford to waste time when their families needed them back home. Search parties could be sent once they safely made it to Pittsburgh.

"Well, we aren't in your *Empire*," Jack growled back. He was still angry at missing the fight. Jack and the guardsmen had remained with the convoy in case anything came out of the forest. They had listened to the sounds of the battle and anxiously watched as the injured wyvern flew away and then followed later by the griffin. Jack had just been about to go in looking for them when Mike and the others had finally emerged from the trees.

"We could stop on our way back," Mike offered.

Baldor scratched his beard and thought about it. "I guessin' we could," he muttered. "They should keep a few days."

"Good," Mike said. "It's settled then."

Jack snorted at that, but didn't say anymore.

****

The miles crawled by, or at least Mike thought so, sitting there in the cramped truck bed in his heavy armor with the hot sun beating down on him. Luckily, he knew they were getting close. They should arrive in the city within half an hour or so, and he was looking forward to getting out and stretching his legs.

Signs of recent conflict grew more common the closer they got, with some buildings still burning. Mike was growing more nervous by the mile. Hopefully, Pittsburgh was still standing when they arrived. The carnage they were seeing was getting worse and it didn't bode well for the city.

They crested another hill when Jack suddenly pointed down below them in the valley. "Look!" he shouted. "There are people down there!"

Liz slowed the truck to a stop as everyone in the back climbed to their feet for a better look at what Jack was pointing at.

Sure enough, down the hill Mike saw there were over a dozen people quickly spreading out in an open field. Something about the way they moved Mike found odd but he couldn't put his finger on it and at this distance it was hard to make out much.

"What are they doing?" Ted asked, as the figures spread out even more.

The answer appeared a moment later when a group of riders on horseback suddenly charged from around another hill beyond the valley. The riders pointed at the people in the valley followed by a horn blast that echoed through the hills.

"What is it with horns?" Jack muttered to himself.

More riders appeared behind the first and the small group quickly grew in size until a large throng of riders was charging into the valley.

As the riders got closer, Mike noticed something strange about them. It took him a moment to figure out what it was.

The riders weren't riders at all, but creatures that were half horse and half man.

Mike knew what these creatures were and they filled him with wonder. Legend told that such beasts were wild and ferocious. That dangerousness became apparent as the leading group of racing creatures drew bows and began firing at the small party of people that were now waiting in a widely spread out formation.

Ted came to the same conclusion. "Centaur," he said excitedly!

The herd grew until there must have been over a hundred centaur down there, kicking up dust as they pounded into the valley.

"Those people are going to get slaughtered," Jack said. "We have to do something."

"I don't be knowin' what these... *centaur* be," Baldor rumbled, "but I agree with Treno." He thumbed his axe eagerly as he spoke.

Jack grinned and looked back to the lead hummer behind them. He motioned for them to continue down the road.

"Hold on!" Liz shouted, just before she hit the gas and cut the wheel hard. The truck veered off the road and sped down the embankment.

In the valley, the air filled with arrows as the centaur launched a concentrated volley at the smattering of people. Those arrows never hit their targets. Bursts of light flashed above the defenders and the falling arrows disintegrated. Undeterred, the centaur continued their charge and fired arrows as they came on hard.

The people drew bows of their own and began firing back at the centaur, but with much more success. The tightly packed centaur were easy targets and many fell to the group's arrows.

The Heroes of Awesome unceremoniously bounced and rattled down the slope.

****

The first wave of centaur hooted and bellowed challenges as they reached the defenders and drew forth long, wicked-looking swords from their backs.

Mike watched in horror as the battle was joined. The centaur drove into the defenders and swarmed them. They broke around the standing figures like a wave against rocks.

The outnumbered people didn't panic and suddenly burst into motion. Spinning and dancing almost faster than the eye could follow, they carved into the surrounding centaur. Explosions ripped through the swarming beasts as some of the defenders cast devastating magical attacks.

Streams of fire, lighting, and pure energy shot out around the people to obliterate any centaur caught in their path. The defenders wove a deadly dance with their blades and fired bows while throwing powerful spells at the same time with ease. It was beautiful to behold.

Thunder filled the valley as Jack brought his machine gun to bare. Fire billowed from the barrel and spat a stream of death at the centaur. Bodies and earth were torn up wherever the bombardment of hot lead passed.

Arrows began pelting off the armored sides of the truck as the centaur became aware of the new threat and retaliated. An arrow whizzed past Ted. Mike stood in the bouncing truck and summoned a protective Svalinn Field around them as the arrows bounced harmlessly away.

Now that they were getting close, Mike could make out some details of the centaur. They were very similar to how the stories portrayed them. They had the head and upper body of a man, with the body of a horse attached at the waist. But they were smaller than Mike had first thought. Instead of the body of a full-sized horse, these centaur were smaller; closer to resembling a large deer than a horse.

They were mostly unarmored with the exception of some leather vests and caps. Their fur was typically some shade of brown or black and they all carried a short bow with a large quiver of brightly colored arrows.

The truck reached the base of the hill and leveled out as they entered the valley. Liz hit the gas and the truck plowed into the centaur. Furry centaur bodies flew through the air as the plow bulldozed its way into the mass of beasts while some unfortunates were impaled on the plow spikes.

"Let me out!" Baldor cried eagerly.

Jack kept up a steady stream of fire as they barreled their way into the thick of the herd.

More arrows and swords bounced off the barrier as the centaur quickly surrounded them. A growing pressure began to build behind Mike's eyes and he knew he couldn't hold his shield for much longer.

A loud click and the thunder of Jack's gun ceased.

"I'm out!" Jack shouted, and unslung his AR-15.

Liz began to slow down and Baldor suddenly leapt out, axes whirling, laughing maniacally.

With a groan, Ted jumped out and followed the crazed dwarf, shooting small bursts of fire to protect the reckless jarl's back.

Mike and Jack jumped out together as Emily dove out of the cab and quickly hauled herself up into the now empty bed. Without waiting, Liz picked up speed again and drove off, plowing into helpless centaur as Emily fired arrow after arrow from the back.

An arrow *thunked* into Mike's shield and the world suddenly shrunk to his immediate surroundings. His concentration became focused on maintaining his protective field.

Mike and Jack stood back-to-back, with Jack firing small bursts into packs of centaur while Mike was busy blocking the arrows that came whizzing at them. None of the beasts would come close enough for Mike to get a good swing at them.

He could see that the centaur were getting frustrated that none of their arrows made it past him. More arrows rained down on them, but Mike's Svalinn Field blocked them all with a faint wall of shimmering blue-tinted energy.

One of the centaur had finally had enough and charged Mike with a wickedly curved long sword. Two more came in behind it and Mike was suddenly surrounded. He blocked one thrust with his shield then dove to the side as another centaur tried to trample him. The beast followed and Mike rolled away and came up swinging.

The centaur was caught off guard and Mike's enchanted mace crushed its chest and blasted the centaur backwards into its companions. They all went down in a tangled heap of legs. Suddenly, Jack appeared beside him and before the two centaur could extract themselves from the corpse, his rifle flashed.

Mike nodded his thanks, but then more centaur charged in. He blocked and parried furiously as Jack shot into the masses until his ammo ran out. Then he drew his black katana and sliced into any creature that came too close.

Time faded away as Mike and Jack worked together to carve through the herd. Arrows flew and explosions ripped through the beasts.

A sudden break in the herd revealed a gorgeous woman weaving through the charging centaur, lashing out with two short swords to hamstring them as she passed.

The woman wore strange clothing of exquisite leather that had been dyed browns and greens. She had a short skirt made of leather strips that resembled leaves blowing in the breeze and a vest of leather straps that was molded tightly to her slender body. Long, dark hair billowed out around her as she twirled and slashed through the herd.

There was an almost liquid-like grace in her actions that Mike couldn't quite believe. Her movements really were like watching a dance.

Entranced, Mike almost lost his head to a centaur' saber, but he ducked at the last second and retaliated with a blow that shattered the beast's front legs. He dispatched the creature, but then lost sight of the strange woman as more centaur came roaring in.

Mike and Jack were hard-pressed as more of the beasts poured in around them. Mike's impact mace sent centaur flying at the slightest touch and Jack's orc sword sliced through flesh as easily as paper, but there were just too many.

Jack suddenly cried out as an arrow lodged in his thigh. But he didn't slow, if anything, the arrow seemed to make him angry and he waded into the herd with renewed ferocity.

****

A large centaur suddenly reared up in front of Mike. Before he could react, the beast crashed into him, bearing him to the ground and began stomping on him. Mike curled up into a defensive ball with his wooden shield over as much of him as he could as more centaur swarmed around and began pounding him with their hooves.

A sharp hoof struck Mike in the head and his vision swam. His wooden shield cracked under the relentless onslaught.

He tried to summon a Svalinn Field, but he couldn't concentrate. Every time he grasped the power, it slipped through his fingers. Mike closed his eyes and tried to focus, but nothing happened. The hooves continued to pound him like sledgehammers.

Sudden, intense heat bathed him and the centaur screamed in pain and the beating ceased. Mike opened his eyes to see that the centaur around him were aflame. He quickly pulled himself up as Ted appeared and shot a jet of liquid fire at another group of nearby centaur. It was like watching a human flamethrower.

"You alright?" Ted shouted to him.

Mike's wooden shield fell apart and crashed to splinters at his feet.

"Yeah," Mike yelled back.

A centaur shot an arrow at Ted's back and Mike managed to summon a small barrier to deflect it just in time.

More centaur stormed in around Mike, swords flashing. He blocked and struck wildly, hard pressed now that he didn't have his shield, barely keeping the slashing blades at bay. One blade snaked past his guard and cut a gash above his eye.

Blood ran down his face and Mike couldn't see. Thinking fast, he created a circular barrier and with a mighty force of will, Mike blasted the wall outward, throwing the centaur away.

Mike swayed dizzily for a moment, the mental exertion taking its toll. He fell to his knees as the world spun crazily around him. The feeling quickly passed and he wiped the blood from his face and looked up.

There before him, surrounded by centaur was the same gorgeous woman he had seen earlier. She was battling furiously against several centaur at once, but as he watched, one of them got behind her unnoticed and struck at her unprotected back.

Still dizzy and half blind from the cut above his eye, Mike hurled himself forward. He crashed into the centaur, mace flailing, pulverizing a centaur with each swing and blasting the last centaur before it could strike her exposed back.

The woman looked surprised for a brief moment before whirling up to Mike. Together they fought side-by-side until another horn blast split the air. Hearing the call, the remaining centaur suddenly broke off their attacks.

Breathing heavily, Mike was confused as he watched the centaur herd retreat. Where were they going? Surely they were about to win… It was then he noticed how few centaur were actually left to retreat. Their herd had been decimated and some of the defenders shot arrows at their backs, downing a few more before they were out of bow range.

Mike smiled when he saw a black truck still chasing a group of centaur. *She is just as bad as Darrell.*

The woman next to him bent down and wiped the blood from her elegant short swords on the fur of the centaur at her feet before sheathing them behind her back.

Mike looked down at her and was struck by how beautiful she was. Her skin was a light, brownish-red that spoke of long hours outdoors. He hadn't noticed before, but her dark hair was actually made of countless small braids. Her large green eyes looked up and regarded him curiously.

"That was rather reckless." The woman had a musical voice and a mischievous sparkle in her eyes. "But I thank you for coming to my aid. I am Galina of Felias."

"Mike Strazney at your service," Mike replied.

Heavy stomping behind Mike told him that Baldor had arrived.

"Durned man-ponies," Baldor grumbled, as he trudged up to Mike.

A look of shock crossed Galina's face when she saw Baldor but it passed so quickly that Mike wasn't sure he had seen it. Perhaps she had never seen a dwarf before. Mike looked down at the jarl and was surprised to see several arrows protruding from the back of his shoulder.

He continued his cursing of the centaur, apparently unaware of the arrows.

"Um... Baldor?" Mike said and motioned to the arrows.

The dwarf craned his neck spying some of the shafts and grunted. Baldor reached around and casually began pulling them out one by one.

"I had heard of the legendary dwarf toughness," Galina said, with a hint of awe in her voice, "but that is truly impressive."

"Bah!" Baldor waved the comment away. "These little things?" He held up a fistful of arrows. "I've fought owlbears with more bite n' that."

Jack came limping over with help from Ted, the arrow still buried in his thigh.

"I think they have plenty of bite," Jack grumbled. He was covered in blood, but other than the thigh wound and a few scrapes, he appeared unhurt.

Ted seemed to sag against Jack, and Mike realized that it was actually Jack keeping Ted up, not the other way around. Ted was pale as a ghost and had blood running from his nose. He saw Mike's concern and gave a weak smile. "I think I may have overdone it again."

"Ya think?" Jack grated, as he set Ted gently on the ground.

Jack looked up at Mike. "So, are you going to introduce us to your pretty friend?"

"I would," Mike answered, "if you would ever quit your complaining." He turned to Galina. "Galina this is Jack, Ted, and Baldor." Each nodded in turn. "Guys, this is Galina of..."

"Felias," she smiled, almost bashfully.

"Felias," Mike smiled back. "And unless I miss my guess, Galina is an elf."

Ted just nodded. He had probably suspected the same thing, but Jack eyed her suspiciously and Baldor only snorted.

Galina's eyes widened in surprise. "How did you know?"

Mike shrugged. "The way you moved caught my attention first. Then there is the strange weapons and armor. Then I noticed th-"

"Oh baloney!" Ted wheezed from the grass. "Don't let this bag of meat fool you. He is almost as big a nerd as me and has been reading about elves forever. Anyone with half a brain could have figured that out." Ted wiped a fresh trickle of blood from his nose. "She is pretty and has pointed ears! What else would she be?"

"What is a… *nerd*?" Galina asked, looking embarrassed. "Is it a type of human?"

Laughter burst from Mike, Ted, and Jack. Their amusement only seemed to embarrass the elf woman further.

"You could say that," Ted chuckled.

"Bah!" Baldor snarled. "I will settle this!" He stomped up to Galina until his barrel chest was almost touching her. His head just came up to her chest, but he probably weighed over twice as much as her slender frame. He jabbed her in the stomach with a thick finger. "How old are ye?"

"Excuse me?" Galina asked.

Baldor scowled. "Everyone knows elves live forever," he growled, and poked her again. "So how old are ye?"

Galina's laughter rang out like bells. "Master Dwarf, elves do *not* live forever."

Baldor's eyes narrowed dangerously and he rested a hand on his axe. "If ye don't live forever, then ye be no elf."

Galina's laughter suddenly vanished and she abruptly looked very dangerous. She bent down and poked Baldor in the chest. "Do not threaten me, dwarf." Her voice had taken on a razors edge. "I *am* an elf and we do *not* live forever."

Mike, Jack, and Ted shared a look of surprise. They had never seen anyone stand up to a dwarf like that. It was impressive.

She straightened up. "But, we do possess an exceptional lifespan compared to most other races that we have encountered."

Baldor didn't back down, but he did seem impressed that the woman stood her ground. "Then how old are ye?"

"If you must know," Galina sighed, "I am 673."

"Nobody lives that long," Baldor growled.

Confusion crossed Galina's face. "But you just said-"

Baldor suddenly spun around and stomped away from her. "She be an elf a' right," he rumbled, and sat down on the grass near Ted.

Jack shook his head in disbelief. "Well, I'm glad that's settled."

Mike looked around and noticed that the surviving elves were wandering the battlefield, gathering arrows and searching for their missing comrades.

Galina still looked confused when Mike asked. "So, what were you doing out here?"

"We were following that herd of centaur," Galina replied. "We were hoping they would lead us to their main force, but it seems they knew we were here and set up this little ambush." She looked out at the carnage surrounding them. "Luckily, centaur are not the most Gifted race, or else this could have ended quite differently."

A growing rumble announced the arrival of Liz and Emily as they drove up with two centaur corpses impaled on the plow spikes. It reminded Mike of an awful parody of when a hunter would hang his deer on the hood of his truck, something Mike had never actually seen, even growing up in the sticks of Clearfield. Blood ruined paint. Everyone knew that.

Mike made introductions again. Liz and Emily were not surprised that the people they had come to help had turned out to be elves. It would take a lot to surprise them anymore. Way too many impossible things had happened in the last months to doubt the existence of anything.

Liz quickly moved to each of them and healed their wounds, spending the most time with Ted even though he didn't have any physical injuries that Mike could see. Perhaps mental fatigue was harder to heal than a cut.

As Liz worked, the surviving elves retrieved their fallen comrades. Surprisingly few elves had died during the skirmish with the centaur, but injuries were common. Once she was finished with her friends, Liz went around and healed the elves.

"Don't you elves have healers?" Mike asked, as he watched Liz work.

"We do," Galina replied, "but this is just a scouting party. We didn't bring any clerics or medicus with us. There should not have been any fighting. All we were meant to do was observe, find the main army and report back."

"Report back to whom?" Ted asked.

"Archmage Talsin, in the Steel City," Galina replied.

"Steel City?" Jack looked confused. "Do you mean Pittsburgh?"

"Yes," Galina said. "That is what you humans called it before the Shearing. But we elves prefer a more fitting title for that metal monstrosity you call Pittsburgh.

"Wait, wait, wait," Ted said, holding up his hands. "What is this *Shearing?*"

"The Shearing is what we have taken to calling the event that brought us to this world." Galina replied.

"And what was this event?" Ted pressed.

"We don't know." Galina gave an exasperated sigh. "We had heard rumors of whole villages disappearing, but thought it was just a joke spread by the Wild Ones. But several weeks ago we were having a Life Celebration when Gaea suddenly began to shake. The air… shimmered and then there was a sensation of falling, and we suddenly appeared in this world, in the woods, a few miles from your Steel City." She shuddered, remembering. "It is said that Archmage Talsin somehow came here on his own so he could discover what was happening. Perhaps he has found an answer to your question."

"Then I suggest we get going and find this Archmage Talsin," Ted said. "We are headed for Pittsburgh anyways."

"Will you join us?" Mike asked the elfin female.

Galina shook her head. "No. We will honor our dead and then continue our mission. We must discover where the enemy is hiding."

She looked up at the sky. "We have wasted too much time here already." Galina turned to Mike and the others. "Thank you again for coming to our aid. I hope to see you again, gods willing."

With that, Galina and the other elves gathered their dead and headed for the woods. The Heroes of Awesome watched them go until they vanished into the trees.

"Well, that was interesting." Ted noted.

"Yeah…" Emily said. "Now, let's get out of here before anything else interesting shows up."

CHAPTER 5

A few miles down the road, they caught up with the convoy and a short while later they found their first signs of civilization. They passed several checkpoints; some guarded by elves, others by dwarves, but most were human soldiers.

They drove through the hills and the deeper they got the more people they found. Houses with lights on, people working in fields, and even a few vehicles were driving around.

They wound their way through a valley and rounded a sharp bend when suddenly the city of Pittsburgh appeared before them. Nestled into the point between three connecting rivers and surrounded by hills sat the magnificent city, its skyscrapers dull and grey in the overcast light.

Liz breathed a sigh of relief. She hadn't realized how afraid she had been of finding Pittsburgh, and their hope, in ruins. But now that the city was in sight, her fears suddenly fled.

Baldor gave a soft whistle of awe. "Well, ain't that a sight," the jarl said. "I can see why they call it the Steel City."

They picked up speed as they rounded the last hill and headed toward one of the many large bridges spanning the wide river before them.

The first thing that Liz noticed was the immense wall that now ringed the city. She had thought the wall that the dwarves were building around Clearfield was impressive, but it was nothing compared to the monstrosity before her.

Standing several stories tall, the wall was made of some type of odd white stone with colossal towers that protruded along its length. Thick, vertical metal bands periodically wrapped sections of the wall. Liz could see markings on the steel bands, but couldn't make out what they were from this distance.

Thankfully, there appeared to be minimal damage to the city itself, but this side of the river had been almost completely destroyed. The football and baseball stadiums still stood, but most everything else was in ruins. Groups of dwarves and men worked together to clear away the destroyed buildings.

Liz couldn't believe the amount of change that had happened in a few short months. It made the changes in Clearfield seem painfully slow. But then Liz had to remind herself that Pittsburgh was infinitely larger than the sleepy little town of Clearfield and had much more resources to work with.

The convoy reached the base of the bridge and found a group of elves wearing long robes standing around what looked to Liz like a pile of bubbling mud. She wasn't sure what they were doing, but it almost seemed like the mud grew as she watched. But before she could inspect it further, they were past them and driving across the bridge.

They reached the other side, and were forced to stop and wait in line to enter the city. A gigantic gate that looked to be made of solid steel and covered in dwarfen runes blocked the entrance.

Now that they were close, Liz noticed there was something strange about the walls. They looked unlike any stone she had seen. Swirls and flecks of color almost seemed to move inside the stone. But that wasn't the only strange thing. It took her a minute to realize she couldn't see any seams where the stones met. It almost looked like one solid piece.

And then there were the massive steel bands strapped along the wall. They were far larger than she had expected and they were also covered with dwarfen runes.

"Baldor, what are those metal bands on the wall for?" Liz asked.

"Those be Warding Belts," Baldor explained. "Most types o' stone can only hold wards o' a certain strength. The greater the ward, the stronger the material needed ter hold it. So, for the most powerful wards o' protection on a wall they must be usin' Warding Belts ter hold the runes."

"I can no believe that such powerful wards have been built so quickly," Baldor added. "There must be many master Runesmiths here for such grand Warding Belts ter be in place."

Baldor inspected the walls closely. "But… I no recognize the type o' stone in that wall. Perhaps Midguard has stone that Svartalfheim does not?"

"I don't recognize it either," Ted muttered thoughtfully, as he too examined the strange white stone.

Liz could see the small figures of men, dwarves, and elves patrolling along the top of the wall while a group of soldiers stood before the gate, checking everyone before they were allowed to enter.

Long banners rippled in the breeze on either side of the gate. The banners were black with a gold bar running vertically down the center. A three-towered fortress of black stood on a shield of gold and was outlined in white.

Liz thought the design looked familiar, but couldn't place it. She also noticed the human soldiers wore tabards of the same design. *Tabards?* Liz wondered. *Who even wears tabards anymore? Besides Scadians, of course.* She figured it must be the dwarves' idea.

They sat on the bridge for several minutes before they finally reached the guards at the gate. After a brief conversation with Jack and the accompanying guardsmen, the gate guards let them enter.

Inside the walls was a riot of activity as humans, elves, and dwarves crowded the streets. The dwarves stomped about in heavy-looking battle plate, like Lord Aurvang and his guard.

The elves, on the other hand, wore a wide variety of clothing. Many wore simple but elegant robes, some were clad in elaborate silvery armor sculpted to look like a bare torso much like ancient Greek statues, while other styles of armor were strips of metal bands that reminded Liz of ancient Roman legionnaries, and others had the brown and green leathers like Galina and her scouts.

Most humans wore an assortment of modern body armor, heavy dwarven plate, and the fine elfin gear, but some chose average clothing.

Liz was shocked at the sheer volume of people. She hadn't dared to hope that so many people had survived. And it looked like they weren't just surviving; to Liz, it looked like they were actually thriving.

In the distance, she saw groups of people standing around a man who stood on the hood of a car. He seemed to be giving a speech. But soon he was lost in the distance as the convoy made its way slowly through the throng, following the directions from the gate guards.

Liz was surprised at how the city looked the same inside the walls. With the exception of elves and dwarves walking around, it looked pretty much like it normally did. There was amazingly very little sign of conflict.

"What kind o'city be this?" Baldor said disgustedly, as they wound their way through the city. "Why must ye keep turning? Can ye no just drive straight ter where we be going?"

"They are called one-way streets," Liz explained. "Pittsburgh is full of them."

Baldor snorted. "Seems dumb ter me."

The companions all got a chuckle out of that.

"And why do ye have so many bridges?" Baldor grumbled. "Do they no realize that each gate be a weak point in the wall?" He snorted again. "Foolish."

It was a short drive to the open square surrounded by a towering glass building where soldiers loaded and unloaded supplies. The convoy entered the square and came to a stop. The people inside the trucks eagerly disembarked and quickly melted into the crowed in search of friends and loved ones.

Liz and her friends stayed in the truck and watched as the Clearfield guardsmen went over to the Pittsburgh soldiers to see what supplies they could get.

"Well, now what?" Emily asked, as they watched the soldiers talking.

"Good question," Liz replied. "I guess we wait."

The guardsmen came back a minute later and walked up to Liz. "You know your way around Pittsburgh, right?"

"Yeah. Why?" Liz asked.

"Those guys," the guardsmen motioned to the soldiers they had been talking to, "say we need to talk to somebody at the Cathedral of Learning to get approval for any supplies. Ever heard of it?"

"Yeah, I know where it is," Liz answered. "I can get you there."

"Great. We will follow you then." The guardsmen looked relieved. "Thanks."

As the guardsmen walked away and got back into their transports, Liz turned back to the open window behind her and said, "Hey Ted?"

"Yessum?"

"You know where the Cathedral of Learning is right?"

"Of course."

"Good. How do we get there?"

"Home sweet home," Ted sighed as the Cathedral came into view.

The Cathedral of Learning was located a short distance east of downtown, in the neighborhood of Oakland. Made of steel and limestone, the Cathedral towered over its neighbors, rising over 500 feet into the air to dominate the skyline.

"About time," Baldor grumbled.

Liz noticed that several teams of dwarves and elves were working around the grounds. It looked to her like they were planning a wall for around the Cathedral. She didn't think that was a bad idea. It looked very exposed standing in the center of a half-acre of trees in the middle of a city block.

They drove up to the main entrance and parked along the street. Liz and her friends got out and were joined by one of the guardsmen while the others stayed behind to watch over the trucks. They didn't think anything would attack them here, but they weren't taking any chances.

Liz felt a slight tremor under her feet as they walked up to the entrance. The huge wooden doors were guarded by a pair of human soldiers in the same black and gold tabards as those at the gate. The guards didn't try to stop them and opened the heavy, wooden doors as the party arrived. Ted led the way as the imposing doors swung open and they entered the Cathedral of Learning.

Liz's breath caught when she saw the majesty of the room they had entered. Immense stone pillars soared several stories above to support a vaulted ceiling. Large iron lamps hung from long chains down the center between each row of pillars. Marvelous stone sculptures and brilliant stained glass windows decorated the walls all along the cavernous chamber.

"Impressive..." Baldor muttered, "fer human work."

Wooden tables and chairs were spread around the chamber where humans, elves, and even a couple of dwarves sat and studied the various books and texts each had laid out before them.

An elf in exquisite silvery armor, holding a short spear and round shield, stood nearby and noticed them enter. The elf hefted his spear and approached Ted.

"Greetings," the elf said warmly. "May I ask what your business is here?"

"We need to speak with whoever is in charge," Ted answered.

The elf eyed them wearily and Liz realized how they must look, armed to the teeth and some of them still splattered with blood from their encounter with the centaur.

"I'm afraid I cannot let you beyond the Commons so armed, friends," the elf said.

Baldor growled deep in his throat. "And who are ye ter be tellin' us what we can 'n can no do, elf?"

"I am Leandros, Paladin of Athena," the elf replied coolly, "and I must insist."

"And if I refuse?" Baldor rumbled threateningly, hefting his axes.

Leandros' eyes narrowed dangerously behind his silvery helm.

Thinking quickly Liz jumped in. "Do you know Galina of Felias?" she asked hurriedly.

A look of surprise crossed the Paladin's face at the mention of Galina's name. The surprise quickly passed. "Yes. Why?" Leandros asked suspiciously.

"Because we saved her and her scouting party from a herd of centaur less than an hour ago in the hills north of the city," Liz said, "and she told us to find Archmage Talsin and tell him what happened." It wasn't quite the truth, but Liz hoped dropping the Archmage's name would get them through.

Her story had the desired effect and Leandros' hostility suddenly vanished. "Why didn't you say so?" the elf said. "Follow me."

Leandros spun on his heel and strode away without looking back. Ted looked down at Liz in surprise and she shot him a quick wink in return.

Baldor grunted and held his axes at the ready as he prowled after the elf as if expecting an ambush at any moment.

They passed several classrooms where Liz saw elves or dwarves who appeared to be teaching groups of humans. She wondered what they were learning. Then in one room, the seats were filled with elves and dwarves and a human woman stood before the class pointing at a large map. Liz couldn't make out much more before the room was out of sight.

Leandros led them to an elevator where they all crammed in and got off on one of the upper floors. He led them down a long, stone hallway with fine carpets lining the floors. The elf stopped before one of the doors and softly knocked. There was a muffled response from within, and Leandros opened the door and led them inside.

It was a small office that was dominated by a large, wooden desk near the window. Seated behind the desk was a middle-aged man with light brown hair that stuck up at wild angles, and bright eyes looking out from under his glasses.

"You aren't an elf," Ted said in surprise.

"An acute observation," the man said with a sly smile. "I am Dr. Daniel Cooper," he said without getting up. "I am the Dean. Welcome to the Cathedral of Learning."

Dr. Cooper looked them over carefully. "I understand you have word from Galina and her scouts?"

"How did you…" Ted began, but Dr. Cooper waved the question away.

"I know everything that goes on within Cathy," Daniel said. "Now, about Galina…"

"Just one minute." Ted eyed the man behind the desk. "What happened to Dr. Z? I thought he was the Dean here."

"He was," Dr. Cooper admitted. "Unfortunately, Dr. Zehner had to resign his post after a small accident when one of his spells went awry. Now, if you would please continue."

Mike recounted how they had found the scouts being attacked by the centaurs and then came to their aid.

"And why were you on the road in the first place?" Daniel asked once Mike had finished.

"We had heard on the radio that Pittsburgh still stood," Mike answered. "So, we came to see for ourselves."

Dr. Cooper looked intrigued. "And where are you coming from?"

"Clearfield."

"Clearfield?" Daniel said. "Can't say I've heard of it."

"I'm not surprised," Ted grunted. "It's a small town a few hours northeast of here."

"I see." Daniel leaned forward in his chair almost eagerly. "I assume Clearfield is intact?" Mike nodded. "Good," Daniel said. "How did Clearfield survive?"

"That is a long story," Mike answered.

"I've got time," Dr. Cooper said easily.

So, together Mike and the others retold Dr. Cooper of their experiences over the last months starting with the strange aurora lights, and how various creatures suddenly appeared and attacked Clearfield. They told him how each of them discovered they had some kind of new ability and how they had met the dwarves. They described the battle against the orcs and goblins, and how they were rebuilding following the victory.

"And that is why we are here," Ted finished. "To get some supplies to finish our construction and, hopefully, become fully self-sufficient."

"Of course, you shall have whatever supplies we can offer." Dr. Copper looked at the elf Paladin. "Leandros, would you be so kind as to take this young man," he motioned to the guardsman, "and make sure he gets whatever he needs. Also, inform Master Titus about the possible captives and see if he can get some scouts up there."

Leandros nodded and left the room with the guardsman following behind.

Once the door closed behind them, Daniel reclined in his chair. "Now, let me tell you what we know, or at least suspect, about this event," he began. "My colleagues and I have a theory that this is the result of a malfunction at the Large Hadron Collider. Somehow the collider ripped a hole in our reality and created a kind of vortex. That vortex has been pulling magic and creatures from other worlds, or realities, into ours to fill the vacuum."

"I believe this magic is also the reason for the sudden appearance of your abilities," Dr. Cooper said. "Have you heard the rumor that humans don't use all their brains?"

"Of course." Ted replied. "But, that's not technically accurate."

"Correct," Daniel said. "Humans do use all of their brains, just not all at once." A note of excitement entered his voice. "What I have found is that this magic has activated parts of the brain and made connections to others where previously there had been none."

"It is my belief that human brains were wired to use magic all along, but there wasn't enough in our world for us to use. But since the Shearing, there is plenty of magic floating around for our brains to connect with."

"Interesting," Ted muttered. "But what is this *Shearing*? Galina mentioned it, too."

"Ahh... of course you wouldn't have heard of this since you just got here," Daniel said. "According to the elves and dwarves, there are many other worlds, perhaps an infinite number, existing alongside our own. But, the only way to access them is to cross this barrier that the elves call the

Veil Between Worlds."

"From what I have been able to piece together, this Veil became impassible for whatever reason around two thousand years ago. Since then, it has been impossible to cross. But like I said earlier, we believe the LHC ripped open this Veil, allowing things to cross again."

"The elves are calling the tearing of the Veil, and its subsequent pulling of magic and beings across, The Shearing."

Dr. Cooper let out a deep sigh. "But, most of this is just conjecture. Without any way to communicate with our European allies, we cannot be sure if the LHC is in fact responsible."

"So, phones and Internet don't work here either?" Mike asked.

"Correct," Daniel said. "We have limited radio usage, but it's spotty, and we are working on getting the Internet back." The doctor smiled ruefully. "I hadn't realized how much I used it until it was gone."

"I assume you saw the fire in the sky a few weeks back?" Daniel asked.

"Of course, we did," Emily said. "How could you miss it?"

"Well," Dr. Cooper said, "that was most of Earth's satellites burning up in the atmosphere." He looked tired. "There are a few left, but their signals are scattered and usually come back in a garbled mess."

"But, that isn't our only problem." He rubbed his eyes tiredly. "What little news that reaches us is rather dire. There are a few towns like your Clearfield out there that have survived this long. Unfortunately, they are few and far between."

"Honestly, this country is in shambles and I suspect the rest of the world is similarly mired in disaster," Daniel admitted. "There is no government anymore. The last partial radio signal we received said that DC is overrun with monsters. There has been no contact with any other states beyond Ohio and the Virginias."

"We are on our own," Daniel shook his head sadly. "The only reason we are still alive at all is because of the arrival of the dwarves and elves that joined us in our fight, and those individuals that discovered they can use magic."

Dr. Cooper went silent and stared blankly at his desk.

After it became apparent the doctor wasn't going to say anymore, Ted cleared his throat. "So, what is it you do here?"

Daniel snapped out of his fog and smiled. "This is the Cathedral of *Learning*," he said. "With the help of the elves and dwarves, we are trying to make sense of all this... craziness."

"Thanks to the elves, we have learned that magic comes to people in different ways, so we started classes to teach people how to use their unique abilities," Daniel said. "We have elves and dwarves teaching magic and combat techniques, while we humans teach the elves and dwarves about our world and how to use our technology."

"And how is that working?" Ted asked.

Daniel shook his head ruefully. "There has been some... *debate*... between the three races."

Baldor snorted, and Mike and Ted grinned. Liz knew what they were thinking. They didn't know much about the elves, but they knew how stubborn dwarves could be.

Dr. Cooper continued. "But, we have created an alliance between the three races and since the United States is effectively no more, we have formally declared Pittsburgh its own independent nation until such a time as this crisis has passed and the States can once again be united. But until that day comes, if it ever does, we will govern ourselves with our new alliance between the humans, elves, and dwarves."

"How does that work?" Jack asked.

"It is administrated by the elected human Governor and the Allied Council that represents all three races," Daniel replied. "That way humans will still rule, but the other races each have a say in how policy is handled."

"So, who is the Governor now?" Emily asked.

"There isn't one." Dr. Cooper made a face. "The city is under martial law for the time being and under the control of the military until an election can be organized. General Adams is the ranking officer in charge of the city at this time. But myself, Arch Battlemage Gwydion, King Anvilborn, and a few others all have a word in any policy before it is implemented."

Baldor made a strangling noise. "King Varnir Anvilborn be here?" he spluttered.

Daniel looked surprised. "Why, yes, he and a large portion of his Clan."

Liz was just as surprised at the jarl's reaction to learning a dwarf king was in the city. "Who is King Anvilborn?" she asked.

"King Varnir and the Anvilborn Clan be one o' the most powerful Clans in the Empire, second only ter Clan Armorthrone," Baldor explained, with a hint of awe in his voice. "Everyone knows that Anvilborn weapons and armor be the finest in the whole o' the Empire."

"He should no be here." The dwarf was almost muttering to himself. "The runes protecting Burdr Geirr should have prevented any transportation."

"Ah, as to that…" Dr. Cooper said, "King Anvilborn wasn't in his city when he was brought here…"

"Well, where he be then?" Baldor thundered.

"From what I heard," Daniel replied calmly, "he was having some kind of feast or something beyond his city when they were transported here."

"A feast…" Baldor groaned miserably.

Completely ignoring the jarl, Jack looked directly at Dr. Cooper. "You said that you know what abilities people have."

"Yes…?" Daniel replied.

"How do you discover that?" Jack asked.

"The elves have some kind of test. I've never watched anyone be tested so I honestly couldn't tell you how it's done. But I know someone who does," Daniel said as he stood up. "Come." He motioned for them to follow as he passed them and left his office.

"Where are we going?" Liz asked, as they all followed him into the hall.

Dr. Cooper smiled. "We are off to see the wizard!"

CHAPTER 6

They got back on the elevator and Dr. Cooper took them down several floors, then they followed him through several winding corridors. He came to a stop in front of one nondescript door in the center of the hallway.

"When we go in, you must keep quiet," Daniel said.

Everyone nodded that they understood and Dr. Cooper opened the door.

Inside was a large auditorium filled with people. They emerged at the top of the stairs in the back of the room looking down on a stage. Mike was surprised at how many people were in here. There must have been dozens, representing all ages and genders.

On the stage stood an elf that Mike could only describe as a wizard. He almost laughed at the stereotypical appearance of the elf on the stage. The wizard wore a robe of dark blue trimmed in silver. Long, silvery hair hung past his shoulders and a silver circlet ringed his brow. All that was missing was a beard and a pointy hat.

"Magic," the elf's voice boomed, "is all around us. It moves through the ground and the air just as it swirls though our very bodies. But," The elf held up a slender finger. "Magic is useless without the ability to control it."

"You all have the natural ability to control it. That is why you are here after all," the elf continued. "That ability is your Will. Only through Will Power can anyone use and control the flows of magic and grow in the Art."

"That means that the way in which you access your Will will depend solely on you. Some need to say a word to bring their spell to life. Others need only to think it. While still others need some object to focus their Will, like a wand or staff," the robed elf said. "There is no 'right' way to access your Art. However," a dangerous note entered his voice, "the use of Blood Magic is expressly forbidden."

"Now, those of you that sufficiently master the Art may even grow to see the actual flows of magic themselves. This is called Magesight. Some of you may experience flashes of it as you progress here. Do not fear." The elf looked around the room. "Fear has no place in the heart of a mage. Fear will consume you and ultimately break your Will."

"But," the elf said, holding up a hand, "that does not mean that emotion cannot be useful. Indeed, most of you, no doubt, experienced your first manifestation of the Art due to some powerful emotion." Mike noticed many of the "students" nodding their heads in agreement.

"As I said, emotion can be useful, but you cannot let it control you. You must control it, focus it, and use that emotion to reinforce your Will."

The elf looked around the room and caught sight of Dr. Cooper and his companions. He scanned the crowd for another moment before waiving his hand dismissively. "You may have a short recess. We will resume in fifteen minutes."

As the students were clearing out the room, Dr. Cooper led Mike and the others down the stairs and over to the stage. The elf smiled at Dr. Cooper and came down off the stage.

Mike noticed that the elf's robes were far more elaborate up-close, with faint symbols that seemed to almost float in the cloth itself.

"Greetings Daniel!" the elf said. "It has been long since you last paid me a visit."

"I know," Dr. Cooper replied. "I have been busy trying to bring some order to this chaos."

"You are not the only one," the elf said mysteriously.

"I'm sure," Dr. Cooper replied, "but I'm afraid I didn't come down here just to visit. These folks have just come from a small town several hours northeast of here and they have some questions."

The elf nodded knowingly, then gave a slight bow. "I am Talsin, Archmage of Hyperborea and I would be glad to answer whatever questions I can before my class resumes."

"*You* are the Archmage?" Ted asked incredulous.

"I am *an* Archmage, yes," Talsin replied easily.

Undeterred Ted pressed on. "Why would an Archmage be teaching what looks to be a basic magic class?"

Mike groaned inwardly. *Leave it to Ted to nitpick such a thing.*

Luckily, the elf didn't seem too put out when he replied. "Normally, I wouldn't concern myself with such trivial matters as teaching the basics of the Art. But you humans are like ignorant children and I cannot, in good conscience, allow you to muddle through the Art untended."

"There is an entire race of humans that haven't the first idea how the Art works. That is unimaginably dangerous," Talsin continued. "However, I only instruct those humans with the most Potential. The remainder are instructed by other mages."

"Potential?" Ted asked.

"Yes," the Archmage replied. "Potential is the measure of one's natural latent abilities. The greater one's Potential, the greater the chance they will become a master of the Art."

"Where is your hat?" Jack asked abruptly.

Mike groaned and Ted rolled his eyes. Liz and Emily tried not to laugh.

The Archmage looked confused. "Why does everyone keep asking me that?"

"How do you discover this Potential?" Ted asked, ignoring Jack's question.

"There is a simple spell to sense for Potential," Talsin replied.

"Can you test me?" Ted asked eagerly.

"If you wish," the Archmage said.

"Please do."

"Very well." Archmage Talsin walked up to Ted and muttered something under his breath as he reached up and put a hand on the side of Ted's head. Ted shivered and the Archmage's eyes grew wide in shock. The elf lowered his hand and stepped back. "Incredible," he whispered.

"What?" Ted asked.

Before the elf could answer Mike jumped in. "What about the rest of us?"

"What?" The elf looked confused a moment then shook himself. "Yes, of course."

Talsin stood before Mike and whispered something again before touching his hand to Mike's head. The elf's hand was warm to the touch and then a sudden icy sensation passed through Mike.

Talsin's eyes widened in surprise again and he stepped back.

Without saying anything, the Archmage repeated the process to Liz, Emily, and Jack.

"Truly incredible," he breathed after testing them.

Last, he approached Baldor, but the dwarf took a step back and held up a hand. "Ye will no be touchin' me, elf," he rumbled meaningfully.

"Very well," Talsin nodded. "I have found that you dwarves have very little Potential as a race and are naturally resistant to magic anyway."

Baldor grinned and tapped his head with a meaty finger. "Thick skulls," he proclaimed proudly.

The Archmage regarded the group before him before saying, "This is truly incredible. As a group, you have more Potential than any humans I have ever encountered, and not just pure Talent in the Art, but each of you has a different Talent."

When the elf saw that they didn't know what he was talking about, he explained. "There are many Talents of the Art and each Talent allows for a unique way of accessing and using magic." Talsin grew more excited as he talked. "But what is truly incredible is that each of you has more than one Talent! There is no telling what you are capable of."

"And you." He looked at Ted. "Your Potential for the Art is immense. With the proper training, I believe you could become an Archmage."

"Wait," Jack said. "You are telling me I *do* have magic?"

"Why, yes," Talsin replied as if it were obvious, "but your main Talent appears to manifest in a Corporal Form."

"What the hell does that mean?" Jack growled.

"It means," the Archmage replied coolly, "you cannot cast spells like a mage, but with proper training your mind and body can become infused with magical energy and become as one. Allowing for greater speed, strength, and stamina."

"I've got plenty of stamina," Jack grumbled.

Emily tried to stifle a laugh and Ted rolled his eyes.

Jack ignored them. "So, you are saying I will be a better fighter than Mike?"

"I imagine you will be better than everyone," Talsin replied. "You all have the Potential to be the best in your respective Talents, but you will not achieve that unless you learn from the Masters here."

"Stay," Talsin suddenly said. "Join the Cathedral. We could use humans with your Potential."

"We can't just stay," Liz said. "We need to make sure the supplies get back to Clearfield."

"Never fear my dear," Dr. Cooper interjected soothingly. "We will send plenty of guards along to ensure they arrive safely."

"Good enough for me," Ted said eagerly. "Sign me up."

"Me, too," said Jack. "It's about time I get to do something cool."

Mike looked over at Liz and shot her a sly grin. "I'm in."

Liz sighed. She wasn't about to go back without her friends. "Me, too, I guess."

Emily looked at them as if they had gone crazy. "Well, I'm not going back alone." She crossed her arms under her breasts defiantly. "I guess I'm staying, too."

Everyone looked down at Baldor. "What?" he growled. "I need ter get back ter me clan. Ye humans can have fun with yer new pointy-eared friends."

The doors suddenly opened and some of the students began coming back in.

Archmage Talsin clapped his hands. "Good. It's settled then." He looked at Dr. Cooper and said, "You will get them situated?"

"Of course," Daniel answered.

"Wonderful. I wish to speak with each of you later. Now, I must get back to my lesson." Talsin spun around and strode back onto the stage. "Ted, I will see you here tomorrow," he said without looking back.

Dr. Cooper motioned for them to follow and led them back out into the hall. He looked at his watch. "Come. Let's find some food and then we will get you a place to stay."

Dr. Cooper led them down a wide hallway and exited the main Cathedral to enter a smaller building attached to the main structure. Inside was a large cafeteria where all three races were represented and sat side-by-side. Mike noticed that the elves and dwarves sat on opposite ends of the room while the humans were in the center and mingled with both sides.

Each of them got a tray filled with food and they drew many looks as they walked in, covered in grime and still carrying their weapons.

Dr. Cooper noticed the people staring. "Perhaps I should have gotten you cleaned up before coming here… oh, well." He shrugged, unconcerned, and led them to an open table.

"Do all the people here have some kind of ability?" Ted asked, looking at all the people surrounding them.

"Why, yes." Daniel answered. "There is a remarkable percentage of individuals within the human population that have unique abilities."

"Do you see that little girl over there?" Daniel motioned with his fork.

Mike saw that the girl he was referring to looked to be only about eight or so.

"She has the ability to make duplicates of herself," Dr. Cooper said. "Kind of like a hologram, only so good you can't tell which one is really her," he said between bites of food. "So far, she has been able to make two of these duplicates simultaneously, but I suspect as she grows her powers will as well. It is quite extraordinary."

"Ah, and that man," he nodded toward a shifty-looking little man in the corner. "He can make himself invisible. And not just himself either, but anyone within a few yards also."

"That could be handy," Jack muttered.

"Indeed," Daniel agreed. "But it only lasts for a few moments. He has been working on keeping it active longer and is hoping to get half a minute soon."

Daniel motioned to another man seated near them. "What do you think he can do?

Mike inspected the man Dr. Cooper indicated. He was enormous. The man was a mountain of hair and muscle.

Emily whistled softly. "Now *that* is a man." Jack scowled at her, but she ignored him. "I bet he is super strong."

"I bet he is super dumb," Jack grumbled.

Dr. Cooper shook his head no.

"Can he fly?" Liz asked hopefully.

Dr. Cooper shook his head again.

"How about teleport?" Ted asked.

"No," Daniel said, "but I know a lady who can." He looked at them eagerly and when none of them offered any other ideas he grinned. "He sings."

Baldor choked. "He what?"

"He sings," Dr. Cooper repeated. "His songs give strength and courage to those around him, and it scares the monsters." Daniel grinned again. "We have taken to calling him Bard," he said, with a sly wink.

The group groaned. "Oh, that's bad," Ted chuckled.

Dr. Cooper laughed. "It seems it's rather common among the elves; they have a whole mess of them. Those warriors that sing while using weapons are called Blade Singers and those that purely use the power of their voice are known as Warsingers. There are even those that use arcane spells along with their song and those elves are Melody Mages.

"All that be *very* interestin'," Baldor rumbled, "but tell me this…" He pointed the small fork at Daniel. "Ye be one o' these… *scientists*, yes? Ye study things ter gain knowledge o' all kinds o' things, yes?"

"That is correct," Daniel replied. "That is how I got to be a doctor."

"Good," the jarl nodded, and leaned forward intently. "What do ye know o' the Bifröst?"

"The Bifröst?" Daniel said, caught momentarily off guard. "Isn't that the rainbow bridge that connects Earth to Asguard."

"So, ye've heard o' it," Baldor grinned. "Good. Now, tell me where I can be findin' it."

Daniel chuckled. "Master Dwarf, the Bifröst is a myth." He waived his hand dismissively. "It is about as real as…"

"Dwarves?" Jack said helpfully.

"Elves?" Mike added with a grin.

"Magic?" Ted smirked with a small flame dancing across his fingers.

Dr. Cooper held up his hands in defeat. "Alright, you got me." He looked at Baldor, "To answer your question, no, I don't know where the Bifröst is. I'm sorry." Baldor's shoulders slumped. "Perhaps you could ask the elves…" Daniel offered. "They know far more about magic than anyone else."

The dwarf scowled. "I would rather eat me own beard than talk about the Bifröst with a bunch o' fairy elves."

"Suit yourself," Dr. Cooper shrugged.

They ate in silence for several minutes until Liz spoke up. "Doctor, when we came in there was a group of elves standing around what looked like a section of… bubbling earth. What were they doing?"

"Ahh," Daniel smiled, "an excellent question. What you saw was a group of Shapers," Dr. Cooper explained. "The elves don't build things like we think of. They… grow them, if you will."

"So, we saw them growing a building?" Emily breathed.

"In a manner of speaking, yes," Dr. Cooper agreed. "But, that isn't the most amazing thing. I'm sure you noticed the wall around downtown?"

"How could we miss it?" Jack said.

"Well, it is made by the elves using some kind of secret process that imbues the stones with some kind of magic essence," Dr. Cooper said excitedly. "Combined with the dwarves' Warding Belts, they say the walls will be nearly impregnable once completed."

"They aren't finished yet?" Jack asked. "They looked done when we came through."

"Oh, my, no," Daniel chuckled. "The walls downtown are not nearly complete. And even when they are there are many more places in need of walls. Including here," Daniel added. "We plan on putting similar fortifications around Cathy to make her a kind of... fortress of knowledge... of sorts."

"Intriguing," Ted replied, "but tell me more about some of these special abilities."

****

The sun was beginning to set when their meal was over and Dr. Cooper led them across the Cathedral's expansive lawn over to several large cylindrical buildings.

"What are these?" Emily asked, eyeing the tube-like buildings.

"These are the dorms that you will be staying in," Dr. Cooper replied.

"Dorms?" Mike grumbled. "I had enough of dorms when I was in college." He looked around. "I'll take a nice hotel, thank you."

"I'm afraid we must insist," Dr. Cooper apologized. "There isn't enough room as it is with all the refugees, not to mention the elves and dwarves. I managed to reserve these dorm buildings for students of the Cathedral only."

"Well, wasn't that sweet," Jack mumbled, as they made their way into the nearest building.

They followed Dr. Cooper up several floors and then down a circular hallway. He stopped next to a row of doors.

"We have these three rooms reserved for you," Dr. Cooper said, and motioned to three doors in a row before them. "You may choose who stays where."

Dr. Cooper then led them into one of the rooms and Mike was

pleasantly surprised. Each dorm room was, in fact, a completely furnished suite; there were two small bedrooms, a little kitchen, and a living area.

"Wow!" Liz breathed. "These are nicer than the dorms I had to stay in."

"I'm glad you approve," Dr. Cooper smiled, "but here is where I leave you." He motioned down the hall. "You will find new clothes in a variety of sizes in the drawers and the laundry is next to the elevator. If you need anything else, there is a phone with a directory in each room. Make yourselves comfortable and I will have somebody get you in the morning for breakfast. Tomorrow, I will show you the rest of the campus and introduce you to the instructors."

"We are looking forward to it," Ted said eagerly.

"Speak for yourself," Emily muttered under her breath.

"Good." Dr. Cooper ignored Emily's comment. He smiled and turned to go. "Oh, one last thing." Daniel turned back to them. "In the morning, please leave your armor and weapons here."

CHAPTER 7

A soft knocking woke Liz up.

She sat up in bed, her dark hair falling loosely around her shoulders as she stretched luxuriously in the first rays of sunlight that streamed in through her window.

Liz slid out of bed, crossed the small room, and shivered when her bare feet touched the cold floor outside her new bedroom.

The soft knocking sounded again.

Liz walked up to the dorm's door and opened it to find Mike standing in the hallway.

Mike smiled at her. "Good morning," he said cheerfully.

"Morning," Liz replied sleepily.

She saw that he had his breastplate strapped to his chest, but she didn't see the mace anywhere. Liz eyed his armor. "I thought Dr. Cooper said no weapons *or* armor?"

Mike shrugged innocently. Knowing him, he had at least one dagger hidden somewhere.

She noticed him look her up and down, and Liz realized she was only wearing a flimsy nightshirt. Suddenly self-conscious, Liz blushed and quickly hid behind the open door. "What do you want?" she demanded.

"One of the doctor's assistants was just here and told us to meet him in the cafeteria in fifteen minutes," Mike said. "Will you guys be ready?"

"Of course," Liz replied. "Was there anything else?"

"Nope," Mike grinned.

Liz slammed the door shut then leaned back against it, eyes closed, embarrassed.

"Who was that?"

Liz's eyes popped open and she saw Emily standing in the doorway, rubbing her eyes sleepily.

"We need to get ready," Liz replied, trying to calm her racing heart. "Breakfast is in fifteen minutes."

****

A short time later, the Heroes of Awesome strode into the cafeteria.

Ted quickly spotted Dr. Cooper seated in the center of a long table, having a discussion with several elves and dwarves. They decided to find a table and eat while the doctor finished his discussion.

Liz was on her last bite when Dr. Cooper finally came over.

"Where is your dwarf friend?" he asked, walking up to their table.

"No idea," Jack answered. "He was gone when I woke up."

"Interesting," Daniel muttered, and then smiled. "Either way, if you are all done I would like to show you around and introduce you to the instructors."

Dr. Cooper's eyes narrowed as everyone got up. "I said you could leave those in your rooms." He motioned to their weapons.

While Liz had left her rifle in their room, Jack had convinced her to bring some weapons. He said that they could never be sure when some "baddie" would appear. She had to acknowledge that he made a good point, so her pistol was strapped to her thigh and a saber hung from her other hip.

Mike didn't have a shield, but that ancient mace now hung from his belt. Ted used the tall pole weapon that he had taken from the orc sorcerer as more of a walking stick than anything else. Jack was covered in assorted weaponry as usual and Emily had her precious bow and arrows.

"And I don't care," Jack replied defiantly. "We aren't going to be the only ones around here unarmed."

Liz wasn't sure what Jack meant until she took a good look around. While the elves mostly wore simple robes, a few did wear armor and swords while daggers could be seen on most of them. The dwarves, on the other hand, were almost all completely encased in their heavy armor and armed to the teeth. And the humans had a variety of weapons between them.

Dr. Cooper seemed to sag before them. "I know," he sighed miserably. "I try to get everyone to leave their weapons, but none of them will. They don't trust each other," Dr. Cooper muttered. "I am afraid something will set off one side or the other and start a war. And *that* is something we cannot afford."

Liz suddenly realized how tenuous this alliance truly was. She almost forgot that these three races had only been living together for a few months. Their similarities plus a shared history had brought them together. But they were all so different. It would take time for them to learn to fully trust each other. Liz just hoped they survived long enough for that to happen.

"The dwarves are a stubborn lot," Dr. Cooper continued as he led them out of the cafeteria. "Once their mind is made up, there is no changing it. And it doesn't seem to matter what clan they are either. Whether they are hill or mountain, they are all just as bull-headed." Daniel smiled. "If you ask them, there is a huge difference, but I haven't seen it."

They made their way across the Cathedral grounds and Liz could see several groups standing around in large circles. Dr. Cooper headed towards them as he talked. "And the elves are an emotional bunch. I haven't been able to figure them out," Dr. Cooper complained. "It seems there are countless classes of elves. They are all named after natural elements as far as I can tell, like wood elves and sky elves," Daniel explained. "You met Leandros. He is a sun elf, but don't ask me what that means because I haven't the slightest idea." He sighed heavily. "They are a secretive bunch and it's like pulling teeth to learn anything about them."

As Dr. Cooper finished talking, they arrived on the edge of one of the rings of people. Liz saw that in the center of the circle were two men sparring with two-handed wooden swords. A tall elf with long, blonde hair who was wrapped in dark red leather armor paced around them and gave instructions as the two humans dueled.

"The short guy is gonna win," Mike noted.

"Pft," Jack snorted. "I'll take that bet! That big dude is gonna crush him."

Liz had to agree with Jack. The larger man attacked furiously, driving the smaller man back with every swing.

Suddenly, the short man deflected a strike and spun away. The wooden sword whistled through the air and connected with the larger man's side with a resounding crack. The large man groaned and fell to his knees. The crowd burst into applause.

Jack cursed.

Mike grinned. "Told ya."

"That was luck," Jack grumbled.

Ted laughed. "No, it wasn't." He pointed to the shorter man. "That is Duke von Jensin, one of the best fighters in the SCA. That big guy didn't stand a chance," he chuckled. "The Duke was messing with him the whole time."

Jack cursed again.

"Go cry about it," Emily teased.

The leather-clad elf instructor took the two practice swords and held them aloft. "Who is next?" he shouted to the crowd.

"What are they doing?" Liz asked.

Dr. Cooper pointed at the tall elf. "That is Darius of Buyan. He is a Blade Dancer and one of the two-handed sword instructors," Dr. Cooper explained. "We are in the Martial Field and these are the Fighting Rings. Each ring has a different weapon mastery being taught."

"The elves use a ladder system to determine skill and ranking," Dr. Cooper said, "and so now we do as well. Everyone who wishes to learn a specific weapon or fighting style is first ranked based on his or her skill in a duel and then training begins. So, if any of you wish to improve your two-handed sword skill..." he said, as he glanced at Jack and his black orc katana, "...you should see Darius."

Emily prodded Jack in the ribs. "I think you and Mike should fight."

"Hey!" Jack rubbed his side. "I would, but I don't want to hurt him."

Mike laughed. "The only person you are likely to hurt is yourself."

"Shall we see about that?" Jack goaded.

Dr. Cooper stepped between them. "Perhaps later."

"Oh, you're no fun," Emily pouted.

"Sorry, my dear," Dr. Cooper said, "but we have places to go and people to see."

They skirted around the crowd as two more men took up the wooden swords as the elf Darius looked on.

Dr. Cooper wound around several rings of people, each with a different weapon being used. "There," he pointed to a black-bearded dwarf holding a huge war hammer, "is Dorf Gloinson, one of the war hammer and great mace instructors."

Emily giggled. "Dorf the Dwarf."

Dr. Cooper ignored her and pointed to a pair of dwarves in another circle. "Those are the Tarheels Brothers. Leif is the one using the axe and shield while Sven wields the mace and shield."

"Over there," Dr. Cooper motioned to another ring, "is the Pole Arm Ring where they teach spear, staff, and other pole weapons."

"Obviously," Emily muttered. "It *is* the Pole Arm Ring."

Dr. Cooper shot her a scathing look before continuing. "Next to it is the Great Axe Ring and then there is the Fencing Ring, Grappling Ring, Knife Ring..." He pointed to each group of people as they passed them. "Pretty much any weapon you could possibly want to learn is taught here."

"We have discovered that the elves, dwarves, and humans have very different fighting styles," Dr. Cooper continued, "and so we try to have instructors from each race to give as complete examples as possible."

They passed the last ring and left the Field behind them. "The Rings are always open for training, so feel free to come here whenever you want,"

Dr. Cooper added as they walked.

He took them down a street that led to a large park. The occasional gunshot could be heard coming from deeper in the trees, and in a clearing near the road Liz could see several people with bows standing in a line.

"That is the Range." Dr. Cooper stopped and looked into the trees. "It used to be a golf course, but it has been converted into where we teach firearms, bows, and other ranged weapons."

"I'm not going to take you inside the Range, but if you want to see for yourself later, just follow the path and it will take you to each station," Dr. Cooper said, and turned back the way they had come. "Now, for the part you are really here for."

He led them back through the Martial Field and into the Cathedral of Learning. Up a flight of stairs guarded by several stoic dwarves, they came to another long hallway. Liz didn't think it looked much different from any other hallway that they had seen, but Dr. Cooper stopped and raised his arms dramatically. "Welcome to the Halls of the Gifted!"

"Halls of the Gifted?" Jack snorted. "Really?"

"What?" Dr. Cooper sniffed. "It's a good name."

"It's a stupid name," Jack retorted. "Sounds like something out of one of Mike's stupid fantasy books."

"Hey!" Mike growled. "My books aren't stupid."

Liz saw this rapidly spiraling out of control and decided to cut it off. "So, what are these *Halls of the Gifted* for?" she asked quickly, even though she was pretty sure she knew the answer.

"It is where anyone who discovered they have some kind of power can learn to unlock their abilities," Dr. Cooper said proudly.

"And just who exactly is teaching these abilities?" Ted asked.

"Elves mostly," Dr. Cooper answered. "They seem to have a complete mastery of all things magical, even though we have discovered a few abilities that even they haven't seen before. And there are a few things that the dwarves excel at, like crafting magical items." Dr. Cooper shook his head in wonder. "I have never seen such craftsmen as these dwarves. Their work is truly unrivaled. But I digress," Dr. Cooper said with a sigh before he motioned dismissively. "Now, back to the matter at hand!" he said with a flourish.

"These lower floors are devoted to defensive spell craft," Dr. Cooper explained. "Anyone trying to get further up must pass through this area. It is partly a defensive measure in case we are attacked, and to keep any accidents on the higher floors from escaping."

"Escaping?" Liz asked. "What do you mean escaping?"

"Oh, it's nothing to worry about my dear," Dr. Cooper said easily, and started walking again. "Now, as I was saying, these are the defensive magic floors. You will find a great many dwarves around here, as they seem to have a unique affinity for such powers and a natural resistance to spells."

Dr. Cooper continued talking as he strode down the hall, but Liz stopped listening as she peered into the rooms as they passed. Many strange sights greeted her.

In one room there was a man who appeared to be trapped inside a glassy box. He pounded futilely on the clear walls and shouted, but no sound came out.

Then, there was a woman surrounded by a shimmering dome as half a dozen people smashed it with various weapons.

Dr. Cooper stopped in front of a door and motioned for them to look.

Inside stood a black-bearded dwarf who stood with arms raised and several glowing runes hovering in the air before him. He was stripped to the waist; his thick-muscled form glistened with sweat. Flickering runic tattoos covered most of his torso and ran down both arms to pulse with an inner glow, but most shocking of all was his eyes. They blazed with a fiery light.

"That," Dr. Cooper pointed at the dwarf, "is Ambrosar the Thunderer, Chief Guardian of Thor and Co-Chair of our Defense Department."

Dr. Cooper turned from the room with the powerful dwarf and directed their attention across the hall to another room. "And that," he said, "is the other Co-Chair. Commander Valerian, Paladin of Athena and Lord of the Ice Leaves.

Liz's breath caught in her throat. Before her stood the most beautiful being she had ever seen. He was tall and lean with ebony skin that contrasted wonderfully with his exquisite silver armor. His black hair was cropped short and his eyes were the most piercing shade of purple.

Although she couldn't hear what they were saying through the door, his stunning good looks, perfect white teeth, and beautiful sparkling eyes entranced Liz as he spoke to the dozen or so humans seated before him.

The beautiful elf glanced up and caught her staring at him, and Liz blushed. He flashed a dazzling smile at her before turning back to his class.

Liz suddenly realized she was alone.

Looking around frantically, she spotted her friends moving off down the hall after Dr. Cooper. They were almost to the elevators.

Liz caught up just as they were getting on and she hurried inside.

"Get his number?" Mike teased.

She punched him as the door slid closed.

Several floors up they got off and followed Dr. Cooper through another maze of hallways. "Here we have lessons for all the 'miscellaneous' abilities," Dr. Cooper said. "Ones that don't seem to relate to any other powers, or only have one use. Like teleportation, invisibility, and our large Bard friend," Dr. Cooper added with a chuckle.

"Now, mages can use teleportation and all those other things as well," Dr. Cooper continued. "However, they use spells to accomplish them. The people here seem to have these abilities naturally. It is quite remarkable."

"But we don't just teach abilities here, we also discover them!" He looked directly at Jack and said, "Perhaps here you will find that you really do have some ability or gain a better understanding of your fighting talent."

"I won't hold my breath," Jack muttered.

Dr. Cooper then led them up a flight of stairs to an area where nearly all the walls were glass.

"This is the R&D floor," Dr. Cooper said excitedly. "My colleague, Dr. Su Yong has made more breakthroughs in robotics and artificial limbs in the last few weeks than we have had in years!"

Dr. Cooper nearly danced with excitement and Liz could see Ted's eyes light up at the mention of robotics. "She has already successfully applied an artificial arm on a soldier and you would swear it was his real arm! Soon she hopes to perfect a bionic eye."

"Really?" Ted said. "How would she interface with the optic nerve?"

The conversation, as they progressed through the lab quickly broke down into a bunch of techno-babble that Liz couldn't follow. So instead of listening, Liz spent her time admiring all of the strange devices being worked on by teams of scientists.

Not quickly enough, they were out of the labs and up to the next floor. As soon as Dr. Cooper opened the door, Liz instantly had the feeling they had stepped into a hospital.

"This is the Medical Bay," Dr. Cooper said.

"Sounds like we are on a spaceship," Mike noted.

Dr. Cooper smiled. "Yes. Yes, it does. But this is where they teach the healing arts, both normal and magical… at least from inside Cathy. There is also a separate building the elves call the Temple of Light, which most of us just refer to as the Healers Tent."

"It's not really a tent anymore since the Shapers worked on it, but the name stuck. It is one of the few places where the elves, dwarves, and humans actually work together," Dr. Cooper continued. "It seems there are many different ways of healing, so everyone is learning something new."

Dr. Cooper pointed into one room where three figures stood around an operating table. One was a very short dwarf with fiery red hair and a long scar running down one cheek. Next to the dwarf was a tall middle-aged human woman in a white lab coat with long, black hair. She seemed to be having an argument with the pretty blonde female elf in blue robes that was standing across from her.

"The tall woman there is Dr. Kilpatrick. She is a brilliant surgeon and in charge of all 'normal' medical procedures here," Dr. Cooper explained. "She is talking to High Priestess Ipheto of the Temple of Demeter. And the dwarf is Fugal Brightrobe, a Master Cleric of Frigg."

"Together the three of them oversee all things related to injuries and healing," Dr. Cooper said, and continued walking. They made a quick circuit around the Bay before heading up to the next floor.

This new area was guarded by several stern-looking elves in black robes, but they recognized the doctor and let them pass without a word. Once inside, it looked more like the usual classrooms they had seen the day before.

"Last, but not least," Dr. Cooper announced grandly, "is the Arcanum. These last several floors are devoted to all things magical and arcane."

Ted grinned like a little kid in a candy store. "This is awesome!" he said, and quickly wandered off to peer into each room gleefully.

The others followed more slowly behind Dr. Cooper.

Emily suddenly spoke up. "Do you have anyone that can make things grow?"

Dr. Cooper smiled. "Of course. The Druids have great knowledge of such things, but they are very secretive. It has been a constant battle just to allow humans to see them," Dr. Cooper sighed. "There is a room here for them. However, the Druids prefer to stay in the forests. You can look for them in either Schenley or Frick Park."

"So, what do you think?" Dr. Cooper asked eagerly.

"Impressive," Mike said, and the others nodded their agreement. "It seems you covered all the bases."

"We try," he said, as he watched them wander the halls and peer into several rooms.

"So..." Dr. Cooper rubbed his hands together eagerly. "Will you be staying?"

CHAPTER 8

A wooden sword whistled though the air and collided with another practice blade with a resounding *crack*. The two men circled each other in the center of the ring as the gathered crowd cheered them on.

A few strikes later and one man doubled over in pain as the other's wooden sword connected with his midsection.

"Good," the red-clad elf said. "Still sloppy, but you both have improved greatly."

The two men seemed pleased with the announcement as they handed the practice swords to the elf. Once they had joined the others around the ring, the elf looked around. "Who's next?"

An enormous dark skinned man came out of the crowd and approached the elf. He held out a massive hand and one of the wooden swords was placed in it.

The blonde elf waited a minute but when nobody stepped forward he shouted. "Who will face the Bear?"

The onlookers shuffled nervously, but none came forward. Then, a black armored figure moved into the ring. "I will," Jack smiled.

"You do not look familiar," the elf said.

"I'm new in town," Jack replied easily, as he strode up to the elf.

"Ah," the elf barely looked at him. "Then welcome." He handed the wooden sword out to Jack. "I am Darius, Blade Master here in the Sword Ring."

"Jack Treno," Jack replied, as he took the offered blade and swung it experimentally. He didn't really like the way it felt in his hands, almost like it didn't sit right, unlike his orc katana. That blade felt like it was made for him. But he knew he didn't really have a choice in the practice area, so he accepted the wooden sword.

Darius eyed him curiously. "There are a few rules you will need to follow," the elf said. "One, there will be no use of magic during the duel. Two, there is to be no strikes to the head or face. Three, the duel ends with a solid strike to the body or by the incapacitation of your opponent. And finally, no armor is permitted."

Jack nodded. "Understood," he said, and quickly stripped off his orc armor and set it in a pile at the edge of the Ring. He hesitated a moment holding his orc katana uncertainly.

"Will you hold this for me?" Jack asked as he held the katana out to the elf.

Darius smiled. "Certainly." And took the sword.

A sudden shadow crossed the elf's features so quickly that Jack wasn't sure he had even seen it.

"Begin!" Darius shouted, never taking his eyes from the black weapon.

The large man raised his sword in a salute and Jack did the same.

Before he was set, the Bear lunged forward. Jack ducked the sweeping blade and stabbed forward with his own sword, thinking to end it quickly, but the large man was surprisingly agile and twisted away.

Without hesitating, Jack pursued and the two men traded several blows before Jack landed a solid hit on the Bear's knee, causing him to stumble. Jack took quick advantage as the large man tried to regain his balance. Jack got around the Bear's guard and delivered a solid strike to his massive chest.

"Well, that was disappointing." Jack muttered as he lowered his wooden blade.

"That was surprising," Darius said, as the two combatants approached him. "It seems you already have some skill at the Dance."

The Bear handed back his practice sword and silently rejoined the crowd, but Jack held on to his. "I have had a little practice," Jack said with a smirk.

"I see…" Darius saw that Jack still held his practice blade. "Do you wish to go again?"

"Sure." Jack looked around at the crowd. "I could use a challenge."

"Oh," Darius smirked, "you want a challenge?" He looked into the crowd and pointed to two men near the front. "Steven, Jeremy, grab a sword and get over here," the elf commanded before turning back to Jack. "How does two against one sound?"

One blonde man and an ugly fellow each picked a sword off a nearby rack and entered the ring. Jack grinned as he turned to face them. "Works for me."

The crowd muttered excitedly as the three men circled each other. Jack closely watched their movements and realized these guys were probably far more skilled with a sword than the Bear had been. Jack scolded himself for a fool. Of course, the elf would set him up against two skilled swordsmen.

Jack took a deep breath. There was only one thing to do in a situation like this. He took a play from Mike's playbook.

He attacked.

Jack charged the ugly man to his left, hoping to overwhelm him quickly before the other man could get there. But the man was ready and danced away, effectively putting Jack in between his two opponents.

"Well, that didn't work," Jack muttered to himself, as he tried to keep both men in his line of sight.

Suddenly, both men charged forward and Jack was caught between them. Acting purely on instinct, Jack lunged to his right and engaged the blonde, creating some space between himself and Ugly for a few precious seconds.

But, all too soon both men were on him and Jack had to use every ounce of skill he could muster to avoid their slashing blades. He ducked, weaved, and blocked madly, taking a few hits to his arms and legs, but nothing serious.

Although he was holding them off for the moment, Jack knew he couldn't keep this up forever. These guys were good and they were wearing him down. He had to end this quickly.

Jack noticed that Ugly favored his right side and that Blondey was slow backing up. Thinking fast Jack wove between their whirling blades and positioned himself on Ugly's left. Then he barreled toward Blondey, exposing his back to Ugly.

His gamble paid off as Ugly was slow to adjust to his left side and gave Jack enough time to take on Blondey alone. They traded several blows, but backing up, Blondy was too slow and Jack pressed his advantage. With a resounding smack, Jack struck Blondey in the ribs.

A soft whistle was all the warning Jack had as Ugly's blade descended. Jack rolled away and caught Ugly by surprise. Ugly stumbled as his swing hit nothing but air and he lost his balance. Coming up swinging in one smooth motion, Jack pressed in.

Ugly froze as Jack's wooden blade rested against his throat.

The crowd erupted in cheers.

"Impressive," Darius said grudgingly.

Breathing hard, Jack waited as Blondey and Ugly put their practice weapons back. Darius noticed that Jack wasn't moving to give up his sword and raised an eyebrow questioningly. "You wish to go again?"

"Yes," Jack breathed. "But this time," he pointed his wooden sword at the elf, "I want you."

Darius laughed. It was a rich, cheerful sound. "Do not be absurd," the elf chuckled. "You may have some skill with a blade... for a human, but I am a Blade Dancer."

"So, you're scared," Jack sneered.

The elf's eyes narrowed dangerously. "You cannot stand against one of the Korybantes."

"Shall we see about that?" Jack pressed.

The crowd began cheering and Darius scowled. "Very well." He sat Jack's katana on his pile of armor and raised a practice sword. "Prepare yourself."

Jack smiled. "I'm ready when yo-"

One moment the elf was standing several paces away and the next his sword was streaking at Jack's chest.

Jack flung himself backwards and brought his blade up just in time to barely deflect the blow. But before he could recover, Darius was a blur as he twirled around and struck again. This time Jack wasn't fast enough and the wooden sword smashed into his chest, sending him crashing to the ground.

Jack laid there, gasping for breath as Darius stood over him. "I am impressed. You actually managed to parry one of my strikes. Perhaps you have the makings of a Dancer in you after all." The elf held out a hand and after a moment Jack accepted and was hauled to his feet.

"A Dancer?" Jack groaned. "Sounds kinda lame to me," he gasped, still trying to catch his breath.

Darius smiled. "Lying dead seems more 'lame' to me."

"Ha!" Jack winced. "You got me there, elf."

Darius led them out of the ring and replaced the practice swords on a nearby rack. The elf motioned with his hand for the sparring to continue before retrieving Jack's sword.

Two women entered the ring, each wielding two short, practice swords.

"Begin," Darius shouted, and then turned to Jack with a look of concern on his face. He held up the oversized, black katana. "Where did you get this?" Darius asked.

"I took it from an orc I killed," Jack replied. "Why?"

Darius ignored him and asked. "Have you noticed anything strange about it?"

"Maybe," Jack groaned, as he rubbed his sore ribs.

"Like what?" Darius pressed.

Jack was suddenly suspicious of the elf's line of questioning, but he didn't see any reason to lie. "Sometimes the blade gives off a kinda red glow, and it cuts through things easier than it should," Jack shrugged. "I figured it's got some kind of enchantment on it."

Darius nodded as he drew the large sword out of its sheath and inspected the blade closely. "Anything else?" The elf looked sharply at Jack. "Does it make you feel any different perhaps?"

"Now that you mention it," Jack nodded, "it feels… good." Jack had trouble putting it into words. "It's like the sword was meant to be in my hands… I feel stronger and quicker." Jack shook his head. "Sounds crazy I know."

Darius's eyes narrowed. "Do you hear anything when you use it?"

Jack looked confused. "Like a voice?"

"A voice or a feeling." It was Darius's turn to shrug. "Or any kind of impression that you should do something?"

"No." Jack lied. Recently he had been getting some strange urges while using the black sword, but he wasn't about to tell the elf about them.

Darius shot Jack a look that said he didn't believe him.

"Why all the questions?" Jack asked defensively.

Darius gripped the long hilt and raised the blade before him before answering. "I suspect there is more to this sword than meets the eye…I am no mage, but I believe this blade has a powerful dark enchantment on it."

"Wonderful," Jack muttered, but he wasn't really surprised. The dwarves had basically said as much and it would take someone really thick to not suspect that a black orc sword that glowed red had something evil about it.

"Gather your armor," Darius said suddenly, as he reached some decision.

Jack put his black orc armor back on as Darius moved away and called another elf in red leather over. They talked briefly and by the time Jack was ready, Darius had returned.

"What are we doing?" Jack asked, suspicious of the sudden activity.

"We are taking this sword to the Forgefather," Darius answered. "He will be able to tell us exactly what we are dealing with."

****

Leaves rustled softly, but sounded like an avalanche in the stillness of the woods and Emily winced as she froze in place. It had taken her hours to find where these Druids were supposedly located. And it had taken hours more to get this close.

They seemed to vanish every time she drew near, but she was determined to find them this time. They could hopefully explain all the strange things she had been hearing and the seemingly random, and useless, abilities she had discovered. Like making grass grow. What good was that?

Emily could just make out the flickering light of a fire off beneath the trees. She would make it this time! Emily took another careful step when suddenly a voice whispered in her ear. "Persistent, aren't we?"

Emily jumped and spun around, drawing an arrow in the same motion and searching for the speaker. But nobody was there.

Breathing deeply, Emily tried to slow her racing heart. She lowered her bow and relaxed a bit. Just another one of the random voices she occasionally heard.

Emily looked back and could still see the flickering light between the trees. She took a step in that direction when the light unexpectedly vanished.

Emily cursed in frustration. "Not again."

Soft laughter whispered through the trees.

"Show yourself!" Emily shouted angrily.

The sounds of birds were abruptly silenced and woods suddenly grew darker, as if night had fallen and a light fog crept in.

More laughter ghosted eerily through the trees.

"Well, that's creepy," Emily muttered and drew her bow.

A black shape suddenly flittered through the darkness toward her.

Without hesitating, Emily fired an arrow. It sped through the air and when it struck, the dark thing blew apart in a billowing black cloud and then dissipated into nothing.

Then, more black shapes appeared with the death of the first one.

The things moved quickly and began to surround her. Emily fired rapidly, each shot destroying a black thing in an explosion of darkness. But it seemed the more things she killed, the more things appeared around her.

Black shapes burst all around as Emily killed them. But she noticed that the things were getting larger, and when they burst, they were less smoky, as if they were getting more solid.

The things were moving ever closer and Emily shot a few more before she realized that it wasn't her imagination, the things were getting more solid.

A horrifying suspicion grew in Emily as she destroyed another of the dark things. Deciding to follow her instincts, Emily stopped shooting the dark shapes.

Now that she wasn't trying to kill them, Emily realized the things were not headed straight for her, but rather they were circling.

The things circled for a few moments until it became apparent that Emily wasn't going to attack anymore, then they moved in.

Emily almost shot then, but held herself back as the black shapes swirled around her and got ever closer.

The things began to wail horribly as they got close enough for her to almost reach out and touch.

Emily closed her eyes and stood her ground as the black things pressed in and swirled around her in a wailing tornado.

The blackness howled in her ears and buffeted her clothes so much that it almost blew her hat off, but Emily refused to budge.

The shrieking wind seemed to last an eternity, but then suddenly it vanished.

Emily opened her eyes and saw that the black things had disappeared. The dark woods were eerily silent once again and she let out a breath that she didn't know she had been holding.

"Very good," the voice whispered all around her.

Emily didn't jump this time. "Who are you?" she demanded.

Instead of an answer, the ground around her erupted.

Vines and branches shot up and wove themselves together, effectively trapping Emily. She pressed against the wall to no effect. She kicked, punched, and clawed at the wood, but it was hard and dead. No amount of force was moving it.

The light abruptly re-appeared in the distant darkness and Emily suddenly realized that this must be some kind of test. All she had to do was get past this wall of dead wood.

Then, Emily had an idea.

She placed her hand on the wall and concentrated. She wasn't quite sure how she did it, but just like the grass, the vines and branches blossomed under her touch. Soon, they were young and alive and she was able to easily bend them out of her way.

Once through the now-blooming wall, Emily set off toward the light in the darkness.

She hadn't gone ten steps before she heard a rustle and saw movement before her. She stopped short and watched as the soft rustling grew and the shape of a person appeared between her and the light.

"Hello?" Emily asked as the figure slowly approached.

There was no response and she noticed there was something odd about the figure as it moved closer. Emily realized it was because the person walked with a pronounced limp.

"Hello?" Emily asked nervously. When there was still no response she raised her bow.

Dread filled her as two more figures appeared from the darkness along with the first and entered a small clearing. There was just enough light for her to get her first good look at them.

White bones stood out from decaying flesh that hung in ribbons from their desiccated frames. They shambled clumsily through the underbrush, tripping over roots and barreling mindlessly through bushes.

"Seriously?" Emily groaned, as the undead creatures stumbled toward her.

She raised her bow and realized to her dismay that she only had two arrows left. She scolded herself for wasting the arrows on those smoke creatures.

Emily let fly and the first monster collapsed with an arrow embedded in its throat. She fired again and another fell, pierced through its eye. But before she could decide what to do about the last one, the two she shot picked themselves back up and regained their feet. The mortally wounded creatures continued their approach with her arrows still lodged in them.

Emily cursed and grabbed the goblin scepter she had hanging from her belt. Suddenly glad she brought it along; she pointed the skull-topped rod at the shambling zombies.

The skull's eye sockets began to glow with a bright green light as the monsters neared. Emily shouted in defiance as a bolt of crackling green energy burst forth and blasted one of the undead creatures into pieces. A second bolt destroyed another monster and engulfed the last of the zombies in green flames.

Emily watched one of the burning zombies stumble towards her, mindlessly unaware as it was slowly consumed by the emerald flames.

The poor creature finally succumbed to the flames and Emily snorted. "Is that all you've got?" she shouted into the darkness.

There was no answer, but the darkness suddenly lifted and the woods returned to their previous state. Birds sang and the beams of sunlight danced through the trees.

"I guess so," Emily muttered as she looked around in amazement. It was as if none of the things had even happened. She walked over to where the undead creatures had been, but there was no sign of them anywhere. No tracks, no pieces of flesh, nor any scorch marks from the flames. It was like it never happened.

If it wasn't for her empty quiver and still glowing scepter, Emily might have thought she imagined the whole thing.

A soft breeze picked up and Emily could just make out a voice on the wind. "Who are you?" it said.

"I asked you first," Emily growled. She was getting tired of all this foolishness.

There was a long silence then the voice whispered. "We are the Watchers."

"Watchers?" Emily muttered. "I'm looking for the Druids. I was told they could help me."

Laughter echoed through the woods. "That they can," the voice laughed.

Emily didn't like being laughed at, especially by an annoying disembodied voice. "So, where are they?" she demanded.

There was no reply, but suddenly a tree branch shot out and pulled the scepter from her hand.

"Hey!" Emily cried, but then more branches shot out and grasped at her. She dove away, but more branches clawed at her.

A root burst from the ground and wrapped around her ankle and she fell hard against a tree. Emily pulled her foot free, but then more branches grabbed ahold of her wrists. She struggled, but the branches pulled her back against the tree as more roots and branches wrapped around her with a mind of their own.

"Let me go!" Emily shouted angrily.

"Command the tree to release you," the voice said.

"What?!" Emily shrieked. "I just did!"

"Only then will you find those you seek," the voice whispered and faded away.

"Let me go!" Emily thrashed wildly, but only managed to get herself locked tighter in the tree's embrace. "Let me goooo!" she shouted again, but the tree didn't budge.

Furious, Emily tried with all her might, but she couldn't move an inch. She was trapped against the cool bark of the old tree.

Deep in the woods, nobody could hear her scream.

****

Sweat glistened off Mike's muscled bulk, as he stood bare-chested in front of a roaring furnace. Sparks flew as he pounded a length of glowing hot metal with a heavy hammer.

A man wearing a heavy leather apron and welding gloves working at a nearby forge stared at Mike in disbelief. "Why don't you wear an apron or something?" the man shouted over the roar.

Mike didn't stop hammering. "Most of the dwarves do it this way," he yelled. "They already think us weak. I'm going to show them differently."

The man just shook his head and went back to his own work.

Mike inspected the piece of metal a moment before jamming it back into the forge. While that one heated, Mike took ahold of another piece of metal that was sticking out of the super-hot coals.

Setting the metal on an anvil, Mike began hammering it into a more curved shape. As he worked, a grey-bearded dwarf trudged over and watched.

The dwarf was larger than most of his race and was covered in elaborate runic tattoos that ran down his bare arms and chest. Immense cords of muscle bulged under his ruddy skin and heavy metal studs were embedded in his flesh.

Mike ignored the pierced dwarf and continued to shape the metal until it was too cool and he jammed it back to the coals. He selected another piece and started shaping that one.

The dwarf grunted in approval. "Ye have some skill at the forge."

Mike kept hammering. "I was apprenticed to a master armor smith in the SCA before you guys showed up."

The dwarf snorted. "I be very much interested ter see a *human* master smith."

"Perhaps *you* could teach me then?" Mike shot back.

The old dwarf snorted again. "T'would be a waste o' me time."

"You don't think a human can be a master smith?"

"Bah!" the old dwarf rumbled. "I no think it. I know it. A human could ne'r even come close ter the skill o' the Sons o' Durinn. Even our apprentices could out-craft yer 'masters,' don't ye doubt."

Mike found the dwarf's casual disregard for humans insulting and shot the dwarf a dark look. "Well, if you're so good, why don't you prove it?"

The grey-bearded dwarf laughed a deep booming laugh. "Lad, do ye even know who I be?" the dwarf chuckled and answered his own question. "No, o' course ye don't."

The old dwarf puffed up his massive chest and proclaimed. "I be

Skapari, Overseer o' the Verkstad."

"Never heard of you," Mike mumbled with a hidden grin.

The old dwarf scowled and Mike knew he was pushing his luck. But he was having too much fun. Dwarves could be an easily offended bunch.

"Obviously, you don't know who *I* am," Mike said as he set the hammer down and picked up his ancient mace from behind the anvil. He puffed up his own thick chest and pointed the mace at the old dwarf. "I am Michael Strazney!" he boomed. "Lord of the Nerds! Slayer of the Digital Hordes! Vanquisher of the Random Baddies and Savior of Stereotypical Damsels in Distress!"

Mike was just screwing around, but the old dwarf was taken aback and lost all his bluster. "I had no idea…" he stammered, his eyes never leaving the ancient mace.

"Never fear," Mike said grandly, as he tried not to laugh. "You are forgiven."

"Thank ye, Lord," Skapari said. "But I must ask… where did ye acquire that mace?"

Mike sighed inwardly. *Why did the dwarves always have to ask about the stupid mace?* "It was given to me by Lord Aurvang Twinpeaks for saving his life."

That wasn't entirely true. Lord Aurvang had let Mike borrow it when his sword had gotten trapped during a battle with goblins. It wasn't until after the dwarf lord had seen the mace react to Mike's touch that he had allowed Mike to keep it.

Skapari's eyes narrowed. "Impossible!" Mike let out another inner sigh. *Why did they always have that reaction?*

The old dwarf shook his head. "No dwarf would ever hand over such a powerful artifact ter a human. And unless me eyes deceive me, especially no a legendary weapon like Rikr Foerah."

So, Skapari knew the name of his mace. Few dwarves seemed to know that, but Mike had had this same argument with almost every dwarf he had met. They all recognized its power even if they didn't know its name and would only ever believe him when he showed them proof that he could unlock the mace's power. So, to cut off a long argument Mike decided to end it now.

"Look," Mike said, "the mace chose me." He held up the mace and it began to glow with a faint white light and the runes inscribed on its head began to burn with a soft inner fire.

Skapari's eyes bulged. "Impossible…"

"You said that already," Mike grinned.

The old dwarf scowled. "Very well. But when next I see Lord Aurvang I will learn the truth o' this."

"Fine with me," Mike said, and meant it. He hoped Aurvang would spread the word about the mace so Mike wouldn't need to have this same discussion with every stubborn dwarf he met. Proving he controlled the mace did have its benefits though; every dwarf showed him a level of respect that Mike didn't see them give any other humans. "Last I saw Lord Aurvang, he was in Clearfield overseeing the construction of the town's defenses."

Skapari nodded and never took his eyes off the mace. "I'm not fer know'n why he would bother with such a small village when this city could use him more, but yer town be lucky then. Lord Aurvang has Keepbuilder blood running through his veins. There be no better engineers in all the Empire." The old dwarf cleared his throat. "May I see it?" he asked easily and held out a large hand.

Although Skapari seemed relaxed, Mike could see the hunger in his eyes. He desperately wanted the mace for some reason and it made Mike uneasy.

"Lord Aurvang entrusted it to me," Mike said, as he turned away from the old dwarf and set the ancient weapon down and picked up his smiths hammer. "I'm not in the habit of handing it to strangers."

The old dwarf snorted. "Lord Aurvang always has been considered rather odd. Perhaps no be much o' a surprise that he would hand out artifacts so carelessly."

Mike ignored that as he pulled a piece of glowing metal out and sparks flew as he began hammering it into shape. When he glanced up a few moments later, the old dwarf was gone.

"Well, that was easy," Mike muttered to himself and continued working.

He wasn't sure how long he had been working, but eventually Mike heard the heavy tread of footsteps coming up behind him. When he looked up from his anvil, Mike saw that the old dwarf overseer, Skapari, had returned, and with him was another dwarf.

Where Skapari was stripped to the waist, this newcomer was draped in heavy, red robes. Under the thick hood was a surprisingly youthful dwarf with a short, braided, black beard that was capped with metal bands. Most surprising of all was that the young dwarf wasn't sweating!

Mike couldn't believe it. It was hotter than a furnace in there and he was dying even without a shirt. He was sure there was some kind of trick there; all Mike had to do was figure out what it was.

"So," the new dwarf said, "this be the human who supposedly wields Rikr Foerah."

"It is, Lord," Skapari said quickly.

So, the old overseer brought a lord back with him eh? Mike smiled. *This should be interesting.*

"Thank ye, Skapari," the robed dwarf said. "Ye may go."

The old dwarf bowed and strode away.

Mike put away his tools and introduced himself with a slight nod to the robed dwarf lord.

"Well met, Mike Strazney," the robed dwarf nodded back. "I be Master Runesmith Nadal Ivaldisson."

"Aren't you a bit young to be a Master Runesmith?" Mike asked before he could help himself.

Nadal smiled. "Age does no matter. Only skill. And I may be young fer a dwarf, but I be willin' ter bet I be far older than yerself," he added with a wink.

Mike decided he liked this Runesmith and he grinned back. "I bet you are."

Nadal pulled back his hood and revealed several silver studs poking out of his skull above his left ear. The sides of his head were shaved and the hair on top was braided back in a long mane.

"Our good overseer tells me ye not only have a dwarf artifact in yer possession, but that ye can also unlock its power." Nadal looked doubtful. "It's not that I don't trust our old friend, but I would like ter see this fer meself."

Mike saw Nadal's eyes sparkle with excitement as he drew the ancient weapon from its resting place. He called forth its power and the Runesmith's mouth dropped open.

"I'm sorry," Nadal apologized. "Rumors no do it justice." The Runesmith gathered himself and continued. "Do ye realize what ye have there?"

"Rikr Foerah," Mike answered. "An old impact mace."

Nadal chuckled. "Rikr Foerah be no just some old impact mace," the Runesmith said excitedly. "It be the Great Hurler. Crafted in the glorious forges o' Holy Agartha, inscribed with the lost runes o' superior impact, and thrice blessed in the waters o' the Urðarbrunnr itself." Nadal stepped forward eagerly. "Do ye know what this means?"

"Um…no?" Mike replied, confused.

"It means that the runes o' superior impact no longer be lost!" Nadal nearly shouted with delight. "All such weapons have either been destroyed or forgotten and the knowledge ter make more has been lost. But by studying Rikr Foerah, I could unlock the secrets o' those runes and we could once again craft weapons o' superior impact."

Mike was confused. "How could these runes be 'lost' when Lord Aurvang had it before me?"

"Ahh," Nadal shook his head sadly. "Ye see, we dwarves are not known fer our sharin'. Quite the opposite really, and ter find a human in possession o' such a powerful artifact…well, it could cause some…tension."

"I've noticed," muttered Mike.

"I'm sure ye have," Nadal nodded, "but the runes being lost is no the fault o' those who held it these last centuries. The runes be hidden. Such be their craftsmanship that I was only able ter see 'em once ye activated 'em. So, unless a Master Runesmith saw it activated, nobody would be knowin' what runes were hidden within."

The Runesmith held out his hand for the mace, but Mike pulled it back to his chest and said, "That's all real nice, but like I told Skapari, I'm not in the habit of handing it to strangers."

Nadal held up his hands. "Oh, no, no, no, don't ye worry. I no want ter keep it. I just be wantin' ter study it."

"And how long will that take?" Mike asked dubiously.

Nadal shrugged. "Who fer knowin'? It may only take hours, or it may be takin' years before I unlock its secrets. I won't be knowin' until I look at it." He held out his hand again.

"I'll make you a deal," Mike said, still clutching the mace to his chest. "You teach me how to make runes, and I will let you study my mace."

Nadal's sudden bark of laughter echoed through the building, causing many men and dwarves to look at him in confusion.

"The crafting o' runes be a secret known only ter the dwarves." Still chuckling, Nadal wiped tears from his eyes. "No human can learn it."

Mike didn't budge. "Well, then, you can't study it."

Nadal's mirth suddenly vanished. "Ye misunderstand me, manling. When I say no human can learn it, I mean it be impossible fer a human. Only a dwarf blessed with Runevision can craft runes."

"Humor me," Mike pressed

Nadal sighed. "Very well," he shook his head slowly, "but we be wasting our time."

"Now, clear yer mind," Nadal instructed. "I hear ye be one o' Thor's Chosen, so this should be easy fer ye."

Nadal was right. Mike quickly cleared his mind and thanks to his training from the veteran Guardian Jerrik Ironforge, he entered a state of detached tranquility.

Seeing the change come over Mike, Nadal nodded and raised a calloused hand. "Watch," he instructed. With one finger extended, the Runesmith began to draw in the air. Wherever his finger went, a thick glowing red line followed.

With a few quick strokes, a sharp, glowing runic symbol floated in the air before Nadal. "Can ye see that? he asked.

Mike nodded and without thinking raised his own hand. A thinner, wavy line followed Mike's finger and soon there was a shaky duplicate of the same rune hovering before Mike.

"Incredible…" Nadal breathed in wonder. "A human Chosen o' Thor that also be blessed with Runevision… the gods must surely be playin' a joke on me."

The Runesmith looked thoughtful. "Or perhaps…" he said as the glowing rune winked out, "perhaps it be no mistake at all. Maybe the gods meant fer us ter meet." Nadal began talking excitedly. "Long have we been searching fer the lost runes, but it has been centuries since the last one was discovered. And ter find it with a human gifted with Runevision no less! It surely be a sign."

"Do ye have dwarf blood in ye?" Nadal asked suddenly.

Mike shrugged. "Not that I know of."

"I see…" Nadal stroked his beard as he contemplated something.

"Why is it so strange that I can use the mace?" Mike asked.

"Weapons such as this were created fer the sole purpose o' defeating the orcs and their muspell allies," Nadal explained, "but ter keep such power from falling into the wrong hands, the ancient Rune Priests placed special blessed Runes o' Warding so that only a dwarf could unlock their full powers."

Understanding dawned on Mike. That explained all the dwarves' shock when he activated the mace.

The Runesmith looked thoughtful. "If the gods will it, then so shall it be," he muttered seemingly to himself.

Nadal drew his hood back up. "I be a Master Runesmith and if ye wish ter learn rune craft, then I will take ye as me apprentice. But I'm not fer knowin' if a human can master such a divine skill."

"The mark of a true master is the ability to train new masters," Mike replied.

"Wise words, fer a human," Nadal muttered.

After a moment's thought, the Master Runesmith nodded. "Very well,"

Nadal's voice had the ring of finality to it. "I will teach ye the secrets o' rune craft in exchange fer studying the superior runes o' impact," Nadal extended his hand, "but ye must tell no one."

Mike clasped the dwarf's thick forearm. "Deal."

CHAPTER 9

BANG!

Three hundred yards away, the target exploded in a brilliant shower of debris.

"Nice shot," Scout Sniper Jason Andrews shouted. "Youz a natural."

"Thank you," Liz shouted back, even though they were only a few feet apart because they were both wearing protective earmuffs. She stood up and beamed at the handsome young army sniper. He wasn't much taller than her, with dark skin and a dazzling smile. She guessed he wasn't much older than her either.

"Now, ya just need ta get faster and you'll be a true sniper in no time," said Jason.

"Oh, so I'm not fast enough for you?" Liz teased.

Jason grinned. "Not quite."

"So, what would be fast enough?" Liz asked.

"I have the same requirements for all my beginner civilian students," Jason replied. "Five shots, five kills, in five seconds."

"Sounds easy enough," Liz smirked.

Jason crossed his arms and leaned against the wall of the range. "Let's see it then."

"Alright." Liz picked the rifle back up and waited as a tiny looking soldier at the far end of the range set up five new targets.

The outdoor firing range was carved between low hills and stretched for over a mile. The individual firing benches were all filled, mostly with humans, but several dwarves were learning how to properly use firearms.

It had been decreed by General Adams and the newly created Allied Council that each race would be required to learn the basics of the other's weapons and tactics. That meant that both elves and dwarves had to learn how to use guns.

The dwarves jumped into it enthusiastically; they seemed to enjoy shooting things, but most of the elves were more reluctant. They distrusted anything that was made by humans, and especially something that exploded in their hands.

Without sitting back down, Liz aimed at the first distant target.

Liz glanced over her shoulder and winked at Jason. She pulled the trigger and the target fell over. The others followed in rapid succession.

"Show off," Jason laughed, as they removed their ear protection. "Looks like we will need to find ya something a wee bit more challenging."

Jason grabbed the radio that was clipped to his shoulder and spoke into it. "Hey, Sarge. I've got a lady here that is ready for Stage Two."

The radio crackled to life. "Affirmative. Bring her over."

"Rodger." Jason let go of the radio and looked at Liz. "Police yinz brass," he said, and pointed to a large blue barrel. "Throw them in there. General Adams wants everything saved so we can reload them. Then we can head out."

"Stage Two?" Liz asked, and bent down and began picking up her shell casings.

"You'll see," Jason laughed.

"Aren't you going to help me?" Liz asked, when she noticed Jason hadn't moved from leaning against the wall.

"Nope," Jason replied easily.

Liz glanced up and saw him watching her. "Enjoying the view?" she teased, as she picked up the last casing.

"Sure am," Jason smirked.

Liz took her small pile of spent brass and dumped them in the large plastic barrel.

"Alright, follow me," Jason said and strode away, forcing Liz to hurry and catch up.

They walked the width of the range, passing stalls filled with people using all sorts of rifles. Once they were beyond the rifle range, Jason removed his earplugs and Liz did the same. When she did, Liz could hear more gunshots coming from the hill in front of them.

It was a short walk down the hill to another firing range, but this one was much shorter. As they got closer, Liz could see people practicing with handguns.

"So, Stage Two is a pistol range?" Liz asked.

"Affirmative," Jason replied. "We want everyone proficient with a rifle before we give them a sidearm."

Liz noticed that there wasn't just one range, but several spaced around a half circle. Each station seemed to be set up differently, one was your basic range, another had swinging targets, and one even looked like a maze.

"So, how many stages are there?" Liz asked as she followed Jason into the circle of ranges.

"Four," Jason answered. "Most can't complete Stage Three though," he said, before heading to the first station that looked like a basic firing range.

"Wait." Liz grabbed his arm. "Let's do this one." She pointed to the stage with dozens of small hanging disk-like targets. A few of the stalls were in use, but there were plenty of open spaces.

Jason shrugged. "Fine with me," he said, and led her to that area where he stopped in front of a long rack filled with handguns of various sizes and styles.

"Choose your poison," Jason instructed, and waved at the rows of pistols.

Although Liz had her pistol still strapped to her thigh, she chose two identical handguns from the rack.

Jason raised a questioning eyebrow. "Dual wielding them eh?" he asked dubiously. "Somebody been watchin' too many movies n' at."

Liz shrugged. "Thought I'd make it interesting."

Jason slowly shook his head. "You sure are something, ya know dat?"

"I know," Liz teased, before walking up to the firing line. "Any special rules here?"

"Nope," Jason answered. "Just break as many targets as you can."

As Liz scanned the targets, she noticed movement heading toward them out of the corner of her eye. She looked back and saw a beautiful female elf dressed in flowing, golden robes striding toward them.

The elf stopped beside Jason and opened her mouth to speak, but before she could say anything Liz quickly turned back to the targets and raised her twin pistols. She briefly remembered that she hadn't put her earmuffs back on… but it was too late now.

She suddenly pulled both triggers and began rapidly firing at the small disks. A storm of gunfire erupted from the barrels as targets began exploding all around her.

Within a few heartbeats, the targets were all destroyed and nothing remained but bits of broken clay and Liz's smoking guns.

"Oooh," Liz breathed, "that felt good."

"Cheese and Crackers!" Jason stared down the range in disbelief. "I think we're done here."

"Good. Then you will come with me," said the beautiful elf woman. "It is time for your next lesson."

Her name was Kassandra, a priestess of Demeter, and she had been assigned as one of Liz's new healing instructors. They had met that morning before Liz had come to the ranges.

Liz reluctantly sat the guns down and flashed a grin at Jason. "Stage Three tomorrow?"

Jason, still looking shocked, smiled back. "Lookin' forward to it."

****

A soft golden light spilled out from under Liz's hands and seeped into the old man lying on the cot before her. His eyes were closed as he shivered violently and sweat streamed down his face. Liz held on to his arm as he shook, the golden light pouring into him.

After a few tense moments, the man's shaking subsided and he stopped sweating. Liz took a relieved breath and sat back, exhausted from her efforts.

"Very good," Kassandra said. She stood on the other side of the old man who now appeared to be sleeping peacefully. Next to Kassandra was a very short, white-robed mountain dwarf named Gretta, who was one of the few female dwarves that Liz had seen.

Gretta's hair was oddly tied under her chin to resemble a beard. Liz had learned that dwarf females rarely left their homes. The males went to war while the females stayed behind and guarded the cities. Strangely, females were considered an adult when they could tie their hair under their chins, and apparently they usually wore full helms to hide their faces. This gave the appearance that they were male, leading many to believe that there were no dwarf women.

"Thanks," Liz breathed. That had been the most difficult healing she had ever done. Even guiding a little girl out of a coma had been easier than that. It was almost like his illness had fought back, but Liz had overwhelmed the darkness and destroyed the poison that had infected the poor man.

Kassandra looked truly pleased. "You have demonstrated all of the various forms of healing." The elven priestess continued, "It seems that you really are a true healer."

"And what is that?" Liz asked.

"While some can only heal one type of malady, a true healer is a person with the gift to cure all conditions," Kassandra explained. "There are three primary types of healers: Menders heal physical wounds, like a sword cut. Curers can banish disease and other illness, while Soothers calm afflictions of the mind and can ultimately restore one's sanity."

"But the true healer can do all of these things and more, although perhaps not as effectively as a primary is at their singular gift," Kassandra said. "The gods have granted you great power."

"I don't believe in your gods," Liz replied.

Gretta's mouth dropped open, but Kassandra laughed. "Obviously, they believe in you. Where do you think the power to heal comes from?"

"From the one true God, of course," Liz said.

Kassandra chuckled and shook her head. "I forget that most of you humans have abandoned the gods and now worship the Creator."

Gretta still looked stunned. "Ye no be believin' in the gods? How do ye still stand? Ye should have been struck down fer yer blasphemy!"

"I may have," Liz replied with a smirk, "if they existed."

"Of course, they exist, child," Kassandra said. "If not, how do you explain our ability to heal also?"

Liz shrugged. "Magic."

"Yes," Kassandra sighed, "healing is a type of magic, but it is divine magic granted by the gods themselves."

"Enough o' this pointless debate," Gretta interrupted. "It be time ter see if this unbeliever can Call the Light." The dwarf crossed her thick arms. "But I think this be a waste o' time. The gods will no answer her pleas if she denies them."

"I'm ready," Liz announced, even though she had no idea what was going on. She was determined to prove herself to these two.

Kassandra looked dubiously at Gretta and shrugged. "Very well."

So Gretta and Kassandra took Liz and led her to a large empty room with glass walls that was devoid of furniture or any kind of decoration.

Liz joined Kassandra on one side of the room as Gretta stomped over to the other and turned to face them.

Gretta rolled back the sleeves of her white robe and then suddenly drew a long dagger.

"What's going on?" Liz asked nervously.

Gretta smiled. "Time ter prove yer faith." She held out one arm, palm up, and then suddenly plunged the dagger into her exposed wrist!

Blood spurted as Gretta pulled the dagger back, slicing a long gash the length of her forearm.

Liz squealed in horror at what she was seeing. "What are you doing?!" she cried, and tried to run to the dwarf, but Kassandra held her back.

"You must heal her," Kassandra said easily.

"Then let me go!" Liz cried, as she struggled in the elf's grip.

"No," Kassandra replied. "You must heal her from here."

Blood pooled around Gretta's feet as the life-giving fluid poured out of her ruined arm.

"Are you insane?" Liz shouted.

"Call the Light human," Gretta ordered. "It be the only way ter save me."

"But I don't know how!" Liz cried, as she watched the dwarf begin to sway dangerously.

"How do you heal?" Kassandra asked calmly.

Liz couldn't believe what was happening. This crazy dwarf was going to die just to prove a point! And the elf was going to let it happen!

"By praying," Liz replied with tears in her eyes.

"Then pray!"

****

"There are countless books on magic," Archmage Talsin said, "and every one of them is wrong." He paused and looked around the room. "However," he held up a long slender finger, "every one of them is also right."

There was a great deal of muttering from those assembled humans seated around the darkened auditorium.

"That is because magic, by its very nature, is indefinable. There are no rules. There are no constants," Talsin said grandly. "Understanding that you know nothing is the first step to becoming a mage."

Talsin's voice dropped. "I have tested each of you and found that you all have the greatest Potential of any humans I have yet encountered. But having Potential is simply not enough."

Everyone seated around him leaned forward eagerly, hanging on to the Archmage's every word. "You must have an all-consuming desire to master your Gift and work tirelessly to achieve perfection in The Art."

Talsin's voice began to swell. "We are all working toward the same goal, but make no mistake, this *is* a competition. And those who fail to compete, fail to survive."

"Unfortunately, time is not on our side," Talsin lamented. "One, because you humans have such a pitifully short life span, I doubt any of you could ever truly master The Art." A low grumbling came from the gathered students but the Archmage ignored it. "And two, because there are dark forces beyond this city that seek to destroy us all."

"I do not have the luxury to properly train you as I would other mages," said Talsin. "Therefore, we will be breaking you into groups based on your current abilities and focusing on perfecting them. Should we survive the coming storm, a more thorough education will begin."

Ted was confused why the Archmage said "we" until he noticed the small group of elves standing in the darkened corner of the stage. He was pretty sure they hadn't been there earlier.

"As much as I am loath to do so," Talsin continued, "and against my better judgment, you will be focusing on mastering battle magic first."

As Talsin spoke, the group of elves lined up in front of the stage next to the Archmage.

There were four of them and an odder grouping Ted had never seen. They were all attractive like every elf Ted had met, but that is where the similarities ended.

The first elf was a tiny female with pale skin and short-cropped, light colored hair. She wore a long, tight fitting white gown with one strap over her left shoulder. A belt of gold links encircled her tiny waist and simple leather sandals hugged her small feet.

Standing next to her was a tall male that was completely bald with extremely dark skin. He was larger than most elves and could almost be considered bulky by elf standards. Surprisingly, this elf wore a coat of silvery scale armor under a brilliant red tabard. A large, silver symbol stood out on his chest that depicted a three-armed spiral. One hand rested on the pommel of a slender sword at his waist and the other clutched a rolled-up scroll.

Another male stood next to the one in armor, but where the first looked more like a soldier, this one looked more like a mage. Tall and slender with brown hair pulled back in a long ponytail, he held a long, ornate staff topped with a brilliant crystal. Long robes of pale blue trimmed in dark green draped over his sparse frame.

Finally, was a stunning female with long, black hair that fell in tight spirals down her back and was held away from her face with a small, bronze diadem. A bronze colored blouse with long, tight sleeves and a plunging neckline was cinched by a black corset and flowed into a long, black skirt that was also trimmed in bronze. Her skin was golden brown that spoke of long hours spent outdoors and seemed to glitter in the low light. She was enchanting and it took a moment for Ted to realize that Archmage Talsin was still speaking.

"-and do not forget it," Talsin announced ominously. "Nothing is more important and death will follow those who do not heed my warning."

Ted cursed for missing what this "important" thing was, but didn't have time to dwell on it as Talsin continued. "Now, I had planned on instructing all of you myself, however, events outside my control have forced my hand. Therefore," he motioned to the four elves standing before him, "you will be instructed by these Masters of the Art as well."

The Archmage walked over and placed a delicate hand on the short female in the white gown. "This is Lady Braelynn, a Supreme Sorceress and the Lady of the Appledoves. For those of you humans with the natural power of Will, you will follow her instruction."

Ted was suddenly interested in this tiny elf woman. The power of Will is what the Archmage had said Ted possessed. It seemed this diminutive sorceress would be his primary mentor.

Talsin moved to the next elf in line, the tall, dark male in armor. "This is Master Pars. Combat Magician and Chief Arbiter of Vlaanderen," Talsin said. "There is no one here better to teach the complicated intricacies of the

Word."

Talsin made his way to the next male elf in pale blue robes. "Lord Quillan here is the High Wizard of the Order of the Gnarled Staff." The Archmage nodded politely to the High Wizard. "His mastery of Focus will be immensely beneficial to those of you with a similar proficiency."

The Archmage turned to the last elf in line. "And as you humans say, last but not least," Talsin said, as he came up to the stunning female, "is Mistress Dianoia of the Psionic Cult." He took Dianoia's hand, then lightly kissed it.

Turning back to the assembled humans, Talsin said. "The power to read another's thoughts or even control another's actions is the most dangerous of powers. It is not to be taken lightly. That is why Mistress Dianoia is here, not only to teach the proper use of such abilities for those rare individuals that have them, but also for everyone to learn how to successfully defend themselves from a psychic attack."

"Now," Archmage Talsin announced grandly, "each of you will join your new master and begin your training. Those with an aptitude for Willpower will join Lady Braelynn first."

The small sorceress beckoned the assembled students to follow her and then proceeded across the stage toward the door.

Over half of the gathered humans stood and made their way to follow the Lady out. Ted waited a moment before he too stood and joined the end of the line.

Ted saw Talsin's eyes sparkle as the line of humans filed out. The Archmage caught Ted's eye and muttered, "Good luck."

"Thanks," Ted replied as he walked by.

"You will need it," Talsin added.

The sorceress led them outside to a small clearing near the Martial Rings and waited as everyone gathered around her.

"Archmage Talsin has informed me that so far you humans have the most Potential," the Lady said, in a soft silky voice, "but I must know where each of you stands in the Art. Therefore, we will have a little test," she smiled wickedly.

"Each of you should have some element that you first discovered you could manipulate. Perhaps it was a burst of flame or a gust of wind. Or maybe it was a wall of stone or a bolt of lightning…" The sorceress looked around as most of the assembled humans nodded in agreement. "And I am guessing that they appeared for some destructive purpose…" More nods. "So, the first thing I must know is where each of you stands in your Gift," Braelynn announced.

"Form a line here in front of me," the sorceress suddenly commanded. "Quickly now, one in front of the other… there you go."

Ted and the other assembled humans jostled about and quickly formed a line stretching away from the sorceress.

"Very good," Lady Braelynn purred. "Now, I will attack each of you with a small plasma bolt, don't worry it will only sting a little," she said easily, as she skipped a few paces away from the first student in line.

The sorceress faced them and grinned impishly. "All you have to do is block it."

Ted saw the young man that was first in line go pale as the Lady Braelynn motioned for him to step away from the others. He did slowly and faced the sorceress alone.

"Are you prepared?" Braelynn purred sweetly.

"Y-yes," the young man stammered nervously.

The sorceress slowly raised her right hand and pointed at the young man. A spark of light appeared at her fingertip and then suddenly shot forward. The crowd gasped as it hurtled toward the young man. Before he could react, the spark found its mark.

"Ouch!" he cried, as the spark struck him in the chest and knocked him backwards with an electrical popping sound.

"You see? It only stings a little," Braelynn teased. "Now, how about you protect yourself this time?" She smiled and raised her hand again. Ted had the distinct impression that the sorceress was enjoying herself.

The small spark shot forward again and Ted winced in anticipation of the strike. But just before the spark connected, it collided with a wall of fire that sprang up just beyond the young man's outstretched hands.

"Very good," beamed the small sorceress. "You may go to the back of the line."

The young man looked relieved as he rejoined the others.

Lady Braelynn eyed the humans hungrily.

"Next."

An old woman stepped forward and to Ted's surprise she blocked the first spark shot at her with a wall of stone.

"Next."

The line moved quickly after that, with each person successfully blocking the sorceress' small plasma bolt. Not all of them blocked it the first time, but none were stuck twice. Everyone else had gone and then it was Ted's turn.

"Um, Lady Braelynn?" Ted said as he stepped forward.

"Just Braelynn, my dear," Braelynn replied sweetly.

"Ehm, Braelynn," Ted began. "I have a request."

Braelynn looked amused. "And what is that, my tall pupil?"

"Could you throw something a little stronger at me?" Ted replied. "I like a challenge."

"Oh really?" Braelynn chuckled almost to herself. "Haven't even proven you can stop the small bolt and you want more...very well."

Ted spread his feet and grinned. He did love a show.

The sorceress didn't raise a hand this time; instead, a spark sprung to life and quickly grew to the size of a baseball. Without any warning, it shot at Ted. This was not his first duel, however, and he quickly summoned a thick wall of revolving fire and laced it in a cage of crackling electricity.

The large bolt struck Ted's shield and exploded in a burst of light.

For a brief instant, a look of surprise crossed Braelynn's face. "I am impressed. You have control of two elements already," she said, as Ted let the shield dissipate. Braelynn then addressed the crowd. "Can anyone else summon more than one element?"

Others stepped forward including the old woman that had gone second, and a tiny little girl that Ted thought looked familiar.

"Nearly half of you." The sorceress looked shocked. "And only-" she looked at Ted questioningly.

"Ted Koldun," Ted said helpfully.

Braelynn smiled thankfully. "Only Ted here chose to show what he could truly do. The rest of you should follow his example."

Ted was pleased by the sorceress' praise. He strove for perfection in all things and he knew that it was through this tiny sorceress that he would unlock the secrets of Will. Ted wanted nothing more than to master his magic.

"It seems that I have underestimated you," Braelynn said to those gathered around her. "I will not make that mistake again."

"The elements are the basis of sorcery." A small flame suddenly appeared floating in the air before her. "Fire is the most common element that a novice first learns. It is usually first discovered by strong emotions of anger or fear. It is destructive and volatile, and it is the job of the sorcerer to master those emotions and channel them."

A glob of water formed alongside the flame as she spoke. "Water gives life, but can also drown it out. Fire is more easily countered with water than any other element. However, the strength of Will is what truly determines the effectiveness of any given element."

Tiny particles formed and revolved into a small lump of stone that hovered next to the water. "Earth is a complex element that includes all types of stones and metals. It is primarily used for its defensive capabilities, but can also be used as a powerful force of destruction."

A small breath of air swirled around, picking up dirt and leaves to blow around in a miniature tornado alongside the stone. "Air is wild. It can gently carry you to safety or it can blow your enemies away. It may seem simple, but Air is not to be taken lightly."

Sparks flared up and a ball of electrical energy crackled into existence. "Electricity is one of the most unpredictable elements and it takes great skill to truly master."

Shadows gathered and formed a dark cloud that floated almost menacingly until a small ball of light appeared next to it. "Darkness and

Light are opposite sides of the same coin. You cannot have one without the other. To master either, you must understand both."

"Now, there are many more than just these few elements," Braelynn said, "but until you can control these seven, I will not teach you any others." There was a low grumbling from the gathered humans but the sorceress ignored it.

"However, each of these elements has many possible states." As Braelynn spoke, a piece of the fire broke off and formed a ball of what looked like liquid fire, similar to what Ted could make.

Then the bottom half of the glob of water froze into a long icicle.

The stone broke into three; one stayed a small stone, another crumbled into dirt, and the last liquefied into a lump of mud.

"Each element can be combined with another. Some are easier than others to create new and wonderful spells," the sorceress said. "The combinations are endless."

A middle-aged woman suddenly spoke. "What about nature? Can we control plants?"

"A good question," Braelynn smiled. "The answer, however, is a complicated one. It is true that we can manipulate living plants, but it is a different mindset and requires a certain skill and compassion that not everyone possesses."

"If you wish to learn the Arts of Nature, then you must seek out the Druids," Braelynn said. "They are the keepers of the living lore and could teach you their Art if you are found worthy."

"I will focus on teaching you the core elements of sorcery and help you strengthen your Will," said the sorceress. "Now, each of you will summon forth as many of the elements that you can."

The students spread out, careful to give plenty of room between each of them before they began casting.

Ted easily summoned a small flame and an orb of liquid fire, along with a ball of crackling lighting. But he could not get any of the other elements to appear.

He looked around and saw that while half of the others could summon two elements, few had a second state for any of theirs like Ted did with his fire and that made him feel better.

But then Ted cursed. There was that old woman and she had three elements floating before her; a chunk of stone, a dancing flame, and a glob of water.

Refusing to be outdone, Ted bent all his willpower into creating a stone. He figured it would be the easiest to create since it was a solid object and something he could imagine holding in his hand.

Ted concentrated and focused everything he had on summoning the stone. He pictured how it felt, the rough edges, and weight of it. His other elements began to flicker as he lost the concentration to keep them together. Veins bulged in Ted's forehead as he threw everything he had into it.

But before the fire and electricity vanished, a tiny pebble suddenly swirled into existence. Ted let out a long breath and smiled. He had done it! The other elements reformed as the tiny pebble joined them in a little dance before Ted.

"Very good."

Ted jumped and nearly lost his elements as the Lady Braelynn walked up to him in her shimmering white gown. Ted stood a little taller at her praise.

"It appears you are tied for the most elements and variants," she said and Ted instantly deflated. *Tied?* Who could have more than him? The old woman had three elements, true, but she didn't have any variants.

Just then, the familiar-looking little girl came dancing though the crowd, happily juggling a stone, a flame, and a glob of water before her. To Ted's dismay he saw that the water was half frozen.

How could this little girl, who must be no more than eight, have as much power as he did?

The girl laughed and suddenly there were two of her! The second girl faced the first, and they both laughed as they began to toss the elements back and forth to each other.

"Of course," Ted muttered, remembering where he had seen her before. She was the little girl that Dr. Cooper had said could make duplicates of herself.

Ted found himself a bit jealous. It seemed making duplicates wasn't her only ability and on top of that, her other power matched his own.

"Everyone release the elements you have summoned," Braelynn commanded, "and choose one that you are unable to create." She glided between the students with hands clasped behind her back. "Focus your Will on that one element and summon it. Become that element. Feel it, be it. Let it fill your mind."

Ted closed his eyes and imagined water as he tried to form it in his mind's eye, but it kept slipping though his fingers. He chuckled. It was water, after all.

A squeal of delight made his eyes pop open.

The little girl clapped happily as a miniature tornado whirled around above her head, causing her long hair to fly madly about.

Ted scowled.

It seemed that he had some practicing to do.

CHAPTER 10

Emily stormed through the woods, furious.

She had spent the last several hours arguing with a tree! A tree!

"And I thought men were stubborn," she grumbled angrily to herself.

To make matters worse, once she escaped the old tree she searched for her arrows, but couldn't find any of them. So now her only weapon was the skull-topped goblin scepter. But even that didn't make her feel much better. She preferred the hard reality of a physical object, not the hoped-for magical weapon.

That pesky voice hadn't been back since either. It was nice not having it floating around laughing at her, but it would be nice to know if she was going in the right direction!

Emily trudged on, still fuming, until she noticed something had changed.

She came to a stop and looked around. It took her a moment to realize what was different.

There was silence in the woods. No bird song, no wind through the trees... nothing. The eerie silence stretched on and a chill passed over Emily.

Her skin prickled and a sudden feeling of dread began to creep in. The silence seemed to grow and Emily was suddenly afraid. Her heart pounded in her chest and her breathing came in sudden gasps.

Terror filled her.

It was all Emily could do to not run from that awful place as fast as she could. She stood rooted to the spot, terror gripping her, as the trees seemed to close in and the silence became deafening.

Emily gritted her teeth and forced the unreasonable fear back. She had never been afraid of the woods in her life. She wasn't about to start now!

As if walking through thick mud, Emily struggled to put one foot in front of the other as she pushed through her fear and plowed onward. She hadn't spent hours trapped by a tree to just run away from some imaginary feeling of dread.

After what seemed like an eternity, the fear subsided and Emily breathed a huge sigh of relief. Birdsong and the sound of the wind suddenly came crashing back. It was almost as if she had crossed some invisible threshold. She shook off the last remnants of her unease and strode boldly further into the trees.

A large squirrel watched her from a low branch as she picked her way through the thick underbrush. It took several minutes for her to get clear of the foliage, but eventually it thinned and the woods opened up before her.

Emily's breath caught. Sunlight lanced through the trees, casting rays of light on the most incredible sight she had ever seen. Spread out before her were more wild animals than she had imagined possible in one place. Deer, squirrels, raccoons, foxes, chipmunks, opossums, turkey, and even bear and wolves, along with many more critters roamed the landscape everywhere Emily could see.

Suddenly, a large, ugly bird swooped down and in a puff of mottled feathers landed heavily on a nearby branch that bent dangerously under its weight. It looked down at her for a moment, then squawked in a horribly nasally voice. "Mine!"

"No, she's mine!" another voice squeaked from behind her.

Emily spun around to see a large squirrel standing on a stump. "I saw her first!" the squirrel squeaked heatedly.

"Mine! Mine!" the ugly bird squawked even louder.

The squirrel shook its tiny fists at the bird. "Oh, no you don't! Come down here and fight me Robadoo, you mangy old vulture!"

Emily stood there in amazement as the two animals argued with each other. "Whoa! Hold on there. I am no one's property." Emily said, but the animals paid no attention to her.

"Mangy?" The ugly bird actually managed to look offended. "Vulture!?" it gurgled. "I'm no vulture!" It stared down its large beak at the defiant squirrel. "If I were, then I would swoop down there and eat a furry little rodent like you, Rabidad!"

"Rodent!?" the squirrel barked angrily. "I'll show you a rodent!"

The squirrel's body abruptly began to bulge and expand at an alarming rate. Its head began to shift and change as its teeth grew into huge fangs. The tiny paws swelled as long claws sprouted from its growing digits. Thick, brown hair burst to life all over the body that was now larger than Emily and kept expanding until an enormous bear stood where the squirrel had been.

The huge bear roared and Emily shrunk back in fear.

"Rabidad!" a strong voice shouted. "Stop that at once!"

Emily searched for the voice and saw a handsome young elf striding confidently through the trees from behind her and realized that she was now surrounded. She gripped her scepter tighter as the elf approached.

He was of average height and his lean body was nicely tanned. A beaded leather vest hung open across his chest and tight, calf-high boots hugged his leather pants. He walked with a tall staff that was wrapped in ivy leaves and topped with a pinecone.

A band of metal encircled his left bicep and blue markings were painted all over his exposed skin. A wolf-headed silver torc hung around his neck. A leather strap held back his surprisingly dark green hair from his face. Nestled into his hair, just above his ears, two small deer antlers poked out giving Emily the impression that he had grown them.

"You are scaring our guest," the handsome elf said to the bear, but he never took his eyes off Emily.

"But Rubadub," the bear called Rabidad growled, "Robadoo started it."

"Rub-a-dub?" Emily laughed. "Like taking a bath?"

"What?" The handsome elf looked confused. "Are you offering to bathe with me?"

"A bath isn't *exactly* what I had in mind," Emily replied sweetly.

The bear and bird both sniggered. "It seems there is more than a bit of the wild ones in her as well," the ugly bird cackled in amusement.

"Yes," Rubadub said, "and that is why she is mine."

Rabidad growled. "I saw her first."

"Mine!" squawked Robadoo.

The three began arguing and Emily just stood there in amazement as they shouted at each other. Here was a good-looking elf, an ugly bird, and a huge bear all fighting over her. It was rather flattering. If only she knew what they wanted her for.

They continued arguing until the elf's voice rose above the others. "Wait, wait. WAIT!" Rubadub shouted over the other two as he motioned for silence. "I have a solution." He smiled at Emily. "Let's let her choose."

"A grand idea," Robadoo chirped from his branch. "There is no way she won't choose me." The ugly bird puffed itself up and preened its feathers regally.

"Um..." Emily looked up at the ugly creature. "I don't even know what I'm choosing for... and why would I choose a bird?"

"I'm no bird," Robadoo chirped and spread his wings grandly. "Behold!"

The bird suddenly exploded like a pack of firecrackers in a shower of feathers. Emily covered her face as fluff flew everywhere. When she looked back up, there was the strangest looking elf perched precariously on the branch were the ugly bird had been.

He was handsome, with features that closely resembled Rubadub. But the resemblance ended there. His hair was short and wild with feathers sticking out of it, looking almost like a straw bird's nest. A thick, feathered cloak hung across his shoulders and a feathered skirt circled his waist that led to calf-high wrapped sandals. Clutched in one hand was a long, wooden staff topped with a large bird's skull and stuffed wings.

Blue paint markings covered his body just like the other elf, only his pattern was wildly different. An eagle-headed silver torc hung around his slender neck and small bones pierced his long, pointed ears.

"You see!" the feathered elf announced. "Behold! Robadoo the Magnificent!"

"Give it a rest Robadoo Birdroppings," the bear rumbled, and stood up on its hind legs. "Feast your eyes on true perfection!"

The bear's long hair began to recede as its body began to deflate. The thick bulk melted and shifted, becoming smaller and leaner with each passing second.

Within a few moments the bear was gone, and in its place stood a third handsome elf. He resembled the other two, but he was taller and much more heavily muscled. And he was completely naked.

The only decorations were the painted blue markings all over his bare skin and a silver torc around his neck, similar to the others only with bear heads on it.

"Rabidad!" Rubadub scolded. "Would you cover yourself up? You know how these humans feel about exposed bodies."

Rabidad grunted and looked around as if searching for something. "Humans are strange," he muttered.

"Oh, I don't mind," Emily said softly, as she stared at the buff elf. "Really."

Apparently, he couldn't find whatever he was looking for and shrugged. With a wave of his hand, a pile of leaves swept off the ground and stuck themselves to his waist in a leafy clump.

"Better?" Rabidad asked, with his hands on hips.

"Not really. No," groaned Rubadub. "Sometimes I wonder if we are really brothers."

"I think that about you two all the time," Robadoo quipped from his branch.

Rubadub and Rabidad scowled up at the third elf who just laughed in the safety of his tree.

"Come now," Robadoo chuckled. "Let's let the pretty little human girl choose."

Rabidad scratched himself and a few leaves fell away. "Yes, let's get this over with, these blasted leaves are getting itchy," he grumbled, and continued to dig through the clinging pile of leaves.

"Well, my dear," Rubadub said kindly. "Which of us do you choose?"

Emily looked around at the three crazy elves that she found herself trapped between. "Um…I don't even know what I'm choosing for…"

"For your new Master. Of course, of course," Robadoo chirped happily.

"What?" Emily held up her hands defensively. "No, no. I just came here to find the Druids… not to be anyone's slave."

"Slave?" Robadoo cocked his head curiously. "Who said anything about slaves?"

"You just said-" Emily began before Rubadub jumped in. "You are in luck my dear," the nude elf said sweetly. "You have found the Druids."

Emily eyed the elf skeptically. "You are a Druid?"

Rubadub stepped forward. "Indeed, we are." The green haired elf suddenly hit himself in the head with the palm of his hand. "But where are my manners? Let me introduce myself. I am Rubadub Sweetwater," he said with a bow, "and these are my idiot brothers." He motioned to the two other elves. "Hiding in that tree is Robadoo and the itchy one is Rabidad."

Emily smiled at the strange elves. "Pleasure to meet you. I'm Emily."

"Welcome to the Glade, Emily," Robadoo chirped, "but now you must choose-choose!"

Emily eyed the elves wearily. "So, I get to pick which one of you teaches me to be a Druid?"

"Yes, yes." Robadoo piped and shifted in his branch eagerly.

"And you are Robadoo, Rabidad, and Rubadub." Emily pointed at each in turn. "Right?"

"Correct," answered Rubadub.

"Ugh," Emily sighed. "Your names are giving me a headache."

Robadoo perked up. "I can help with that!" he said excitedly, and began rustling through one of the small pouches hidden in the feathers of his skirt. "I've got some kerfluffin worms around here somewhere."

"She doesn't want worms, you dolt," Rabidad chided. "Snorkwallow root will take away the pain much faster anyway."

"Ha!" Rubadub laughed. "It will knock her out for several hours too." He winked at Emily. "But I have some fine Themiscyran wine back in my tent. That will take away a headache in no time."

"She is not going back to your tent with you Rubadub," Rabidad growled.

"She will when she chooses me," Rubadub retorted hotly.

"Boys, boys." Emily smiled sweetly at each one. "I'm flattered that you are fighting over me, really I am, but I don't think I can choose between you."

Emily saw the disappointment in each of them. It was almost comical how defeated they all looked. Like heartbroken children after their favorite toy broke.

Suddenly, Rubadub perked up. "I have an idea!" he said excitedly. "We can let Belenos decide!"

"Yes, yes!" Robadoo squealed. "The High Druid will know who to choose!"

"Works for me," Rabidad grumbled. "Follow me." He motioned to Emily and began marching away without waiting to see if anyone was following.

Emily shrugged to herself and hurried after the elf. She smiled as she followed him. While the pile of leaves covered his front half, his perfectly shaped backside was not.

Emily settled in and enjoyed the view as they made their way deeper into the forest.

It was several minutes before Emily realized that the other two elves were not following them. She was alone following the mostly nude elf. *Where had the others gone?*

They passed many more animals on their short hike through the trees before they reached an area that had several tents and small shacks nestled under the branches. They blended in so well that Emily almost didn't see them until she was right next to one.

Instead of going into one of the structures like Emily thought they were going to do, Rabidad led her through the camp and further into the woods.

He came to a stop before an unusually large, but rather uninteresting tree.

Rabidad knocked on the trunk of the tree and then stepped back to wait.

Emily wondered what was going on when a large shape suddenly burst out of the tree. Startled, Emily jumped back in alarm. The shape stepped forward and revealed itself to be another elf dressed in a long, hooded cloak that had the appearance of moss-covered bark. She suspected that if the elf stood very still that he would blend in perfectly with the large tree behind him.

Rabidad bowed low to the newcomer. "Greetings High One. We have another human that made it across the PANic Line."

The robed elf eyed her. "Good. I knew this one would make it."

Emily was surprised to discover that this elf's voice was the same that had teased her earlier that day. This must be the Belenos that the brothers had mentioned.

"You!" Emily growled. "You left me trapped in a tree for hours!" She pointed an accusing finger at the robed elf.

"Now, now," Belenos said soothingly. "You were not trapped *in* the tree. Merely trapped by the tree. There is a significant difference."

"I don't care what word I used!" she fumed. "And what was with all the garbage before that, huh? Walls of sticks in my way, swarms of shadow monsters, and even freakin' zombies!"

"Those were tests," Belenos said easily, seemingly not bothered by her outburst in the least. "I had to see if you possessed the heart and courage to join our ancient order." The elf smiled down at her. "I am pleased that you passed each one marvelously."

Emily was about to say more, but just then green-haired Rubadub stepped out of a nearby tree followed immediately by Robadoo in mid-conversation.

"-don't care if you saw her first," Robadoo was saying. "There is no way-" he cut off when he saw Emily and the others standing there. "Oh, hello there." He bobbed awkwardly.

"I told you we would be late," Rubadub whispered loudly to Robadoo.

Rabidad grinned. "Looks like she is mine since you two sloths couldn't get here on time."

Rubadub opened his mouth to argue, but Belenos cut him off. "I see what is going on here." He looked down at Emily. "They each claim you as their new novice, and they wish for me to choose between them, yes?"

Emily nodded her agreement.

"I see." Belenos looked thoughtful. "I think I may have a solution," he said, and a mischievous glint entered his eyes.

"She will be the novice for all of you," Belenos stated. "Together."

"What?!" Rubadub cried. "One novice per Druid. It has always been that way!"

"Well, not anymore," Belenos replied easily.

"The Great Stag would not approve of this," Rubadub argued.

"Then it is a good thing that Lord Cernunnos isn't here," Belenos smiled. "Besides, you three are nearly inseparable anyways. And I would hate to torture three souls to your shenanigans when one will do." Belenos looked apologetically at Emily. "Sorry, my dear, but I'm confident that you can handle these three."

"Wonderful," Emily muttered. "I would get a bunch of stooges..."

"Good." Belenos clapped his hand. "Now that that is settled, I have important matters to attend to."

"Now, off with you." He made a shooing motion. "And good luck," he said to Emily, and with that turned away and walked back into his tree.

The three elves just stood there and looked at each other. "Now what?" Robadoo mumbled.

"How should I know?" Rabidad grumbled. "We have never had an apprentice before."

"Well, that's just wonderful," Emily gave a resigned sigh. "How about you teach me something Druid-y," she offered helpfully.

"Like what?" Rabidad asked her.

"How should I know?" Emily replied. "*You* are the Druids."

The three brothers just stood there, looked at each other in confusion and Emily sighed heavily. "How about moving through trees like you two did?"

"Treewalking?" Rubadub shrugged. "That is as good a place to start as any."

"That's a good idea," Rabidad agreed. "It would take far too long to walk her to everywhere we would want to go."

"Okay, then," smiled Emily. "Let's get started."

Rubadub held up a hand. "Not so fast," he said, and pointed to the ground. "Have a seat. First we need to explain how treewalking works and its benefits and dangers."

Emily groaned and plopped unceremoniously on the ground.

"You and Ted would get along great," Emily moaned.

"Who?" Robadoo asked owlishly.

"Ted," Emily answered. "A friend of mine."

"Who?" Robadoo repeated.

"Don't encourage him," Rabidad muttered. "He likes the attention."

****

"Are we there yet?" Jack moaned as he trudged along behind the elf.

"Patience human," Darius chided.

They had been walking for miles and with each passing minute Jack grew more annoyed.

"You know we humans have a little thing called cars, right?" Jack grumbled. "We could have been there twenty minutes ago."

Darius grunted. "I will not be contained in one of your human death machines."

Jack followed Darius in brooding silence after that as they came to one of the many old factories that had been repurposed since The Shearing. This one had been turned into a massive smithy where dwarves, elves, and men worked side-by-side creating and repairing all types of weapons and armor.

When they entered the hot interior, Jack saw the large space had been converted into several stations. The nearest one had a group of human gunsmiths instructing a large crowed of dwarves.

Jack and Darius marched through the factory until Darius strode up to a small group of elves that were showing something to a few humans that was glowing in front of them. Jack tried to see what it was, but he couldn't make it out through the crowd.

One of the elves looked up and saw them approaching.

"Greetings Darius," the elf said, as he moved away from the crowd and approached them. He had long, blonde hair and a regal bearing. "What brings you here?"

"Greetings Quintus," Darius replied. "I must speak with the Forgefather."

Quintus looked curiously from Darius, to Jack, to the black sword and back again. "Forgefather Polynices is meeting with Rune Lord Starmantle to discuss… differences in forging techniques." Quintus glanced back to a closed room down the aisle. "It has been… heated to say the least."

"I would not interrupt without good reason," Darius assured the other elf. "I am sure he will want to see this."

Quintus didn't look like he believed Darius, but he sighed and shrugged his slender shoulders. "Very well. Follow me."

They snaked their way through several work stations filled with numerous tools and objects in various states of repair. The elves in this section moved about purposefully and some carried strange objects that Jack couldn't identify.

Once through the maze of workstations, they came to the closed door that Quintus had glanced at earlier.

Muffled voices cut off as Quintus knocked on the thick door.

"Enter!" a deep muffled voice bellowed.

Quintus opened the door and inside was an ancient dwarf that stood across from the largest elf Jack had ever seen.

The dwarf's grey beard was almost white and it was so long that it brushed the floor. Bright eyes looked out from bushy eyebrows and tufts of white hair poked out from around his thick leather apron. Dark, runic tattoos scarred his ruddy flesh and heavy, metal rune-studs stood out on his thick brow.

The elf was taller than Jack and built like Mike - broad shoulders and corded muscles. His long, dark hair was tied back in a series of intricate braids. An exquisitely tooled leather vest hung open revealing a heavy necklace made of many large links, each of a different metal.

"What is it Quintus?" the large elf growled. "I said I was not to be disturbed."

Quintus bowed low. "Apologies Forgefather. But Darius here has something he believes you will want to see immediately."

Forgefather Polynices turned his penetrating gaze on Darius and the Blade Dancer bowed low. "I am sorry for the intrusion Forgefather," Darius said quickly, "but I believed this to be urgent."

"It had better be," the large elf snarled, and spied the black sword Darius held and scowled. "That will be all Quintus." Polynices dismissed the other elf with a wave. Quintus bowed quickly and closed the door behind him.

The old dwarf didn't say anything and looked on curiously with a mischievous twinkle in his eye.

Once the door closed, the anger seemed to drain out of the Forgefather and he smiled. "It is good to see you Darius. It has been too long."

Darius smiled back. "Yes, it has Polynices, far too long. But my oath to train the humans has taken all of my time."

"And how is that progressing?" Polynices asked.

"Surprisingly well, actually," Darius replied grudgingly. "There is much talent among the humans; however, they are all in a rush to learn more before they are ready."

The Forgefather smiled. "You must remember that the humans do not have a thousand years to master their skills like we do, my friend."

"I know," Darius sighed, "but it is difficult… they are so hasty." Darius glanced back at Jack. "And confrontational."

Polynices saw the look and seemed to notice Jack for the first time.

"And who is this?" Polynices asked gently.

"This is Jack," Darius answered, "and he is the reason we are here."

"Oh?" Polynices said. "Explain."

"The human asked me to hold his sword while he sparred in my Ring," Darius explained. "When I took it in my hand… I felt… something…" The Blade Dancer's brow furrowed in concentration. "…. It was all I could do to keep from drawing it right there." Darius shook his head in disbelief. "I knew the blade had some kind of enchantment on it, so I brought it to you."

Darius held out the long, curved sword to the Forgefather and was careful not to touch the long hilt. Polynices approached the offered weapon, but made no move to touch it.

"It appears to be of orc design," Polynices muttered, as he carefully inspected the sheathed weapon, still without touching it. He looked at Darius. "What exactly did you feel?"

"Pride," Darius replied, "and anger."

"Could you hear a voice?" Polynices asked. "Did it speak to you?"

"No. Just a feeling," Darius mumbled softly.

"You, Jack," Polynices said without taking his eyes off the sword. "Do you feel the same urges from the blade?"

"Um… no. Not really," Jack shrugged. "It feels… good in my hands. Like it was meant to be there… I feel faster and stronger when I'm using it."

"Humm…" Polynices muttered. "Interesting…" He reached out to grasp the sword when the old dwarf suddenly spoke.

"I would no do that if I were ye," he rumbled with a surprisingly strong voice.

Polynices' hand froze a hair's breadth away from the sword. He looked back at the dwarf. "And why is that Eitri?"

Instead of answering the ancient dwarf called Eitri addressed Jack. "Be the blade black?"

"Yes," Jack replied.

"And does it ever glow?" the dwarf pressed.

"Sometimes," Jack muttered carefully.

Polynices lowly pulled his hand away from the wrapped weapon. "What do you know about this blade?" he asked the ancient dwarf.

"I'm not fer knowin' anything elf," Eitri rumbled, "but I have me suspicions." The ancient dwarf suddenly strode forward and grabbed the hilt, and drew the black blade before anyone could stop him.

Everyone stood around in shocked silence as Eitri held the dark blade up before him. "Ancient lore mentions weapons such as this," he rumbled. "I have only ever read about such legendary blades."

"Well, what is it?" the Forgefather asked.

"This," Eitri held up the black blade, as a soft red glow spread along its curved length, "be an orc soul sword, the weapon o' orc Bloodthirstiers."

"It be said they were forged from tamahagane by the powerful Muramasa Tribe," Eitri said. "Me ancestors record that such a weapon could cut through nearly anythin'. Only adamantine-forged dwarf steel or rune-protected weapons could resist the bite o' a Muramasa soul sword."

"How do you know for sure that this is such a weapon?" Polynices asked.

Eitri smiled. "There be only one way ter find out," he smiled wickedly. "Human, be a good lad and fetch me a sword."

Normally, Jack would have argued, but he was curious to see what the ancient dwarf was up too. So, Jack opened the door and saw a nearby barrel full of finished weapons. He rushed over, grabbed the first sword he saw and came back into the room.

"Now, hold it out and don't move," Eitri rumbled, and Jack did as he was asked.

"But…" Jack began.

The ancient dwarf suddenly bellowed a battle cry and the black sword flashed through the air.

With a shriek of tearing metal, the orc blade sheared through the other sword. The broken blade clanged to the floor.

"And that be why every dwarf weapon has a rune o' protection on it," Eitri rumbled.

"Impressive," Polynices muttered, as he picked up and inspected the sheared off piece of metal. "There must be immensely powerful enchantments in that blade. How did the orcs manage it? From what I know of the beasts, they are a primitive species."

"Ancient lore tells that the Muramasa Tribe be no regular orcs, but oni and they took their name from the demon Muramasa that taught them how ter create the soul swords," rumbled Eitri.

"I do not know this term... oni," said Polynices.

"I be no surprised," Eitri replied. "The oni be huge, red-skinned beasts that be half orc n' half demon," Eitri explained. "They more closely resemble a troll er ogre than they do an orc. And they be completely evil. Oni be extremely hard ter kill, wielding both immense physical strength as well as dark demonic powers."

"Luckily, they were rather rare creatures, so the chances o' ever seeing one was extraordinary," Eitri sighed. "At least that be the case before we cleansed our world o' the orc filth."

Eitri took the sheath and carefully slid the black blade back inside. "How did ye come across such a weapon?"

"I killed the orc who had it after he cut my rifle in half," Jack answered. The loss of his favorite gun still disappointed him.

"And how long have ye been wielding it?" the ancient dwarf asked.

Jack shrugged. "A few months."

A furry eyebrow rose curiously. "And ye haven't felt any urges ter needlessly kill or harm those around ye whilst wielding the sword?"

"Just whoever I'm fighting at the time," Jack replied. He wasn't quite lying, but he wasn't about to tell the dwarf everything. It wasn't like he wanted to kill his friends or anything... he just sometimes didn't want the fight to end.

Eitri looked hard at him and suspected the deception in Jacks words but let it go. "Very well," he rumbled, and handed the weapon back to Jack.

Jack snatched it from the dwarf and held it close.

"What are you doing?" Polynices cried. "We should destroy it!"

"And many o' me ancestors did just that," replied Eitri. "Most soul swords were destroyed after the orcs were eradicated from Svartalfheim. But it be said that a few Muramasa blades still remain in the trophy rooms o' several clans."

Eitri shook his bald head. "But after centuries o' study, I can tell ye that the blade itself no be evil," the ancient dwarf explained. "It magnifies and takes on the characteristics and emotions o' the wielder. That be why they be called soul swords, they bind with the wielder ter become one with 'em. This blade has been used by orcs fer so long that it be filled with rage and hate. But I believe that someone with a strong enough will could overcome the evil that be stored inside."

"You are willing to risk this human being corrupted by an evil weapon?" Polynices said, aghast.

"Aye," Eitri nodded. "He has carried it this long with no apparent ill effects." The ancient dwarf looked hard at Jack. "If he can overcome its influence, then it will be a powerful weapon against the coming darkness."

Polynices shook his head in disbelief. "Very well Eitri. It will be as you say. But if he becomes corrupted, then it will be your head."

The ancient dwarf nodded his consent.

"Return to your Ring," Polynices addressed Darius, "but keep a close eye on this one. If you see anything suspicious, report to me immediately."

Darius bowed. "As you wish, Forgefather."

PART II

CHAPTER 11

With a heavy thud, Mike landed hard on his hands and knees. Hot sweat rained down and splattered on the scorched earth beneath him. His breath came in gasps as he shook his head to try and clear it.

What was that? Mike wondered as he climbed unsteadily to his feet.

Steam rose in faint wisps off his armor and the metal shield strapped to his arm had a long, jagged crack running down its center.

Mike tore the shield off in disgust and discarded it into a growing pile of broken metal heaped nearby.

"Ye be improving," a deep voice rumbled.

Mike glanced over his shoulder at the speaker. Nadal sat on a low bench, carefully tinkering with Mike's mace in his large hands.

"But not good enough," Mike growled, and turned back to face the elf in front of him.

Leandros was resplendent in his silvery armor. "Your powers have grown remarkably these past weeks," the Paladin said. "If I had not seen it for myself, I would not believe it."

"It doesn't feel like I've made any progress," scowled Mike. "You still beat me, and these stupid runes are proving difficult to master."

Behind him, Nadal flinched at the mention of the runes. "I still think it

127

unwise that this elf knows about our agreement," he rumbled.

Mike sighed. It was an argument they had been having for days. "Look, I needed someone to help test my new runes in battle and Leandros and I have been training together for weeks. I trust him."

Nadal snorted derisively and continued tinkering.

Leandros nodded graciously. "I am honored. Your secret is safe with me."

"You see Nadal?" Mike smiled. "Leandros won't spill the beans."

"Beans?" the dwarf grumbled. "What does this have ter do with the spilling o' beans?"

"Never mind," Mike chuckled, and put the cautious dwarf from his mind.

"So, what was it you hit me with?" he asked Leandros.

"That was the corona," Leandros explained with a hint of embarrassment. "A blast of holy power to be used as a last resort."

"A last resort?" asked Mike.

"Yes," Leandros gave a sly smile. "You almost had me there."

"Really?" Mike said in disbelief. "I thought you were just messing with me."

The elf shook his head. "There was no 'messing' this time. It was all I could do to keep you from striking me."

Mike brightened at the news. When they had started training together, Mike had felt like he was fighting through mud, his moves slow and sluggish, while the elf Paladin was a blur around him. But as the days wore on, Mike slowly began to catch up, although he had suspected Leandros was actually slowing down to make him feel better. But it seems that that wasn't the case. He actually was getting faster.

A large grin split Mike's face. "Almost had you eh?"

Leandros nodded. "I must admit, I find it... agitating... that you are nearly a match for me when you have only had your powers for a few months and I have been a Paladin of Athena for hundreds of years."

Mike shrugged. "Well, I don't have hundreds of years like you. I guess we humans need to learn quickly to keep up."

The elf looked thoughtful. "I had never considered that…perhaps you are right."

"Of course, I'm right," Mike laughed. "Now, show me how you did that."

The Paladin looked thoughtful for a moment. "Since you have trusted me to keep your rune secret, I will require you to keep one as well." Leandros became very serious. "I will try to teach you the corona, but I must warn you that it is one of the most dangerous powers a Paladin can access."

"I'm ready," said Mike eagerly. "Do you think I can learn it? You know my skills don't exactly line up with you Paladins."

"True," Leandros replied, "but neither do you truly identify with those rigid Guardians. It seems that you are something of a hybrid."

"Let's just hope I have enough Paladin in me to learn his corona," Mike said with a wink.

Nadal abruptly stood up and stomped over to the pair. "I'm afraid ye will have ter attempt this another time. We must be gettin' back afore someone comes lookin' fer us."

"The dwarf speaks true," Leandros said. "We will be missed."

"Ugh," groaned Mike. "Fine. We can continue this tomorrow and, hopefully, I will have finished a new rune shield that won't break."

"One can only hope," Leandros smiled. "Farewell."

Without waiting for a reply, the elf Paladin glided away and quickly disappeared into the trees surrounding the little clearing that they were using as a secret training area.

"I still no be trustin' him," Nadal grumbled.

"I know," Mike sighed, and put his hand on the dwarf's broad shoulder. "Come on, let's get back to the Foundry."

When Mike and Nadal arrived back at the forges, one of Nadal's burly dwarf apprentices ran up to them. "Master." He quickly bowed. "There be a messenger waitin' fer ye in yer private chambers."

"A messenger?" Nadal rumbled in surprise. "A messenger from who?"

"I'm not fer knowin' Master," the apprentice said hurriedly, "but he carries a royal seal!"

Nadal's eyes narrowed and he suddenly stormed off towards his study without a word. Mike was forced to almost run, despite his much longer legs, to catch up to the Runesmith.

"What's going on?" Mike asked as he hurried along through the maze of forges and crafting stations filled with men, elves, and dwarves hard at work crafting all sorts of things.

"I'm not fer knowin'," Nadal muttered, "but if he carries a royal seal then it must be important..." A note of concern entered his voice. "Perhaps they have discovered our little... agreement."

A feeling of dread began to creep through Mike. If someone discovered that Nadal was teaching him to craft runes then his friend was surely in a world of trouble.

"What would happen if they found out?" Mike asked.

"Strip me o' me rank and forbid me from ever putting hammer ter anvil again, if they be merciful," Nadal snorted. "The Anvilborn Clan no be known fer its mercy." He shook his head. "I may be executed. Or worse, exiled."

"Surely they wouldn't do that just for just teaching me rune craft?" Mike argued.

"*Just* rune craft?" Nadal's sharp bark of laughter made many heads turn as they rushed by and he dropped his voice to a whisper. "Lad, rune lore was given ter us by the Allfather himself. There be no art more sacred er well-guarded than the secrets o' craftin' runes."

"Since you already possess Runevision, I believe the gods have granted ye permission ter learn the secrets o' runes." Nadal glanced about suspiciously as they hurried through the forges. "But just because *I* believe it no mean the Rune Priests will agree."

"I'm sure they will understand." Mike tried to make the distraught dwarf feel better. "Maybe they don't even know about it and the messenger is here for something else."

Nadal snorted scornfully. "I be much comforted," he growled, as they finally approached the door to his small private chambers.

"Do you want me to come in with you?" Mike asked, hoping the answer would be no.

The dwarf stopped before his door and took a deep breath. "Ye may as well come along," he sighed. "This more' n likely involves us both."

Nadal squared his shoulders before opening the door and striding into the small room with Mike close behind.

Seated at one of the small stools along the wall was a large dwarf with a fiery red beard and blue runic tattoos covering his baldpate and running down his right arm. He twirled what looked to be a huge steel coin between his thick fingers.

"'Bout time ye showed up!" the dwarf boomed. "I been sittin' here on me arse near all day!"

"Baldor?" Mike blurted at the sight of his old companion. "What are you doing here?"

A huge grin split Baldor's face as he held up the huge coin. "I'm here with a message from King Varnir emself."

"Jarl Deathkettle?" Nadal looked dumbfounded. "Since when are ye a messenger fer the Anvilborn King?"

"Since I gave his highness some very important information that he found ter be quite helpful," Baldor replied cryptically.

"Now, I be here fer a summons," Baldor announced, "and the king does no like ter be kept waitin'."

"I be ready when ye be," Nadal replied.

"No you, ye dolt," Baldor grumbled. "I'm here fer him." He pointed a thick finger directly at Mike's chest.

"Me?" Mike choked. "What does the king want with me?"

"Oh, it's not just ye lad," Baldor chuckled and stood up. "It be all the Heroes o' Awesome. Now come on, we have ter go find the rest o' yer friends."

Without waiting for a response, Baldor suddenly stood up and shouldered his way through Mike and Nadal.

Confused, Mike followed Baldor out and left a stunned Nadal standing alone in his study.

"Do ye know where the rest o' em be?" Baldor asked, as they made their way out of the forges.

"Not really," Mike admitted. "But I can guess."

"Lead on then," motioned Baldor.

It was a short walk from the forges to one of the firing ranges so Mike decided to try there first. As luck would have it, when they entered the handgun range Mike immediately spotted Liz.

"Well, hello!" Liz beamed when she saw Mike and Baldor approaching. "I'm glad you're here," she said excitedly. "I've got something to show you."

"Oh?" Mike replied curiously, as he and the jarl joined Liz at the firing line. "Where is Jason?" he asked.

"Trying to talk some elves into shooting a gun," Liz chuckled at the absurdity of it. The elves wouldn't have anything to do with guns, at least not guns made by *humans*. Rumor had it that some elves had forged their own firearms and were practicing with them in secret.

Mike looked around and something seemed strange, and it took a minute for him to realize what exactly it was.

A normal range had clear firing lanes so you could see your target at the other end. But about half way down the lane, this one had a wide steel beam standing in the center of it.

"Stay here," Liz said. "I'll be right back."

Liz marched down the lane and when she reached the end, she placed a small golden apple on a raised pedestal before rejoining Mike and Baldor at the line.

"Um..." Mike began, "you know the apple is behind the beam, right?"

"Yup," Liz replied with a mysterious grin.

"Oh, ok," said Mike. "Just so you know..."

Liz drew the pistol strapped to her thigh and pointed it down the range in one smooth motion. She looked over at Mike and winked just before pulling the trigger.

Mike flinched, expecting the bullet to smash into the steel beam. But to his surprise the apple exploded in a shower of juicy bits.

"What sort o' spell be that?" Baldor asked in amazement.

"No spell," Liz replied proudly "I bent the bullet."

Mike raised a curious eyebrow. "You *bent* the bullet?"

"Yup," Liz grinned proudly.

"That's a neat trick." Mike was impressed. "And how do you do that?"

Still grinning, Liz tapped a finger against her forehead.

"Ahh," Mike laughed. "I should have known."

Baldor scowled. "So, it be a spell."

Liz shook her head. "I don't think so…. it's like I can guide the bullet… almost as if it were a part of me. I don't think there is anything really magical about it." Liz pulled a few stands of hair from her face and holstered her pistol. "It's hard to explain," she shrugged. "So, what did you guys need? It's nice to see you again Baldor. It's been ages."

Baldor nodded in greeting. "I come ter gather the Heroes o' Awesome fer their audience with King Varnir Anvilborn."

"An audience?" Liz looked questioningly at Mike. "What did you and Ted do this time?"

Mike shrugged. "Got me."

"We must be findin' the others so I can present ye ter the king," Baldor rumbled. "Do ye know where they be?"

Liz thought a moment. "Emily is probably with the Druids, as usual. Good luck finding her."

Baldor mumbled something under his breath that sounded like "tree huggers," but Mike couldn't quite make it out.

"Jack is most likely up at those training rings," Liz continued. "Last I heard he was trying to be the champion of each one… and doing pretty well at it, too."

"How do you know that?" Mike asked.

Liz laughed. "Honestly Mike, don't you pay attention to anything?"

Mike sighed. "I pay attention just fine."

"Sure you do," Liz chuckled. "and where is Ted then?"

"Easy," Mike said confidently. "He is either learning from the mages or in his lab tinkering on those gizmos he's been working on."

"Wrong," Liz's laughter chimed through the range. "I know *exactly* where Ted will be. Today he is taking his test."

Mike slapped himself in the forehead. "Oh, that's right! He was taking his test for Apprentice Battlemage or something today."

"Yes, and if we hurry we can probably pick up Jack on the way and get there in time to watch his test," Liz said.

"Fine, fine," Baldor interrupted. "Just get ter movin'. I dun want ter keep the king waitin' any longer than I have ta."

Grey clouds covered the sky in a hazy blanket as Mike, Liz, and Baldor reached the Cathedral of Learning.

"May as well live Under with all the sunlight this Steel City o' yers gets," Baldor grumbled.

"It's always cloudy in Pittsburgh," Mike quipped, and glanced up at the gloom.

"I thought dwarves liked being underground?" Liz asked.

"Aye, that be true," Baldor replied as he stomped up to the newly built gatehouse around Cathy's grounds. "But it be our mountain cousins that prefer their darkness while we o' the hills also enjoy the sun on our skin and the wind in our beards."

The gate guards in their black and gold tabards let the trio pass as Mike, Liz, and Baldor entered the Cathedral grounds.

Inside was brewing with activity. In the past weeks, more refugees had come streaming in along with two lesser dwarf Clans and a small force of elves.

More Martial Rings had been added to include all possible weapon combinations and every one was filled. Enchanted lights, created by the elves, hung above each Ring so that training could continue even at night. And other areas had been sectioned off for use by the mages and other groups due to the increase in population. A lot had changed in the weeks that the friends had been here and it was hard to keep track of the constantly evolving city.

"So where do you think Jack is?" Liz asked, as she searched through the masses of people milling about.

"Over there." Mike pointed through the throng. "That Ring has the largest crowd. No doubt Jack will be in the middle of it."

They made their way to the outskirts of the large ring of people and could just catch a glance of several individuals sparring in the Ring. Baldor led the way and pushed his way through the crowd to a chorus of curses.

"Oy, go cry," Baldor snarled back, as he used his thick form to barrel himself forward.

Mike and Liz followed close behind as the sea of people was forcefully parted before the jarl until they finally reached the edge of the Ring.

Sure enough, Mike's prediction was proven correct. Inside the circle, Jack dueled against a homely woman with long, black hair that was taller than he was. They each wielded a bo staff with marvelous dexterity. Jack and the woman were each a blur of motion as they struck and dodged nearly faster than the eye could follow.

Jack thrust out, but the woman spun away, barely missing getting punched in the chest. Continuing her spin, the woman's staff whistled through the air at Jack's head.

At the last moment, Jack blocked the strike inches from his face. He pushed her back and the two were separated for the moment.

Jack smiled at her and she smiled back. Suddenly, they both lunged at each other, staves whirling. The crack of wood on wood echoed around them in rapid succession.

The pair danced around each other, their weapons a blur around them, as the crowd cheered them on.

Then abruptly it was over.

The woman was on her back with Jack standing over her with his staff resting lightly against her throat.

The crowd erupted in applause.

Jack acknowledged the onlookers with a wave and then spotted Mike, Liz, and Baldor at the Ring's edge. He smiled and nodded to them before helping the woman to her feet.

Jack and the woman spoke softly together for a moment before she picked up her staff and walked back into the crowd. As she departed, an elf in dark leather armor that had been watching the match spoke up. "We have a new Staff Champion!" he thundered.

Jack beamed and raised his staff in victory and let the applause wash over him.

After a long moment, Jack lowered his weapon and nodded to the elf before walking toward his friends. "Who is next?" the elf shouted.

Jack placed the staff on a rack full of other staves before joining the others.

"Congratulations." Liz gave Jack a hug when he reached them.

"Thanks," he beamed.

"Yes, yes, all well 'n good, but we need ter be off," Baldor grumbled.

"Off where?" Jack asked.

Mike shrugged. "The dwarf king wants to see us."

Jack looked surprised. "What for?"

"That is what we all want to know," Liz replied. "Any idea where Emily is?"

Jack shrugged. "In the woods?" he replied with a smirk.

"Well, that's helpful." Liz grated.

"I try," Jack smiled back. He looked around as if searching for something. "So where is the Beard of Knowledge?"

Mike chuckled. "We are going to get him next. Come on."

They set off with Baldor again clearing a path through the throng. Once clear of the press of bodies, it was a short walk around to the other side of the Cathedral to the mage's training fields. To Mike's surprise, they found an even larger gathering around one particular field. Thanks to the much larger scale of the circular training area, they didn't have to fight through the crowd to get up close.

In the center of the circle Ted sat cross-legged and appeared to be meditating with what looked like a modified poleaxe resting across his knees.

Nearby, two elves stood in conversation as the crowd gathered. One elf was shorter and blonde, and was encased in sculpted armor that was so detailed he could have been mistaken for being nearly naked if it wasn't for the silvery shine.

The other elf was taller with dark hair and had similarly sculpted armor, but where the blonde elf's was unadorned silver, his was exquisitely detailed with gems and arcane symbols that were a brilliant reddish-gold color, which Mike thought closely resembled copper.

Surely nobody would wear flimsy copper armor, Mike thought. *It would be suicide.* Now curious, he resolved to discover what that armor was made of.

It looked to Mike that they were having an argument, but they were too far away for him to make anything out. But it was clear the blonde elf in silver wasn't happy about something.

Eventually, the blonde elf calmed down and the copper-armored elf walked off the field, leaving the blonde alone facing a still-seated Ted.

As if on cue, Ted stood up and faced the silver-clad elf. Ted bowed and the blonde elf stiffly returned it.

Without warning, the sky erupted as a huge bolt of lightning streaked down. Ted didn't move as the bolt crashed into a glowing golden shield just above his head.

Before the lightning bolt had faded, the blonde elf drew two short swords and rushed at Ted.

Ted raised his poleaxe to defend, but while the elf was still a few paces away, a fireball formed in front of the charging elf and shot out with blinding speed. Ted deflected the fireball with a word, but immediately after the elf was on him.

Blades flashed as Ted parried, but was forced to backpedal from the furious assault. A coil of crackling energy appeared behind Ted and lashed out to wrap itself around one of his arms.

Ted fought desperately to free his immobile arm and keep the elf's swords at bay. Ted rammed his poleaxe into the ground and it erupted in a wave around him, knocking the elf backwards and giving him a moment's reprieve.

The blade of the poleaxe began to glow a cherry red and Ted reached up and with one arm used the glowing blade to slice through the magical cord in a shower of sparks.

Just as the cord faded away to nothing, the elf leapt back in, short swords flashing.

Ted fought furiously, but Mike could tell he was out-matched. The elf was just too fast. Ted must have realized this as well because he suddenly pushed the elf back and then dove into a roll that gave him some much-needed space.

Ted waved his hand and darts of magical energy took shape and launched themselves at the blonde elf. Seemingly unconcerned, the elf didn't move and with a contemptuous flick of his wrist, the darts vanished.

Liz moaned in dismay at the ease at which Ted's spell had been defeated, but Mike suspected that the darts had just been a distraction because as they disappeared, Ted finished a spell he had been muttering and released it.

Nothing happened.

The elf smirked and Ted suddenly looked nervous.

The elf thrust a hand down towards the ground and made a pulling motion as the earth began to shake. Large chunks of rock erupted from the ground in fountains of dirt and stone. The elf swung his arm around and the massive stones flew at Ted.

Ted pointed his glowing poleaxe at the rocks, and red bolts of energy shot out and impacted the stones. The explosions destroyed the boulders in an intense shower of fire and dust.

Before the pieces of stone stopped falling, the ones lying on the ground began to quiver. The quivering grew and the pieces began moving. Slow at first, then with frightening speed, the stones flowed together into a towering pillar of living stone. The rocks shifted and formed into a rough humanoid shape before finally coming to rest.

"Golem," Mike muttered at the sight.

The construct's roar shook the ground and sounded like an avalanche.

Streams of air formed around Ted and whipped out at the monster.

They wrapped themselves around its arms and legs, but after a moment's struggle, the golem ripped free of the cords of air and advanced on Ted.

Gouts of water poured from Ted's outstretched hand and blasted into the stone monster. Smaller pebbles and stones were washed away by the torrent, but the larger blocks were unmoved and still the golem advanced.

Lightning crackled and popped around the construct with little damage. Streaks of blistering light and darts of energy all had little effect. The monster shrugged off every elemental spell Ted threw at it.

Desperately, Ted fired the red energy from his poleaxe that had originally destroyed the boulders. But each impact only tore a fist-sized chunk from the living stones.

The rock golem roared and with surprising speed, struck out with a massive fist of stone.

Ted slipped on the slick mud created from his water spells and before he could dodge, he caught a glancing blow from the huge fist that sent him sprawling.

But he quickly recovered and came up firing more spells as he tried to get some space between him and the monster. Chunks of stone blew off the construct's body as it slowly turned to face him.

A jet of liquid fire flowed from Ted and washed over the construct. At first nothing happened and the stone golem continued its lumbering advance, but then Mike noticed that the living stones were starting to glow red from the heat.

Ted gritted his teeth as he forced more liquid fire at the monster. Superheated stone began to melt like candle wax down the roaring construct.

Its heavy footfalls slowed as more and more of its body melted away under the intense heat. The golem roared as its legs finally gave out and the molten construct crashed to the earth and then dissolved in a bubbling pile of melted stone.

Exhausted, Ted let the fire go out and he collapsed to the ground beside the glowing pile of slag that had once been the golem.

The blonde elf hadn't moved since summoning the golem and gave

Ted a slight nod of respect.

"Very well done!" said the dark-haired elf in the reddish-gold armor as he strode over to Ted. "I was doubtful at first, but you have proven yourself worthy to join us."

The elf handed something to Ted, but Mike couldn't make out what it was.

"Welcome to the brotherhood, Apprentice Battlemage Koldun," the elf shouted for all to hear.

The crowd cheered and Mike noticed a few elves leave the crowd, obviously not happy at how the test had ended. He put the upset elves from his mind as a pale and shaking Ted slowly made his way over to them.

"I need a nap," Ted moaned, and leaned heavily on his poleaxe.

Mike laughed. "It will have to wait." He thumbed toward Baldor. "We have been summoned to see King Varnir"

Mike quickly held up a hand as Ted opened his mouth. "Before you ask," Mike said quickly, "we don't know what he wants."

Ted's mouth snapped shut with an audible click.

Liz chuckled. "I wish we could get him to stop talking that fast all the time," she teased.

"If I weren't exhausted I would have a comeback for that," Ted smiled tiredly back.

Jack scanned the crowd. "Now we just need to find Emily and we can get this show on the road," he said.

"Aye," Baldor agreed. "Whatever that be meaning."

"I'm not looking forward to searching the woods for her," Ted grumbled. "But I bet I know who will be able to help us." He pointed over to a group of elves standing nearby.

"How can they help?" Liz asked.

"See that elf that looks like a tree?" Ted replied. "Well, he's a master Druid. He will know where she is."

When nobody made a move, Liz sighed and rolled her eyes. "I guess I'll go ask." She walked off muttering something about "so much for tough guys…" as she made her way toward the elf and Mike breathed a sigh of relief. He disliked talking to people he didn't know.

As they waited for Liz, Mike asked, "So, who was that you were fighting? He seemed nice," he said with a smirk.

"Battlemage Regulus," Ted replied smugly. "He doesn't think humans should be allowed to become Battlemages. But I think I may have just changed his mind."

Mike was only half listening as he watched Liz talk to the Druid. He saw the elf nod to something Liz said then get a far-away look in his eyes for a moment before walking over to a nearby tree and placing his hand on it. He looked to be whispering something before removing his hand and rejoining Liz and his companions.

The Druid said something to Liz and from her reaction she was confused about something. She thanked the Druid and then went to stand by the tree the Druid had touched.

Liz looked back and saw them all staring at her. She waved and motioned for them to join her.

"This should be good," Jack muttered, as they made their way to her.

"What's the deal?" Mike asked Liz, as they gathered around the old tree.

"He just said to wait by this tree," Liz answered with a shrug.

"Bloody elves," Baldor grumbled impatiently. "All their mysterious-"

The tree abruptly rippled like water.

"What the...?" Baldor jumped away from the tree in surprise.

The tree rippled again and suddenly a figure stepped out of the tree.

Everyone's hands flew to their weapons, none faster than Baldor, who had his twin axes drawn and was ready to charge the intruder.

"Thank the spirits you called!" Emily rambled, unaware of everyone's surprise. "Those three morons are going to get me killed!"

Emily looked around at everyone gathered about. "Well, this is quite the party." She put her hands on her hips. "So, what do you want anyways?"

"We have been summoned by King Varnir," Liz explained.

"King Who?" Emily scowled. "And nobody *summons* me."

"King Varnir Anvilborn," Baldor rumbled. "And ye *will* answer his summons," he said dangerously.

Emily glared at the dwarf and stormed up to him until they were nose-to-nose. "And what if I refuse?" Emily growled.

"Nobody refuses the king," snarled Baldor, as his face began to turn red.

They glared at each other for a long moment before Emily abruptly smiled and all of her apparent anger suddenly vanished.

"You're lucky I like you, dwarf," she said sweetly, and suddenly kissed his wide nose

Baldor stood there dumbfounded, unsure of what had just happened.

Everyone shared a laugh at the confused dwarf, and while Baldor tried to come to terms with the sudden emotional reversal, Liz touched the tree where Emily had stepped out. "Can you take somebody with you?" Liz asked.

"No," Emily replied. "Some of the more powerful Druids can bring somebody with them when they treewalk, but I'm not that good at it yet." She admitted. "It actually took me a few jumps to get here."

"Could you teach me?" asked Liz.

Emily shrugged. "I doubt I could teach it, but if you want I can introduce you to some Druids who could. So long as you have the ability to learn it."

"And how will I know if I have the ability?" Liz pressed.

"That is a bit hard to explain." Emily scratched her head thoughtfully. "But I'll tell you it ain't fun." She shuddered involuntarily at some memory. "Definitely, not fun."

"Bah!" Baldor finally seemed to have recovered. "Who would want ter learn such a thin' anyhow?" he grumbled, but Mike saw the bluster for what it was. "Nobody in their right mind would want ter walk through a tree!"

Ted stroked his beard thoughtfully. "It would be very useful…"

"Can it get us to the king?" Jack asked. "I need to get back to my training."

"Don't be stupid, human," Baldor barked a laugh. "There be no trees inside the Great Hall. Or anywhere else in a fortress fer that matter."

"Well, how should I know?" Jack argued. "It's not like you dwarves will let anybody inside to see it anyways."

Baldor snorted, "I'm takin' ye there now, aren't I?"

"Only because the king is making you," Jack retorted.

"Oh, give it a rest you guys." Mike rubbed his temples wearily. "We are all here, so let's just get this over with."

"I second that," added Ted.

Baldor nodded, propped his axe on his shoulder, and stomped away. "Come," he rumbled over his shoulder. "The king awaits."

CHAPTER 12

The long hill of Mount Washington streached along the south of Pittsburgh and formed the border of the Monongahela and Ohio Rivers. Part of the Alliance Agreement had granted Mt. Washington to the dwarves and they had wasted no time making it their own.

Fortresses were taking shape along the length of the hill and the skeleton of heavy walls lined the ridge, but it was deep below where the real work was being done.

The dwarves had descended on Mt. Washington like a swarm of ants and using the Fort Pitt Tunnels, they had burrowed into the rock and carved out a city for themselves.

It was here, deep below the surface, that the Heroes of Awesome were led to the massive steel doors guarding the great hall of the Anvilborn Clan.

Liz looked up at the immense door in amazement. It must have stood a good two stories tall and looked to be made of solid steel. A mural of astounding detail stood out of the polished surface depicting humans and dwarves shaking hands as they stood on the heaped corpses of what appeared to be scores of orcs with the city of Pittsburgh beautifully depicted in the background.

Four dwarves incased in heavy plate armor stood silent guard before the door with huge war hammers clutched in their armored fists.

"Welcome ter Varnirborg!" Baldor rumbled proudly, as they advanced on the massive doors.

Liz raised a questioning eyebrow. "Varnirborg?"

Baldor shrugged his massive shoulders. "It no be every day a king gets ter found a new city."

"No," Liz chuckled, "I suppose it's not."

The guards must have known they were coming because they didn't budge as the jarl led the group of humans forward. A few paces away and the massive doors began to silently swing open on their own.

Hot air buffeted the companions as they made their way through the growing opening. Inside was cavernous space lit by rows of huge braziers set between massive columns that supported the ribbed ceiling high above.

The ceiling was shrouded in shadows, but Liz could still make out the exquisite detail of the stonework and she marveled at its beauty. The massive columns were equally detailed at the top, but became rougher until the bottoms appeared as coarse, natural stone.

Heavy scaffolding lined the walls and columns as chunks of stone and tools lay scattered about the foot of them. It looked to Liz as though the workers that were still carving out this marvelous chamber had left in an awful hurry.

Her companions' footfalls sounded horrendous to Liz's ears as they marched through the eerily silent chamber. Liz had the distinct impression of a tomb and tried to suppress a shiver.

But they were not alone. At the far end of the hall, a figure sat atop a raised dais with a great furnace billowing behind it.

As they got closer, Liz saw that it was a dwarf of fantastic proportions. His large frame was made even larger by the thick armor and heavy cloak he was wrapped in.

A long, bearded axe of immense size rested at his feet and his huge hands where crossed upon its haft. At first, Liz thought the blade was made of stone, but upon closer inspection she realized that it was only made to *look* like chiseled stone. The blade was long with only the slightest taper towards the bottom. Carved runes glowed along the length of the weapon and a strange nub set behind the blade. Opposite of the axe blade was a wide hammerhead that alone looked heavier than anything Liz could ever hope to lift.

"An impressive weapon," Mike muttered, as he took note of the axe as well.

Baldor snorted softly as they marched along. "That be no ordinary weapon, human. That be the legendary Axe o' Perun! Forged by Perun the Thunderer, one o' the First Dwarves and father o' the Anvilborn Clan."

The mighty dwarf holding the legendary weapon was no less impressive. He had rugged features with a long, braided beard the color of burnished copper. Striking blue eyes peered out from beneath bushy eyebrows set upon a heavy brow. His simple circlet of steel set with runes and precious gems sat regally upon his bald head.

His armor was of a dark, blue-tinted metal that Liz had heard Mike call dwarf steel. Intricate runes glowed softly over every inch of the dark plate. Gold and silver trim accented the sharp angles and gentle curves of every detailed piece of metal. The armor was a work of art, but it only accented the imposing stature of the dwarf who wore it.

"King Varnir!" Baldor bellowed, as he came to a halt before the dais. "May I present the-"

The king raised a hand and Baldor's jaw snapped shut.

King Varnir Anvilborn leaned forward and looked hard at each one of them in turn. "So ye be the mighty Heroes o' Awesome that I been hearin' so much about." the king rumbled in a powerfully deep voice. "No very impressive looking…"

"I was about to say the same thing about you," Jack quipped.

The dwarf king's eyes narrowed dangerously and Liz was afraid Jack had just made a new enemy. But then the king's laughter suddenly boomed throughout the great hall. "Bwahaha!" he bellowed. "Finally! A human with a backbone!"

Liz breathed a sigh of relief and saw the others do the same.

Emily leaned over to Liz and whispered. "Since when are we 'mighty heroes'?"

Liz nodded toward Baldor. "I think somebody has been telling stories about us."

Emily discreetly nodded her understanding before turning her attention back to the mighty dwarf seated before them.

"Now that ye have arrived," the dwarf king's powerful voice echoed through the huge chamber, "we have important matters ter discuss." King Varnir motioned with one massive hand and a guard, that Liz hadn't even noticed, marched away through a small side passage.

"The things ye be about ter hear are ter no be repeated ter anyone outside these halls," King Varnir warned menacingly. "Do I have yer word that ye will no speak o' this ter anyone?"

The companions shared a look, each wondering what could be so important that they were sworn to secrecy. "Very well," Mike replied first. "You have my word." And the others all voiced their agreement.

The king inclined his head in thanks. "Good. Now come, we must join the others." King Varnir stood and rested the immense axe on his shoulder as easily as if it were a walking stick before unceremoniously marching down the steps and heading off to the same side passage the guard had taken a few moments before.

Mike glanced back questioningly at Liz and she shrugged helplessly. "After you," she said.

Mike started off after the king and the others followed close behind.

Liz tried to suppress a smile. As much as he didn't want to be, Mike was the unofficial leader of their little group and the others wouldn't make a move unless Mike did first. Which wasn't usually a problem since Mike had a tendency to charge off into danger whenever he was given half a chance.

As they followed the king, more dwarf guards in dark, heavy armor detached themselves from the shadows and silently followed the companions. Liz wondered how many guards were actually in the chamber. She hadn't seen any when they walked in and it was almost like they stepped right out of the stone.

It was a short walk through the narrow passageway to a small, well lit, side chamber that was dominated by a large circular table in its center.

Several figures were already seated around the table when they entered.

Liz recognized most of them.

Three dwarves sat across from them. Ambrosar, the Chief Guardian was tall with a thick, black beard and encased in heavy rune armor draped in a long, white tabard. Next to him, was an ancient looking dwarf with a grey beard and a thick leather apron. Liz recalled Mike talking about him. Rune Lord Eitri Starmantle she thought his name was. There was an empty seat and then next to it was a dwarf Liz knew well. Short with fiery red hair and a long scar running down one cheek was Fugal Brightrobe, Master Cleric of Frigg.

It was a surprising gathering of dwarves, but what was even more surprising was the group of elves seated across from them.

Archmage Talsin looked as mysterious as ever in his dark blue robes that silver symbols eerily floated across like lost spirits. Seated beside the Archmage was the dark-haired Battlemage in sculpted reddish-copper armor that they had seen at Ted's test. Next to the Battlemage was the gorgeous Commander Valerian. The Paladin was exquisite in his brilliant silver armor and lustrous dark skin. And last was the High Priestess Ipheto, seated regally in her sky-blue healer's robes.

Positioned around the table's curve, separating the elves and dwarves, were a group of humans.

Dr. Cooper's light brown hair stuck out in wild angles and he waved enthusiastically when they entered. Next to Cooper, in her white lab coat, was Dr. Kilpatrick and beside her was a dark-skinned Army officer that Liz didn't recognize.

"Ah, good, you found them!" Dr. Cooper exclaimed as the companions entered the room and took seats between the elves and dwarves, across from Dr. Cooper and the other humans.

"No easy task, that," Baldor grumbled, as he plopped heavily into the chair next to Ambrosar.

"I dislike this *round* table," King Varnir complained, as he joined the dwarves in the vacant chair between Eitri and Fugal.

"I'm sorry me King," Eitri said. "But ye did agree ter it in the Alliance Agreement," the ancient dwarf pointed out.

"I be well aware o' what I agreed ter, Eitri," growled King Varnir. "Now, let us get this over with." The huge dwarf king looked at Liz and her companions. "Do ye know why ye been summoned here?" he asked.

"No," Mike answered, "but I bet you are going to tell us."

Dr. Cooper laughed. "You've got that right."

King Varnir scowled at Cooper, but otherwise ignored him and instead addressed Mike and the others. "I wish ter recruit ye fer a very sensitive mission."

The king paused and gauged their reaction to the news. When there were no refusals he continued. "Me son, Brokkr, was scoutin' northwest o' this city with a group o' our best hunters when they did no check in, four days ago."

Commander Valerian leaned forward. "We sent a scouting party after them, but two days ago they similarly vanished." The Paladin looked disturbed. "This morning, a second scouting party found traces of a struggle and kefali arrows, but no sign of either elf or dwarf."

"I suspect they were captured," King Varnir continued. "If these... *kefali* somehow discovered me son was a prince, then perhaps they abducted him fer a ransom." The king sounded almost hopeful.

"No," Talsin said grimly, "if the kefali knew your son was of royal blood, then they will have taken him to be sacrificed to their foul gods."

King Varnir pounded his huge fist on the table. "I refuse ter believe me son be dead!" he bellowed.

The Archmage raised his hands in a sign of peace. "I am not suggesting your son is dead," Talsin replied gently. "They captured both parties, which leads me to believe they took them for some other purpose."

"So, there be hope?" King Varnir sounded relieved.

The copper-armored elf shook his head. "Or they are going to sacrifice all of them."

Silence followed the grim speculation.

"I'm sorry," Mike suddenly spoke up, breaking the silence, "but what are the kefali and what does any of this have to do with us?"

"The kefali," began Talsin, "are a race of brutal, anthropomorphic creatures that come in a wide variety of species."

"Millennia ago, the kefali and their gods, the Ma'at, invaded our world by traversing the Veil. During the war, we encountered numerous species, each deadly in its own way. But the vast majority of the kefali forces were Cynocephali soldiers."

"The Cynocephali stood on two legs, but resembled enormous dogs, or wolves, and stood taller than most elves. But the legions of dog soldiers were not alone. Enormous bull-headed creatures we named minotaur and the half-horse centaurs also fought alongside them."

"But warriors were not all that invaded. Countless priests and mages were integrated into their armies and they deployed a style of war we had never encountered before."

The copper-clad Battlemage joined in. "Not since the Shadow War had we seen devastation on such a scale. Whole city-states were destroyed as the unending hordes of kefali pillaged their way across our world in their attempt to bring Order," the elf snorted in derision. "The *Divine Order* they called it. Slavery is what it was. They believed that it was their duty to conquer everything so that there was Order and peace throughout the universe!"

The seated elves all scowled at such a ridiculous notion and for the first time the High Priestess Ipheto spoke. "However misguided their intentions, their threat was very real. It was not only a war of lands and lives, but also of hearts and minds.

"Their priests secretly spread throughout our cities ahead of their armies, preaching the Divine Order and trying to convert us to their faith. It was a laughable cause; no elf would turn from the Blessed Olympians to worship the Ma'at." Ipheto shook her head in wonder and fell silent.

Talsin continued, "Their magic was powerful and the war raged for many years, but eventually we recovered from our surprise and rallied together in Hyperborea. We finally defeated them at the gates of the White City and drove them back. From there, we controlled the seas and using our superior naval power we were able to trap the kefali on the islands they had captured and eventually push them back."

"With defeat imminent, most of the kefali retreated back through portals to their home world. But not all of them left. Some centaur and faun were allowed to stay in Themiscyra with the Druids, and a few of the minotaur escaped into the forests and hills where they still roam to this day."

"Their invasion did come with an added boon. We discovered the existence of Veil and the ancient mages were able to shield our world from any future invasions. Eventually, we even learned how to travel it ourselves." Talsin looked over at the copper-armored elf next to him. "Gwydion, one of your ancestors was one of the first Stewards, was he not?"

So, Liz thought, *the dark-haired elf in copper was Arch Battlemage Gwydion.* She should have guessed.

Gwydion nodded. "Yes, he was. And when he and his mages pulled the whole of Atlantis across the Veil for the first time, it was said to have been marvelous to behold."

Talsin sighed wistfully. "I wish I could have seen it."

"Perhaps you will get the chance again," Gwydion replied. "Now that the Veil is in tatters, my father may try to come back. He always talked of somehow returning."

"Ehem," Ted coughed. "Excuse me, but did you say *Atlantis?*"

Gwydion blinked. "Yes. I did. It is my home. Why?"

"We have legends of the Lost City of Atlantis," Ted said excitedly, "but nobody has ever been able to find it and now you are telling me it is real and that *you* are an Atlantian! This is awesome!" Ted exclaimed in glee.

"Well, yes," Gwydion smiled at Ted's enthusiasm, "we first discovered this world thousands of years ago. But when we got here, we also discovered that the hated kefali were already here."

"Yes," added Ipheto, "but they had learned from their mistake after their defeat on Gaea, and instead of a military invasion they sent their priests and prophets out to convert the humans to their cause before they came in force."

Gwydion nodded. "Despite our noninterference laws, it was decided that we could not let the humans fall under the kefali's sway. So, we launched our own secret war to counter them."

"Until the Veil began to harden that is," Talsin added. "Then it was decided to abandon all the worlds we had discovered and return to Gaea before the Veil became impassable."

"And the kefali came to the same conclusion and also gave up their dreams of conquest," said Gwydion. "That is, it seems, until now."

"Indeed," murmured Talsin. "They are back and amassing northwest of here in the lands that you call Ohio. So far, they seem to be content to gather more and more to them, but I fear that when they have sufficient numbers they will march upon this city."

"As if we didn't have enough problems," Dr. Cooper muttered.

"What do you mean?" asked Liz.

The assembled leaders shared a look, but said nothing until King Varnir growled, "They may as well know. They be sworn ter secrecy."

Talsin rubbed his eyes wearily. "The kefali are not the only threat to this city."

The Guardian Ambrosar growled. "To the east, the orcs be rapidly gaining territory and gathering all the goblin and kobold tribes ter their banner. They be slowly pushing west and we estimate that within a few months they will be at our gates."

"Hence our rapid construction efforts," Dr. Cooper added.

Gwydion nodded. "And if that wasn't bad enough, there have been reports of mysterious disappearances to the south. Refugees report seeing an army of darkness moving through the shadows at night, and where it passes, those villages are devoid of any living soul."

"They destroy an entire town each night?" Liz gasped.

"Not destroy," Gwydion said. "The villages are intact, but there are no living and no dead. It is as though everyone simply vanished."

"We have our suspicions about this mysterious darkness," Talsin said grimly, "but until we have more evidence we cannot say for sure. All we know is that it is also slowly making its way toward us."

Dr. Cooper leaned back in his chair. "So, it seems as though we are caught in a vice. These kefali to the north and west, orcs and their lackeys to the east, and this darkness to the south." He chuckled without mirth. "Pittsburgh always has been a point of convergence, but now it may also be its undoing."

The Heroes of Awesome suddenly didn't feel so awesome in the face of this dire news. Everything seemed to have been going so well, but now the flurry of activity in building new defenses and the intensive training suddenly made sense. They were preparing for several invasions that the vast majority of the population was completely unaware of.

"I'm still confused," said Mike. "What do you need us for?"

"Because," the man in the Army uniform said, "the dwarves and elves both tried to get intel on the large force of these kefali that is sneaking around eight to ten klicks west of the airport. But now it is our turn. Unfortunately, we are spread too thin as it is and cannot afford to send any soldiers. But then Dr. Cooper had an idea."

Dr. Cooper nodded. "Like General Adams said, we couldn't afford to send any *soldiers,* but we *do* have plenty of civilians with wondrous powers. So, I thought we could send some of them," he smiled. "*That* is where you come in."

Talsin spoke up. "I remember testing you when you first arrived and seeing an immense Potential in each of you. Since then, we have watched as your powers have grown and we believe that you 'Heroes' have the best chance of success."

The dwarf cleric Fugal waived the comment away. "Ye be here because the five o' ye be the most Gifted group o' humans we have found," he said bluntly, and Liz could almost see Jack's head swell.

"Along with the testimony o' the good jarl here," he motioned to Baldor, "we believe it be Fate that five humans with such power arrive together."

"But we aren't done training," Liz argued and Fugal smiled. "Lass, training will never end. There always be more ter learn."

King Varnir leaned heavily on the solid table. "If ye return with me son ye will be greatly rewarded."

"You think you need to bribe us?" Liz scowled.

Jack looked around at his friends. "I don't know about the rest of these clowns, but I can be bribed," he noted, and Liz glared at him. "What?" he laughed. "I can be." He looked at King Varnir. "I'm in."

"Wonderful," bellowed King Varnir. "And the rest o' ye?"

"I can't let Jack get all the reward," Emily said. "Besides, he would get lost without me."

Mike sighed and Liz knew he was going before he said anything. "If we get your son back," Mike said, "you owe me one."

The king smiled. "Deal." Then he looked to her and Ted.

"Fine," Liz breathed. "But I don't need a reward. I will go because it is the right thing to do."

Ted shrugged. "When do we leave?"

King Varnir nodded his thanks.

"Immediately."

CHAPTER 13

Liz took a deep breath as they finally came out of the tunnel and were back outside. She stood there a moment, letting the sun warm her skin as a gentle breeze played with her hair.

"Much better," Emily sighed, as she joined Liz at the tunnel entrance. "If I never go back in there, I will be a happy girl."

"Agree," said Liz, and she meant it. The dwarves could keep their dark, confined tunnels. She would take the sunshine every time. Not that there was much sunshine to be had around here, but even Pittsburgh's near-perpetual gloom was better than the underground lair.

"Well, this day just got interesting," Jack said cheerfully, as he and the others emerged.

Emily snorted. "You would be happy about this."

"Of course, I am," Jack smiled. "I'm tired of all these practice fights. There is no challenge... no excitement."

"And no threat of dying." Liz rolled her eyes. "Or killing."

"Exactly!" Jack said, completely missing Liz's sarcasm.

Emily shook her head. "I'm all for fighting for our home and killing so we don't die, but going out and *looking* for a fight isn't my idea of a good time."

"You girls don't know what's fun," Jack chided good-naturedly. "Right Mike?"

"Erm, yeah," Mike replied noncommittally. Liz suspected Mike hadn't a clue what had been said and had been off in his own little world. He did that sometimes and she wondered what he had been thinking about.

"I, for one, enjoy my lessons," Ted grumbled. "I will lose valuable study time on this little expedition."

"Oh, stop your complaining," Emily chided. "Between Liz and me it shouldn't take long for us to find the missing prince."

Liz appreciated Emily's confidence, but wasn't so sure herself.

Between time spent at the range and with the healers, Liz had precious little free time. But in what spare time Liz and Emily could get together, they had been teaching each other some of the things they had learned.

It turned out that Emily had some skill with healing, although hers was altogether different than what Liz was used to. And while it was true they both had been competent hunters and trackers before, their skills had greatly improved with Emily's new wood lore courtesy of the Druids.

"If he still lives," Ted grumbled. "He is probably dead already and we will all be wasting our time."

"Well, there is no point standing here arguing about it," Mike said. "The sooner we get going the sooner we get back."

"Here, here!" Ted raised his poleaxe in salute and then suddenly he marched off.

"Hey!" Emily shouted after him. "Where are you going?"

"To get a few things," floated the reply.

The others all shared a look as Ted reached the bridge and started across toward the city.

"Should I tell him there is a truck here?" Mike nodded behind him, toward a military transport parked nearby.

"Nah," Liz grinned. "A little exercise will do him good."

"He's got a point though," said Jack. "I need to grab my armor and a few other things before we go."

"Same here," Emily replied. "I left in a hurry and am not ready for an adventure."

Mike nodded. "Agreed, let's all gather what we need and meet back at The Point in, say, half an hour?"

Everyone agreed to that so Jack wandered over to the transport and peeked in the window. "Keys are here," he noted. "I may as well drop off each of you where we need to go to speed things up a little bit."

"Sounds good to me," agreed Mike. "We can pick up the Beard of Knowledge on the way."

In less than the agreed upon half hour, the Heroes of Awesome were together again at The Point.

The Point was the very tip of Pittsburgh where all three rivers came together. It had changed quite a bit since Liz was last there.

The huge fountain still sprayed water several stories into the air, but where the rivers were before it now looked like a thick wall was being constructed.

But The Point wasn't the only thing that looked different, Liz thought. Her friends made quite an interesting mix.

Liz had her hair tied back in a half ponytail and although it was a hot summer day, she was dressed in a black trench coat that was reinforced with metal plates for increased protection while still keeping the weight down. A military issue MK13 sniper rifle was slung on her back and her pistol was strapped to her right thigh. Against her better judgment, a slender saber hung from her left hip. She wasn't very skilled with it, but Mike had insisted she bring it in case she ran out of bullets.

Liz hoped that didn't happen. She had several magazines for both the rifle and pistol. If she had to shot enough to use them all up then they were in trouble.

Nearby was Ted, tall and lanky, wrapped in an elaborate robe of dark red that hung below his knees. A formed steel cuirass covered his chest and simple steel pauldrons protected his shoulders. Matching steel bracers circled his forearms and his modified poleaxe rested lightly on his armored shoulder.

Sitting nearby sharpening a long dagger was Jack. His military camo helmet and body armor had been modified to incorporate large pieces of black orcish armor. An M4 carbine hung from his shoulder and the oversized black katana was strapped to his back. Other weapons poked out from all over and Liz wondered how he could move, let alone fight, with all that gear.

Talking to Jack was Emily, and Liz had to shake her head. While everyone else was suited for battle, Emily looked like she was going to a club. She wore a tiny black mini skirt and a scandalously low-cut, white shirt with a waist clinching brown leather corset over top. Tall, snug leather boots and her usual black fedora completed the ensemble. A compound bow rested next to her and the full quiver peaked over her shoulder. The goblin scepter hung from her waist; bones and stones rattling softly in the breeze.

Nearby, Mike was staring out over the water, lost in thought. He was encased in heavy armor with the telltale dwarf collar that rose up from the cuirass to encircle the neck and rise up to be about even with his chin. Liz headed towards him and noticed that there were a few faint runes inscribed into parts of the armor.

"Are you ready for this?" Liz asked, as she joined Mike looking out over the water.

Mike looked over at her and smiled. "I'm always ready for a good fight. What about you? I'm surprised you agreed to this."

Liz sighed. "To tell you the truth, I am going a little stir crazy here."

Mike laughed. "You never do like to sit still for very long."

"And you are perfectly content to stay here, aren't you?" It wasn't a question.

Mike shrugged. "I just have a higher boredom tolerance," he said with a hint of a smile.

"I'm sure you do," Liz chuckled softly.

A low rumbling slowly built up and soon a military transport arrived. Liz wasn't sure if it was the same one they had been in earlier but she did know that the driver was a soldier she didn't recognize.

"Looks like our ride is here," Jack said, as he stood up and placed the sharpened knife back in its sheath.

"I didn't know we were getting a ride," said Emily, as the companions gathered together.

"I got a call on the radio after I dropped you all off," Jack replied. "They said one of the scouts was going to drive us to the last known location and from there we would be on our own."

Liz didn't like the sound of that. "We can't drive the whole way?"

"Nope." Jack shook his head. "The general says they lost 'em in Raccoon Park. Only way to find them will be on foot. Besides, any baddies will hear us coming a mile away if we are driving around in one of those things." Jack thumbed toward the approaching transport.

As much as she hated to admit it, Jack had a point, but Liz didn't relish the idea of searching for something that could avoid the elves.

Liz forced the thought from her mind as the transport pulled up, and she and her friends piled in. Luckily there was plenty of room since the truck was made to carry a lot more than five passengers. But Liz soon discovered that even driving on paved roads was an awful bumpy ride.

The drive passed uneventfully, and within an hour they turned down a narrow road and entered Raccoon Creek State Park.

They were taken several miles back on the winding road until the transport finally came to a stop. Liz and her friends spilled out of the back and were led by the driver into the woods. A few dozen yards into the brush and the driver told them that the last evidence of the scouts was "around here somewhere" and he waved vaguely in front of him before he abruptly turned away and left in a hurry.

"Well, he was helpful," Emily muttered, as the driver disappeared back into the brush.

Ted watched him go. "He probably heard the stories how everyone vanishes out here and he didn't want to be next."

"We are wasting daylight," Mike grumbled. "Let's get this show on the road." He turned to Emily and Liz and said, "Do you see anything?"

Liz looked around and at first glance didn't see anything, but after a moment she spotted a few displaced leaves and a broken stick.

"I can tell someone was through here," she said, "but I couldn't tell you how long ago or what direction they were going."

Mike accepted this with a nod. "Emily?"

There was no reply.

"Emily?"

Liz looked back and saw Emily standing with her eyes closed and her hands resting on a tree.

"Emily?" Mike asked again and took a step toward her.

"Wait." Liz held up a hand and Mike froze. He looked at her questioningly. "Just wait," Liz sternly replied to his unspoken question.

After a few moments, Emily opened her eyes and slowly took her hand off the tree. "They went this way," she said, and glided off through the trees.

Liz and the others shared a look before heading off after her.

"How do you know where they went?" Jack asked when they finally caught up to her.

"The trees told me," Emily answered easily. "They saw the whole thing."

Jack chuckled. "Of course, they did."

Emily glared back at him and Jack raised his hands in surrender. "Whatever you say, honey," Jack smiled.

Emily groaned and rolled her eyes before charging off deeper into the woods following a trail only she could see.

"I wouldn't give her too much of a hard time," Liz counseled.

"She knows I'm just teasing," Jack said defensively.

"I'm sure she does," Liz replied, "but you may not want to upset the person training to be a Druid that can control plants, walk through trees, and talk to animals, while you are in the middle of a forest."

Jack looked around at their green surroundings suspiciously. "Good point," he grunted, and pulled his gun a little tighter to his shoulder as they continued to follow Emily deeper into the forest.

"Are we there yet?" Ted growled, as he tripped over a hidden root for what seemed like the hundredth time.

They had been walking for hours with no proof that they were even going in the right direction except for Emily's insistence that they *were* on the right track.

"We are getting close," Emily assured him, also for the hundredth time.

"How could we be close?" Ted argued. "We haven't a single indication that anyone has been through here besides us." He heaved himself over a small boulder. "And I think I've seen this rock before…"

"Oh, be quiet," Emily chided. "The trees say a large group of animals leading others came through here not that long ago."

"Animals?" Ted scoffed. "So, you aren't even sure *what* we are following?"

Emily looked almost embarrassed as she shrugged. "These trees are young. It is hard to understand them, but I'm sure we are on the right path."

"I'm glad someone is…" Ted muttered as he used his poleaxe to hack through some low hanging branches.

Emily scowled. "Well, I don't see you doing anything to help."

"And what exactly should I be doing?" Ted shot back.

"Oh, I dunno." Emily hopped over a fallen log. "Cast a finding spell or something."

Ted laughed. "I'm a *Battlemage*, not a find-it mage."

"Fat lot of good you are then," Emily retorted hotly.

The mentioning of a finding spell gave Liz an idea. "Could they have covered their tracks with a spell?" she asked.

"I suppose," Ted replied uneasily.

"So, couldn't you dispel it or something so we could see it?" Liz pressed on excitedly.

"Erm… well, yes." Ted said softly, and then muttered something.

"What was that?" Emily asked.

Ted scowled. "I said I don't know any dispel magic." It was his turn to look embarrassed.

That figures, Liz sighed. She had thought her idea would have paid off and stopped the bickering by finding this mysterious trail so all the pressure would be off Emily's slender shoulders. But it seemed that was not meant to be.

"Well, that's just great," Emily grumbled, as she scampered over a pile of boulders.

Ted suddenly stopped and snapped his fingers. "I have an idea."

"Ugh," Mike groaned. "Not one of your ideas…"

Ted ignored him and closed his eyes. He bowed his head and began muttering something under his breath. Ted then made a few quick gestures with his free hand and then dramatically said a loud word that Liz didn't recognize.

Nothing happened.

"Well, that was exciting," Jack grumbled.

Ted slowly opened his eyes and looked around. His eyes grew wide in surprise. "It worked," he breathed, and then grinned ear to ear. Everyone else looked confused.

"What worked?" Emily asked.

"The dispel magic gave me an idea," Ted explained excitedly. "You see, I cannot dispel any concealment spells yet." He held up a finger. "But I can see them."

"I used magesight to see the flows of magic," Ted said, "and all around us is an amazingly complex weave of spells that I couldn't hope to unravel." Ted said sadly, but then brightened up. "However, I don't need to unravel it, I only need to follow it."

"So, we *are* on the right path?" asked Mike.

"I should think so," Ted confirmed. "I don't know what else would require a spell of concealment in the middle of a forest."

"Good enough for me." Jack started marching off again. "Let's get this over with."

"Um, Jack?" Ted said.

"What?" Jack stopped and looked back.

Ted pointed away from Jack. "Trail bends that way."

Jack scowled and marched off in the direction Ted had indicated, grumbling all the while.

Now that the trail that Emily's trees had them following was confirmed by Ted's magesight, there was less doubting if they were on the right path, and more eagerness to find their quarry.

Another hour passed and the trail wound drunkenly through the trees and between hills on a seemingly random course.

"This is getting a bit ridiculous," Mike muttered as they wandered along behind Emily and Ted through a clearing that Liz was sure they had been through before. "It's like following the trail of a drunk raccoon."

Liz smiled. "You have a lot of experience doing that?" she asked sweetly.

"As a matter of fact," Mike shot back.

They followed the trail through the clearing and back into the woods. The ground began to slope and soon they were walking up a small hill.

Emily was the first to the top and as she crested the hill she suddenly stopped and dropped to the ground. The others immediately did the same.

Now that they weren't moving, Liz could hear the sounds of many bodies moving through the brush down the other side of the hill. There were even grunts and snorts of what Liz thought sounded an awful lot like cows. But what would a herd of cows be doing this deep in a forest?

After a few moments of tense silence, Liz crawled forward to join Emily just behind the ridge. "What is it?" she whispered.

Emily shrugged. "I'm not sure," she whispered back, as the others crept up and gathered around her. "At the base of the hill I saw a lot of movement, but I hid before I could get a good look."

Jack flicked the safety off on his rifle. "Well, whatever it is they must not have seen you or we would have had company by now."

"Jack's right," Mike nodded, "but we need to know what's down there."

"I'll go take a peek," Jack replied, and without waiting for a reply he dropped to his belly and stealthily crawled up the slope.

Near the top, he stopped and slowly stuffed a few pieces of grass and leaves into his helmet, then he inched his head over the crest of the hill.

Liz held her breath for what seemed an eternity until Jack finally lowered his head and slinked back down to them.

"What did you see?" Emily asked, as Jack settled in next to her.

"Minotaur," Jack answered grimly. "There are dozens of 'em and I'll bet there are more I couldn't see." He shook his head in disbelief. "It looks like they have a huge camp set up down there."

"Did you see any captives?" Mike asked.

"No," came the reply, "but I did see the heads of two elves staked outside one of the tents."

"It must be them," Ted muttered. "It can't be a coincidence that the trail led to them."

"Yes," Mike agreed, "but we don't know if the prince or anyone else is even captive down there. They could all be dead for all we know."

"But they might kill them if we wait too long," Emily argued.

"And what do you suggest?" Liz retorted. "Go in all 'guns ablazin'?"

Jack grinned. "Sounds good to me."

"No," Mike stated flatly. "We need proof they are down there before we go charging in."

As they discussed what to do, Liz noticed Emily glance around like she was searching the surrounding trees for something. Liz looked around but didn't see anything of note. "What is it?" Liz whispered to Emily as not to alarm the others.

Emily shrugged. "I dunno… it's like I can hear really faint voices in the distance, but I can't make anything out."

"Like animals?" Liz asked. She knew Emily could understand animals and even hear their thoughts sometimes.

Emily shook her head. "I don't think so. It's different… almost like it's not quite an animal I'm hearing…" She shrugged again. "I'm probably just imagining it."

"Or maybe you are picking up on those minotaur down the hill," Liz offered.

"Yeah, maybe," Emily said easily, but Liz could tell she didn't quite believe it.

"Fine, I'll do it," Jack grumbled, as Liz turned back to the conversation.

Jack quietly crawled back up the slope and peered down the hill. The minutes passed by and as Jack kept watch on the minotaur camp below, Emily grew more nervous.

"Well, how about that..." Jack muttered softly.

"What is it?" Mike whispered up to him.

"Minotaur aren't the only beasties down there," Jack whispered back. "Just saw a pair of lions walk out of the tent. Both robed up like a priest or mage."

"The elves said minotaur aren't very Gifted," Ted muttered. "That explains how they managed to cover their tracks."

"That's all wonderful," Liz whispered, "but isn't it going to be hard to get past a pair of mages?"

"Depends on how good they are," Ted grinned back. "Besides, all I have to do is distract them and you can blast them from here."

"Wait a minute," Emily scowled. "Who said we are going down there? I think we should wait until it gets dark, then sneak in."

Ted was shaking his head before she finished. "Cows can see in the dark better than humans can, and if minotaur are anything similar then they will probably have the advantage at night."

"Fantastic," Emily muttered, and glanced back into the woods nervously. "I didn't want to wait that long anyways."

A few more minutes went by as Jack watched the camp. Emily was getting jumpier with each passing second and Liz was starting to imagine things moving in the trees around them.

You are just being ridiculous, she told herself. *Em has you seeing ghosts.*

A slight rustle off to her left made her jump.

"What's wrong?" Mike asked, taking note of her and Emily's demeanor.

"Emily hears something behind us," Liz whispered back.

Mike scowled. "What kind of something?"

Emily slowly drew an arrow and set in on the bow. "Animals maybe, and they are getting closer."

"We've got action!" Jack whispered suddenly and everyone tensed. "A couple of elves were just led into the big tent."

Liz caught movement out of the corner of her eye, but when she looked there wasn't anything there.

"And there are some dwarves!" Jack whispered excitedly. "We are definitely in the right place."

Emily knocked an arrow and watched the woods carefully. The foliage was too thick on the hill for Liz to see very far, so she slung her rifle and drew her pistol and saber. Mike noticed what they were doing and unslung his shield and gripped his ancient mace. Ted hefted his poleaxe as Jack remained laying on the ground with his back to the others, oblivious to what was going on behind him.

"Oh, man..." Jack whispered. "You guys aren't gonna believe this."

Liz thought she saw movement, but when she looked there was nothing there. But when she looked back again, a large figure was standing barely a few paces away. Liz was surprised, but kept her cool and swiftly pointed her pistol at the figure. At first, she thought she was mistaken and that an animal had just snuck up on her, but it quickly became apparent that this was no wild animal.

Tall as Mike, the creature could only be described as a bear. It stood upright and had a thick body covered in coarse black fur. Rough leathers wrapped around its waist while a vest of leather and beads hung open revealing a pipe bone breastplate and beaded choker.

Feathers and multicolored beads were woven into its thick black fur and in one huge paw it held a longbow with an arrow pointed directly at her.

In the time it took her to blink, more figures appeared around them and suddenly Liz and her friends found themselves surrounded by over a dozen of the large bear creatures, each aiming a drawn arrow.

"Guys..." Jack whispered. "There aren't just elves and dwarves down there."

"Um, Jack," Ted whispered loudly. "I think you should get down here.

Jack grumbled under his breath as he inched backwards away from the peak. Once he was far enough down that no one from the camp below would see him, he stood up and turned around to find dozens of arrows pointed at him.

"Well, this isn't good," he mumbled.

CHAPTER 14

No one moved.

The leaves rustled as the two groups faced off with weapons drawn.

"We can take 'em," Jack whispered, but in front of him Mike shook his head.

"And what happens when that army of minotaur hears us and comes to investigate?" Mike muttered back, not taking his eyes off the bear-men.

"We kill them too," Jack replied softly.

Suddenly a deep accented voice spoke. "I would not recommend that."

From behind the black furred warriors appeared another bear-man, but this one was dressed differently than the others. A triangular piece of beaded leather encircled its chest and a long skirt of pelts hung from its waist. The newcomer was slimmer than the other bear-men and had a hint of grey shot through its black fur. Mike realized that this was actually an older bear-woman.

Designs in thick white paint decorated her face and body. A headband of beads and pipe bone encircled her brow. Where the other bear-men held bows, this one carried a small round leather buckler and a slender spear that looked more like a javelin. The buckler was decorated with more beads and feathers so it jingled softly as she moved closer.

"Listen to your companion," she addressed Jack, "for there are more than just Tiraan below this hill."

"Tiraan?" Ted muttered to himself, but somehow the old she-bear heard him.

"Yes." The bear-woman stopped just behind the nearest warrior. "The elves call them *minotaur,* but they call themselves the Tiraan."

"But you do not appear to be elves…" She looked at Mike and each of his companions closely. "You are humans, yes?"

"That's right," Mike replied cautiously, "and what are you supposed to be?"

The bear-woman smiled, revealing her large, sharp yellow teeth. "We are kefali," she said proudly. "Baribal Kaakuush of the Hoonaw Tribe. And we are no friend of the Tiraan below."

"It would seem we have that in common then," Liz replied carefully. "But that doesn't mean you are a friend of ours."

The old bear-woman nodded her agreement. "This is true. But I believe we have a similar goal and it would be foolish for us to compete with each other."

"What do you mean 'similar goal'?" Liz asked.

The old bear-woman turned to her. "You are here to rescue others of your species, are you not?"

"We are," replied Liz.

"As are we," the painted bear-woman said, and then moved past the bear-warrior she had been standing next to and approached Mike. The large warrior scowled as she moved past him. "Elder," he growled at the old bear-woman. "Do not go near these creatures; they cannot be trusted."

But the old bear-woman waved his comment away. "Nonsense." She eyed the humans before her. "These are the ones I have foreseen while in my spirit walk. I am sure of it."

A look of surprise crossed his bear-like features. "These creatures are the ones that will aid us in our quest?" he sounded disgusted.

"Yes." She turned back to the warrior. "The vision with the five symbols is clear to me now. But we must be cautious, for they will either be our saviors, or our destruction."

The large warrior did not look pleased with that news, but accepted it with a curt nod and the old bear-woman turned back to Mike. "I am Pipaluk, Elder Shaman of the Hoonaw Tribe," she said. "You speak for your tribe?"

"You could say that," Mike answered carefully.

"Very good," Pipaluk nodded. "I speak for the Hoonaw Tribe, but I may not speak for us all. Will you return with us to our camp? We have much to discuss."

Mike didn't know what to make of that offer. This kefali's friendly manner was in contrast to the hostile weapons pointed at them from the kefali warriors that virtually surrounded them. Now, she wanted them to go back to their camp with them.

Mike glanced back at his friends for what to do. Jack shook his head a curt "no" while Emily nodded an excited "yes." Ted and Liz both just shrugged and were no help at all.

With a sigh, Mike turned back to the old bear-woman. "Very well," he said, as he heard Jack groan loudly. "We will accompany you."

"Wonderful," Pipaluk smiled, showing her large teeth again. "Will you hand over your weapons?" she asked.

"Not a chance," Mike replied.

"I thought as much," Pipaluk sighed. "The alpha would not like that," she said almost to herself. "Then again, I do not answer to him," she added with a mischievous smirk.

But then her smile faded. "However, I am afraid I must insist. We cannot let a group of strangers into our midst so well-armed."

"And why should we hand over our weapons *to* strangers?" Mike countered. "Why don't you hand your weapons over to us and then we will follow you?"

Pipaluk chuckled deep in her throat. "I can see you are not easily swayed. But as the ancient saying goes; the enemy of my enemy-"

"Is my friend," Mike finished.

"Precisely," Pipaluk smiled. "We both want the same thing. The Isfet raided our village and when we went after them, we were transported to this world; but so, too, had the Isfet. With no other choice, we continued our quest to retrieve our villagers before they were all sacrificed."

"And now they have some of your people as well," Pipaluk continued. "But there are far too many of them for us to challenge directly. But together we could succeed."

Mike had to admit that it did make some sense, but that didn't mean he trusted these kefali. Although there was something about Pipaluk that made Mike want to believe her.

She must have been able to read Mike's expression because she quickly added. "You have my word that you and your tribe will not be harmed and your weapons will be returned to you."

Mike looked around at the assembled warriors and all the arrows pointed at him and his companions. He was relatively sure he could block nearly all of them if they were all fired at the same time. But "nearly" wasn't quite good enough. And even if they did defeat these kefali, there was still the problem of the noise attracting those minotaur down the hill.

"What of the captives?" Liz asked. "Won't they be sacrificed?"

Pipaluk shook her head. "They have already made their blood sacrifices this day. They will not again until the sun reaches its peak tomorrow."

"So, we could already be too late," Liz moaned, but Pipaluk shook her head. "No. They sacrificed one of our villagers." The old bear-woman's face fell. "We attempted a rescue, but we were repelled."

Mike looked back at Emily and she lowered her bow. "There is no deception in her thoughts that I can tell," she said.

Surprise momentarily crossed the bear-woman's face. "You are a psykik?" Pipaluk asked, eyeing Emily suspiciously.

"No," Emily answered truthfully. But she didn't offer any explanation and Mike was glad she didn't reveal any more to these creatures. The less they knew the better.

Mike suddenly made up his mind and to everyone's surprise he lowered his guard. He slung his shield over his back and presented the hilt of his ancient dwarf mace to Pipaluk. As she reached out a strange hand-like paw he said, "You *will* return this to me."

Her hand clenched around the hilt. "You have my word."

Pipaluk gasped as sudden pain crossed her face and she almost dropped the weapon. "What have you done to me?" She cried as the kefali bear-warriors prepared to fire.

"I have done nothing," Mike replied quickly. "That is a powerfully enchanted mace that will hold you to your word. Should you break it, then it will kill you."

Pipaluk waved her warriors down and they reluctantly lowered their bows. "You did not need to resort to such measures," she chided, "but I cannot fault you for not completely trusting me. After all, we have much to learn about each other."

The Heroes of Awesome followed Mike's example and handed over their weapons to the bear-like kefali. There was a minor scuffle as Jack refused to give up his black sword, but eventually Liz convinced him to hand it over.

Once the weapons were all confiscated, Pipaluk turned and motioned for them to follow. "This way," she said, and set off back the way she had come.

Mike paused a moment, waiting as the bear-like kefali warriors cleared a path for their Elder before he lowered his guard and slowly followed after her.

The other Heroes fell in line as the kefali formed up on either side of them.

They left the minotaur camp behind as Mike wondered at this strange turn of events. He wasn't sure why he believed this strange bear-woman, but he did. And now they were all risking their lives on his gut feeling.

"I would just like to say," said Jack, "that this is one of your dumbest ideas ever."

"For once I agree with Jack." Liz added.

"Calm down." Mike dropped his voice to a whisper. "We all know that they didn't get all of Jack's weapons," Jack shot him a sly wink.

"And I am sure that even without weapons we could escape," Mike added quietly.

Liz nodded. "Maybe, but we don't know what these kefali can do," she whispered. "They may have some power we can't beat."

Ted snorted softly. "If that was the case, they would have rescued their villagers already."

"Or maybe the minotaur down there are even more powerful," Emily argued, but Ted was shaking his head before she even finished.

"According to the elves," Ted whispered, "minotaur aren't very Gifted in the Art. Therefore, it is highly improbable that they would be of any true arcane threat."

"You are forgetting that they weren't the only ones down there," Jack interjected. "There were some that looked kinda like lions."

"Well, there is only one way to find out," Emily muttered, as she picked up her pace. The others followed until they caught up to the old bear-woman.

Mike was surprised that he couldn't hear her walking even though she was right next to him, and now that he was close, he could smell an odd odor that reminded him of cinnamon. Out of the corner of his eye, Mike noticed the bear-warriors tense as he and his friends closed in around their leader.

"Um…Pipaluk," Liz began awkwardly, "do the minotaur use magic?"

Pipaluk chuckled softly. "The *Tiraan* have the ability, yes. But they have very little talent, or desire to master it," she replied. "Their true strength lies in their physical might. The Tiraan are not the most intelligent of kefali, but they are among the strongest and most stubborn. Once a Tiraan sets its mind to something, there is no changing it. We Kaakuush have used this stubbornness to our advantage numerous times."

"So, you have fought them before?" Liz asked.

"You could say that," the old bear-woman chuckled again. "We Kaakuush have hunted the Tiraan as prey for millennia, although that has usually fallen to our larger cousins. We Baribal prefer smaller prey."

Emily scratched her head. "Wait," she said, confused. "Are you kefali, Kaakuush, or Baribal?"

"We are all of these," Pipaluk answered as if it were obvious, but when she saw the confused looks she elaborated. "All sentient beings on our home world of Nibiru are kefali. When the Ma'at first discovered our world, they considered it a paradise and wondered at the abundance of life upon it."

"Many of the Ma'at then chose an animal that best alighted with their own personality and bestowed gifts upon their chosen creatures."

"When the Creator formed the Ideal Template, nearly all the Ma'at incorporated it into their followers, although they did not all distribute the Template evenly. For example; Atepomarus chose for his Hisaan to maintain the lower body of the horses that he loved and to gain the upper Template body, while Mnevis formed his favored bulls more evenly into the Template, similarly to how Great Ursa gave us our form."

"Now, Kaakuush was the name given to all those bears that had been granted the Template. Those bears that did not worship the Great Bear were not granted the Template and remained in their base form. But there were many species of bear that were lifted, so they were broken into four Great Families and each Family is made up of numerous Tribes."

Emily leaned toward Jack and whispered softly. "Does this make any sense to you?"

Jack shook his head. "Not one bit."

"Good," Emily whispered. "I'm glad it's not just me."

"Our Hoonaw Tribe is but one of the many tribes that makes up the Great Baribal Family," Pipaluk continued ahead of them, "and with each god granting the Template in his or her own way, thus the first Great Houses were created."

Mike could see Liz's eyes begin to glaze over at all this confusing information and he had to admit that he was somewhat lost as well. Ted, on the other hand, seemed to be hanging on to every word the strange bear-woman said. Obviously, he found something she was saying quite interesting.

"Those first Great Houses built the Seven Golden Cities to honor their gods," Pipaluk said. "Those cities remain the capitols of several kefali realms to this day."

Ted pushed his way to the front so he was close to Pipaluk. "Do you Kaakuush have one of these cities of gold?" he asked.

"Why yes," Pipaluk said proudly. "Cahokia is admittedly one of the smallest golden cities, but it is the Kaakuush themselves that make it great."

"What are the other cities?" Ted leaned in eagerly to learn more.

"As I said, Cahokia is the seat of the Kaakuush Nation," the old shaman began, "and there is Thinis, the heart of the Feloran's Pride Lands; Cibola, the Cyno's capital in Lemuria; Paititi, the Avian stronghold in the lands of Mu; Quivira, home of the Gurkan and fortress-capital of the Ratel Empire; Mahoroba, the secluded home of the Primat deep in the jungles of Fusang; and finally, the grandest of them all, hidden deep within Shambhala lies Kalapa, dominion of the Hathi."

One of the Baribal warriors growled. "Elder, do not tell these humans of our home. We cannot trust them."

Pipaluk shook her head sadly. "Ah, Shikoba, do you not see? Only by sharing our culture can the humans understand us. It is through understanding that trust is formed."

The warrior called Shikoba lowered his eyes. "As you say, Elder."

"You would do well to remember it," Pipaluk scolded. "For we are lost and alone on this world and we must trust someone or else we are truly lost."

Shikoba's small, furry ears drooped.

The old bear-woman's tone softened. "You are young and have much to learn, Shikoba," she smiled gently. "Do not be so quick to mistrust."

"Yes, Elder," Shikoba murmured softly.

Pipaluk suddenly stopped and sniffed the air and the other Baribal did the same.

"What is it? Liz asked.

The old bear-woman said something in an oddly familiar language Mike couldn't quite recognize and one of the warriors moved off and melted into the brush.

"Come," Pipaluk said, and set a quick pace through the trees.

She took a winding course through valleys and across streams. The Kaakuush moved so stealthily that Mike only caught glimpses of them around him and he could almost believe that they weren't even there. The warriors made no sound that Mike could hear, although it could have just been covered up by the noise Mike and his friends were making.

To Mike, the strange bear-men seemed nervous. They kept glancing back over their shoulders and sniffing the air. Something was out there and Mike didn't like not having a weapon close at hand. He could see the others felt the same way and he hoped they didn't encounter whatever it was that had these Kaakuush so spooked.

After several minutes, Pipaluk stopped and sniffed the air again. She growled deep in her throat before setting off again, this time at a run.

Mike was hard-pressed to keep up to the surprisingly nimble old bear-woman. It was hot and his armor was heavy. He was not prepared for a dash through the forest. Looking back, Mike was glad to see that Ted wasn't faring much better. Jack, Liz, and Emily on the other hand didn't seem to mind the fast pace at all. They charged through the brush as easily as if they were taking a jog along a sidewalk.

Pipaluk set a grueling pace and after what seemed like an eternity she finally came to a halt. Mike stopped gratefully and leaned against a tree, gasping for breath. Ted stumbled over and plopped unceremoniously on the ground, exhausted.

Liz was breathing heavily, but seemed comfortable. To Mike's disgust, Jack and Emily weren't even breathing hard. Jack saw Mike's face and smiled. "Well, that was fun," he said. "Let's do it again."

"Oh, shut it," gasped Mike.

"What?" Jack said with mock innocence. "I'm enjoying the first time I've beat you in a race."

"It wasn't a race," Mike breathed, "and my armor is a lot heavier than yours."

Jack shrugged. "Whatever helps you sleep at night."

Liz rolled her eyes and rounded on Pipaluk who was still sniffing the air. "Care to explain what that was all about?" she asked the old bear-woman

Pipaluk lowered her long snout. "I apologize for our sudden flight," she replied, "but we had very little time. There were Feloran approaching."

"And what exactly is a Feloran?" asked Liz.

"Cats," Emily said suddenly. "Big cats."

Pipaluk looked surprised but nodded. "That is accurate," she said, "but how did you know?"

Emily put her hands on her hips. "The trees told me," she said, as if daring Pipaluk to challenge her.

"The trees told you…" Pipaluk murmured. "And you can hear my thoughts…" She looked thoughtful. "You must be a Druid."

Emily grinned impishly. "Guilty."

"Don't tell them what you are," Jack growled. "The less they know the better."

"Oh, Jack," Liz chided. "Like Pipaluk said, they need to understand us before they can trust us."

Jack scowled at the old bear-woman. "Last time I checked *we* were the prisoners," he grumbled.

"Exactly," Liz retorted. "They won't let us go until they can trust us, you dolt."

Understanding dawned on Jack's face. "Ohhh…" he said, and had the decency to look somewhat ashamed. But Liz had the sneaking suspicion that he was faking it.

Pipaluk smiled and motioned them to follow before moving off again. "Come. Our camp is not far."

The Heroes of Awesome fell in line behind the old bear-woman and made their way through the forest much more slowly this time.

"Sooo…" Ted interjected, "about these cat people…?"

"Ah, yes, the Lions of Thinis," Pipaluk nodded, without breaking stride. "A proud and noble people, the Feloran. They think of themselves as better than all other kefali and have made several attempts to conquer our world."

"However, they have never been successful." It could have been Mike's imagination, but he thought Pipaluk looked relieved. It was hard to read the expressions on her bear-like face. "It took an alliance of Cyno, Kaakuush, and Hathi to stop their advance last time." Pipaluk shivered at the thought. "That was hundreds of years ago. They are perhaps even stronger now."

"Feloran are a large and varied race with villages in nearly every land, except for Lemuria, of course. The Cyno cannot tolerate the Feloran and they are in a near-constant state of war," Pipaluk shrugged. "There are a few Feloran villages in the Kaakuush Nation, but for the most part they leave us alone and we leave them alone. It is only when one of their Pharaohs gains too much power do the Feloran rally together and try to expand their territory."

"Their true strength does not lie in numbers, but in diversity and arcane power." The old bear-woman nimbly jumped over a fallen log. "You see, there are a great many types of Feloran, from the small but cunning Miw, to the huge and powerful Jolbar."

They began to climb a small hill covered in a dense thicket of holly bushes. "But the Feloran searching for us do not follow the ways of the Ma'at," a dangerous growl entered Pipaluk's voice. "They have forsaken the Divine Order and thrown their lot in with Chaos. They are no longer kefali."

The brush was so thick Mike couldn't see more than a few feet in front of him and Pipaluk had vanished from his sight. He pushed his way through the particularly thick section of brush and emerged into a sudden clearing.

The light was failing as the sun dropped below the distant hills, painting the sky with brilliant streaks of red and orange. Mike could see tents scattered around the trees at the top of the hill and the faint smell of wood smoke filled his nostrils. It seemed they had finally reached Pipaluk's camp.

"So, if they are not kefali, what are they?" Liz asked, as she too emerged from the brush.

"Those are Isfet," a deep voice barked. "Zealots of Chaos. Terrorists and anarchists the lot of them."

A shadow suddenly detached itself from one of the nearby trees and revolved itself into a huge looming shape. The shadows fell away, revealing a tall, muscular creature with long, grey fur and huge clawed hands. Intelligent eyes peered out from a large, dog-like face with small, drooping ears.

It wore a long chainmail coat with a thick leather belt around its waist from which several long, curved daggers hung.

"Werewolf…" Ted breathed excitedly. Leave it to Ted to be excited about encountering a creature straight out of nightmares.

The large creature snorted. "I am no wolf," it growled angrily. "I am Canis." It pounded a clawed fist against its chest. "I am Madra."

As it spoke, more shadows detached around them and formed into five more of the tall dog-men. They each clutched a long dagger in each hand and were armored in a suit of chainmail with heavy cloth wrapped around their heads.

"Still think this was a good idea?" Jack whispered.

Pipaluk stepped forward and addressed the dog-man that had spoken. "Greetings Cennetig," she said. "We are taking these humans to Alpha Gadhar."

The dog-man called Cennetig eyed them suspiciously. "What would the alpha want with a bunch of *humans*?" he spat.

"They will help us rescue the captives," Pipaluk answered.

Cennetig snorted. "We shall see about that." The dog-man spun on his heels and marched away with Pipaluk close behind. Mike and the others followed a little more slowly as the large dog-men eyed them darkly.

The Baribal were joined by the dog-men in their circle around Mike and his friends as they made their way toward the camp.

The light was fading rapidly now and the air was growing cold. They reached the edge of the camp and it was the strangest thing Mike had ever seen. Bear-men and dog-men sat around small fires fletching arrows and sharpening blades. They looked up and watched the humans pass with a mixture of curiosity and distrust.

The camp wasn't very large and it only took a moment for them to reach a tent that was larger than the others.

"Wait here," Pipaluk ordered, before slipping inside the tent after Cennetig.

A moment later the flap parted and an enormous figure emerged. Taller even than Ted, but far more heavily muscled, a monster stepped out into the failing light.

Liz gasped and Emily took an involuntary step back. Fear filled Mike, but he refused to show any weakness in front of this beast. Together, Mike and Jack stood their ground as a true monster rose up before them.

Making the dog-men look tame, this creature radiated violence. It resembled a massive wolf encased in heavy black armor with large, yellow fangs protruding from its long snout. Pointed ears rose from its wide skull and golden eyes glittered menacingly in the firelight. Wicked-looking spikes jutted from various places on the black armor making the beast's form look even more savage.

The enormous creature stepped aside as Pipaluk followed it out, seeming tiny in comparison. Mike was about to address the huge wolf-man, but before he could speak the tent flap moved again and a tall dog-man emerged.

This dog-man's armor was more elaborate than the others Mike had seen. A large, circular metal disk was set into the chest of the chainmail and a sculpted helm that looked like a snarling dog complete with laid-back ears covered its mangy head as a long aventail obscured its face. Gold filigree decorated the helm and chest plate in strange interlocking patterns.

The masked dog-man's eyes narrowed behind his helm. "What are these creatures that you have brought before me?" its muffled voice growled.

"They are humans," Pipaluk answered quickly. "They track the Isfet as we do."

"I do not trust them," the alpha growled, and nodded to the huge wolf. "Kill them."

The beast bared his teeth in a wicked grin and stepped forward as the dog-men around them drew their weapons.

Pipaluk jumped between Mike and the huge wolf-man with her paw-like hands upraised. "Wait!" she cried. "Alpha, please listen to me! I have seen these humans during my spirit walks. The gods have sent them to aid us!"

The alpha held up his hand and the dog-men halted. "Why would the Glorious Ma'at send *humans* to aid us?" he growled. "How do we know they are not spies or assassins sent by the Destroyer?"

"Because the visions of the spirit walk do not lie," Pipaluk pleaded. "Five symbols dance around an altar. Either the symbols vanish and the altar is bathed in blood and all becomes dark or the symbols are joined by a sharpened claw and destroy the altar."

"One is a shield," Pipaluk turned and pointed to the shield strapped to Mike's back. "Another is a screaming black sword." She pointed to one of the Baribal warriors and he held aloft Jack's black orc blade. "The others are a leaf pierced by a metal arrow, a river of molten fire, and a beam of brilliant golden sunlight." Pipaluk looked back at the alpha. "Five symbols, five humans. The Great Bear has sent me a vision that these humans will help us save our villagers or else we will fail."

The alpha's eyes narrowed dangerously as he studied Mike and his friends.

"You are positive these are the creatures from your vision, Elder?" Alpha Gadhar's muffled voice growled questioningly.

Pipaluk nodded eagerly. "Yes, Alpha."

"Very well, Elder," Gadhar snarled, "but these humans are your responsibility."

Elder Pipaluk nodded gratefully.

The alpha spun on his heel and made to enter his tent. "Throw them in the cage!" he barked over his shoulder and the warriors leapt to obey.

CHAPTER 15

The Heroes of Awesome were escorted to the cage, which turned out to actually be a deep hole in the ground with a heavy lid made of lashed-together logs.

"Well, this is nice," Jack grumbled, as they sat together at the bottom of the pit. "First, we get captured by a bunch of talking bears, and now some dogs have thrown us in a cage!"

"Brilliant idea, Mike," Jack griped. "Just brilliant."

Mike slumped into the corner. "And you have a better idea?"

"As a matter of fact, I do." Jack reached into a pocket and pulled out several round devices.

"Are those grenades?" Liz asked.

"Yup," grinned Jack. "Ted can blow this door off of us, then I lob a few of these bad boys out, we can get our weapons back, and cut our way out of here."

"A wonderful idea," Ted replied heavily. "Only we don't know where our weapons are up there and who's to say we can find them before we are overrun." Ted settled down on the hard dirt floor. "Besides, it's getting dark. Do you want to run around in the pitch-black woods with a bunch of angry dogs and bears after you?"

Liz joined Mike in one corner of the pit. "And I'm sure all those explosions won't alert anyone to where we are," she said, dripping sarcasm.

"That's even better," argued Jack. "Maybe those minotaur back there will show up and do our fighting for us."

"Then we will have to fight both?" Liz shook her head. "You are trying to get us killed, aren't you?"

"I'm *trying* to get us out of here," Jack grumbled. "Unlike the rest of you who seem content to be locked up." He plopped himself down angrily on the rough dirt floor of the pit.

"Don't pout," Liz chided. "It's unmanly."

"I'm not *pouting*," Jack muttered. "I'm *brooding*. And brooding is sexy."

Emily snorted. "Not when you're doing it it's not," she laughed.

Jack glowered at her, but it just made her laugh harder. "I'm glad you find this so amusing," he grumbled.

"Don't worry," said Mike. "If they decide to kill us, then we will fight. Until then, we don't need to make any more enemies. We have enough of those as it is."

"He's got a point," Ted added.

"And what if they pour some boiling oil on us while we wait down here, eh?" Jack argued. "Or shoot us full of arrows while we can't escape." He shook his head. "We are sitting ducks down here and all of you are idiots."

"Do you think they would do that?" Liz asked nervously, and watched the cage roof suspiciously.

"Of course not," Emily replied. "There was no deception in the bear Elder's thoughts. She truly will not harm us."

"I'm not worried about her," Jack said. "It's that dog guy I don't like." He scowled. "Him and that big, bad wolf."

"Yeah," Liz tried to suppress a shiver, "that wolf guy gives me the creeps."

"Same here," Emily nodded. "And his thoughts were so… wild. That alpha guy though, he seemed pretty trustworthy."

"Trustworthy!" Jack gagged. "He wanted to have us killed!"

"Yes," Emily allowed, "but only because he wants to protect his people. He has no reason to trust us and is suspicious of a trick."

Jack threw his hands into the air. "Oh, well, that makes it 'ok' then."

"How would you like to have your friends snatched away for some horrible sacrifice, and when you go after them you are all transported to another world full of strange beings that will kill you as soon as they see you?" Emily retorted hotly.

Not backing down an inch Jack growled back. "I would feel the same as if a bunch of monsters from other worlds invaded my home and tried to kill me as soon as they saw me."

"Enough you two," Liz pleaded. "Arguing isn't going to get us anywhere."

They lapsed into silence as the gathering darkness settled in and soon the pit was pitch black until Ted summoned a tiny flame that danced above his hand. One of the dog-men appeared for a brief moment to see what was making the light, but then quickly disappeared again without a word.

Some time passed before a dark shape finally appeared through the cage slats. The faint glow from Ted's flame revealed a solitary bear-warrior. He motioned something with a paw-like hand, and then with a groaning creak the cage lid was slowly pulled back. Once clear, a rope was dropped down and the bear-warrior motioned for them to climb up.

Mike was the first up, followed by Jack and then the others. Up above stood several Baribal bear-warriors, some carried torches while the others held the heavy wooden lid.

Once all five of them were out, the lid was put back on the pit and the Baribal motioned for them to follow, but Mike didn't move. When the Baribal noticed that they were not following he turned back, confused.

Mike crossed his arms over his broad chest. "We aren't going anywhere until you tell us where we are headed."

The bear-warrior scowled and moved toward them. Once he got closer Mike realized it was Shikoba, the same Baribal that had questioned Pipaluk's wisdom earlier that day.

"The Elder Shaman has taken responsibility for you and convinced the alpha to put you into our keeping." Shikoba obviously didn't care for that arrangement. "I have been tasked with bringing you to the Elder's tent."

"Now, if you will follow me…" Shikoba motioned them forward again, and this time Mike and his friends followed.

It was a short walk through the dark camp to a relatively small tent that Shikoba stopped at. The Baribal said something in a strange language and a muffled reply came from within. Shikoba pulled the tent flap aside and motioned them in. Mike entered first with his friends close behind.

Inside, the tent smelled strongly of wood smoke and incense. Tall, wooden bear totems lined the walls and seemed to dance in the flickering light of the small fire in the center of the tent. Numerous talismans and charms hung from the ceiling and swayed softly in the smoky haze above them.

The old shaman sat on a low log bench near the fire. Pipaluk looked up and smiled as they entered. "Come," she said, and motioned to the other logs around the small fire. "Sit."

And so, the Heroes sat. Ted eagerly, Emily curiously, and the rest slowly and cautiously.

"I am sorry that you were thrown into that pit," Pipaluk began. "The alpha can be… overly protective sometimes."

"Yeah, we noticed," Jack grumbled.

Ted leaned forward eagerly. "So, this *alpha* is your leader?"

"No." Pipaluk shook her head and then smiled ruefully. "Although he thinks he is." Her smiled faded. "The Cyno have a very rigid hierarchy while we Kaakuush have a very loose one. Cyno gain rank by defeating their superiors in combat and then taking their place within the pack. The leader of each group is called the alpha with more titles depending on the status of the individual and the pack as a whole."

"There is a separate ranking system for the military but it is all very complicated and I'm afraid most of it is beyond me," Pipaluk confessed. "I admit that I am not very well versed in the intricacies of Cyno society. It would take an actual Cyno to explain it better."

Emily nudged Jack with her elbow. "Why don't you go ask the big wolf guy?" she teased.

"Ah, yes... Lorcan," Pipaluk sighed. "He is unlike the others."

"Yeah, we noticed," Jack remarked.

"Lorcan is not of House Canis like Gadhar and the others," Pipaluk explained. "He is a Warg. Much like how we Kaakuush have different tribes, the Cyno have packs. The Cyno here are Canis, as I am Baribal. But their pack is Madra, as my tribe is Hoonaw. Do you understand?"

"I think I've got it." Ted leaned forward. "These Canis are descended from dogs, yes?"

Pipaluk nodded.

"And the species of dog they came from makes them Madra?"

Again, Pipaluk nodded.

"But this Lorcan is a descendant of wolves, making him a Warg..."

"Correct," Pipaluk smiled. "You are a fast learner."

Ted beamed at the compliment and Jack groaned. "All this nonsense is giving me a headache." He rubbed his temples wearily.

Emily scowled at Jack before turning back to the old bear-woman. "I think it's fascinating," she said excitedly. "To think that there is an entire race of beings out there descended from all different types of animals is amazing."

"Is there really *every* type of animal represented?" Liz asked.

"Once," Pipaluk replied. "Some have been destroyed or lost over the centuries."

"How do you keep them all straight?" asked Ted.

The old bear-woman smiled. "I do not," she admitted slyly. "I worry about the Kaakuush and those nations along our borders. The others are of little concern to me or my people."

"So why is the Warg here with a pack of Madra?" Ted asked.

"That is an excellent question," Pipaluk answered. "However, you will have to ask the alpha. I do not know why Lorcan is with them. I have my suspicions of course," she said slyly.

"And what would those be?" Emily pressed.

"Well..." the old bear-woman thought a moment. "He could simply be a mercenary that Gadhar hired to help them track the Isfet, or he could just be a bodyguard."

"But you don't believe that," Ted surmised.

"I do not know." Pipaluk shrugged her large, furry shoulders. "There is something going on there that I do not understand. Or perhaps it is simply that Wargs and Baribal do not get along."

"But you do with the Canis?" Ted asked.

"Not always." Pipaluk shook her head. "The alliance between the Cyno and the Kaakuush is a fairly recent development. It took the threat of the Feloran to force us to put our differences aside and unite. There is, of course, still some conflict, but not like there once was."

"We are stronger together," Pipaluk said proudly. "The vast, loyal legions of Cyno, ever watchful, reinforced by the great strength and ferocity of the Kaakuush make for a powerful alliance that benefits both sides."

"So, you don't want to conquer this world?" Mike asked suddenly.

Pipaluk looked taken aback. "Of course not," she said quickly. "Where would you acquire such an idea?"

"The elves," Liz answered. "They say the kefali once invaded their world and tried to take over this one as well."

"So, it's true…" the old shaman whispered softly almost to herself.

"What is true?" Ted asked.

Pipaluk seemed distracted. "Legends tell of a time when the kefali strode across the stars with the Ma'at, like gods ourselves, bringing the Divine Order to new worlds." The old Baribal sighed. "Most thought those legends were nothing but stories told to children. But here I sit, on another world, surrounded by humans who say we kefali were here before. It is… unbelievable."

Mike and Jack shared a look and Pipaluk saw it and quickly added. "I cannot speak for all kefali, but let me assure you that those of us here, in this camp, have no intention of trying to continue where our ancestors left off."

"We were brought here by accident," Pipaluk said passionately. "We only wish to retrieve our captive villagers and return home."

"That is good to hear," Ted said. "There are enough races warring for this planet already."

"Speaking of the captives," said Liz. "Who are these *Isfet*?"

Pipaluk sighed. "The vast majority of kefali follow the Divine Order set forth by the Glorious Ma'at. But there are those that believe that the Divine Order will not last and that all things must eventually succumb to Chaos. These are the Isfet. They use living sacrifices to power their dark magic granted to them by their foul gods."

"The army of Isfet that you saw had snuck into Kaakuush lands and abducted several of our villagers," Pipaluk continued. "The Isfet were being monitored by this pack of Madra and once the villagers were taken we joined forces. However, the world shook and a heavy fog settled on us in the middle of day. When the fog lifted, we were on this world along with the Isfet."

"We tracked them for days and made several attempts at rescue, but their numbers were too great and with an abundance of sacrifices, their priests are far stronger than I." The old bear-woman's shoulders sagged. "No matter what I did, their spells defeated it. I was worthless," she growled angrily. "But they will not best me again!" She looked around at Mike and his friends. "This time we have you to aid us."

"How do you know we will be any help?" queried Emily.

Pipaluk turned to her. "I know you are a Druid. That will be invaluable while we are in the forest." She looked at Ted. "And you have magic," she said to him. "One of my warriors saw you with a flame in your hand."

"That doesn't mean I'm any good in a fight," Ted pointed out.

"True," Pipaluk agreed with a grin, "but you are here on a rescue mission of your own. And the five of you must be formidable indeed to make such an attempt against so large a force."

"Or we are just stupid," Jack offered.

Pipaluk grinned again. "This could also be true. But I do not think that is the case."

In the distance, a wolf howled.

A heartbeat later another howl, and then another. Soon the air was filled with the eerie cry of a pack of wolves.

"It has begun," Pipaluk said.

"What's going on?" asked Mike.

"The Tiraan are generally afraid of all Cyno and of the Warg especially," the old Baribal said. "So, the Madra are imitating Warg calls and will take shifts and will continue to do so all night to keep the Tiraan awake."

"They won't notice the difference?" asked Emily.

Pipaluk waved the question away. "The Tiraan are not the smartest kefali," she chuckled. "They would believe *I* was a Cyno if I howled loud enough."

"But what is one night without sleep going to accomplish?" Liz asked.

"It isn't just tonight," Pipaluk replied. "We have been hounding them every night for the last several days. A few hours before daybreak they will stop, allowing the Tiraan to rest and when they do, we will strike."

Liz looked confused. "Why would you let them rest before you attack?"

"We are not attacking," Pipaluk corrected. "We are going to sneak in and steal the villagers back while they sleep."

"Sounds wonderful," said Mike, "but what if they wake up early and find us?"

"The Madra will be positioned around the Isfet camp to draw them away should we be discovered," Pipaluk answered easily.

"And just how many captives are there?" Jack asked.

Pipaluk shrugged guiltily. "We do not know." The old shaman's small ears drooped. "A dozen or more, hopefully. We do not know exactly how many have already been sacrificed."

"That doesn't count the elves and the angry bearded midgets," Pipaluk added. "I am unsure of how many of them there are as well."

"Well, you are just a wealth of helpful information," Jack grumbled.

"I am sorry." If a bear could look ashamed, Pipaluk did. "It is difficult. The Isfet try to keep the captives hidden so we cannot rescue them before they reach the Destroyer and are lost to us."

"The *Destroyer*?" Jack scoffed. "Not a very creative name."

Liz shot Jack a look before turning back to Pipaluk. "Who is the Destroyer?" Liz asked. "The alpha mentioned him also."

"You do not know?" Pipaluk shuddered. "Malek the Destroyer is a Champion of Chaos. He leads an army of zealots that call themselves the Horned Legion. He and his legion have terrorized much of our world for the last thousand years."

"A thousand years?" Ted scoffed. "How is that possible?"

Pipaluk looked nervously around the tent as if afraid someone would over hear. "Some say he is a powerful sorcerer. Others say he is an immortal demigod. Many say he is both." Her voice dropped to a whisper. "They say he is the son of Apep himself."

"The Destroyer has lusted for control of one of the Golden Cities for ages, but he has never been successful. Thankfully, the followers of Ma'at have always managed to defeat him," the old bear-woman explained. "Some have claimed to have killed him, but always he returns."

"That's all just dandy," Jack grumbled, "but what does this jagoff have to do with us? He sounds like a problem for your world."

"But he is no longer on our world," Pipaluk replied softly. "He is here."

"Here!" Emily squeaked.

Pipaluk nodded. "It is true. The Isfet we are after are but a small fraction of the vast legion he is gathering. We believe once all the scattered fragments of his army are rejoined, they will make war on this world."

"But we don't have any golden cities for him to conquer," Liz said. "What could he want?"

Pipaluk shrugged her furry shoulders. "I cannot speak for the Destroyer, but if I were to guess I would say he will try and conquer the whole of this world. He will realize the chaos that has befallen this world and will see it as a sign."

"What kind of sign?" Liz asked.

"That this world is blessed by Chaos," Pipaluk said, "and that it is free for the taking."

"Screw that!" Jack growled. "If this clown thinks he can take over *my* planet, then he's got another thing comin'!"

"I am glad to hear that," Pipaluk said. "The Destroyer cannot be allowed to gain a hold on this or any world."

The old shaman shifted uncomfortably. "Will you aid us in getting back our captives?"

"So long as we get ours back as well," Mike countered. "And we will need our weapons back."

Pipaluk nodded as if she had expected no less. "Of course." She pulled out a small flute made of many small wooden reeds and put it to her lips. A soft tune whistled through the tent for a brief moment before the old shaman hid the flute again.

There was a long pause, and then the tent flap was pulled aside and a large Baribal warrior entered with a large sack hanging from Ted's poleaxe. The warrior's black fur was grey around his snout and his pipe bone armor was decorated with feathers and claws.

"Thank you Skatew." Pipaluk smiled at the newcomer as he set the large sack on the ground at the shaman's feet.

The warrior put a large paw on Pipaluk's shoulder. "Are you sure of this Elder?" he asked softly.

Pipaluk smiled at him. "Of course. Trust in the Great Bear."

The warrior smiled back and nodded before turning away and exiting the tent.

"That was War Chief Kaneonuskatew," Pipaluk explained, as she worked out the knot in the sack at her feet. "He will be leading our warriors in the coming raid."

With a final tug, the sack came apart and the contents spilled out onto the floor. There, spread out before them, were their weapons. Mike's ancient mace sparkled in the firelight while Jack's black orc sword seemed to absorb it.

Pipaluk bent down and retrieved Jack's rifle and turned it around in her hands. "How does this device work?" she asked, as she inspected it closely. "I have never seen such a strange weapon."

"Stop!" Jack jumped up as the shaman's hands neared the trigger.

Pipaluk froze.

The howling outside continued.

She stared down at the rifle in surprise, suddenly afraid to move.

"Be careful with that," Jack cautioned. "If you touch the wrong place it could kill us all."

The color seemed to drain from her face and she held the rifle away from her as if it were suddenly poisonous. Jack reached over the fire and snatched if from her trembling grasp.

Pipaluk breathed a sigh of relief. "What kind of weapon is that?" she asked. "Is it truly a mythical Thunder-Stick, as some of my warriors claim?"

"I don't know what a thunder-stick is," Jack replied, "but this is a rifle, and when I… activate it, it will kill anything standing in front of this end." He pointed to the tip of the barrel. "It is not safe to handle unless you know what you are doing."

Pipaluk nodded her understanding. "Thank you for the warning. I will remember it."

Liz and the others retrieved their weapons before returning to their seats around the fire. Pipaluk looked between Jack's and Liz's rifles, obviously curious.

"What is it?" Liz asked gently.

The old bear-woman pointed at the MK13 slung over Liz's shoulder. "That is a Thunder-Stick as well? It has a similar appearance but is different."

"Yes," Liz replied, "but where Jack's will spray death quickly, mine can kill a single enemy from further than the eye can see."

Pipaluk's eyes grew wide. "Truly? It must have powerful magic."

Liz shook her head. "Not magic. Technology."

Pipaluk tilted her head curiously. "What is *technology*?"

"Technology," Ted began in what Jack called his 'lecturing voice,' "is the techniques and processes used in producing goods. It is the advancement of current methods and materials to create new and better products."

Pipaluk listened intently. "Fascinating. We have artifacts of the lost O'Saurs that resemble such weapons, but even our greatest scholars could not decipher their purpose. You must tell me more about this technology and this world once the captives are safely returned to us."

"But now it is time to rest." The old shaman abruptly stood. "You will sleep here." She began pulling the log bench she had been sitting on away from the fire. Liz and the others stood as well and began moving their benches away from the fire as well, and lined them along the walls of the tent.

"Do not leave this tent," Pipaluk instructed. "You will be retrieved when it is time."

"Thank you, Elder," said Liz sweetly.

The old bear-woman smiled and ducked out of the tent without another word.

No sooner had she left than the ground began to shake. The totems swayed dangerously and the hanging talismans rattled together.

The tremor slowly faded away.

"That wasn't ominous," Emily muttered.

CHAPTER 16

Mike groaned and sat up at the sound of the tent flap rustling.

The accursed howling had finally stopped an hour ago and Mike had just begun to doze off.

Jack was still seated by the fire, absently poking the burning logs with a stick. He had insisted on keeping watch while the others slept. Emily had maintained that nothing would happen to them, but Jack was taking no chances and he looked up at the rustling as well. His hand slowly moved to the M4 on his lap.

A Baribal's bear-like head poked through the opening and saw Jack and Mike. "Come, break your fast with us," he growled, before ducking back out.

Jack looked at Mike. "Did he just invite us to breakfast?"

Mike threw off the blanket and sat up. "I think so."

"Good. I'm starving."

"You're always hungry," Mike laughed as he rolled up the blanket.

"I'm a growing boy," Jack grinned, and began rousting the others.

Within a few minutes the Heroes of Awesome were ready and quickly emerged from their tent stepping out into the early morning darkness.

Outside, the kefali camp was a beehive of activity.

Baribal Kaakuush, looking like large black bears, moved silently about in their leather and pipe bone armor as the tall, dog-like Canis Madra prowled around in their heavy chainmail and pointed helmets.

Low cook fires burned everywhere and the smell of roasting meat greeted them.

"Mmm," Emily sighed, "that smells good. I'm so hungry I could eat a cow."

Jack wrinkled his nose. "All I smell is wet dog- Ow!" Emily punched him in the arm.

Two golden eyes suddenly appeared out of the darkness and moved toward them. Liz and her friends clutched their weapons as the eyes drew closer.

Out of the darkness, the towering Warg, Lorcan, appeared before them. His black, spiked armor blended in with the darkness almost completely, making him extremely difficult to see, even though he was only a few steps away.

"This way," his deep voice growled, and he turned away.

Without seeing his golden eyes, Lorcan was almost invisible in the darkness. Only the soft light of the cook fires made him partially visible. But even then, it was challenging. It was as if his black armor absorbed the light instead of reflecting it like it should have.

He led them to a small camp that was somewhat secluded from the others. A small fire burned in a pit and what looked like a small deer was roasting above on a spit.

The huge Warg pointed a clawed hand at the carcass and then at a stack of wooden bowls resting on a nearby log. "Eat," he growled.

"Good," Emily sighed, and pushed her way to the front of the group. "I'm *starving*." She found a long, curved knife and proceeded to deftly slice several large strips of steaming meat off the body and drop them into one of the wooden bowls.

Liz followed and before long they were all seated around the fire, relishing a meal of hot, roasted venison.

Upon further inspection, Emily discovered a water skin behind one of the logs and they shared it between them.

Lorcan did not partake of the meal. Instead the huge Warg remained back in the shadows. Liz could almost have truly enjoyed the meal if it wasn't for the unmoving golden eyes glowing in the darkness behind her.

They ate quickly and once they were all finished Lorcan moved into the light. "Come," he growled, and the darkness swallowed him again.

"I'm getting real tired of that…" Mike grumbled before they followed the dark shape into the night. The black armored Warg was hard to follow, but luckily it was a short trip to another tent where the Canis alpha was having a heated conversation with the two Kaakuush leaders, Elder Pipaluk and War Chief Kaneonuskatew.

"That is unwise," Pipaluk was saying. "Nothing good will come of it."

"Have you had a vision?" the alpha asked.

Pipaluk shook her head. "No, but it does not take a vision to know that something foolish will fail."

The kefali commanders noticed Liz and the others arrive. "About time you got here," the alpha growled. "Let's get this over with."

"Elder Pipaluk tells me that you will aid us," the alpha snorted derisively. "She says you can be trusted, but I do not trust you. So tell me, why should I?"

"Well… we didn't try to escape," Liz offered.

"And we didn't kill you once we got our weapons back," Jack added.

The alpha scowled at Jack. "I do not believe you five could have killed us all, but your point is noted. However, I still do not understand your motives for coming here. From what my scouts have reported, there are no human captives. There are only elves and the angry bearded midgets"

"Dwarves," Liz said. "Your angry bearded midgets are called dwarves."

The alpha waved the comment away. "Regardless. Why are you here?"

"Those elves and dwarves are our allies," Mike answered defiantly. "We came to rescue them."

"So, it's true then," the alpha growled. "You are allied with our ancient enemies."

"Really, Gadhar?" Pipaluk sighed. "That was thousands of years ago. I doubt the elves even remember us."

"Oh, they remember all right," said Ted, "but we have no quarrel with you. All we want is to rescue our allies and return home."

"He is correct," Pipaluk said. "Our battle is not with the humans. It is with the Isfet. We cannot afford more enemies on this strange world." The old bear-woman pleaded. "Accept their aid so that we may be reunited with our loved ones before it is too late."

Alpha Gadhar looked into the flames of the dying fire for long moments, deep in thought.

"Very well," the tall dog-man sighed wearily.

"You must be quick," Lorcan's deep voice growled from the shadows. "There are only a few hours until daybreak."

The alpha nodded to the giant wolf beast. "Go. Gather the warriors, we march immediately."

The golden eyes blinked once in confirmation before vanishing.

"And what are we going to do?" Mike asked, as the alpha picked up a round metal shield worked with delicate engravings.

"We will tell you our plans on the way." Alpha Gadhar slung the shield on his back and marched away into the night with two Canis warriors right behind. Pipaluk and Kaneonuskatew followed closely, and suddenly Liz and the others found themselves trailing along.

A short walk through the dark camp saw many beastly figures strapping on armor and gathering weapons by the light of small fires.

"I'm glad these guys are on our side," Emily muttered, as a large bear-warrior with fur matted down with heavy streaks of white paint brushed passed them.

"That has yet to be proven," Ted replied warily.

"If they were going to fight us, they would have done so already," Liz pointed out.

"True enough," Ted conceded, "but I won't feel better until we are back in Pittsburgh with the freed captives."

They made their way past the last tent on the edge of the camp, but instead of stopping like Liz had figured, they continued on through the dense barrier of brush and down the hill out into the thick of the forest.

"Aren't we going to wait for the others?" Emily asked loudly.

The alpha and his two guards slowed down and allowed the humans to catch up before answering. "All our warriors know their positions already. We will meet the main insertion force outside the Isfet camp. Once there, we will proceed with the extraction at the appointed time."

"And how exactly is this extraction going to work?" demanded Ted.

Gadhar looked unhappy and Liz thought he wouldn't answer, but he eventually sighed. "My Madra are already positioning themselves around the Isfet camp as we speak. They will remain there until they are needed."

"Hopefully, they will not be needed," the war chief breathed.

"Indeed," the alpha nodded. "Chief Kaneonuskatew and a team of his Baribal along with you humans, myself, and my guards, will sneak into the camp and free the captives while the Isfet slumber."

"I still do not agree with this plan," Pipaluk growled. "You are the alpha, you should not be leading the rescue."

"And that is precisely why I must lead it," Alpha Gadhar retorted hotly. "I am the alpha. It is for me to lead my pack. Cowards lead from behind."

"It is not cowardice to let those more skilled do this task," Kaneonuskatew added. "I mean no disrespect alpha, but we Baribal are far more gifted in the art of stealth than you and your armored soldiers."

Gadhar snorted. "And you would bring these humans with you? They sound like a herd of Hathi on parade."

"That may be," Pipaluk agreed, "but the vision said they must be part of this for us to be successful. The Great Bear will see us through."

"You may be wise, Elder," Alpha Gadhar growled, "but in this my mind is made up. I will lead this rescue. And that is final."

Pipaluk's shoulders sagged in defeat. "Very well… but know this; you put us all in danger by your actions."

Gadhar barked a laugh. "We are already in danger."

The trek to the Isfet camp took far less time than Liz had expected.

After such a long and winding journey to the Baribal camp earlier, she thought the distance between the two to be greater. They must have wandered in circles to prevent anyone from following them, and perhaps to confuse Liz and her friends so they couldn't find their way back.

It was hard to tell in the darkness, but when they stopped just before cresting a small knoll, Liz realized they were back on the same hill that she and her friends had been on the day before when the Baribal had found them.

Chief Kaneonuskatew crouched down and silently crawled to the crest of the hill, followed by several of his warriors. They remained there for what seemed like an eternity before quietly rejoining the others.

"There are Feloran patrols circling the camp," Kaneonuskatew reported. "There are too many to sneak past with so large a force. We will need to eliminate them before we can attempt the rescue."

"Droppings!" Gadhar cursed. "The Feloran will assuredly either hear us or see us long before we can get close."

"If I take only one or two warriors we could sneak past them." Kaneonuskatew whispered.

But the alpha was already shaking his head. "It won't work," he grumbled. "Even if you manage to elude them and free the captives, you will still need to get back out with all the captives in tow."

Kaneonuskatew unslung his wooden bow and drew an arrow. "Then we must eliminate them first." Six Baribal warriors also knocked arrows. "We will need to get closer, but we can silence them before they realize we are here. Luckily, the Feloran patrol alone so we can pick them off one at a time."

"I don't like it," Gadhar muttered. "Feloran are almost impossible to sneak up on. If they so much as sense you they will sound the alarm."

"Perhaps I can help," said Liz, and she unslung her MK13 sniper rifle.

"That won't work," Jack said. "The noise would wake the whole camp even with that suppressor on it. This isn't some movie."

"I know that," Liz retorted. "You will just have to trust me."

Jack threw his hands up in defeat. "Fine. Wake the whole bloody camp.

It's our funeral."

"Stop being such a drama queen," Liz chided softly.

"I must agree with the other human," the alpha said. "A Thunder Stick has its name for a reason. If you use it, we will be discovered."

Liz sighed. "Listen, I can eliminate those patrols for you from here without getting any closer and I can make it quiet. It is your best option. Trust me."

Alpha Gadhar's eyes narrowed dangerously.

Pipaluk suddenly spoke up. "Listen to her," she pleaded. "They are here for a reason."

Gadhar snorted. "Very well," he growled softly. "But if you are wrong, you will die."

Liz turned away and began to crawl up the slight slope to the hillcrest. "If I'm wrong, we will all probably die anyways."

"That makes me feel better…" Emily muttered softly, as Liz positioned herself on the crest of the hill under some thick brush.

The woods were nearly pitch dark, but that didn't worry Liz. The United States Army had spared no expense when equipping their soldiers, which meant that the MK13 she pulled up to her shoulder was equipped with not only night vision, but infrared as well.

Looking through the scope brought the world to life. Where once there was nothing but darkness, now there was an entire panorama displayed before her.

The Isfet camp was a glowing mass of heat from the numerous cook fires and she could even see the sleeping forms of the massive minotaur inside their tents. But more pressing than their sleeping heat signatures were the glowing forms prowling the woods around the camp.

Liz counted five guards walking around the camp. She watched them for several minutes until she thought she had their patrol patterns memorized.

They walked in overlapping loops that left very little openings. She would have to be quick and there was no room for error.

"Get ready," Liz whispered behind her.

She bent back over her rifle and she could hear the creak and rattle of armor and weapons as her friends, and reluctant allies, prepared to move.

Liz found her first target and waited for the opportune moment. The opening appeared and she took the shot.

A sharp crack, like the sound of a snapping stick, echoed through the silent night and Liz cursed under her breath. The four remaining guards' tall ears perked up and they all turned her way, searching for the sound.

Liz held her breath for what seemed like an eternity until finally the guards lost interest and resumed their patrols.

That first shot had been way too loud and Liz knew that if the next shot was the same, then the guards would know something was up and sound the alarm.

She couldn't let that happen.

With a supreme effort of will, Liz clamped down on her emotions and focused all her thoughts on the silence of the gun and the target before her.

Her next shot was barely a whisper as the second guard fell.

The third guard's body jerked once and then collapsed.

Liz moved quickly, but the fourth guard proved elusive. Every time she got a bead on him, he would disappear behind a tree.

The guard ducked behind what must have been his sixth tree and Liz grew worried. At first, she had thought it was just bad luck that put the guard behind a tree every time it stopped. But now Liz was afraid he had discovered something was wrong and was purposefully hiding.

The elusive guard was getting dangerously close to one of the bodies and Liz knew she was running out of time.

Liz had never bent a bullet and silenced the shot at the same time before, and she didn't know if such a thing was even possible. But it looked like she wouldn't have much choice. If she waited any longer the guard would discover the body of one of his comrades.

The guard stopped behind another tree and with every ounce of concentration Liz could muster she fired.

The soft crack of the shot sounded loud in her ears, but she didn't waiver. The bullet arched around the tree and struck true. The guard pitched forward and lay still.

However, the last remaining guard heard the shot and must have discovered his companions were missing for he lunged away and bounded away towards the camp.

Liz cursed under her breath and tried to get a bead on the fleeing guard.

This Feloran creature proved to be remarkably fast. Try as she might, Liz couldn't keep up with the darting figure. The brush was thick and it was hard to make out anything.

She fired in desperation, but her shot stuck a tree just behind the retreating form.

Liz pulled back and scanned the whole area to get an idea of where the racing guard was headed. Seeing a path the guard was headed gave Liz a glimmer of hope.

There was a slight clearing just before the outskirts of the Isfet camp. Liz hoped the guard would take the easier route in hopes of reaching the camp sooner. But if the guard took a different route, or if she missed, then the guard would be in camp and any chance of rescue would be lost.

Liz dialed up her scope until her vision was filled with the place she prayed the guard would pass by.

Her heartbeat pounded in her ears as she lay there, frozen like a statue, praying that she was right and that the guard would take the quickest path to the camp.

The seconds dragged out and Liz feared she had guessed wrong. In her mind, she could hear the shouts of warning as the camp woke up and all hope of rescue vanished.

Just then, movement appeared in the corner of her sight and without hesitating, she fired.

The last guard stumbled and took a few steps before crashing to the ground only a few paces away from the first tents.

Liz didn't move for several heartbeats until she was sure that no alarm would sound. When nothing happened, Liz let out a breath that she hadn't known she had been holding.

"All clear," she whispered behind her.

The rustling and clanking of her companions climbing the hill to join her sounded loud to her ears after the long silence.

Alpha Gadhar was the first to the top of the hill. He surveyed the area closely and then snorted. "Impressive," he growled at Liz. "I didn't think such a feat was possible. In this case, I am glad to be wrong."

Once the others had all reached the crest, the alpha waved them forwards. "Quickly," he snarled. "We haven't much time."

Mike grinned and took off down the hill with Jack and Ted close behind. Gadhar scowled at Mike's back before following with his two armored guards and the black shadow that was Lorcan. The Baribal chief Kaneonuskatew brought up the rear with four of his own black-furred warriors.

Liz started to get up, but then Emily plopped down next to her and Pipaluk sat gracefully down on Liz's other side as the two remaining Baribal warriors took up positions on either side of the trio.

"We aren't going down, too?" Liz asked the old bear woman.

Pipaluk shook her head. "No. We will remain here and make sure the way back is clear.

"Well, that doesn't make me feel very good." Liz watched as Mike, Jack, and Ted slowly disappeared down the hill into the darkness. "Those clowns will pull a Leroy Jenkins if they get half a chance."

Oh no," Emily groaned. "You're right… Mike especially."

"Yeah," Liz sighed, "and he will call it 'strategy'."

Pipaluk looked confused. "What is a *Leroy Jenkins?*"

Liz just shook her head. "You don't want to know."

CHAPTER 17

The darkness was nearly complete beneath the trees. If it weren't for the light of the full moon, Mike wouldn't have been able to navigate through the forest at all. He could however, see the faint light from the dying campfires of the enemy camp and he made his way toward them.

When he reached the slight open space just before the camp itself, Mike stopped and waited as the others joined him at the edge of the shadows.

"I will go in first," Alpha Gadhar whispered.

"It would be wise to allow my warriors to scout the way first," Kaneonuskatew whispered back.

Gadhar thought a moment before nodding his agreement.

The Baribal chief made a quick motion and two of his black-furred warriors drew long daggers as they crept out into the moonlight and silently approached the first of the Isfet tents.

Mike was surprised to discover just how large the campsite was. Tents stretched out through the trees for as far as Mike could see. The sprawling Isfet encampment must have been well over five times the size of the Baribal/Canis camp.

The warrior reached the first tent then crouched down and peered around it as the second scout snuck past and disappeared into the camp.

A few moments later, the first scout looked back and motioned them forward.

Kaneonuskatew and his four remaining warriors quickly crept forward and earned a scowl of annoyance from Gadhar before he, too, snuck toward the camp with his two soldiers and the huge Lorcan in tow.

Mike, Jack, and Ted waited in the shadows until the Baribal had all disappeared and the Canis were moving into the camp before they too moved into the clearing.

They were halfway across the clearing when one of the tent flaps suddenly opened and a massive figure stepped out.

Mike and his friends froze, completely exposed in the bright moonlight.

The beast must have stood over eight feet tall and was a mass of solid, corded muscle. Thick fur covered its hulking body and its legs ended in massive black hooves. Two wickedly curved long horns protruded from its wide, bull-like head.

A look of confusion crossed the minotaur's face as it noticed the three humans standing before it. It obviously hadn't expected to see anyone outside its tent. But before it could react there was a soft whistling through the trees and the minotaur jerked as something slammed into it.

It stood there for a few heartbeats before its heavy body fell to the ground with a dull thud.

Jack breathed a soft sigh of relief. "Shit, am I glad Liz is up there."

"Come on," Mike whispered, and then quickly finished crossing the field with Jack and Ted close behind. They crouched down at the corner of the first tent and waited to make sure no one had seen them.

When no alarm was raised, Mike peered around the tent and saw the kefali snaking their way through the maze towards one extremely long tent. Surely that was where all the prisoners were being held.

Mike and his friends set off after their allies as quietly as they could. He was constantly impressed at how stealthily these kefali moved.

They passed the body of a minotaur lying face down in the grass and then a few paces later they saw one of the Baribal warriors keeping watch from the shadows of a dark tent.

They were half way to the long tent and had crossed the bodies of two more minotaur, and one creature that Mike couldn't identify, before finding a second Baribal warrior hiding in the shadows.

Ahead of them, Kaneonuskatew and his remaining warriors ducked into the long tent and vanished from sight. A moment later one of the warriors popped his head out and said something to Gadhar just before the alpha was about to enter the long tent.

Mike couldn't hear what was said, but Gadhar nodded once and the Baribal ducked back inside.

The alpha gave an order to his soldiers and they snuck off into the camp just as Mike, Ted, and Jack caught up.

"What are they doing?" Mike asked as he watched the Canis soldiers each creep up to a tent.

"The captives have been located and the Baribal are freeing them as we speak," Gadhar whispered, "but their gear and weapons are missing. My soldiers are searching for them."

"Why even worry about it?" Ted asked quietly. "Why not just free the captives and go?"

"Because we are short on supplies as it is," Gadhar growled softly. "Besides, if the Isfet discover us, the captives will need a way to defend themselves."

"Let's hope that doesn't happen," said Mike, as he watched the sleeping camp around them anxiously.

"Fear not human. I won't let anything happen to you."

Before Mike could answer, one of the Canis soldiers returned. "Alpha, we have found the supplies."

"Very good," Gadhar replied. "Now gather it all and bring it here."

"Yes, Alpha." The soldier saluted with a fist to his chest before turning away and disappearing back into the camp.

Lorcan moved away and faded into a patch of darkness across from the captive's tent. Ted and Jack took the hint and spread out to cover all directions, leaving Mike and Gadhar next to the large tent entrance.

The pair of Canis soldiers returned a few moments later, laden with weapons and other pieces of gear. They set the items down next to the alpha and retreated back for more. When they came back, they were dragging something heavy between them.

"What is that?" Gadhar demanded.

"A war hammer," one of the soldiers gasped.

They struggled with the massive weapon until they finally managed to drop it next to the other items and head back for more.

The soldiers made several trips and the pile grew large before the first captives finally emerged from the tent.

First was a tiny little Baribal cub, followed closely by a large adult that Mike assumed was a parent of the child. They looked half-starved, each with large patches of fur missing.

Gadhar handed the cub a small pack from the pile and put a long dagger in the hand of the adult before directing them down the path. One of the hidden Baribal warriors appeared and motioned silently, directing them through the camp and out to safety.

The process repeated itself as more freed captives emerged and were handed weapons before being shown the way out. Soon, a steady stream of captives was sneaking out of the camp.

Things were moving smoothly, but with each passing minute Mike grew more anxious as the possibility of discovery grew.

Over two dozen captives had been freed, mostly Baribal, when suddenly a pair of large minotaur strode around one of the tents and stopped abruptly in surprise at what they saw.

They opened their mouths to shout a warning but Ted acted first. He summoned a column of air and pushed it into their faces, and both beasts choked on the sudden blast.

Jack lunged forward and quickly stabbed one in the chest and then beheaded the other with a viscous slash before it could recover.

The two bodies fell with heavy thuds.

"Well done human," Gadhar said approvingly, as a trio of dwarves stormed out of the tent. The dwarves seemed irritated, but otherwise unharmed. Two of them had dark beards, but even in the faint light Mike could make out the coppery luster of the central dwarf.

Gadhar offered a sword to the first dwarf, and the dwarf snorted and bent over the pile and began noisily rummaging through it.

"Quietly you fool," Alpha Gadhar growled softly.

The dwarf finally pulled a short handled, but very wide, double bladed axe out from the depths of the pile. "I dun take orders from no dog," he rumbled menacingly.

Gadhar and the defiant dwarf glared at each other as the copper-haired dwarf bent down and easily picked up the war hammer with one hand that had taken both Canis soldiers to drag over.

The copper-haired dwarf stood and placed his other hand on the defiant dwarf's shoulder. "Come, brother," he said gently. "Let us escape this wretched place."

"O' course my- er.. brother," the defiant dwarf rumbled, but still glared at the alpha for another moment before he reluctantly turned away and followed the other captives on the way out of the camp.

The two Canis soldiers finished gathering the captives' supplies, and from a signal by Gadhar they ducked into the long tent to assist in freeing the remaining prisoners.

Mike couldn't believe how many captives there were. There seemed to be a never-ending line of them. They had been lucky so far, but Mike knew that sooner or later their luck would run out.

"How many captives are there?" Mike whispered.

"Over fifty Baribal villages were taken," Gadhar replied grimly, "but I do not know how many have already been sacrificed, nor do I know how many of these *dwarves* or elves were taken."

"Wonderful…" Mike groaned.

"Fear not human," Gadhar said. "Already over half of the villagers have reached the safety of the forest and more make it every minute." The alpha gave a strangely curved sword to a small Baribal. "Soon, they will be out and we can make our escape."

"I hope you're right," Mike breathed.

"Trust me." Gadhar handed a staff to a battered-looking elf. "The Tiraan sleep soundly and those few that are up can be easily overwhelmed."

Mike wasn't convinced, but he kept these thoughts to himself.

A few minutes later and the captives were streaming out of the long tent and the pile of supplies began to dwindle. For the first time, Mike actually felt hopeful that this crazy mission would succeed.

The two Canis soldiers exited the long tent and rushed to the alpha. "There are less than a dozen captives remaining," one of them reported.

"Very good," Gadhar smiled, and Mike could see his long, yellow fangs in the gloom. "That should put our human friend here at ease."

"Not really," Mike muttered under his breath.

Just then, one of the Canis soldier's ears perked up and swiveled around as if searching for a sound. The alpha sniffed the air and then growled low in his throat. The three Canis were suddenly on alert with weapons drawn and at the ready.

"What is it?" Mike whispered.

"Feloran," spat Gadhar.

No sooner than the words had left his mouth than three figures appeared from between two tents. They were tall creatures, each a head taller than Mike and covered in light brown, almost blonde, fur. The two on either side had faces of lionesses, and their bodies were curvy and obviously feminine while the central creature was a larger male and had faint black stripes in its fur.

Ted threw a column at the trio like he had done earlier to the minotaur to keep them from sounding a warning, but the striped Feloran waved his hand dismissively and the air suddenly vanished.

All three wore white kilts that hung past their knees and were shirtless except for a white sash that hung across their chests. But where the two smaller creatures' clothing was plain, the central Feloran's dress was embroidered in gold and it wore a tall, elaborate golden headpiece and a wide, gold necklace set with a massive ruby. A huge book hung from a gold chain around the striped Feloran's waist and each wore a large, gold gauntlet with extended claws on one hand.

The striped Feloran smiled menacingly, revealing long, white fangs. "I thought I smelled wet dog," it purred at Gadhar. "And look," it glared at the captives that had frozen in fright, "they are taking our toys away." Its eyes narrowed and the wicked smile faded. "We can't let that happen, now can we?"

"Of course, you can," Gadhar quickly said, as the Feloran were ready to pounce.

"Oh," purred the striped leader, "and why would that be?"

One of the Canis soldiers pushed the captives back into motion and freed them from their paralysis, and they scurried away.

"Because these are the last of your prisoners." It was Gadhar's turn to grin. "I am sorry, Lector Priest, but you have already lost them."

The Lector Priest shrugged unconcerned. "They can be recaptured, but now I have an even better prize," he purred. "The sacrifice of you, hated Cyno, will please Lord Apedemak greatly."

"You think I'll let you take us alive?" Gadhar barked a laugh. "Foolish furball."

"Foolish?" the Feloran Lector Priest sneered. "I am not the one that has allied myself with a bunch of filthy *humans*. You must be desperate indeed to use such creatures."

Jack scowled at how the Lector Priest had used the word humans, but somehow managed to hold his tongue.

Mike leaned over to the nearest Canis soldier and whispered, "What is going on?"

The soldier scowled at him but answered, "Felorans are a boastful lot. The alpha is distracting them while the last captives are freed."

A pair of battered elves came out of the tent and stumbled in the darkness. The Lector Priest saw them and his eyes bulged. "Elves!" he howled. "Your disparity knows no bounds. Rescuing elves! The great enemy of all kefali! How dare you!" the Lector Priest thundered.

The three Felorans roared in anger as orbs of crackling energy and tongues of fire erupted from their clawed hands.

****

Liz pulled away from her scope and stared down into the darkness.

She hated waiting. Hated it with a passion. There was nothing worse than sitting around while your friends were in danger and you had to sit back and watch. But she also knew her role was important. If not for her, they would have been discovered long ago and all these fleeing individuals would still be captives. She had eliminated three more of the monstrous minotaur since Mike and the others had disappeared into the bowels of the camp.

That was little consolation however.

The stream of freed captives seemed never-ending. Just when she thought they were done, more would stumble out into the forest. The vast majority of them were the bear-like Baribal, but there were a few dwarves and a small but growing number of elves.

Many were injured, especially the elves, who all seemed to have been severely beaten. But she couldn't get up to heal them. If she moved and they were discovered, then all this would have been wasted. So, with a sigh Liz peered back into her scope to wait and watch.

"Someone's coming," Emily suddenly whispered.

"How do you know?" Pipaluk asked softly. "I do not see anything."

Liz could just make out Emily tap the side of her head with a heavily ringed finger. "I can hear them," she answered quietly.

"Where are they?" Liz whispered.

Emily shrugged sheepishly. "I don't know. It's not like hearing with your ears that you can pick out what direction the thoughts are coming from."

"Well, that's not helpful," Liz muttered. "Do you know how many there are?"

"Not exactly," Emily hissed, "but there must be a lot of them for me to hear it over all the other noise."

Liz wasn't sure what Emily meant by that. It was very nearly silent on the hill even with all the new arrivals.

Emily must have seen the confusion on her face because she pointed at the milling throng of Baribal behind them and then tapped her forehead again.

"Ahh," Liz nodded, "I gotcha."

Pipaluk was muttering under her breath and then waived her hand around her head. She closed her eyes and sniffed the air. After a moment, she pointed down to their left. "There are Tiraan approaching from that direction," she whispered.

Liz followed the old bear-woman's instruction and quickly spotted the figures stalking through the trees. "I see them," Liz muttered.

"How many?" Emily whispered.

"Over a dozen, I'd say," Liz whispered back. "It's hard to tell though."

"Well, what are you waiting for?" Emily grinned in the darkness. "Take 'em out."

Liz shook her head. "If I shoot one, the others will know and run faster. I doubt I can get them all before they reach us."

"So?" Emily knocked an arrow. "You aren't the only one up here."

"True enough," Liz grinned, and took aim through the powerful scope.

With a small flash and a whisper of sound, one of the beasts dropped from her sight. The other minotaur stood there dumbly for a moment until another fell. Realizing they were under attack, the remaining minotaur charged.

Liz got two more shots off before she could hear the herd crashing through the brush.

"Here they come…" she muttered and pulled the trigger again.

More minotaur appeared behind the first and joined the charge up the hill. Liz fired again and her vision blurred. She blinked rapidly to clear it before firing again.

This time, the shot sounded like a soft crack and a dull ache grew behind her eyes. Liz realized that she wouldn't be able to keep the rifle silent for much longer.

Emily abruptly lowered her bow and looked around as if confused. "Something's not right."

"I agree," Pipaluk muttered.

One of the former captive Baribal suddenly pointed down the other side of the hill and began talking very excitedly to its companions.

Pipaluk ran over and looked down to where the other Baribal was pointing. The old shaman growled deep in her throat. "Feloran," she snarled.

Liz jumped up and her vision swam.

She held on to a tree to steady herself until the dizziness passed. "Where?" she stumbled to Pipaluk's side.

"There," the old bear-woman pointed and then scowled. "How did they get past our sentries?" she muttered almost to herself.

Liz didn't know, but she knew they would soon be trapped. Her head was pounding with the effort of keeping the shots silent and she was having a hard time concentrating. The Isfet camp was in front of them and with the minotaur charging up the left and now the Feloran approaching from the right, it seemed that they were indeed trapped.

"I don't know how they snuck up on us." Emily fired her bow into the darkness. "But if we hurry we can get the captives out behind us before we are surrounded."

Pipaluk swiftly said something to one of the former captives and he nodded. Pipaluk turned back to Emily. "Shakur will lead them away."

"Good." Liz fired again and this time the shot was a louder crack. She rubbed her temples, but the pain only grew.

Emily unleashed a hail of arrows down the hill on the charging minotaur while Liz concentrated on the pack of bounding Feloran.

The lion-like creatures moved remarkably fast and Liz knew they would reach them even before the herd of minotaur would.

A roar suddenly echoed through the hills followed by a brilliant explosion in the Isfet camp.

"Well, I think our element of surprise just ended," Emily yelled.

"Thank God!" Liz shouted, and fired her rifle without suppressing it. The weapon roared to life and Liz's headache immediately began to subside.

Emily took the cue, slung her bow, and instead drew the skull-topped goblin scepter. She sent a streak of crackling green energy lancing down into the charging minotaur that were almost to the top of the hill.

A look of concentration briefly crossed Emily's face and suddenly the roots and branches of the surrounding trees began clawing at the huge minotaur. Wooden limbs grasped at the beasts, but the minotaur were too strong and were hardly slowed as they bulled their way through the living snares.

The former captives were rushing away down the other side of the hill as even more continued to arrive from the Isfet camp. Further explosions and shouts of warning erupted as the camp came fully awake.

The Feloran were now too close for Liz to see in her scope, so she swung the rifle over her back and drew her pistol and slender saber. A spray of bullets dropped two lion-faced warriors as they mounted the hill, but more bounded over the fallen. Those that survived the hail of bullets were met with a roar by Pipaluk and her warriors.

Emily continued to fire bursts of green energy as she was forced backwards as several of the towering minotaur crested the hill in front of her. She stopped when she backed into Liz who was unloading her pistol in the opposite direction.

Back-to-back, Liz and Emily desperately unleashed death as their enemies surrounded them.

CHAPTER 18

Everything happened at once.

The churning ball of energy collided with Gadhar's upraised shield in a brilliant explosion of arcing power. Mike was closest to the alpha and the force of the blast knocked him backwards into the large tent.

Jack dove away as a barrage of multi-colored, magical bolts flashed past him and destroyed a nearby tent.

Ted stood his ground as a column of fire washed over him to crackle harmlessly over his glittering arcane shield.

The two Canis soldiers stumbled, but quickly recovered and barked challenges as they charged the distracted Feloran casters. But before they could reach them, several lion-like Feloran pounced from the darkness. Several hulking minotaur lumbered in behind them and the battle was joined.

Mike extracted himself from the tent just in time to see Chief Kaneonuskatew and his warriors emerge from the prison tent behind what must have been the last of the captives. The Baribal saw all of the Isfet battling with their allies and with a roar they charged into the melee.

The Isfet wore very little in the way of body armor. While a few had scaled vests or wrapped leather, most just sported a long kilt and sandals, leaving their furry torsos exposed. But where they didn't have much in the way of armor they made up for with a wide variety of weapons.

It seemed to Mike that no two Isfet dressed the same or carried the same weapon. This contrasted greatly with what he had seen of the Canis and Baribal so far.

Each Canis soldier wore a coat of interlocking plates and a tall helm while wielding a metal round shield and a curved scimitar. They were obviously soldiers that were part of a larger and well-disciplined army. The Baribal were also alike in that they all wore similar pipe bone armor with beads of the same color and each carried a pair of long daggers.

The Feloran and minotaur, on the other hand, were all different and that difference was what bound them together. Weapons of all sizes and styles were on display. Tall leaf-headed spears and wickedly hooked sickle swords were in abundance, but there were also narrow axes, serrated daggers, bone clubs, slings, wicker shields, and even a few claw weapons.

Without hesitation, Mike dove into the fray with his ancient mace leading the way. His connection to the dwarven weapon grew daily; where once it was little more than a basic mace, it was now a mighty weapon. The force of his blows was multiplied to the point where anything that contacted it would be propelled backwards. But if he wasn't careful, all the force in the world wouldn't protect him from a blade in the back, and there were plenty of blades looking to do just that.

The mace was a blur as Mike struck left and right, sending Isfet flying like rag dolls. Mike ducked and a spear scraped off his pilfered dwarf helm. He punched out and the Feloran at the other end of the spear crumpled.

A sickle-like khopesh sword snaked out and Mike parried, but before he could do anything else a huge minotaur lowered its horns and tried to gore him. Mike lowered his shield just in time, but the power of the beast's charge drove him back. Mike struggled to hold on as he was pushed back. With a mighty swing, Mike brought his mace down hard on the minotaur's skull. With a loud crack, the beast crumpled to the ground at Mike's feet.

Freed from the minotaur's horns, Mike waded back in. However, he hadn't gone three steps when two hulking figures loomed up out of the gloom before him.

They were towering minotaur, both easily eight feet tall and thick with corded muscles. Unlike the other minotaur that Mike had seen so far, these two were covered from head to hoof in heavy, overlapping plate armor festooned with blades and spikes. What was worse was that they each carried the largest weapons Mike had ever seen. One wielded a long-handled war hammer that Mike doubted even a dwarf could carry, while the other minotaur held a serrated greatsword whose blade was longer than Mike was tall.

The monstrous armored minotaur bellowed eagerly when they saw Mike alone before them.

"Oh wonderful…" Mike groaned, and the minotaur charged.

****

More magical missiles flew at Jack, but he danced away, barely avoiding their sting. The Feloran priestess growled in frustration as Jack dodged yet another flurry of spells.

"Hold still and die!" she hissed angrily.

Jack just laughed and bounded away, a hair's breadth ahead of a beam of searing light. As much fun as it was to agitate the priestess, Jack was growing tired of the chase and was eager to join his friends in the battle. Unfortunately, this determined Feloran wasn't giving him a moment's rest and he was slowly getting pushed further away from his friends. All he needed was a second to sheath his sword and grab his M4 from his back and he would end this dance with an orchestra of hot lead.

A Feloran warrior suddenly bound out of the darkness and lunged at him. Jack twisted away and slashed with his black orc sword and sliced into the Feloran's back. The lion-man howled and crumpled to the ground, its spine severed.

The warrior proved to be just enough of a distraction to slow Jack down a step and the priestess smiled as the next swarm of magical darts found their mark.

Jack grunted in pain as the darts seared through his orc armor into the flesh beneath.

As much pain as he was in, Jack remained on his feet, wisps of smoke wafting off his charred armor. This must not have been what the priestess had expected because her smile fell away and she growled deep in her throat as she prepared to hurl another spell.

Jack clenched his teeth and raised his black sword before him. He was tired of running. It was time to end this once and for all.

Then, out of the corner of his eye, Jack saw a section of darkness break away behind the priestess. The darkness solidified into a huge, armored shape with glowing golden eyes.

Lorcan bound forward and seemed to vanish and then reappear several steps ahead of where he should have been. He phased in and out several times between strides, crossing the distance to the priestess remarkably fast.

The Feloran was so engrossed in the spell casting that she didn't realize the danger until she heard the hidden, twin blades scrape out of Lorcan's heavy gauntlets. The priestess started to turn, but it was too late. The massive Warg rammed a bladed fist into the Feloran's back and the weapon burst from her chest in a shower of dark blood.

The priestess slid bonelessly off the long blades and fell in a heap at Lorcan's feet. The huge Warg tilted his head back and unleashed a deep and bone-chilling howl.

The Canis surrounding the camp took up the call and soon the night was full of the eerie call of the wolf.

The large Feloran Lector Priest ceased his assault on Gadhar and turned to find the source of the haunting sound. Although Pipaluk had said that the minotaur couldn't tell the difference between the cry of a Warg and a Canis, Jack could tell the difference, and apparently so could the large Feloran priest.

The Lector Priest found Lorcan through the chaos of the battle and seeing the body of the priestess at his feet, the striped Feloran snarled in rage. With the alpha forgotten, he spun to face the Warg.

Lorcan met the Lector Priest's eyes and bared his long, yellow fangs eagerly. The huge Warg bellowed a challenge and bound toward the priest with Jack a few steps behind. Together they raced at the large, striped Feloran as the priest began muttering a spell and tracing arcane shapes in the air.

Just before they reached the priest, Jack realized they were going to be too late as the striped Feloran smiled wickedly and uttered one last word and released his spell.

A distorted wave, like the heat shimmering off a road in the summer, radiated outward from the priest and the full force struck the defenseless Lorcan and then hammered into Jack.

Jack's mind shattered and he lost all comprehension of who and where he was.

Pain ripped through his mind and threatened to tear him apart as a sudden, unknown presence pressed in. Instinctively Jack pushed back, but his fragmented thoughts couldn't compete with the invading force and he was being overwhelmed.

Jack's mind screamed in protest as it scrambled to find purchase.

The presence slid relentlessly into Jack's thoughts and the urge to kill Lorcan suddenly overcame him. A haze filled his vision as Jack struggled powerlessly against the invading presence. He was forced to watch helplessly as his hands slowly raised his black sword behind the unsuspecting Warg's back.

Seeing the black soul sword before him gave Jack's fragmented thoughts something to cling to. He felt the blade in his hands and could just barely sense the power of the orc weapon. Desperately, Jack's mind frantically pulled the forces contained inside the blade to himself.

The currents of power inside the blade were unlike anything Jack had ever experienced and the sudden release of energy threatened to overwhelm him. Enough of Jack remained to feel fear, as he understood that if he lost this battle, he would be utterly consumed.

The powers in the blade raged around a diamond-hard fragment of Jack's will that refused to be consumed. Pulling on his last strength, Jack gathered every ounce of willpower he could summon and grabbed the wild hurricane of power that was the soul sword and clamped it down.

Ever so slowly, and with a supreme effort of will, Jack somehow brought the chaotic forces under his control.

The new power seeped into the cracks in his spirit and bound them together again. Jack's thoughts cleared and he was able to see the dark presence latched onto his mind.

Sword and man fused together, rammed a spear of pure, white-hot willpower into the parasitic other-mind.

The other presence screamed and burst apart, flaring brilliantly in a shower of released energy and outside the Lector Priest winced in pain.

Jack's fragmented parts came crashing back together and the fog lifted from his vision.

His body and mind once again his own, Jack lowered his sword and was surprised to discover that barely a few seconds had passed since the spell had hit him. It seemed like it had taken an eternity to free himself.

Lorcan stood frozen a few steps ahead, between Jack and the Feloran caster.

Jack angrily advanced on the Lector Priest. "You are going to pay for that," he growled.

The striped Feloran ignored him and stood rooted to the spot, seemingly lost in his own little world. Jack grinned wickedly and strode toward the immobile priest. This was going to be easier than he had thought.

But before Jack could reach the priest, Lorcan turned and blocked his path.

"Get out of my way," Jack snarled, but the huge Warg didn't move.

It was then that Jack looked up at Lorcan and noticed something odd about him. Where his eyes were usually a brilliant gold, they were now solid black, like staring into an abyss.

Jack had a sudden sinking feeling as he realized what had happened. Lorcan had fallen to the mind control spell of the Feloran priest.

The Warg growled and without warning, slashed at Jack's head with his gauntlet blades.

Jack threw himself backwards, barely avoiding being decapitated.

"He is controlling your mind!" Jack cried at the Warg. "Fight it!"

But Lorcan didn't acknowledge that Jack had even spoke and instead lunged at him.

The huge Warg's form blurred and he became like a shadow as he streaked forward. Lorcan abruptly reappeared and stabbed savagely at Jack, but again Jack dodged away. Blades dropped out of Lorcan's other gauntlet and the huge Warg redoubled his assault.

Jack deflected the blows, but every time he tried to strike back, Lorcan became like smoke and Jack found himself dueling with a shadow by the light of the full moon.

****

Farther down the line of tents, Ted found himself in his own duel with the remaining Feloran priestess as a hail of flaming arrows began to rain down on the waking camp. Ted smiled, as it seemed that the Canis distraction had begun.

Nearby, the Baribal chief and several of his warriors were struggling against a number of Feloran. Ted could see the Baribal were hard pressed and as he watched, one of them was gutted by a Feloran's bronze khopesh.

Another volley of destructive magic flew from the priestess and hammered at Ted's shield, but he was confident that it would hold for a few more moments. So instead of attacking the priestess, Ted concentrated on the Feloran warriors.

Bolts of deadly magic fanned out from Ted's outstretched fingers and connected with several of the cat-like Isfet. Their bodies fell in smoking ruins and the Baribal seized the sudden advantage and slew the remaining Isfet warriors.

Chief Kaneonuskatew and his warriors then charged the priestess. Before they had gone two paces, the ground erupted at their feet and sent them crashing to the ground. They landed hard and Kaneonuskatew rolled to a stop next to Ted.

The priestess threw balls of fire at the pair, but Ted said a word and the fireballs vanished in a puff of smoke.

The Isfet priestess hissed at him and flexed her golden gauntleted hand. Wicked-looking golden claws protruded from each of the gloved digits as she drew a slender rod from her belt. She quickly twisted the rod, and it suddenly elongated and became a long, slender staff.

"Don't let the claws touch you," Kaneonuskatew rumbled, as he stood up beside Ted. "They are poisoned."

More Feloran and minotaur came charging in and the Baribal warriors were abruptly caught again in a furious melee.

Ted nodded his understanding and hefted his poleaxe. Together they charged the Feloran priestess.

A minotaur abruptly rushed out of the darkness and swung a massive club at Ted. The poleaxe caught the heavy weapon, and Ted roughly twisted his body and put the beast off balance. Ted swept his leg and the minotaur landed hard on his back. The club fell from the beast's surprised hand and without hesitating, Ted stabbed down and drove the spike into the minotaur's chest.

Kaneonuskatew charged ahead and met the priestess with a roar of hatred and flashing steel. The Baribal chief's twin daggers were a blur as they slashed at the Isfet priestess, but a twirling staff met them at every turn. Sparks flew as the weapons collided and a furious dance of death had begun.

With a grunt, Ted extracted his poleaxe from the minotaur's chest just in time for a pair of Feloran to bound into the light of a nearby burning tent. They saw him and roared in unison. Together they rushed him, weapons gleaming.

A blast of ice flowed out from Ted's hand and struck one of the warriors. The Feloran froze instantly in place, encased in a wave of ice. The other warrior pounced at Ted with axe raised.

Ted deftly turned the stroke with a twist of his poleaxe. The Feloran proved remarkably fast and surged with a flurry of blows that Ted was hard pressed to block. Over the Feloran's shoulder, Ted could see

Kaneonuskatew battling the priestess and it wasn't going well for the Baribal chief.

The fur on Kaneonuskatew's shoulder was charred and smoking as he was forced backward under the priestess's assault.

Ted chopped down hard at the warrior before him, but the Feloran dodged it and countered with a vicious swipe at Ted's head.

Kaneonuskatew threw himself at the priestess and he managed to knock the staff from the priestess's hands. But before he could deliver a killing blow with his daggers, the priestess struck with her golden gauntlet and drew four bright lines of blood across Kaneonuskatew's chest.

"No!" Ted cried as he saw the Baribal chief stumble. An axe dove at the distracted Ted and nearly split him in two, but Ted reacted just in time and spun away, swinging his poleaxe in the same motion. The move caught the Feloran warrior off guard and it stumbled. The longer reach of the poleaxe carried it into the lion-man's side as it tried to get away.

The priestess leisurely walked away from the wounded chief and daintily retrieved her staff as he struggled to stand upright.

Not waiting to see if the warrior was dead, Ted raced to the stricken Baribal chief. Kaneonuskatew collapsed just before he reached him and Ted bent over the prone form, but he was too late. The Baribal chief was dead.

Ted clenched his fist and spun to face the sneering Feloran priestess.

"Now you die," Ted growled, and energy crackled to life around him.

****

With a crash, Mike landed hard on his back.

Blood ran down his face from a gash on his forehead and there was a large dent in his breastplate.

Mike gasped and tried to get air into his lungs, but the impact had robbed him of breath.

Chaos swirled everywhere, but right here was a peaceful calm. Mike looked up at the stars as he listened to the sound of battle all around him. His whole body ached and he couldn't find the strength to pick himself up.

But that was OK. It was nice here in the grass, watching the stars… Mike scowled. Perhaps he had gotten hit harder than he realized.

A blaring roar sounded and still lying on his back, Mike picked his throbbing head up to look down between his feet. The tent before him suddenly burst apart as a massive, armored minotaur with a huge war hammer crashed through, reducing the shelter to splinters.

It saw Mike and roared again.

"Wonderful…" Mike groaned, and set his head back down as the armored beast advanced on him.

The massive minotaur's armored bulk sparkled in the darkness, reflecting the flickering light of burning tents. It howled in victory and raised its massive war hammer above Mike's prone form.

"I've had just about enough of you…" Mike groaned.

The enormous weapon descended in a fatal arc and Mike didn't move.

The war hammer struck.

Barely a foot above Mike, the huge weapon rebounded off an invisible wall.

The minotaur howled in rage and furiously hammered on the shield, but to no avail.

Still on his back, Mike grinned and pointed his mace at the raging beast. Electricity sparked to life and began to curl around the ancient, flanged head.

The minotaur stopped his assault and stared stupidly at the lightning wreathed mace.

"A little trick I picked up from the dwarves," Mike said, and with a crack like thunder, the lightning shot out from the mace and caught the armored minotaur full in the chest. Spasms wracked its huge body as the electricity coursed through it.

The beast was dead before it hit the ground, a charred hole burned through its chest.

Mike slowly hauled himself to his feet.

Appearing around the bend in the darkness, Mike saw Gadhar trying to herd the last of the freed captives out of the embattled camp.

A small Baribal cub stumbled and the alpha bent to pick up the child, but as he was doing that a group of Feloran archers emerged from the darkness behind them.

They drew their bows back and Mike shouted a warning, but he was too late. Gadhar looked up at Mike's shout and saw the archers. He clutched the cub protectively to his chest as they fired.

The arrows slammed into a faint shield-wall that flickered to life just inches away from their targets and dropped harmlessly at Gadhar's feet.

The alpha looked up in surprise and saw Mike struggling to maintain the shield as the Isfet knocked more arrows. "Run!" Mike shouted.

Alpha Gadhar didn't need to be told twice. He pushed the frightened villagers along as another volley of arrows collided with Mike's Svalinn Field.

A Baribal warrior stepped out of the darkness and the alpha handed over the cub. The warrior took the cub and vanished back into the darkness, leading the last captives away.

Gadhar turned back and howled. He drew his saber and bounded toward the archers. Just before he reached the Feloran, Mike pushed his wall into them and the archers were knocked off their feet by the surprising move.

The alpha waded into them, saber flashing and was joined by Mike a moment later. The pair made quick work of the helpless archers, but a few of them managed to escape and vanished into the dark maze of tents.

Gadhar bounded after them with Mike close behind. They rounded a bend and found themselves back in the center of the growing melee.

All around, Baribal and Canis were locked in vicious combat against swarms of Feloran and minotaur warriors. Mike was shocked to see Jack battling furiously with Lorcan as Ted and a Feloran priestess traded devastating spells. In the center of the chaos stood the tall Lector Priest, surrounded by a protective ring of Feloran warriors. Mike noticed something strange about the priest - he wasn't moving. It was almost like he was watching something far off.

"Oh no…" Gadhar growled, when he saw what was happening. "The priest has Lorcan under his spell."

Mike could see that the battle was quickly growing into a rout. If they remained much longer they would be slaughtered. Even as he watched, a pair of lion-like warriors cut down a Baribal as more Isfet joined the fray.

"What do we do?" Mike asked.

The large Canis snarled as he advanced on the Feloran and his ring of guards.

"Kill the priest."

CHAPTER 19

Jack fought brilliantly, but even his skill was outmatched by the prowess of the massive Warg he faced. There was no time for him to even think of attack. Lorcan's strikes came so fast that Jack was constantly on the defensive. What was worse was that every blow got just a little bit closer to landing.

Jack knew he couldn't keep this up and sooner or later Lorcan's claws would get through. If only he would get the chance to draw his pistol. Even the big, bad wolf wasn't faster than a speeding bullet.

Long, steel claws slashed at Jack from what seemed like everywhere at once. But then Jack noticed what was almost a rhythm to the Warg's strikes. Jack effortlessly moved into the dance and found a rhythm of his own.

Lorcan was still faster and stronger, but Jack suddenly found himself actually enjoying the fight. The crash of steel on steel was music to his ears and every movement was a joy to perform. Jack wasn't sure where these strange feelings were coming from, but he embraced them and met the Warg blow for blow.

Blades descended in a blur, but Jack was ready. He had anticipated the strike and just before they landed, Jack slid away and slashed at the blades with his black sword.

There was a scream of tearing metal as the orc blade carved through the dark steel claws.

Robbed of a pair of claws and clearly frustrated at not easily killing the pathetic human before him, Lorcan snarled and suddenly lunged at Jack's throat.

Unprepared, Jack threw his forearm up just in time to keep the huge Warg's teeth from ripping his throat out, but the powerful jaws clamped down on Jack's arm. Long fangs punched through tough orc armor to slice into the soft flesh beneath.

Jack grunted in pain as Lorcan shook his head violently and ripped into his arm. Jack's vision swam as pain threatened to overwhelm him.

Then Lorcan abruptly released him. Suddenly free, Jack stumbled backwards, confused.

The huge Warg unexpectedly spun around and bounded away, leaving Jack standing there.

"Hey!" Jack shouted. "Where the hell are you going? I'm not done with you yet!"

But Lorcan ignored him and continued toward a large group of Feloran. At first Jack thought that he had broken the spell, but soon realized that wasn't the case when he saw Mike and Gadhar battling their way through the guards around the Lector Priest.

"Oh, no you don't," Jack muttered, as he set off after Lorcan. "Your furry hide is mine."

****

Feloran warriors flew through the air, tossed like dolls by the force of the ancient mace. In such a tight formation, Mike couldn't help but hit at least a few warriors as he waded into them.

The last guards were knocked aside and the Lector Priest appeared before him. He rushed forward, mace ready to strike when a huge body slammed into him.

Mike and the assailant crashed to the ground and rolled around with snapping jaws just inches from his face. Lorcan clawed and bit viciously, but Mike had created a protective field around himself and the huge Warg's attacks slid harmlessly away.

The Svalinn Field pushed Lorcan up and way, allowing Mike to quickly regain his feet and face the massive beast. The Warg was an ally and Mike didn't want to hurt him, but he also wasn't about to let the wolf-man kill him either. Lorcan howled and lunged at Mike, his huge form blurring and fading into smoke between slashes as the alpha cut his way through the last guard and stalked toward the Lector Priest. A bolt of deadly energy lanced out from the Feloran priest and Gadhar was forced to dive away as the beam carved a smoking trench where he had been standing.

Mike noticed Lorcan's movement significantly slow down when the priest cast his spell. "Keep him occupied!" Mike yelled. "He can't keep control and cast at the same time!"

"Easy for you to say!" Gadhar snarled, as a blast of energy hammered against his upraised shield.

Lorcan slashed at Mike half-heartedly and he avoided it easily. But as the huge Warg attacked, his pace increased and soon Mike found himself hard-pressed once again.

The blades on one gauntlet were sheared away, but that didn't stop Lorcan from using his own claws. Mike didn't try to hit Lorcan; instead, he focused on blocking the huge Warg's attacks.

Suddenly, two large minotaur barreled their way in and joined Lorcan, flanking him.

Now three-on-one, they surrounded him and Mike was in trouble. The three worked in unison and didn't give him a chance to escape. Mike took comfort in knowing he was keeping these three occupied while the alpha would hopefully take care of the priest.

But when Mike stole a glance back, his heart sank. Gadhar hung in the air, bound in glowing red cords before the Feloran priest.

A club crashed into Mike's shield and a large axe drove toward his head. Mike pushed the club away and caught the axe with his shield. The axe sunk into the shield and with a mighty heave, the huge minotaur ripped the shield off Mike's arm.

Off balance, Mike couldn't avoid the next swing from the minotaur's heavy club and it threw him to the ground. On his back, with a minotaur standing on either side of him and the huge Warg in front, Mike groaned in pain and tried to get up. But he had taken a beating and his battered body wouldn't respond.

The minotaur on either side sneered and looked down on Mike as Lorcan advanced.

****

All around, more of the Isfet were joining the fight as the camp came fully awake and they were slowly encircling the last of the raiding party. Only one Canis soldier still stood alongside the few remaining Baribal.

The alpha hung, suspended in the air a few feet off the ground and fought futilely against his bonds. The Lector Priest smiled wickedly and drew a long, curved dagger. "Struggle all you like, but it will avail you none," the Feloran purred. "I am going to gut you like the mangy dog you are and devour your beating heart right before your eyes. Your life will power my spells that will destroy your precious pack." He grinned, revealing long, gleaming fangs. "How does it feel to know that you will be responsible for the destruction of your own?"

"Has anyone ever told you that you shouldn't play with your food?" The Lector Priest spun to find who had spoken. His large eyes grew wide when he found Jack standing there.

Jack held a pistol leveled at the tall Feloran and clutched his injured arm close to his chest. The gun burst to life, spitting fire.

A jolt passed through the Lector Priest's body and he stood there a moment looking confused. He slowly looked down and found a hole in his chest. The priest let out his last breath and his body crumpled.

The bindings around Gadhar suddenly vanished and he fell hard to the ground.

Lorcan stood over Mike and froze, his blades raised. The blackness suddenly drained from his eyes and they glowed a brilliant gold again. He howled, and in a blur he slashed left and right, stabbing each minotaur in the throat before they knew what was happening.

The huge Warg offered his large hand and Mike accepted it gladly as Lorcan helped him to his feet.

Nearby, Ted was wreathed in fire as the priestess hurled spell after devastating spell at him. Mike could see the strain on Ted's face as he struggled to keep the hexes at bay.

With a loud bang, Jack fired, taking the priestess between the eyes. She collapsed and her spells winked out as she died.

"What the hell, Jack?" Ted shouted. "I almost had her!"

"You can thank me later," Jack yelled back. "We have to go!"

Ted looked around and for the first time realized the situation they were in. The Isfet nearly had them surrounded, and only he and a few others remained alive. He had been so focused on his duel with the priestess that he had lost track of everything else. More white-sashed Feloran priests could be seen approaching through the darkness with each surrounded by a large cadre of warriors.

Needing to create some space, Ted acted fast and summoned a jet of fire that he sprayed in a great arc. Any Feloran or minotaur that were caught in the inferno were instantly cooked by the heat.

Freed from immediate combat, Jack used the opportunity to sheath his sword and painfully unslung his rifle. His injured arm made it difficult to grip, but eventually Jack got a hold of it and a hail of bullets carved through the Isfet.

Abruptly separated from their reinforcements, the Isfet on this side of the fire were quickly cut down by blade and bullet.

Without any immediate threats, the surviving raiders took the opportunity and broke for the safety of the forest. The burning wall that Ted had created was snuffed out as the priests advanced and the army of Isfet charged after the fleeing raiders.

It was a mad dash back through the maze of tents and Lorcan led the way, fading into the gloom and silencing any foes that appeared in their path. Mike and Ted brought up the rear with Ted throwing spells of fire and lightning to try and slow their enemies, while Mike blocked any arrows or spells that the Isfet tried to fling at them.

They moved as quickly as they could, but with every step the Isfet closed in around them.

****

Liz slashed wildly with her saber, hacking at anything that came too close. She resolved that if she survived this she would take her sword training more seriously from now on.

Her pistol was almost out of ammunition, and she had been forced to rely on her blade work and use the gun only sparingly.

She and Emily stood back-to-back in the center of an insane nightmare. Dog-man battled lion-man battled bear-man battled bull-man in a chaotic storm of slaughter in the fading gloom all around the two humans.

Dawn was finally approaching as the sky began to lighten. They still held the hill, but just barely. Many of the former captives had chosen to fight rather than flee, making it more of a fair fight. But if it hadn't been for the party of dwarves making it up the hill and joining the fray with wild abandon, she doubted they would have survived this long.

Worryingly, the stream of freed captives had slowed to a trickle and then stopped altogether some time ago. With their reinforcements gone, Liz didn't think they could hold out much longer.

"We should fall back!" Pipaluk shouted, as she clubbed a minotaur across its cow-like face.

"Not until my friends get back!" Liz yelled over the sounds of battle.

Pipaluk shook her head sadly as she dueled with another minotaur that had followed the first one. She slid around behind it and slit its throat with an expert twist of her long claws. "They may already be dead."

Liz knew the old shaman could be right, but she refused to accept that. Her friends were alive and Liz was determined to hold this hill for them as long as necessary. That determination was put to the test when three hulking minotaur suddenly crashed through the brush and came roaring at her.

Emily heard the roars and looked back over her shoulder. She saw the beasts coming and calmly fired another bolt of green energy down the hill before turning to face the new threat. Together, Liz and Emily confronted the howling monsters.

Liz fired and a minotaur collapsed, clutching its throat. A green beam blasted the second full in the chest and it fell in a smoking heap. The third minotaur howled in rage and was almost on them when roots suddenly erupted form the ground and wrapped themselves around the beast's thick legs. The minotaur lost its balance and fell, landing on hands and knees as more roots snaked their way around its body.

The beast roared and struggled, even managing to snap a few of the living roots, but more took their place and soon the monster was tightly bound on its hands and knees. A slender root slithered its way around the immobile minotaur's thick neck and began to tighten.

Liz turned away, unable to watch the minotaur's slow death. It was one thing to kill an enemy quickly before they could kill you, but to die slowly and helplessly knowing what was about to happen… Liz shuddered. Her thoughts were interrupted as more minotaur and Feloran gained the hilltop.

A group of battered elves rushed in and dove into the enemy kefali with steely determination. Liz was shocked at the fury of the elf assault. She had never seen such rage by the elves before. They were usually calm and reserved, but now they attacked like beings possessed. Liz was glad the elves were on her side. She couldn't imagine facing such brutal savagery.

Although the Isfet had greater numbers, the enraged elves carved through them in a whirlwind of blood and death. Within moments, the Isfet were dead and the battered elves vanished back into the woods like some vengeful spirit.

Liz heard a light scratching sound above her and that was all the warning she had. Suddenly, a heavy weight crashed down into her and bore her to the ground. Claws slashed at her neck as she tumbled down the hill.

****

Emily stood there in shock as Liz and a Feloran warrior rolled down the backside of the hill, away from the camp.

Emily heard a rustling behind her and as she turned around another lion-like warrior lunged out of the trees with a spear stabbing directly at her. Emily twisted away, but the wide blade sliced though her corset and drew a bright red line along her ribs.

Emily hissed in pain and clutched her bleeding side as she desperately tried to get some distance between her and the lion-man. The Feloran snarled and pressed its attack, stabbing wildly after her. Pain raced through her side and she stumbled into a large tree.

Abruptly, Emily found herself backed against the tree with nowhere to run. The Feloran knew she couldn't get away and it sneered as it advanced on her. With a snarl of bestial satisfaction, the Feloran drove the spear at Emily's chest.

The spear drove deep into the tree where Emily had been only a moment before and the Feloran howled in confusion. The howl was cut short, however, when Emily abruptly stepped out of a tree behind the angry cat-creature and unleashed a blast from her scepter.

"I hate cats," Emily muttered, as the charred corpse hit the ground.

She picked her way back to where she had last seen Liz, but she didn't see any sign of her friend or the Feloran she had been grappling with. Emily started down the hill in search of her, but just then Liz stumbled out of the brush. She was bruised and covered in scratches, but otherwise seemed unharmed.

"Are you alright?" Liz asked, concerned when she noticed Emily holding her side.

"Merely a flesh wound," Emily winced.

Liz rolled her eyes. "You are starting to sound like Mike." She shook her head as she reached Emily and put a hand over the wound. Emily sighed contentedly as the golden light filled her and the gash closed up.

Emily took the brief respite to look down onto the Isfet camp. She was partially surprised when she could see much further into the camp than she had before. She had lost track of time in the chaos and found herself looking in wonder as dawn was fast approaching and the darkness faded into a twilight gloom.

Fires burned unchecked all across the camp as the rain of flaming arrows continued to pummel the site. Roars and howls echoed up through the hills alongside the clash of weapons and the powerful boom of deadly explosions.

Emily could see figures scurrying madly through the camp, all headed in the same direction. Oddly they were going *away* from her and the hill. That could only mean one thing… Emily searched desperately for what seemed like an eternity until she caught a glimpse of an arcing fireball that exploded amidst several rushing minotaur.

"I see them!" Liz cried excitedly, as she pointed down in the camp.

"Finally," Emily sighed, although she hadn't seen them yet. The brush nearby rustled and Liz and Emily both spun around to face the newest threat.

Instead it was a tired-looking Pipaluk and a bloodied Baribal warrior that appeared. Emily relaxed and lowered her scepter at the sight of her allies.

Pipaluk raised a hand in greeting. Suddenly, a Feloran dropped out of the trees directly above the old shaman.

"Look out!" Emily cried, but she was too late. Pipaluk looked up in surprise as the Feloran's dagger plunged into her chest.

The Feloran warrior yanked the dagger out of Pipaluk's chest and she fell to the ground. The Feloran spun and kicked the surprised Baribal warrior down the hill before turning to face Liz and Emily.

Liz fired her pistol and took the lion-man square in the face before he had a chance to move. He dropped like a sack of hammers beside his victim.

Liz and Emily rushed to Pipaluk's side and were surprised to find her still alive, if just barely.

"Go," Pipaluk gasped. "Leave me," she sighed, as blood trickled out of the corner of her mouth.

"This is no time to be dramatic," Liz chided, as she bent over the stricken shaman.

Pipaluk smiled sadly. "I'm af-" Her eyes grew wide and she shuddered as a soft golden light spilled out from under Liz's hand and seeped into her ruined chest. The bleeding slowed and then stopped as the wound neatly knit itself back together.

"You are a healer," Pipaluk breathed in amazement.

Liz smiled. "You don't think they keep me around because I'm any good with this silly sword, do you?"

"I... thank you," the old shaman breathed.

"You're welcome," Liz said, as she helped Pipaluk to her feet. "Now, let's clear a path for our friends so we can get the hell out of here."

****

Liz's skin burned all over from the scratches she had received from the Feloran's claws, but she pushed the pain aside as she, Emily, Pipaluk and the Baribal warrior moved through the forest gathering any survivors they could find.

The battle had become scattered all along the hill into dozens of small skirmishes and that was how they found them. Liz and her group acted as a kind of magnet. Everywhere they went they gathered up whomever they found until a significant force had assembled.

But a magnet could work both ways, picking up the good as well as the bad. Where before the fragmented forces had proved beneficial by spreading out the Isfet and forcing them to search the woods, the enemy could now concentrate on the main force. Liz realized this as more and more Isfet appeared out of the trees to attack her ragtag forces.

Positioned at the top of the hill, Liz had a good view of the burning camp and the surrounding area as the sky grew ever lighter and the darkness faded.

Her heart leapt when she spotted Mike and the others charge out of the camp and begin the long climb up the wooded hill. Her feeling of joy at seeing her friends alive quickly vanished as a horde of screaming Isfet came pouring out of the camp behind them.

Arrows and spells flew at the retreating party, but thankfully they were all blocked by either Mike's shields or Ted's counter spells. However, the Isfet were gaining on them and Liz wasn't sure if they would reach her.

Liz grabbed her sniper rifle, even though it only had a few rounds left. Everything grew larger in the scope and she found one of the sashed Feloran priests as he prepared another spell. He never finished it.

Liz began systematically picking off the leading Isfet to give her friends as much space as possible, along with eliminating any Isfet that she saw using magic.

The growing battle swirled around Liz, Emily, and Pipaluk, but a ring of dwarves surrounded them and nothing made it through their flashing weapons. Picking her shots between the wall of dwarves, Emily launched volleys of energy from her scepter into the largest groups of Isfet.

"We can't stay here much longer!" Pipaluk shouted over the din of battle and laughing dwarves. "We will be overwhelmed!"

"We don't have to stay long." Liz pointed down the hill. "Just until they reach us."

Her friends were nearly halfway up the hill now and there was an acceptable distance between them and the Isfet thanks to her shooting. Liz fired her last shot and with a sigh, drew her pistol and saber again.

"Come on, come on…" Liz muttered anxiously, as she watched the slow progress up the hill.

Movement suddenly caught her eye.

Liz's heart stopped and she abruptly pushed her way through the protective ring of dwarves toward her friends.

"Look out!" she screamed down the hill. "They're in the trees!"

Jack looked up at Liz's shout and saw the Feloran hiding among the branches. Discovered, a score of Feloran roared and dropped to the forest floor between Liz's force and her escaping friends.

"Oh, no," Emily moaned. "They're trapped."

"We have to go get them!" Liz cried.

"Are you mad?" Pipaluk growled. "We will never escape them."

"I'm going down there!" Liz shouted, and then shot a minotaur that came too close. "Who's with me?"

The dwarves gave a hearty cheer and the rest of the battered survivors joined in.

"Fer the Allfather!" cried the dwarves.

"Alala!" shouted the elves.

"Hokahey!" hollered the Baribal.

The Canis howled alongside the others and the whole force leapt forward, eager to meet the hated Isfet.

Liz shouted her own wordless battle cry and charged down the hill, pistol blazing, leading the tiny, ragtag army of freed elves, dwarves, and kefali down the hill. Emily raced right beside her, laughing wildly as she bound over fallen logs and fired her scepter into the fast-approaching Feloran.

The two sides crashed together with thunderous impact. Liz fired her pistol point blank into the face of the first Feloran to appear before her and stabbed the second before it knew she was there. A third Feloran slashed at her with a large axe that nearly knocked the saber out of her hand before she shot that one in the chest. She got off two more shots before she drained the magazine. Liz cursed and rammed the empty gun into the holster and replaced it with a small dagger from her belt.

A tall lion-man wearing only a white kilt and wielding a long two-handed sword found Liz through the melee. The tall Feloran smiled and licked his lips at what he saw as an easy victory over the smaller human female.

His first swing was lazy and Liz deflected it easily. She quickly slashed at him with her dagger and nearly gutted the overconfident beast. The Feloran dodged the dagger and came on harder this time.

They traded blows and Liz was forced backwards by the power of the Feloran's strikes. He was far stronger than she was and his great sword was much larger than her own slender blade. She did have one advantage though - she was quicker. The lion-man was fast, but the large sword was slower to wield and Liz used that to her advantage.

Liz danced around the tall Feloran and dodged his broad strokes. She darted in after each swing and delivered a small cut with each strike. The Feloran grew angry at the constant sting of her small blade and his inability to hit her. His attacks grew wilder and Liz found even more openings. Finally, the Feloran lunged at her and Liz had her opening, she slid around the clumsy strike and drove her saber and dagger into the Feloran's furry body.

Liz looked around and saw that her forces were hard pressed against the Isfet warriors. Now that they were off the hill, she saw that her forces were caught between those who were now racing down to them and the Feloran that they were currently battling. Soon, they would be trapped as the entire Isfet army poured out of the camp after them.

Relief came when Jack and the alpha finally reached them and drove the Canis and freed captives into the backs of the Feloran. They brutally carved a path to Liz and the others.

The Feloran were caught between two forces and were quickly overwhelmed. A lion-man dropped dead and Liz found herself face-to-face with Mike. His face was bloody and his armor was covered in dents and gouges.

"You're late," Liz scolded.

Mike shrugged guiltily. "There was some unplanned excitement."

The last Feloran fell as the two sides joined together, but there was no time to celebrate. The camp was quickly emptying and the army of angry Isfet grew by the moment. Liz looked up the hill in dismay. Above them a large force of minotaur and Feloran had gathered and was blocking their retreat. Even if they did manage to beat them, the army below would catch up and it would all be over.

"Sound the retreat!" Alpha Gadhar roared.

From nearby, Pipaluk raised a small flute to her lips and blew a surprisingly shrill note that rang through the hills and echoed for what seemed like far longer than it should have.

Mike looked back at the swiftly approaching army behind them and the small force above them. "We'll never make it through them in time," he noted.

"I believe I may be of assistance," said Pipaluk.

"Well, if you are going to do something, do it now," Jack grumbled, still clutching his injured arm close to his chest.

The old shaman closed her eyes, raised her hands in the air and began speaking in a musical language that Liz didn't understand.

The hairs on the back of her neck stood up and it seemed as though the temperature had suddenly dropped. Mist began to form along the ground and it grew into a light fog.

Pipaluk's voice grew louder and the fog began to shift and writhe in the air. It gathered together and formed into shapes. Suddenly, there must have been a dozen ghostly figures standing around the old shaman.

Each ghost looked like a Baribal warrior, armed and ready for battle.

"Spirits, heed me!" cried Pipaluk. "Your brothers and sisters have need of you again! Clear a path for us so that we may escape this place!"

A deep, echoing voice rang out, seeming from nowhere and everywhere at once. "We will do as you ask, honored Elder."

The spirits abruptly turned and swiftly glided up the hill, phantom blades hazy in the growing light. Pipaluk lowered her arms and took a deep, shuddering breath before following the ghosts.

The shaman's movement broke the thrall and suddenly everyone was moving through the light fog, racing back up the hill behind the Baribal spirits.

"How are a few ghosts going to help us?" Jack grumbled, as he struggled through the brush.

Liz didn't have an answer for him and had been wondering the same thing. She glanced back nervously, afraid she would see the Isfet army bearing down on them from their brief stop. But when she looked back, she couldn't see anything. The fog behind them was surprisingly heavy and obscured her view of anything. Liz breathed a sigh of relief and continued her dash up the hill.

Jack's question was answered a moment later when a ghostly Baribal slashed a minotaur with his ethereal daggers. The minotaur howled and clutched at the wound, even though Liz couldn't see blood or any evidence that the ghostly blade had touched it.

More spirits drove into the Isfet on the hill as howls of pain and fear filled the air. The spirits washed over the Isfet and slew many, although their ethereal blades left no mark on the living flesh.

The Isfet fought desperately and a few of the spirits howled eerily as their spectral forms unraveled under the assault, but the damage had been done. Many of the minotaur had fled at the sight of the deadly ghosts and those Feloran that remained were confused and demoralized.

Liz and the other survivors reached the hilltop and made quick work of the few remaining Isfet. When the last one fell, the spirits silently faded away as if they had never been.

Liz discovered that the fog didn't reach to the top of the hill. When she looked back a wall of white obscured everything from view; it was as if an invisible line had been drawn. The eerie sight gave Liz a chill, but she didn't have long to think about it.

Without pausing, the battered party hurried down the other side and vanished into the woods, leaving the shrouded Isfet camp behind.

CHAPTER 20

The day proved to be gloomy and overcast - a typical day around Pittsburgh.

"Where are we?" Liz asked, as they trudged along a trail through the woods.

Mike and the other survivors had met up with the majority of the former captives and the Canis soldiers a mile out from the camp. Reunited, the party set out to put as much distance between themselves and the Isfet as possible. They had been making slow progress away from the camp for a few hours now with no sign of pursuit.

Liz had worked her way through the line, performing healing on those that had serious injuries. She had dark circles under her eyes and looked like she hadn't slept in days.

When Mike had tried to get her to stop and rest, she had waived him away saying, "I'm fine." Knowing better than to argue with her, Mike let her continue to help the injured.

"As far as I can tell, we have been mainly traveling east," Mike answered. "I would guess we are somewhere west of the airport."

"I concur," Ted nodded. "It is hard to tell with all these darned clouds, but I suspect we will be out of the woods soon. At our current pace, we will reach the airport within a few hours."

"Good," Liz sighed. "I'm tired of sneaking through these trees and looking over my shoulder every other step."

Up ahead, Alpha Gadhar called a halt and everyone gratefully found a place along the path to rest and eat. Liz looked around and appeared confused. "Where's Jack?" she asked.

It was then that Mike realized that Jack wasn't with them. So Mike, Liz, Ted, and Emily spread out and began searching the length of the party.

It was several minutes before they found him near the front of the line. Mike was surprised to discover him having a conversation with the elves.

"There you are!" Emily punched Jack hard on his uninjured arm.

"Ow!" Jack cried in mock pain. "What was that for?"

"For disappearing on us," Emily replied hotly. "We were worried about you."

Still rubbing his arm Jack smiled. "Aw, you actually care about me."

"Oh, shut it," Emily smirked.

"Jack, you're hurt." Liz rushed forward when she saw the gouges in his forearm, but Jack quickly pulled his arm away.

"I'm fine," he grumbled. "Just leave me be."

"Stop being a little baby," Liz chided, "and let me heal you."

"Save your prayers for somebody who believes in that crap," Jack retorted defiantly, still keeping his injured arm close to his chest.

Liz groaned. "I don't have time for this." Suddenly, she grabbed Jack's arm.

"Hey!" Jack cried as he tried to pull away, but Liz held tight. He struggled and twisted, but nothing could break Liz's hold. Within moments, the golden light seeped into Jack and his ruined arm began to mend.

Liz's brow furrowed in concentration as the wound closed up until only a faint scar remained. Instead of letting go, Liz held on to Jack and closed her eyes.

"What is it?" Emily asked, noticing Liz's strange behavior.

"I'm not sure..." Liz muttered with her eyes pinched shut in concentration. "It's like there is a... shadow that I can't get rid of..."

Jack abruptly yanked his arm away. "Thanks for the healing," he said quickly. "I feel much better now."

Mike had noticed a look of panic cross Jack's face when Liz had mentioned a shadow just before he pulled away. Jack knew something that he didn't want Liz to find, but instead of confronting him about it now, Mike decided to wait. Jack would tell him eventually.

"What are you doing up here, anyway?" Mike said suddenly.

"Oh, right!" Jack laughed, obviously relieved about the change of subject. "I found somebody we know." He moved aside and standing before them, despite her battered appearance, was a beautiful elf woman. She had long, dark hair that cascaded in countless fine braids down her back and brilliant green eyes. Mike found her familiar, but couldn't quite place her.

Her clothing was torn and bloodied, but the fine quality of the leather was obvious. Her ripped skirt was made to look like leaves and the molded leather vest hugged her abused body.

"Galina?" Ted asked in surprise.

"Hello Ted," Galina smiled shyly. "It is good to see you again."

"It is good to see you, too," Ted beamed back. "We didn't know that you were one of the captives."

"What?" Galina feigned surprise. "You mean you didn't come here to rescue me?" she added with a sly grin.

"Trust me," Ted replied hurriedly. "If I'd known…"

Galina laughed. "I know who they really sent you here for." She looked at the nearby group of dwarves. Everyone joined her in staring at the burly warriors. As if sensing the eyes on them, the dwarves stopped what they were doing and turned to glare right back.

An awkward silence filled the air as the two groups stared at each other.

Finally, the copper-bearded dwarf muttered something to the others before hefting his huge hammer, propping it easily on his shoulder, and striding toward the group of humans and elves. Two black-bearded dwarves hustled to catch up and flanked him just as he stopped before Jack and the others.

"I take it ye know who I be?" the copper-bearded dwarf rumbled without preamble.

Ted nodded. "You are Prince Brokkr Anvilborn."

"Aye, laddie," Brokkr nodded. "I take it me father sent ye ter find me?"

Ted nodded again. "He did."

"Well, I'm glad it twas humans and not a bunch o' elves. I couldn't bare ter be rescued by those pointy-ears." Brokkr looked at Galina. "No offense, mind ye."

Galina smiled. "None taken, your Highness."

"Shhh," Brokkr whispered. "No, 'Yer Highnessin' me." He looked around suspiciously. "We don't need these animals knowin' who I be."

"We can trust Pipaluk and Gadhar," Emily argued, but Brokkr shook his coppery head. "I'm not about ter be trustin' any o' these overstuffed fleabags."

Mike heard rustling behind him and when he looked back he saw the alpha, Pipaluk, and Lorcan approaching. "Speak of the devil…" he muttered.

Silence fell as the kefali joined the small group. There was a long, awkward silence until the alpha nudged the huge Warg.

Lorcan cleared his throat. "I apologize for any injury I may have caused you," he mumbled, staring at Jack's boots.

Mike was stunned. He didn't take the imposing Lorcan for one that would apologize about anything, especially to a human. Looking around, Mike saw that everyone else had a similar reaction. It must have been Pipaluk's idea. Mike doubted the huge Warg would have come over otherwise, but it made Mike suspicious. *Why would Gadhar bring Lorcan over to apologize?* It seemed out of character for both of them.

Recovering from his shock, Jack nodded. "Apology accepted." He waved a finger at the huge Warg. "But next time I won't go easy on you."

Lorcan's eyes flashed and he looked up from Jack's boots. "Going easy on me? That is not how I remember it."

"Trust me." Jack held up his arm and showed off the ruined orc armor. "I wouldn't have gotten this if I wasn't going easy on you."

Lorcan snorted derisively.

"How *did* you overcome the mind control spell?" Alpha Gadhar asked.

Jack looked suddenly sheepish. "I dunno," he shrugged. "I'm just more stubborn I guess."

"I see…" the alpha murmured. He obviously didn't believe Jack and Mike couldn't blame him. He didn't believe Jack either. There was something Jack wasn't telling.

The dwarf prince eyed the big Warg up and down. "The Cult o' Fenrir would love ter get a look at yerself," Brokkr chuckled.

Lorcan's ears perked up. "Cult of Fenrir? What do you know of the Great Wolf?"

Brokkr shrugged. "Legend says that Gleipnir still holds him ter the isle o' Lyngvi," Brokkr smiled, "even if those mad cultists wish it be otherwise." The other dwarves sniggered behind him.

"What!?" Lorcan suddenly flew into a rage. "I demand the release of the Great Wolf at once!" the Warg roared.

"Oh, sure," Brokkr chuckled, not showing any concern in the face of the raging Warg before him. "Lemme just fly up ter Asguard n' tell Odin ter release the very beast that be fated ter kill him."

"You dare mock me!?" howled Lorcan.

"I would never dream o' it, ye great flea-bitten mongrel," Brokkr laughed back. "Why do ye care anyway?"

Before Lorcan could answer, the alpha quickly answered. "Holy Fenrir is the god of all Wargs and he vanished without a trace ages ago."

"Well, he's no vanished any longer," Brokkr replied. "He remains right where the Æsir left him."

"Who are these Æsir, so that I may kill them?" Lorcan snarled.

"Good luck with that, lad," Brokkr chuckled. "The Æsir be gods, ye silly pup. So, unless ye can enter their heavenly realm, I no be thinkin' ye'll get yer wish."

Lorcan scowled darkly, but it was Gadhar who spoke. "I am more concerned with how such a powerful being as Holy Fenrir could possibly be contained."

"Ahh!" A twinkle entered Brokkr's eyes. "Now that be the trick. Old Fenrir broke the first chain the gods put on him so Odin had me forefathers craft an unbreakable ribbon, called Gleipnir, ter bind him. But Old Fenrir wasn't about ter let anyone tie him up, oh, no. So, the Æsir devised a trick. They said Old Fenrir wasn't strong enough ter break the ribbon and a coward besides. Ter prove 'em wrong, Old Fenrir allowed Gleipnir ter be tied ter him. But when he could no break the ribbon, Old Fenrir bit off Lord Tyr's hand. But it no availed him and he been held there ever since."

"Nooo," howled Lorcan. "I don't believe it. Why would the Great Wolf abandon us only to become ensnared by these... *Æsir*?"

"I may be able to answer that," Galina said softly.

Lorcan bared his teeth. "What could a filthy elf know of Holy Fenrir?" he snarled.

Galina took a deep breath before answering. "I know that Fenrir didn't abandon you because he was searching for his lost half-brother, Cerberus."

Gadhar snorted. "Blessed Cerberus was killed during the War in Heaven.

"No," Galina shook her head, "he survived The War and when it was over he desired to be the Guardian of the Ma'at underworld. However, Anubis was chosen instead, so Cerberus abandoned the Ma'at and wandered aimlessly until he encountered the Olympians. Seeing his potential, Hades offered him the role of Guardian of their underworld. Cerberus gladly accepted and he is still there to this day."

"No," Lorcan growled stubbornly. "Blessed Cerberus is dead and Holy Fenrir *will* return to us."

"Not until he breaks Gleipnir," Brokkr muttered.

"I will cut out your lying tongue," Lorcan snarled, and took a threatening step forward. Brokkr hefted his war hammer and smiled. "Let's see ye try, pup."

The blades slid from Lorcan's gauntlet, but the alpha hastily stepped between them and placed a restraining hand on the angry Warg's chest. "Calm yourself, cousin," Gadhar said soothingly.

"What if what the dwarf says is true?" he whispered excitedly. "Then this is glorious news! All of Lemuria will rejoice in the knowledge that Holy Fenrir is alive and did not abandon us."

Lorcan snorted. "Even if what they say is true, we must still find our way off this cursed world and get back to Nibiru."

"Fear not, cousin," the alpha smiled. "We will see our home again."

"I do not share your confidence," Lorcan growled.

"Cease yer petty moaning," Brokkr butted in. "Yer no the only ones that be far from home."

Galina stepped in. "At least we have a place to go, thanks to the kindness of the humans." The elf looked at the kefali. "Perhaps they will grant you sanctuary inside their walls as well."

Lorcan scowled. "I have no desire to be trapped within a city full of *humans* and *elves.*"

"Don't be forgettin' us dwarves," Brokkr added cheerfully.

"Ugh." Lorcan wrinkled his nose. "And definitely not *dwarves.*"

"Fine," Brokkr shrugged easily. "We don't want ter get yer fleas anyhow."

"I don't have fleas!" Lorcan growled.

"No, you don't," Brokkr itched himself, "because they all jumped over ter me."

"Why you little..." The huge Warg rose up menacingly, but Pipaluk placed a hand on him and Lorcan quieted.

"There is too much bad blood between our races," said Pipaluk, looking around the gathered elves, dwarves, humans, and kefali. "Although I believe we have taken the first steps on the path to understanding."

A crowd was gathering around them as members of every race packed around shoulder-to-shoulder to hear the exchange.

Pipaluk addressed Galina and the elves. "I am sorry for what the Isfet did to you back in the camp. That is not the way of the Ma'at." The old shaman looked sad. "I know that the elves and kefali have been enemies in the past, but I hope that we may one day overcome our rivalry and find peace."

Galina smiled. "I cannot speak for all elves, but I share your hope."

"It gladdens my heart to hear that," Pipaluk beamed, and turned to the humans. "And know that today you have gained the trust and friendship of the Hoonaw Tribe. We cannot thank you enough for aiding us in the rescue of our villagers. We are forever in your debt."

Liz smiled back. "We were glad to help, although we were there to find our allies as well."

"Indeed you were," Pipaluk said, "and you have left with more allies than you arrived with."

The old shaman unhooked a beaded pipe bone armband and placed it around Liz's arm. Other Baribal did likewise, giving one to Mike, Emily, Jack, and Ted. "A small token of our gratitude," Pipaluk smiled. "Perhaps our next meeting will be more cheerful than our first."

Emily looked confused. "You aren't coming with us?"

"No," Pipaluk smiled sadly. "As I said, there is still too much bad blood. Spread the word of our friendship amongst each of your peoples as I will tell mine. Perhaps we can plant the seeds of trust that will someday benefit us all."

"We will.," Liz promised.

"As will we," added Galina.

Brokkr grunted. "I suppose I can put in a good word fer ye." The dwarf prince eyed Lorcan. "I'm not sure about this one though."

Lorcan bared his teeth in a parody of a smile. "I look forward to meeting you again on the field of battle, runt."

Alpha Gadhar stepped forward. "The Madra of Pack Daithi thanks you for your assistance." He reached into a small pouch on his belt and drew out a large silver coin. "A token of our trust." He handed it to Liz. "Show this to any Canis and you will have an ally."

"Thank you," Liz said taking the coin, "but I'm afraid I have nothing to give you in return."

"Nothing is required," the alpha replied.

Mike stepped up. "I have an idea."

"There is a city several miles southeast of here that lies between the meeting point of three rivers," Mike began. "It's called Pittsburgh or as some like to call it, the Steel City. If you change your mind about joining us, or run into any humans, tell them that you are a Steelers fan. That should at least stop them from shooting you on sight. Then ask for the Heroes of Awesome."

"That is… strange," Gadhar replied, "but we will remember. Thank you." The alpha saluted with a fist to his chest and then suddenly spun on his heel. "Alright you lot!" he barked. "It's time to move out."

The assembled kefali dispersed and gathered up what meager supplies they had. The alpha led the band of kefali as they set out on the trail once again. Pipaluk and the Baribal warrior Shikoba remained behind a moment longer.

"Where will you go?" Emily asked.

"Away," Pipaluk shrugged sadly, "with Kaneonuskatew gone we will need to appoint a new War Chief, then we will search for others of our kind and hopefully discover a way home."

"Good luck." Emily suddenly wrapped the old shaman in a tight hug. Pipaluk tensed at first, but then relaxed and returned the gesture warmly. When they separated, Pipaluk caught Jack's eye.

"Oh, no." Jack crossed his arms over his chest. "I'm not going to hug you."

Pipaluk smiled. "I didn't expect you to."

Shikoba offered the old shaman his arm and she gratefully took it.

"Farewell." Pipaluk waved and together they joined the last of the retreating kefali.

When the last kefali vanished into the trees, Brokkr blew a sigh of relief. "Boy, am I glad ter be rid o' them." He easily propped his massive hammer on his shoulder once again. "Now, how about we find this *airport* o' yours so we can get back ter the Steel City afore any other critters be showin' up?"

"Sounds good to me," Jack muttered, "but first I need a bite to eat."

****

The kefali headed south, staying in the woods whenever possible to avoid notice. The smaller party of humans, elves, and dwarves struck out east, in search of Pittsburgh International Airport.

Mike had always found it entertaining how the airport sat out in the middle of nowhere. He suspected that with all the hills around it was difficult to find any kind of flat place big enough for an airport and that was why it was so far out.

Even though it was only a few miles to the airport, the hilly terrain made for slow going. Mike knew they were getting close when the land started to level out and he spotted some cornfields in the distance.

The party reached the top of the last large hill in the area and what greeted them took their collective breath away.

Mike couldn't quite believe what he saw.

Below them in the valley filled with cornfields was a massive hole. And there rising up out of the pit and towering before them was an immense, twisted fortress of black stone.

"Where the hell did that come from?" Jack muttered in disbelief.

Perhaps it was Mike's imagination, but the sky seemed to be darker here around the dreadful structure. The fortress soared high into the air, so high that its jagged towers rose taller than the surrounding hills. High walls made of impossibly large, black stones surrounded the central keep while the keep itself was a twisted parody of a castle. Faces and deformed shapes were carved into the walls. Even from this distance, Mike could make out the hideous statues adorning the walls and towers that depicted humanoid figures engaged in grotesque sexual acts intertwined with scenes of brutal carnage.

There was something odd about the fortress, besides its twisted appearance, but Mike couldn't quite put his finger on it. It almost seemed out of scale somehow. The doors and arrow slits were too tall, and the parapets too wide.

Long banners hung from the towers and rippled gently in the breeze. A winged falling star in the deepest black was emblazoned on a field of dark red, like dried blood.

"Oh, gods…" Galina whispered in horror. "It cannot be!"

Nervous chattering erupted from the elves as they pointed at the twisted fortress and angry mutterings rumbled from the gathered dwarves.

"What is it?" Liz asked with growing concern.

"That symbol…." Galina breathed. "It is a sign of the nephilim."

"*Nephilim?*" Emily struggled with the strange word. "Who are they?"

"They be an enemy o' legend," Brokkr answered. "They be the lords o' giants."

CHAPTER 21

Giants.

That explained the strange proportions of the twisted fortress. It was to scale for a much larger being. But so far Ted hadn't seen any living things in or around the structure. By nature, Ted was skeptical, so until he saw what was actually in there, he wasn't about to jump to conclusions.

"How can you be so sure?" he asked. "I don't see anything that looks like a giant."

"Look at the banner," Galina replied. "Do you see the falling star? And the wings on either side of it? The nephilim are the offspring of The Fallen."

"That doesn't prove anything," Ted argued. "Anyone could use a falling star with angel wings."

"This is true," Galina agreed, "but what about that one?" She pointed to the top of the central keep where a black banner hung from the tallest tower. Ted was surprised. He hadn't noticed that one before. It depicted what appeared to be a deformed goat's head with curled horns and a pentagram on its forehead.

"Now, that one I recognize," Ted replied, eager to show his knowledge. "That is the symbol for Baphomet."

"Correct," Galina said, "and Baphomet is one of The Fallen"

"Yes, yes, I know who Baphomet is," Ted replied impatiently, "but what does that have to do with the nephilim?"

"Baphomet is one of *The Fallen*," Galina repeated, as if that explained everything.

"Ok...?" Ted prodded.

"Don't you humans know anything?" Galina sighed heavily.

"When the worlds were young and without war, a number of angels, led by Samyaza, saw the mortal women and lusted after them. Those angels fled Heaven and entered the mortal realms, where they raped the women and taught the men how to make war," Galina shuddered. "Many of those poor women actually gave birth and those children were the first nephilim."

"The Creator was angry at the angels, and as punishment he cast them into Tartarus, where they are to remain until Judgment," Galina continued. "But that was only the Fist Fall. Later, a second group of angels rebelled and ignited the War in Heaven. But when their rebellion failed, they too were cast into the Nine Hells. Those imprisoned angels are now known collectively as The Fallen."

Emily eyed the distant fortress quizzically. "So, this Baphomet was an angel that left Heaven to get some and ended up fathering some giants."

"Almost," Galina replied. "Nephilim are technically demigods, fathered by a Celestial and birthed by a mortal. But when the nephilim mated with each other, they gave birth to giants."

"Ah, I got it," Ted stroked his beard thoughtfully. "I assume there are far less nephilim than there are giants."

"Correct," Galina said, "and the nephilim are far more powerful than any of their offspring. Nephilim are said to be master sorcerers and lords of the arcane. I would be-"

"Wait just one second," Liz interrupted. "The Earth was flooded to be rid of the nephilim."

"At least you know that much," Galina breathed. "It is true. The nephilim are completely evil and they bring nothing but darkness and pain. So, the Creator brought the Deluge to wash away their taint. Yet it seems somehow they survived."

"Aye," Brokkr jumped in. "A group o' foul gods callin' themselves the Jotun saw an opportunity and gathered as many o' the nephilim and their giant spawn as they could. Having no followers o' their own, the Jotun hid them from the flood and claimed the giants as their own."

"How could these Jotun hide anything from the Creator?" Galina asked.

"I'm not fer knowin'," Brokkr shrugged. "Mayhaps He let them live. Who am I ter say? But what I do know be that the giants invaded Svartalfheim ages ago and we be at war with them ter this day."

"Ehm," Galina cleared her throat. "I believe I was telling this story."

"Sorry lass," Brokkr gave her a big, toothy grin. "Just makin' sure ye get the facts right." Galina's eyes flashed, but the dwarf prince just winked.

"As I was saying…" Galina ignored the dwarf, "the banners lead me to believe that there are either nephilim or giants in the fortress."

"Or both," Brokkr muttered.

Jack grinned wolfishly. "Well, there is only one way to find out."

"Are you insane?" Emily cried. "Did you not just hear what they said? That evil-looking castle is either full of evil half-demon demigods or their giant kids." Emily crossed her arms under her breasts defiantly. "There is *no way* I'm getting any closer to that thing. I say we sneak away and keep as far away from it as we can get."

"I'm no much fer sneakin'," Brokkr rumbled. "I say we go and knock on the front door." This was greeted with enthusiastic cheers from the dwarves and looks of horror from the elves and humans.

"And what do you plan to do once you knock on the door?" Emily asked. "There are only like twenty of us and they probably have an entire castle full of giants."

"It no be the first time I've fought giants," Brokkr said proudly and the other dwarves rumbled their agreement.

"If we got close, would we even be able to tell the difference between a nephilim and a giant?" Mike asked.

"Aye," Brokkr answered. "The nephilim are said ter have long heads and pale, blue-ish skin. They be also said ter be surprisingly purdy fer bein' some o' the vilest creatures living." The dwarf prince shrugged. "I ain't seen one meself, but I have seen plenty o' giants. And giants usually look just like yerself… only fifteen feet tall and smelly."

"Wait just one moment," Liz interjected. "We don't even know for sure that someone is in that ugly castle. It could be empty for all we know."

"Like I said," Jack grinned again, "only one way to find out."

"And how *exactly* do you plan on doing that?" Emily shot back.

"First," Jack replied, "we get to the bottom of this hill. It's all wooded so nobody will see us. Second, the cornfield butts right up against the trees and the corn will hide us as well. Third, we sneak through the corn until we reach that pit around the fortress. Finally, we search for any sign of who, or what, lives in there."

"A sound plan, human," Brokkr nodded, and without waiting for anybody else, he suddenly set off down the hill with his dwarves close behind. The elves and humans each shared a look before slowly following the eager dwarf prince.

"Isn't this exciting!" Ted rubbed his hands together eagerly as they trudged down through the trees. "I've never seen a giant before."

"Me either," Emily muttered, "and I don't want to start now."

"I'm with Em," Liz added.

"Cheer up you two," Mike laughed. "We are just going to take a quick peek and be back out before you know it."

"Riiight." Liz rolled her eyes. "When has *that* ever happened?"

At the base of the hill the trees suddenly ended and ran right up against a virtual wall of corn. "Should we hold hands or something?" Jack asked with a grin and put his arm around Emily.

Emily pushed him away. "I don't think any raptors are going to get us."

Jack shrugged as he headed into the cornfield. "You never know…"

They picked their way slowly through the tightly-pack stalks and stayed parallel with the small, dirt road leading up to the castle.

"Interesting…" Ted muttered.

"What is it?" asked Mike.

"The road lines up perfectly with the castle gate," Ted replied. "That seems rather unlikely. What are the chances that a human road perfectly lines up with a castle that materializes out of nowhere?"

Emily snorted. "You would notice something stupid like that."

****

The corn seemed to go on forever and Ted was beginning to wonder if they had gotten turned around, even though the twisted black fortress still loomed high above them. It was an unnerving sight from far away, but it was positively revolting up close.

The walls were so tall it was like looking up at a black mountain with tortured people trapped inside the stone. Faces stared out of the wall, some in agony, others in terror, and even some in ecstasy. Writhing stone figures were frozen in varying stages of pain and pleasure. The entire scene was quite repulsive, but Ted found it alarmingly alluring at the same time.

The party was over halfway to the pit surrounding the dark fortress when rustling could be heard in the trees behind them. The entire party froze and ducked down, hiding in the corn along the roadside as the rustling drew closer.

Suddenly, out of the trees appeared what could only be described as a giant. The huge, bearded giant must have stood well over ten feet tall and was dressed in ancient-looking armor. It wore tall sandals, an armored skirt and sculpted breastplate very similar to the ones the elves wore. But where the elves' armor was either silver or bronze, the giant's was black and decorated with spikes and skulls. It carried a spear that was even taller than it was and the giant's long hair was tied back in a long, elaborate braid.

The ground quivered with each of the giant's heavy footsteps, as its long strides carried it down the road remarkably fast even though it didn't seem to be walking very quickly. In no time the giant was striding past the hidden party and toward the twisted fortress.

"Ugh." Jack wrinkled his nose as the breeze from the passing giant washed over them. "What's that smell?"

"I told ye they stink," Brokkr whispered back.

The giant suddenly stopped and turned back.

It stared directly where the party was hidden and took several steps toward them.

Brokkr clenched his war hammer and the entire party prepared to fight.

Ted considered what spell would be best to take down a giant, but he didn't know enough about the creatures. Since it was wearing armor that was probably metal, Ted decided on a lightning bolt.

The spell was on his lips as the giant scanned the cornfield, obviously searching for something, but after a tense minute it lost interest and continued toward the castle.

Everyone breathed a sigh of relief as the giant strode away.

Emily leaned over to Jack. "Next time you have the urge to talk, don't."

"That should be the rule all the time," Mike added.

"Hey!" Jack argued. "He heard the dwarf, not me."

Brokkr opened his mouth, but before the dwarf prince could reply, the giant stopped at the edge of the pit and bellowed something in a harsh language that Ted didn't recognize. The sound of it hurt their ears but when the giant was done speaking there was a long moment of silence until an answering shout echoed from the dark fortress. A few seconds later, there was a loud grinding noise as the massive drawbridge began to lower.

The drawbridge hit the ground on the other side of the pit with a resounding bang right in front of the waiting giant.

The down drawbridge revealed massive doors that must have been over five stories tall. Ted was in awe of the fortress. The vast scale of the thing was just mind-boggling.

The mammoth gate slowly ground open giving the hidden party their first look inside the twisted fortress.

The outer walls were so large that it was almost like looking down a tunnel. The other side of the tunnel-like wall opened into a large courtyard that was filled with giants. They were all armed differently, but they were all similar in that each wore blackened armor that was decorated with spikes and skulls. Many wore helmets shaped like screaming demons and carried huge, wicked-looking weapons.

A few of the giants clutched arcane staves and were wrapped in jet-black robes that hid their faces in a deep, unnatural darkness.

The hair on the back of Ted's neck stood on end. It looked like the mouth of Hell had just opened up before them and Hell was prepared for war.

The giant at the gate strode across the bridge and entered the teeming courtyard, immediately becoming lost in the crowd.

The gate only remained open for a brief minute before slowly drawing closed again, but that minute was more than enough.

"I guess that answers that question," Jack muttered, as the massive doors thundered closed.

"We have to get back and warn everyone," Liz said urgently.

"Aye," Brokkr agreed. "Me father must be informed immediately."

"Oh, you don't want to charge in there and fight them all right now?" Emily teased.

"Bah!" Brokkr snorted. "Only a fool would attack a giant fortress!"

"I agree," Mike said. "Let's get out of here before somebody sees us. I don't think we can outrun giants."

"We are close to the airport." Ted pointed back beyond the twisted castle. "You can see the control tower from here."

"Then what are we waiting for?" Galina didn't wait for a response and began working her way through the cornfield. The entire party picked up and followed, carefully picking their way through the corn and around the twisted fortress.

"I can't believe we haven't been seen from the castle yet," Liz muttered, pushing her way through an extra dense section of corn.

"Giants no keep a close watch," Brokkr rumbled from up ahead. "Who would be stupid enough ter attack 'em? And even if they did see us, they may no care. What danger be we ter them?"

"We could be scouts and report them," Liz replied.

Ted couldn't see the dwarf, but he heard Brokkr's chuckle. "Giants be nothin' if no arrogant. They may want us ter bring back an army. Then they no have ter go lookin' fer us."

"But you said you've fought giants before," Liz argued. "How did you beat them?"

"Dwarves no attack giant fortresses," Brokkr answered, as if it were the most obvious thing in the world. "We let 'em come ter us. An' then we ambush 'em."

Eventually, the small party found its way out of the cornfield and into the sparse trees on the opposite hillside. They crossed that small hill and put it safely between themselves and the menacing fortress, although it still took up a large portion of the sky behind them.

They made good time through the last of the small hills until they finally found themselves on the edge of a long airstrip. Apparently, their approach had been spotted, for when they stepped out onto the runway, a small army of human soldiers, elven mages, and dwarf Guardians greeted them.

"I don't believe it," one of the human soldiers said. "They actually came back."

Another solider held out a hand to the soldier that had spoken. The first soldier groaned and placed something in the second soldier's open hand.

"Taking bets on us I see," Jack grinned. "Stupid grunts should know better than to bet against a Marine."

Mike stepped forward. "We need to get back to Pittsburgh ASAP."

"Rodger," one of the soldiers replied. "We have transport on standby."

"Great," Mike answered. "Let's go."

The weary party was lead to the 911th Air Reserve Station where they gratefully climbed into the waiting transports. After such a long time walking, it seemed like the trucks were going way too fast, but Ted wasn't about to complain. He didn't care for being out in the wild and civilization was calling to him.

He must have dozed off because one minute they were driving down the runway and the next they were coming to a stop in the Fort Pitt Tunnel in front of the large doors leading to the dwarf realm.

Ted groaned as they came to a stop. The only thing worse than being in the woods was being underground.

"You guys go ahead," Ted grumbled. "I'll stay here and guard the trucks."

"If I have to go in, so do you," Emily replied.

Ted smiled. "You have my permission to stay here."

"Ye both be comin'," Brokkr rumbled. "Me father will have words with all o' ye."

"Fine…" Ted groaned, and hauled himself to his feet and followed the others off the truck and into the dwarf tunnel. He tried to ignore the hollow boom of the doors that sounded like a tomb closing behind him.

They made the long descent into the bowels of the earth and finally entered the immense chamber where they had met the king the day before, but the throne room looked very different than it had then.

Was it really yesterday that they had been here? Ted wondered. It seemed like a lifetime ago that they had set out on their mission.

The rough stone pillars that had been only half carved two days before were smooth and polished now and gleamed in the torchlight. The walls and floor were immaculate and covered with fine carvings of dwarves in battle. More surprisingly, humans were depicted fighting beside the dwarves.

"This is new," Mike muttered, as they all stared in wonder at the changes that had come over the cavernous chamber. It was magnificent. Long banners of various dwarf clans hung from the ceiling and large crystal chandeliers provided much of the light. Gold and silver decorated everything and it truly looked the part of a throne room now.

They were led through the chamber and to the same small door that they had followed the dwarf king through once before. The journey had come full circle to end in the same meeting room that they had agreed to the mission in the first place.

To their surprise, already seated at the table was King Varnir Anvilborn.

CHAPTER 22

"Brokkr, me son!" King Varnir Anvilborn boomed cheerfully, and pushed himself up from the table. "Praise the Allfather fer yer safe return!"

The king and his son embraced briefly. "It be good ter be back," Brokkr replied gruffly.

"I know it be no Burdr Geirr," King Varnir rumbled, "but it will suffice fer now."

Brokkr nodded. "It will indeed. Anything will be better than that flea infested, dung heap I been stuck in."

"Ye must tell me o' it," the dwarf king said eagerly.

"I will father," Brokkr held up a hand, "but first ye need ter call the Council together. I'm afeared we bring grave news that all will need ter hear."

"Very well." King Varnir then barked an order and several guards that had been stationed around the room hurried out. After the guards left, the king turned to Mike and his friends. "I do believe I owe ye a reward," King Varnir smiled. "Name yer price, and if it be in me power ter grant, it shall be yers."

"Thank you, your Majesty," Liz answered first, "but as I said before, we require no reward."

"Aye," King Varnir nodded slyly, "but ye would no insult us by refusing a gift would ye?"

Liz scowled, but then sighed in resignation. "No, we could not refuse a gift."

"Wonderful!" The dwarf king clapped his large hands and a moment later a dwarf warrior entered carrying a large folded cloth. The warrior then presented the cloth to Liz. Looking slightly confused, she accepted the gift.

"Open it," King Varnir waved her on eagerly. "Open it."

Slowly, Liz unfolded the large cloth. She held one end as the opposite edge of the material dropped and touched the floor. The cloth was revealed to be a heavy cloak made of a strange looking material that looked almost like scales, whose color seemed to shift in the light.

Brokkr's eyes grew wide and he looked at his father in surprise. "Ye be given her yer dragon skin Cloak o' Concealment?"

King Varnir nodded. "I have no need o' such an item and I believe she will put it ter far better use than I ever will."

"What does it do?" Liz asked, holding the strange cloak up before her.

"The cloak will take on any shape ye wish and it blends in with its surroundin's," Brokkr explained. "It will no make ye invisible, mind ye, but it be the next best thing."

Liz eyed the cloak in wonder. "I couldn't possibly accept-" King Varnir's eyes flashed and Liz swallowed what she was going to say. "Thank you," she breathed instead.

"Ye be most welcome, lass," the dwarf king boomed happily and then turned to Mike. "And what would the Guardian have o' me?"

Mike took a deep breath. "I wish to learn Runecraft."

"Runecraft!" King Varnir sputtered. "No human can learn Runecraft. The secrets were given ter the dwarves by Odin himself."

Mike wasn't about to tell the king that he already knew how. "That may be," he said, "but I wish to try."

King Varnir laughed. "Very well, Guardian. Ye have me permission ter try and learn a skill that only a dwarf can be knowin'. But I am afraid ye will be wasting yer reward."

"We'll see," Mike replied confidently.

This gave the king pause, but the dwarf dismissed it and turned to Ted. "And what about you, Wizard?"

"I have a similar request," Ted answered. "I wish to learn the dwarven tongue."

King Varnir looked confused. "Ye mean Svarty?"

Ted nodded. "Indeed."

"I fear that too be impossible," the dwarf king said solemnly. "Only dwarves be permitted ter know our language. And at me last check, yer no dwarf," King Varnir said with a smirk.

"That's twice now I have heard you say that you are afraid," Ted quipped. "I'm starting to think you are scared."

King Varnir's mirth melted away. "Afraid?" the copper-haired dwarf monarch rumbled dangerously. "I be no afraid o' anythin'."

"Could've fooled me," Ted sniggered.

"Very well, Wizard," King Varnir snarled. "I will send a Loremaster ter ye so that ye may try and learn our tongue." The king smiled. "But I have no doubt that it will prove beyond yer limited human comprehension."

"We shall see about that," Ted replied.

Just then, the chamber door opened and three elves strode in. The first was the silvery-haired Archmage Talsin in his midnight blue robes, followed by Arch Battlemage Gwydion suited up in sculpted, reddish-gold armor. Last came the diminutive Sorceress Supreme, Braelynn, in her form-fitting, white gown.

Behind the elves were two dwarves. The first was large and encased in heavy rune armor. Chief Guardian Ambrosar scowled at the elves' backs as they took their seats across from King Varnir. Behind the black-bearded Guardian came the ancient-looking Eitri Starmantle in his worn leather apron and with heavy metal studs protruding from his brow.

The dwarves took seats on either side of their king as Brokkr remained standing behind his father's chair. Before the door could swing closed, a disheveled Dr. Cooper pushed his way through followed by the grim-looking Army officer from the last gathering that Mike knew to be General

Adams.

Dr. Cooper and the general took their customary seats at the round table between the elves and dwarves.

"Welcome me friends," King Varnir boomed. "I was just granting some well-deserved rewards ter ar young heroes here." The dwarf king looked at Emily. "And what would ye have o' me, lass?"

"Well, Santa, one of those cloaks would be nice," Emily replied.

"Alas, that be the only one I had," King Varnir answered. "Perhaps a fine rune axe? Or a suit o' Dwarf Steel?"

Emily shook her head. "No. I don't use axes and I wouldn't be caught dead in some smelly tin can."

King Varnir looked taken aback. "Dwarf Steel be no *tin can*," he sputtered. "It be the finest metal in all the world!" He waved his thick arms in the air. "In all the worlds fer that matter! It be given ter only the greatest heroes and champions. Anyone would be honored if-"

"Perhaps..." Archmage Talsin interrupted gently. "I may be of some service."

King Varnir fumed at being cut off, but nodded his assent to the elven Archmage.

Talsin bowed graciously from his seat before turning and addressing Emily. "I noticed that your quiver is empty," he began softly. "I assume you exhausted your arrows during the rescue of Prince Brokkr and the other captives?"

"Yes..." Emily answered cautiously.

"Perhaps you would like new arrows for your bow then?" Talsin offered.

King Varnir snorted. "Dwarves don't use bows. We only have crossbow bolts."

Talsin ignored the dwarf king. "Would you like new arrows?" he repeated.

Emily shrugged. "I have a habit of losing my arrows, so I use plain ones that are easily replaced. I would hate to lose any nice ones."

"Never fear." Talsin reached into a small pocket worked into his robes.

"I have just the thing." He began rummaging around in the small pocket and his hand moved in ever deeper. Soon he was up to his elbow in pocket that should have fit little more than his hand. The Archmage continued his search and his whole arm was lost in the bowels of the small pocket.

"I know it's around here somewhere…" Talsin muttered as he leaned forward and was nearly swallowed by his own tiny pocket. His head and shoulders vanished into the pocket that somehow managed to stretch out to impossible proportions.

"Ah, ha!" came a muffled shout from inside the pocket.

A moment later Archmage Talsin emerged proudly grasping an exquisite quiver. Vines and scrolling silver knotwork wrapped around the tooled leather case and glittering blue gems encrusted its rim. A clutch of silver-shafted arrows entwined with fine golden vines rested easily inside the elegant quiver.

"Is that what I think it is?" Gwydion gasped.

Talsin grinned and handed the beautiful quiver to Emily. "It is indeed."

"What are you doing with an Endless Quiver in your pocket?" Gwydion exclaimed.

Talsin shrugged innocently. "I came across it some years ago and had hoped to learn the secrets of its creation," the Archmage sighed. "But alas, I have yet to find the time and I fear that I may never get around to it now that we are trapped on this ungodly world. Thus, I believe that it will do more good in the hands of a skilled archer than safely tucked away in my pocket."

Emily eyed the marvelous quiver in her hands. "What does it do?"

"Once fired, the arrows will return to the quiver after a set amount of time," Talsin explained.

The quiver came complete with a matching belt and Emily quickly took off her old quiver and cinched the new one around her slender waist.

"I don't suppose you have a Bow-of-Never-Missing or something?" Emily asked hopefully.

The Archmage smiled. "I'm afraid not."

"Dang," Emily sighed. "I suppose that would have made things too easy."

"Like you need it," Liz laughed. "You hardly miss anyways."

"Yeah, but that's because I practice a lot," replied Emily. "With a Bow-of-Never-Missing I could spend my time on other things."

"That be all well n' good," King Varnir rumbled, "but I'm no about ter let some durned elf give away a reward that I promised ter bestow."

"And you cannot give such a weapon as an Endless Quiver to a human!" Gwydion added hotly. "It should go to one of the Spell Archers or at least a Ranger…. Not some human child."

Emily put her fists on her hips. "I am no child," she retorted defiantly. "And as for you," she turned to the dwarf king, "I don't think you have anything that I could use more than this quiver. I will accept this as my reward and call your debt paid."

King Varnir scowled and waved his hand dismissively in disgust. "So, be it."

But the Arch Battlemage wasn't done yet. "You cannot do this," Gwydion argued.

"Can't I?" A dangerous edge entered the Archmage's voice. "Last time I checked Gwydion, *I* was a High Archmage of Hyperborea, not you."

"Ehrm," Chief Guardian Ambrosar coughed. "May we get back to the task at hand?"

"Indeed," King Varnir boomed. "I have one more reward ter bestow." He turned to Jack. "And what would you have o' me?"

Jack thought a moment before answering. "I'll take a rain check."

King Varnir and Brokkr shared a confused look. "And what be a *rain check*?" King Varnir asked suspiciously.

"It means you owe me one," Jack laughed. "I figure someday I will want or need something and you won't want to help. So, I'm going to hold on to this favor until I need it."

The copper-bearded dwarf king scowled. "I dislike owing favors," he grumbled, but after a moment he nodded. "Very well. Ye may have yer… *rain check*."

Dr. Cooper leaned forward eagerly. "Now that all that is settled, let us get down to business, shall we?"

"Yes," King Varnir rumbled. "How were ye able ter find and rescue me son when none o' our scouts could find nary a trace?"

"By listening to the trees," Emily answered.

The Heroes of Awesome then proceeded to tell the gathered leaders how they had followed the hidden trail that eventually led them to the kefali camp and how they were then captured by a different faction of kefali that were also on a rescue mission. The Heroes detailed their experience in the kefali camp and how they came to an agreement.

"You allied yourselves with *kefali*?" Arch Battlemage Gwydion looked stunned. "Impossible! They are one of the most devious and vile races in existence!" Gwydion snarled. "They cannot be trusted."

"It may be as you say," Liz argued, "but we helped them and they helped us."

The Heroes told of their early morning raid and the rescue of the prisoners that turned into a battle when the priests discovered them. They detailed the battle and eventual escape from the camp thanks to Pipaluk's spectral reinforcements and concealing fog.

"And they actually let you leave once they had their villagers back?" Gwydion asked in amazement.

"We're here, aren't we?" Mike retorted.

"That be an impressive story," King Varnir rumbled, "but what was the point o' taking the captives?"

"Sacrifices," Brokkr answered grimly. "The lion-men would place a captive at the top o' a small, mobile pyramid each day and cut out their hearts ter power their dark spells."

"To what end?" Talsin mused.

"They be storin' it up somehow," Brokkr answered. "They be trying ter join forces with someone called the Destroyer. Once this Destroyer has gathered a large enough host, he will march on this city."

"You are sure about this?" Talsin asked.

"Aye," Brokkr nodded. "I heard it from the chief priest's own furry mouth. He seemed ter think that this Destroyer be some kind o' god and that this world be theirs fer the takin." Brokkr grinned darkly. "It seems that our little alliance here has been noticed. I also overheard the chief priest say that the Steel City will fall afore the year be out."

"What are they waiting for?" General Adams asked. "Our outer walls are nearly complete. Why not attack us before our defenses are ready?"

"Because these kefali be waiting fer their allies ter get here," Brokkr answered grimly.

Dr. Cooper ran his hand through his wild hair. "Allies? What kind of allies could they be waiting for that would warrant letting us finish our defenses?"

"I don't know," Mike said, "but we have a more pressing issue."

Ambrosar chuckled. "What could be more pressing than an army o' unknown strength that is seeking yer destruction?"

"Giants," Mike answered simply. "An entire fortress full of giants near the airport."

"So, it be true then," King Varnir smiled almost eagerly.

Liz looked confused. "You knew?"

"Err...yes," Dr. Cooper answered quickly. "Not long after you set out yesterday we received a report that a mysterious fortress had appeared beyond the airport. The scouts were unable to see inside or tell us anything other than the impossible scale of the thing. But just this morning a giant was spotted on the edge of the airfield."

Mike found it hard to believe that they had only left yesterday. So much had happened in such a short amount of time that Mike hadn't yet had time to process it all.

General Adams leaned forward. "Now that we know there is in fact a giant castle dangerously close to the airport, we must act."

King Varnir chuckled. "And what would ye have us do? March out there and fight 'em?"

"If that is what it takes," General Adams replied.

King Varnir shook his head. "Attacking a giant fortress be suicide."

"So, what would your Highness suggest?" the diminutive Lady of the Appledoves asked.

"Simple," the dwarf king answered the small sorceress. "We wait fer 'em ter come ter us."

General Adams shook his head. "Unfortunately, my troops are spread thin as it is, leaving the airbase just lightly defended. It is far too valuable to just let these giants take." The general looked at each person around the table. "We cannot wait. We should attack at once."

The dwarf prince snorted. "Then ye will die."

"Me son speaks the truth," King Varnir added. "Trust us. We dwarves have been at war with the stinkin' giants fer centuries. We have learned that giants be immensely strong and fast, but they be also rather dull. They rely too much on their sheer strength ter overpower their enemies. That be how we defeat 'em."

"And how exactly is that?" General Adams pressed.

Brokkr tapped his forehead with a thick finger. "By outsmartin' 'em."

"How many of these giants are there?" asked the general.

The dwarf prince shrugged. "Several dozen that we could see at least. I would guess by the size o' the fortress that there could be over a hunnerd o' the smelly buggers."

"A hundred giants..." General Adams breathed. "What I would give for a single Raptor or even a Super Hornet..."

"But we have none of those things," Dr. Cooper said. "None of our calls for aid have been answered and our Air Force Reserve Base is only a resupply wing. We only have a few fuel tankers and support craft." The doctor thought a moment. "We could use the two attack helicopters?"

General Adams shook his head. "No. I won't take the gunships away from the city. They are too important to our defenses. If something were to attack us,... we will have to assault them by land only."

"You are forgetting something," Galina suddenly spoke up and Mike was surprised. He had almost forgotten that she had followed them down here. She had remained quiet most of the time.

"And what is that my dear?" Braelynn asked gently.

"There are nephilim banners on the fortress," Galina explained. "There may be more than just regular giants in there."

"Then we will destroy them as well," General Adams replied quickly.

Ambrosar laughed. "Are ye seriously still considering attacking the giants and possibly nephilim? The last time the dwarves encountered a nephilim it be said that it took a team o' Wardens ter finally take it down. And the Wardens be no more. What makes ye think that ye have a chance o' killin a demigod?"

"I don't see how we have much choice," General Adams replied grimly. "If we leave them there, they will assuredly destroy our airport and everything between here and there. I can't let that happen."

"Besides," Dr. Cooper added. "We have a few things you dwarves don't."

"And what be that?" rumbled Brokkr.

General Adams grinned. "Guns."

"And magic," Talsin added.

"With our firearms, the elves magic, and your knowledge of giants, we should be able to destroy them easily," Dr. Cooper said excitedly.

"I have a few Abrams tanks at my command plus other AFV's." General Adams said. "I can pull a company off the wall, and then if we can scrounge up a few hundred volunteers we can take this fortress."

"The Battlemages will join you," Gwydion announced.

"And any elf that wishes to volunteer may do so," Talsin added, and General Adams nodded his thanks.

"Bah!" King Varnir snorted. "Ye'll get yerselves killed if ye go out there." The dwarf king shook his head regretfully. "But it can no be said that the dwarves sat back as their allies marched ter war. So as much as I disagree with this foolish course o' action, I will dispatch a clan ter aid ye." He let out a deep breath. "And I be sure there will be more than a few volunteers fer this suicide mission."

"Wonderful!" General Adams said. "Together we are sure to crush these giants." The elves all nodded their agreement, but the dwarf king snorted derisively.

"It will take time to spread the word and get all the volunteers together," Braelynn said.

Dr. Cooper nodded. "And even more to gather all the transports and supplies that we will need."

"Luckily, it will take less than half an hour to reach this fortress by truck," General Adams smiled. "We can march in the morning, destroy them, and be back before dinner."

Eitri chuckled darkly. "Wishful thinkin', human."

The general ignored him. "We will pass the word for volunteers starting immediately. We have no time to waste," he announced. "Tomorrow at dawn we march."

CHAPTER 23

The weary Heroes of Awesome exited the dwarf halls beneath Mt. Washington a short time later as the commanders remained below to finalize their battle plans that would continue late into the day.

By the time the Heroes reached the Cathedral of Learning, word had somehow spread about the coming battle and volunteers were already lining up to join tomorrow's campaign.

"Well, that was fast," Emily muttered at all the activity.

They made their way through the multitudes of volunteers and pushed towards the cafeteria. Instead of getting thinner the farther away from the recruiting areas, the crowd actually got thicker.

Up ahead of them near the cafeteria doors, a man could be seen standing up on a crate speaking to the gathering. He wore a long, white robe trimmed in royal blue and was preaching something to an eager crowd.

"What's going on?" Jack growled, as he forced his way through the press of bodies.

"Good question," Mike grunted, as he bulled his way into the crowd to a chorus of complaints.

The grumbling grew louder as Mike and Jack led the way through the press toward their destination. As they drew closer to the speaker, they could hear what was being said.

"It is time to cast off our burdens of religious dogma and accept the new truth, the Universal Truth!" the robed man shouted to the masses. "Before we were fragmented and broken, forced to cobble together what truths we could and try to make sense of them. From those fragments religions were formed, and although they were meant to uplift and guide us, they have done little but cause war and death!"

Angry shouts bubbled up from the crowd.

"It is true!" the robed man shouted back. "How many wars have been fought over religion? How many have died to prove their religion is superior to all others? How many atrocities committed in the name of faith?" The cries of denial quieted as the robed man continued.

"Now is not the time for faith! Now is the time for Truth!" he proclaimed grandly. "All religions have been proven to be wrong! The ancient gods of antiquity have come back with their followers, our new friends the elves and dwarves. Their gods bless and answer their prayers! The truth of their existence cannot be denied!"

A few angry mutterings arose from those gathered, but not as strongly as before.

"But all religions have also been proven right! For all of the human faithful have also been given miraculous power. The proof is all around us! All religions are right, and all are wrong! Only by combining the fragments of religion can we piece together the whole and Final Truth!"

Liz snorted as they pushed beyond the speaker. "What a load of crap."

Mike shrugged. "Kinda makes sense to me."

"You can't be serious?" Liz growled. "That clown was wrong on so many levels I can't even begin to correct him."

"He did make a good point," Ted added. "The elves and dwarves both worship different gods and their clerics are just as efficient. It does beg the question."

Liz rolled her eyes. "The answer is simple. The elves and dwarves heal using their natural powers. They were trained to use their healing ability through prayer, so they associate it with their chosen deity."

"That argument could be applied to you as well," Ted noted. "We have no proof that God is responsible for your healing powers. It could very well be that you simply have that gift, much like my own spellcasting."

"If you could feel the power of prayer like I do, then you wouldn't be saying that," Liz replied sharply. "It does not come from within. I am just a conduit for God's power."

"I agree with Liz," Jack said suddenly. "That guy was an idiot."

"Thank you," Liz smiled at him.

Jack laughed. "He is wrong because there is no God or gods at all. It is like you said, just magic and people's own natural abilities."

"Ever the atheist," Liz sighed.

They finally pushed through the last of the onlookers and reached the cafeteria doors. Mike thought better of arguing, and let the matter drop as he went inside. But he could see that the robed man's words had affected everyone. *Was he right? Or was he just another in the long line of false prophets?*

Mike didn't know the answer and as he entered the cafeteria all thoughts of religion were forced from his mind. The smell of cooking food greeted him and he suddenly realized how long it had been since he had had a proper meal. The gods could wait; right now, it was time to eat!

A short time later, they were all seated around a table enjoying a much-needed meal. It was rather quiet inside the cafeteria with everyone either signing up for the campaign or just outside listening to the speaker.

"I can't believe anyone would actually *want* to volunteer for a battle," Liz mused over her steak. "Who would do that?"

Mike and Jack guiltily raised their hands, and Liz rolled her eyes and laughed. "Of course, you two would."

"I would much rather go out there and kill them before they come here and kill any innocent people," Jack replied.

"I'm with him," Mike nodded, and swallowed a mouthful of hamburger. "Best to kill them first and as far away from our homes as possible."

"I guess I can agree with that," Liz said thoughtfully.

"Some people probably want to finally try out their powers in combat,"

Ted added. "Actually, using them against an enemy would appeal to a lot of folks. Besides that, the mages have been pushing battle magic from day one. It will be a good test."

"Unless you all die," Emily muttered.

Jack looked at her funny. "You aren't coming?"

"Oh, I'm going," Emily replied, "but I won't be doing any dying."

They all shared a laugh at that. "Nobody plans on dying," Jack chuckled, "and there won't be any trees around for you to jump into."

Emily waived the comment away. "I won't need any trees. If things get ugly, I'll just turn myself into a bird and fly away."

Jack choked on his food. "You can do that?" he sputtered.

Emily grinned wickedly at him. "Wouldn't you like to know?"

Mike took the last bite of his burger and leaned back contentedly. "Ahh, that's better," he sighed, patting his stomach. "Now, it's time to get to work."

"What work?" Liz asked.

"My armor needs fixing after the beating it took in the camp," Mike explained, as he pointed to a few large dents in his breastplate. "That and I need to tell Nadal the good news that we don't have to practice runes in secret anymore."

"You what?" Liz asked in shock.

"Since when?" Emily asked at the same time.

Jack only laughed and Ted continued eating without so much as a blink. Liz saw the lack of reaction and rounded on Ted. "You knew?"

Ted shrugged. "I suspected. No dwarf would make such ugly runes as Mike has on his armor."

"Hey now!" Mike protested. "They aren't ugly."

"No," Ted laughed, "they just look like a crying baby carved them with a plastic spoon."

Mike suddenly stood and picked his tray up. "Well, just for that I'm leaving," he huffed with a slight grin. "I need to go sharpen my spoon."

Ted laughed and stood as well. "I'm coming along, too. I have a few projects of my own I would like to tinker with before we leave again."

Together Mike and Ted put their trays back and then headed for the door.

"You just go beat your metal," Jack shouted after them. "I'm sure you can give each other a hand."

Without turning around, Mike and Ted both gave Jack a one-fingered salute before going out the door.

A few minutes later, Emily finished her salad and stood as well. "I think I'm gonna go try out my new toy," she said, as she patted her new quiver.

"Mind if I tag along? Liz asked.

"Nope," Emily replied with a smile. "What about you Jack?"

Jack shook his head. "Nah. I think I'm going to get seconds. Been pretty hungry lately. Besides, I got other things to do before tomorrow."

Emily and Liz put their trays back. "Whatever you say," Emily said sweetly. "But if you change your mind, we will be at the archery ranges."

Jack smiled. "Of course."

Liz and Emily waved as they left him alone at the table.

Jack's smile faded as the door closed behind them.

****

It was a bit of a walk to the archery ranges, but Emily was glad for the exercise. She usually felt sluggish after eating, so it was good to be up and moving. The sky was still overcast and grey as the sun began its descent, but that was fine with her. Her pale skin didn't like the sun anyways. The last thing she needed was a sunburn.

The range was surprisingly busy for so late in the afternoon. Emily guessed it was everyone trying to get in that last bit of practice before the attack tomorrow and she couldn't blame them. For many, it would be their first real battle and unfortunately for some, also their last.

"We could just go someplace else," Emily said, when they found all the stations in use.

But Liz shook her head. "No. We can just wait for one. I'm sure it won't take long," Emily chaffed at the delay, but she reminded herself that there really wasn't any hurry.

It turned out that they had to wait a lot longer than either of them would have liked. The sun was dropping rapidly and they barely had a few hours of daylight left by the time they found an open booth.

"I told you we should have just gone someplace else." Emily moaned, as she drew her first silvery arrow from the elaborate quiver.

"We have plenty of time," Liz chided with a grin. "Stop your whining."

"But I like to whine," Emily laughed, as she released the silvery arrow from her compound bow with a soft twang.

The arrow struck true and before it had stopped quivering a second and third followed it. Emily fired as fast as she could and soon there was only one arrow left in the quiver. She drew and fired. "So much for endless," Emily muttered. But when she looked down in the quiver she found another arrow.

She fired that one and when she looked down again there was still one more arrow left. Emily drew and fired as fast as she could, but there was always one arrow left in the quiver.

"That's a neat trick," Liz whistled, as Emily was a blur as she tried unsuccessfully to completely empty the quiver.

Breathing heavily, Emily finally set the bow down as the sun began to set, with one arrow still in the quiver. "I guess it really is endless," she gasped.

"My turn?" Liz asked and Emily set the bow and the now-full quiver down and waved her forward breathlessly.

Liz wasn't nearly as fast on the draw as Emily, but she still fired at a rapid pace. However, there was always one arrow left.

With the light failing, Liz finally set the quiver down. "That is amazing. I need to get something like this for my rifle."

"Endless bullets would be nice." Emily agreed. "But you heard what the Archmage said. Even he doesn't know how they made the quiver."

"Well, he needs to hurry up and figure it out." Liz muttered.

Emily smiled as the two of them gathered up their things and left the range as the sun began to set. The sky was painted in brilliant streaks of orange, red, and pink as the two of them strolled down the forested trail leading away from the range and back toward the Cathedral.

They were half way across a small bridge that spanned a tiny stream when Emily suddenly stopped. "Do you think we'll win tomorrow?" Emily abruptly asked, looking out over the railing.

Liz joined her along the rail. "I hope so. The dwarves seem to know how to beat them and they will be with us."

"Yeah I guess..." Emily muttered. "But they said we should wait for the giants to come to us... we didn't listen to them there."

Liz didn't have an answer for that.

"No point in dwelling on it," she said instead. "The elves and their magic will take care of any surprises. And you are forgetting all the people that have powers. It won't be just a bunch of regular humans versus giants."

Emily took a deep breath. "I suppose you're right... I just don't like the idea of attacking a castle full of giants I guess..."

Liz's soft laughter chimed through the surrounding trees. "I can't say I'm a huge fan of the plan either."

"I just have this bad feeling about tomorrow," Emily admitted. "Something is going to happen to us."

"Its just nerves," Liz tried to reassure her. "It's normal to be afraid before a battle."

"I'm not afraid," Emily insisted. "I just have a bad feeling... it's like... it's like some huge darkness is slowly creeping up on us."

Liz put her arm around Emily's slender shoulders. "Everything will be fine. You just need something to take your mind off it."

"You know what..." Emily suddenly grinned. "You are exactly right. And I have just the thing!" A mischievous glint entered her eyes. "I think I'll pay Jack a visit tonight."

"You're not serious," Liz groaned light heartedly.

"Hey," Emily shrugged innocently, "a girl has needs."

"You *always* have needs," Liz laughed.

"And you should take a lesson," Emily teased. "Stop being such a prude and live a little. You never know when it will be your last chance."

"I would go find Mike," Emily mused. "He is a lot of man…" Emily elbowed Liz playfully, "but I've seen the way he looks at you. I don't think I have a chance."

"Oh, stop it," Liz laughed. "He does not."

"He does," Emily insisted, "and you are blind if you don't see it. If he looked at me like that just once, I would be on him so fast…" she grinned wickedly. "You better make a move before I do."

Liz shook her head. "You are impossible."

"Maybe," Emily grinned, "but I have fun."

She pushed herself from the railing. "Jack is in for a pleasant surprise tonight… and into the morning if I have my way." She laughed and started walking away, but Liz didn't move. Instead she continued to stare out over the bridge as Emily strolled away.

"Don't wait too long," Emily shouted back over her shoulder. "He might not be there when you finally realize what you want."

Liz leaned against the wooden railing, staring out into the gathering gloom, lost in thought as the darkness slowly crept in around her.

CHAPTER 24

The morning arrived dark and gloomy, and below the churning sky an impromptu army gathered around the Point. Dozens of troop transports lined the streets as humans, elves, and dwarves scrambled into them.

"It better not rain," Mike grumbled, as he looked out of one of the transports and up at the oppressive canopy.

"Of course, it will rain," Ted chuckled across from him. "Like any good DM knows, you can't go fight a bunch of giants in an evil castle without it raining."

Emily rolled her eyes next to Ted. "There is no rule that says it has to rain," she chided. "Besides, it could clear up before we get there," she added hopefully.

"I sure hope not," Ted mused, watching the low clouds slide by. "It would ruin the mood."

Mike, Ted, Liz, and Emily were crammed into the back of one of the numerous transport trucks with other human volunteers. A few armored personnel carriers were scattered about the staging area, but the majority of recruits were squeezed into the average heavy truck.

There was standing room only in the back of the transport as Mike shifted to try and make a little more room for Liz who was pressed tight against him. Not that he was complaining, but he didn't want her hurting herself from banging against his hastily repaired armor should they hit a bump in the road.

Mike's armor had a few new runes scribed into the dented metal and the worst of the damage had been beaten out of the heavy plate. He had chosen to forgo a helmet. Mike disliked helmets; they were hot, heavy, and limited his vision.

He hoped that he wouldn't regret that decision.

Next to Mike, Liz wore her new dragon skin cloak that had taken on the appearance of a black leather jacket. Across from them, Ted was half armored in sculpted, elvish plate underneath his long lab coat. Emily was in her usual; leather corset, mini-skirt, and black fedora, but now the beautiful enchanted quiver hung at her slender waist.

"Where is Jack?" Mike muttered, as he searched the hustling throng around them. "We should be leaving soon."

As if his words were prophecy, a trumpet sounded in the distance, announcing the order to move out. The trucks all suddenly rumbled to life and filled the air with a low growl.

Somewhere the first truck began moving and the line began to inch forward, slowly at first but picking up speed, one truck at a time. It was like watching some giant spring unravel. Their truck shuddered as the driver pressed the gas and the transport began to creep forward.

Then out of the surrounding crowd of onlookers, a soldier appeared, dressed in dark combat fatigues and black orcish armor with a long katana strapped to his back.

"Jack!" Mike shouted and waved. Jack saw them and quickly rushed to the truck as it pulled away. Jack reached out, and Mike and Ted hauled him in just in time. The transport lurched ahead as it suddenly picked up speed and rumbled down the road.

"You look like hell," Mike noted from Jack's bloodshot eyes and scruffy appearance. "Didn't you get any sleep last night?" he asked, and Emily sniggered wickedly.

The makeshift army reached the airport less than twenty minutes later. The elves, dwarves, and humans quickly deployed across the runway and formed into one large, combined force. General Adams sat atop one of the four M1A2 Abrams tanks that he had pulled from the city defenses.

Elf scouts were sent to survey the area as the rest of the army positioned itself along the empty runway.

A short time later the scouts returned and reported no sign of any giants outside the twisted fortress. With the dark monstrosity stabbing the sky in the distance, General Adams and his four tanks led the way with the allied army drudging along behind.

The tanks drove four abreast as they plowed a path through the small trees and brush that stood in their way. The path blazed by the tanks made it easier for Mike and the others on foot to follow the general.

The sky grew darker as the army traversed the low hills and swung wide around until they were finally positioned at the front of the castle and climbed the last peak.

There before them, jutting out of the bottomless pit in the center of the valley like a colossal splinter from hell was the giants' twisted fortress.

The general called a stop at the crest of the hill and more scouts were sent out as the rag-tag army quickly fanned out in front of the main battle tanks.

The two hundred or so heavily armored Rockfist Clan dwarves formed ranks first, locking shields and creating a solid wall of dark steel, sharp blades, and bushy beards. Behind them in a large mass were the human, elf, and dwarf volunteers. A few companies of Scadian Knights were also in attendance, making up the backbone of the volunteer forces. Bringing up the rear were ranks of Army soldiers and elven archers.

Spears bristled from two groups of elven hoplites that formed a tight phalanx that flanked the central force. Battlemages and clerics were scattered throughout the entire army to provide unified support across the whole line.

Liz wished her friends good luck before she joined a squad of Marine Snipers that positioned themselves in a heavy clump of brush along the ridge.

As an official member of the Battlemages, Ted was dispersed along the line with all the other mages.

With a wink, Emily fell back and took up position with the other archers. That left Mike and Jack in the central mass of volunteers. Somehow the two of them found themselves not only in the center of the formation, but also near the front, just a few rows behind the dwarf line.

"Next time I get to pick where we stand." Mike grumbled, when he realized where they were.

"Don't lie to me," Jack smiled wolfishly. "I know you like being right in the center of it."

Mike couldn't hold back a sly grin of his own.

Jack scratched his scruffy chin stubble. "Ever wonder why the girls always get to stay back and safely shoot from a distance while we have to be on the front lines?"

"Probably because they are smarter than we are," Mike chuckled.

A dwarf lord gave the signal and the dwarf line moved forward in unison with the rest of the allied forces following behind. The battle tanks drove half way down the hill and stopped, but the rest of the strike force, including the armored vehicles, continued toward the massive fortress.

The army was half way across the field when the immense drawbridge rattled to life and suddenly began to lower.

"Seems the dwarves were right," Jack muttered. "Those bloody giants will come out to get us."

Mike grunted his agreement, but wasn't really paying attention; instead he was focused on the dark clouds churning above the castle. "Is it just me or are those clouds getting darker?" Mike asked to no one in particular.

Jack laughed at his friend's concern. "Of course it's getting darker. It's called a storm. It's what they do."

He was right, but Mike still didn't like the way they seemed to swirl above the twisted castle. Mike smiled to himself. *I've read too many fantasy stories.* Putting the clouds out of his mind, Mike focused on the upcoming battle just as the towering draw bridge crashed into place to span the endless pit.

The Rockfist lord finally called a halt a mere hundred yards away from the towering entrance.

The army held its breath as they all waited for the massive gates to open and their enemy to come charging out.

After several minutes, nothing happened and the gate remained closed.

"Come on…" Jack's trigger finger twitched anxiously. "What are those smelly bastards waiting for?"

"Aye," a grey-bearded dwarf answered next to him. "Mayhaps we can nudge em a bit eh?" The old dwarf pulled out a battered war horn and winked before putting it to his lips.

"Wait, no-" Jack started to say, but it was too late. A deep call echoed through the hills as the old dwarf blew a long note on his battered horn.

As the note faded, Mike and the rest of the army anticipated the onslaught that must surely come.

But after several moments, the massive gate remained closed and they realized that no giants were going to come charging out at them.

"Odin's breath," the old dwarf cursed. "A giant can no resist the chance ter fight dwarves," the greybeard said in wonder. "There must be somethin' awful important behind them walls."

Another dwarf, this one in the heavy rune armor and brow studs that marked him as some kind of Rune Priest, nodded. "Ye may be on ter somethin' there." The Rune Priest raised a heavily gilded hammer above his head and shouted. "If these buggers won't come out, then we'll go in and git em!"

A raucous cheer erupted from the throats of the gathered dwarves. As the dwarves cheered, the Rune Priest raised his hammer and began to chant. It was soft at first, but grew louder. Other Rune Priests also raised their hammers and joined their voices with his. As the cheering subsided, more dwarves joined in the deep, hypnotizing chant.

As one, all the Rune Priests made the same slow motions in time with the pulsing chant. The air began to shimmer before each of them and soon brightly glowing runes appeared in front across the allied line. The hovering runes grew brighter as the chant grew ever louder.

The air thrummed with power and the runes blazed like suns before each of the Rune Priests. Suddenly, the chant reached a glorious crescendo and the Rune Priests shouted the last word as they all swung their hammers in unison into the brilliant runes.

The floating runes exploded in a dazzling release of powerful, crackling energies and a thunderous clang split the air as if a thousand bells had all been stuck at once.

The air vibrated with the powerful ringing and to everyone's shock and horror the stone figures in the titanic walls suddenly began to move. The bodies twisted in agony and the faces screamed wordlessly in the throes of some unknown torment.

Cracks split a number of the lewd figures and some of them crumbled under the vibrations' onslaught. Massive stone bodies fragmented and broke loose from the cliff-like walls to tumble into the endless pit below.

When the ringing finally ended, the towering black stone walls still stood. A few scars marked where tortured figures had broken away, but overall the fortress remained untouched.

"Loki's Balls," the Rune Priest breathed in awe. "Nothin' made by giants could withstand so many Runes o' Breaking."

A tall elf in silvery chainmail under a white tabard scoffed. "It may be that your precious runes are not as powerful as you would have us believe."

The Rune Priest's face turned red and then purple, but his voice was deathly cold. "Or mayhaps there be a darker power at work here." The dwarf struggled to keep his anger in check. "Ye think ye *mages* can do any better?"

The elf Battlemage's laughter was a light chiming sound. He raised his slender staff and shouted for all to hear. "Battlemages! Let us show these dwarves how the elves make war!"

The entire host of elves cheered wildly and an abrupt wave of destructive magics were unleashed upon the twisted fortress. The display was truly awe-inspiring and terrifying. Fireballs, lightning, arcane bolts, beams of power, globs of acid, and all manner of sorcery slammed into the immense gate. Explosions detonated along its black length, obscuring much of the barrier as more and more spells ripped into it.

The majority of the spells were concentrated on the gate itself and the towering doors vanished as powerful incantations hammered into them. Smoke and debris filled the air, further obscuring the wall.

The dazzling display slowly ended as the Battlemages ceased their barrage to inspect their handy work.

As the smoke cleared, the elves were shocked; the gate and walls still stood. Nearly all the figures in the walls had been seared away along with several large gouges torn into the dark stone, but even the magical might of the elves had proven insufficient against the giants' twisted fortress.

The Battlemage lowered his staff in disbelief. "It cannot be…"

"Heh," the Rune Priest snorted derisively. "So much fer the way ye elves make war."

Before the Battlemage could reply, an Army commander spoke up. "It was a valiant attempt by both dwarves and elves," he shouted, "but now it is *our* turn."

The commander said something into his radio.

The Battlemage laughed. "Surely you commanders do not think that your human *technology* will have any success where our spells did not?"

His answer came a moment later when the four M1A2-Abrams main battle tanks unleashed hell.

The roar of their cannons was deafening and the ground shook with the force of their concussions. Columns of fire billowed from the long barrels as the 120-mm rounds came screaming out.

A fraction of a second later, the colossal gate that had withstood both the dwarven runes and the elven spells exploded in a shower of wood and twisted metal.

The gathered humans punched the air and cheered wildly as the huge doors were obliterated. "That's how *we* do it!" the Army commander shouted proudly.

The elves and dwarves stared in shock at the destruction wrought by the battle tanks.

The Rune Priest stared open-mouthed at the billowing cloud of smoke where the impenetrable doors had stood only moments before. "I've got ta get me one o' those," he mumbled in awe.

The celebration was cut short when horrible cries and eerie baying were issued from beyond the shattered opening. The smoke still swirled around the gaping hole when suddenly a horde of screaming demons burst through the ruined gate.

CHAPTER 25

The creatures that charged through the smoke were not at all what the allies had expected. Instead of the towering giants, these monsters were of varying sizes and shapes. Some were as small as goblins while others could have challenged a giant in height. They were red-skinned and covered in coarse, black hair. Each of the creatures had the legs and head of a goat with a long, forked tail.

"What the hell are those things?" Ted wondered aloud.

"Those are Fomorians; half-demons in the service of Baphomet," a nearby elf answered grimly. "Each was once a mortal being, but they were damned when they pledged their souls to the Goat of Mendes."

One of the tanks roared to life and fired into the charging demon host, vaporizing a dozen of the red-skinned beasts.

"Paladins and Guardians to the fore!" one of the dwarf lords bellowed.

The allies reacted immediately as the dwarf Guardians, elf Paladins, and any human with the powers of either moved forward to stand right behind the dwarf shield wall as another 120-mm round pulverized more Fomorians.

Ted noticed that the tank operators were alternating shots and were being careful to not hit the bridge. Instead, they focused on the ruined gate so that many of the demons were destroyed before they could set foot on the long drawbridge. So instead of a continuous stream of Fomorians, they were broken up as groups made it through between shots.

"How do you know what they are?" Ted shouted over the thunder of the tanks and the screams of the goat-headed demons.

"Because I have faced such creatures before," the elf mage shouted back. "On this very world actually, near four thousand years ago it was."

Ted's jaw dropped open. Four thousand years ago? He must have heard wrong.

An ugly little dwarf with a long spear spat between them. "I dun care what they be," he growled. "I just needs ter know how ta kill 'em."

The first wave of hooting Fomorians reached the other side of the bridge and charged across the open field toward the allied army.

"Blessed weapons work best," the elf shouted. "They are tough, with thick skin, incredible endurance, and a vicious attitude, but they die just like any other living thing."

The ugly dwarf grinned with crooked yellow teeth. "Sos if I poke 'em all full o' holes they die?"

The elf mage sighed. "Yes. Poke them full of holes and they will die."

The Fomorians screamed and howled madly as they rushed across the field, tearing gouges in the soft earth with their sharp hooves.

A fat dwarf with a bushy, black beard streaked with grey shook his head. "It be unlike giants ter use lesser creatures fer their dirty work," he grumbled darkly.

Somewhere an elf shouted an order and the archers knocked their arrows. Another shout and the air thrummed as arrows soared through the air. They fell with amazing accuracy among the charging demons, dropping them by the score. But there were just too many. Even after the horrendous losses, the remaining Fomorians drove onward with reckless abandon.

The first pack of demons was nearly upon them when the order was given. A storm of hot lead erupted from the barrels of the soldiers and the hills rang with their thunderous retorts.

Fomorians were cut down in great swathes as the hail of bullets punched through them. Within moments, the first wave of demons was cut down, leaving a pile of red-skinned bodies scattered across the bloody field.

The elves launched volley after volley of arrows into the clusters of demons, thinning their numbers as they came relentlessly on. Once they were close enough, the human soldiers took over cutting down the last demons with organized bursts of controlled gunfire.

Between the tanks, arrows, and guns, the Fomorians were being slaughtered in droves. A few of the larger beasts got close, but even the giant ones fell short.

When the tide of demons finally began to slow, the allied army was ordered forward. An eerie silence fell as the main battle tanks finally ceased their bombardment. The allied army made slow progress across the bloody field as they trudged over rotting corpses that were filling the air with a foul stench as their twisted bodies decomposed far more rapidly than was natural.

Ted pinched his nose closed with his free hand as he used his poleaxe to carefully pick his way through a pile of putrefying corpses. All around him men and elves stopped and were forced to empty their stomachs as the cloying aroma overwhelmed their senses. The dwarves, however, didn't seem to notice the smell at all, plowing through the carpet of corpses as if it were an everyday experience.

Which it may have been for some of them, Ted mused.

The allies crossed the slaughter ground and arrived at the huge drawbridge. To Ted's surprise it remained down, as if inviting them inside. Still unable to see inside the fortress with the chocking clouds of dust and smoke, and not waiting for the giants to change their minds, the commanders ordered the allied army across.

The allies were forced to form into a long column to fit across the bridge with the dwarves first, an elven phalanx close behind, and then the armored vehicles lined up single file down the center, flanked by the mass of volunteers with another elven phalanx bringing up the rear.

They were halfway across the long drawbridge when maniacal laughter suddenly bubbled up from the endless pit below them.

Those individuals near the edge cautiously leaned over the side and peered into the consuming blackness underneath.

A woman shouted and was suddenly pulled from her feet and tumbled into the pit. Her screams faded as she vanished into the dark oblivion.

Movement exploded all around as Fomorians swung themselves up from under the bridge and slashed wildly at the allies. Shouts and gunshots erupted as the demons spilled onto the drawbridge and the battle was joined.

"Push forward!" one of the Army commanders was shouting from his armored transport. "Don't let them trap us!"

Chaos swirled around as more howling demons swung themselves up to join their brethren.

The lead vehicles inched forward as the front lines began moving toward the ruined gate, even as the bulk of the allied forces were still locked in battle with the demons.

Spells arced across the span and blasted demons back into the abyss. Those Fomorians that survived the spells laughed maniacally even as they fell to certain death.

Ted threw fireballs at any demon that got too close, but the allies were crammed so tightly that few Fomorians ever got near him.

"Here they come!" someone shouted, and Ted turned to see a veritable tide of red-skinned Fomorians come pouring out of the ruined gate.

This time, the battle tanks didn't fire. The allied army was too close, so it was up to the soldiers to punch their way through.

Humvees and the other armored vehicles unleashed their machine guns in a thunderous storm of fire and death that tore through the charging demons.

But Fomorians came on relentlessly, and their vast numbers drove them over the bodies of their fallen and into the teeth of the dwarf line. The Rockfist Clan roared gleefully and charged the demons, eager to join the battle at last.

****

The dark clouds swirled above the fortress and Liz watched in horror as the allied forces were being surrounded. She could see the demons hanging under the bridge as they moved closer to the edge and pulled themselves up.

Her MK13 barked and one of the beasts fell into the bottomless pit.

Liz and the other sharpshooters focused their fire on the hanging demons. The monsters dropped like red rain from under the drawbridge as the snipers did their work.

The majority of soldiers and archers were thankfully not on the bridge yet, so they were free to support the embattled allies trapped on the drawbridge.

Flights of arrows soared the length of the bridge and fell in a deadly rain with amazing accuracy on the Fomorians still flowing out of the breach.

In the front of the allied forces, Liz spotted Mike and Jack right where she knew they would be - in the thick of the fight. Mike was surrounded and Jack dueled with a massive demon with several arms. Liz took two shots at the huge creature's head, but the demon didn't even seem to notice. Apparently, its huge skull was too thick for her bullets to penetrate. Hoping that Jack could handle it, she fired a few quick shots to clear some space around them before moving her sight down the besieged line.

Liz tried to find Emily in the mass of archers still waiting to get onto the drawbridge, but she didn't see any sign of her. Hoping that Emily was safe, Liz went back to picking off the Fomorians still hanging under the bridge.

****

An exceptionally deformed Fomorian appeared before Mike. Its lumpy, red body was covered in large warts the color of dried blood. Long streams of snot ran down its goat-like snout as it flailed about with a thick club clenched in its fists.

Mike was engaged with two other beasts as the lumpy one advanced on him. Nearby, Jack was in a duel with a four-armed demon of immense proportions, nearly a giant itself.

Rikr Foerah slammed into the chest of one of the Fomorians and rocketed it backwards. The demon crashed into its comrades like a bowling ball knocking down pins.

Mike spun to face the other demon, but it collapsed at his feet, a hole punched through its ugly head. The lumpy Fomorian charged in, but suddenly buckled as a bullet took it in the eye and it landed beside the other demon.

Two more demons fell with well-placed shots, and Mike looked back at the hill and waved his thanks to Liz. Even though he couldn't see her, Mike was glad she was out there, watching over him, even if he wouldn't admit it.

The press of demons thinned and the line advanced as the Guardians and Paladins made short work of the demons. "Forward!" a dwarf Guardian shouted, and waved his battle hammer above his head. The allies cheered and pressed forward, spells and bullets leading the way.

****

Old Four-Arms was proving to be a better challenge than Jack could have hoped for. Most of these demons were rather unskilled and attacked recklessly, but this giant-of-a-Fomorian was another matter entirely. It had even been unfazed after taking a sniper round to the forehead.

Jack concentrated as Four-Arms slashed at him from four directions at once. He caught the first and second blade with his black soul sword and twisted away from the following two.

A black-bearded dwarf wielding a huge war hammer suddenly slammed his weapon into Four-Arms, but the blubber on the beast absorbed the blow. Dorf Gloinson tried to recover, but the giant Fomorian's blades flashed out and gutted the great weapons instructor. The beast carelessly cast him aside, eager to finish its duel with Jack.

Explosions and war cries mingled with the clash of steel and screams of the dying in a brilliant symphony of battle that sang in Jack's ears.

The song was the most beautiful thing he had ever heard and Jack danced along with it, contributing his own music, as his tamahagane blade was a blur around him.

The giant Fomorian was clearly getting frustrated at being unable to kill this small human that danced around him and that made Jack laugh. But when he heard the order to move forward, Jack knew it was time to end this dance. He was sad it had to end, but truthfully he was growing bored with it. Four-Arms had been a fun challenge for a time, but once Jack realized he could beat the huge demon, some of the fun had left the dance.

It was time to sing the song of death.

Jack called forth the powers held within the Muramasa sword and when Four-Arms' blades descended again, the tamahagane blade cut through the demon's steel like a hot knife through butter. The huge Fomorian's goat-like face screwed up in confusion as it stared at its ruined swords. Jack sprang into action during the beast's confusion and bound up its bloated body. The blade flashed and Four-Arms' head was still looking confused as it fell from his shoulders.

Jack landed lightly on his feet and a moment later the giant body hit the ground with a tremendous crash. The fall of the giant Fomorian was met with a cheer from the surrounding allies and Jack gave an elaborate bow before rejoining his part in the deadly symphony.

****

With the element of surprise lost, the Fomorians were quickly pushed back by spell and blade. The last of the demons still hanging under the bridge were picked off by the snipers and soldiers that had yet to set foot on the titanic drawbridge.

The allied army streamed across the bridge as the Fomorians were pushed back. The mounted machine guns tore through the packed demons that still charged out of the ruined gate and any that survived were quickly cut down by sword and spell.

Emily was impressed at the coordination and discipline of the allied force. The potential for disaster had been huge, but the humans, elves, and dwarves had somehow withstood the surprise assault and not only survived, but were actually routing the demons.

The first row of dwarves reached the foot of the bridge and set foot on the other side just as Emily and the last of the elven archers set foot on the massive drawbridge. The allies drove a bloody path through the demons and pushed into the cavernous gatehouse.

Emily and the archers moved rapidly across the scarred bridge when suddenly a loud grinding sound filled the air above them.

The mammoth chains slowly drew taught and the massive drawbridge shuddered.

"They are going to raise the bridge!" an elf shouted in alarm.

Almost to emphasize the words, the huge drawbridge shuddered again and then shook violently as it broke loose from where it had been resting in the earth and slowly began to rise.

People screamed and rushed for the safety of the gatehouse as the far end of the drawbridge slowly rose.

Emily and most of the allied army were still on the huge bridge as its angle steadily increased. The allies began to slip and slide as they lost their footing on the increasing slope. Some poor souls slid right off the bridge to plunge, screaming, into the blackness below. Some soldiers grabbed onto the vehicles, hoping they would provide some kind of protection, but as the incline grew, the vehicles also began to slide.

The angle was getting dangerously steep and Emily knew she would never make it across in time, so she dropped to her knees and dug her nails into the bridge to try and find purchase. She wasn't sure what good hanging on would do her. The drawbridge would eventually come to a rest against the gatehouse and if she hung on that long it would likely crush her.

Her other option was to let go and take her chances sliding down the bridge, hoping that she didn't slide off into the abyss.

Emily's fingers began to cramp and she knew she wouldn't be able to hold on much longer. She took a deep breath and prepared to let go.

Thunder echoed all around followed by a sudden explosion on the towering gatehouse high above them. Chunks of stone rained down as Emily clung on desperately as another explosion rocked the swaying raise chains.

The next detonation severed the huge raise chain and the drawbridge twisted as the support on one side was cut. The army slid dangerously sideways toward the bottomless pit far below.

A second later, more explosions ripped into the gatehouse, cleaving through the other titanic raise chain.

The drawbridge rocked wildly from the explosion and plummeted back to the ground with a thunderous crash. The allies bounded and tumbled as the huge drawbridge came to a rest across the pit once again.

Emily climbed unsteadily to her feet and looked back across the field. The battle tanks drove through clouds of smoke from their cannons as they barreled down the hill.

"Bout time you showed up," Emily muttered, as she dusted herself off.

Booming roars echoed out of the gatehouse and reverberated through the hills. The allied forces quickly gathered themselves back up and Emily joined them as they hurried to get across the drawbridge.

****

The allied army streamed through the shattered gate and into the cavernous gatehouse to face the unknown.

Liz took one more shot before finally lowering her rifle. The last of the Fomorians in her sight were cut down and the leading units of the army drove boldly forward and vanished into the colossal fortress.

The battle tanks churned across the field and two of them proceeded slowly across the drawbridge while the other two came to a stop and took positions on either side of the bridge.

Liz stood and slung her rifle over her shoulder.

"Where are you going?" Jason asked from behind his AX50 .50 caliber sniper rifle.

"Down there," Liz replied simply. "There is nothing left for us to shoot out here."

Jason shook his head. "But what if somethin' does come out? We need to provide cover incase yinz forces have to escape n'at."

Liz smiled. "Then I'm sure you and your snipers will do a fine job. But I am not about to let everyone else do all the fighting." She turned and started down the hill.

Rustling behind her made her glance back. Other volunteers where picking up their rifles and following her. Glad for the company, Liz hurriedly continued her descent, not wanting to waste any more time. Even if she didn't do any fighting, she was sure people down there could use her healing ability. If she could save even one life, then the risk was worth it.

Under the stormy sky, Liz and a handful of other sharpshooters marched toward the unknown with roars and gunshots punctuated with sharp explosions echoing from inside the twisted fortress.

CHAPTER 26

It was dark inside the cavernous gatehouse as Mike and Jack marched beside the front line of dwarves and carved through the demons, killing any Fomorian that was unfortunate enough to get in their way.

The demons proved to be no match for the combined might of the humans, elves, and dwarves. The allied forces fanned out as they emerged into the expansive bailey on the other side of the towering gatehouse, pushing the demons before them.

Mike was in awe at the sheer scale of the fortress. The bailey they entered was enormous. He guessed that you could fit several football fields comfortably inside the towering curtain walls. Tall, twisted spires that looked like massive dagger blades stabbed up into the sky at seemingly random intervals all across the courtyard.

But there was something amiss and it took Mike a moment to realize what it was.

Besides the last few demons, the huge fortress was empty. There wasn't a single giant anywhere in sight.

Mike was still wondering at the purpose of the strange, bladed spires when the last Fomorian was struck down and a sudden, eerie quiet descended over the army.

The only sound was the rumbling squeal of the two Abrams tanks as they entered the expansive bailey. The ragtag army stopped and at first looked around in confusion, but then eyed the bare battlements suspiciously.

An unsettling howl arose as a hot breeze gusted through the bailey and whistled through the haunting forest of blades. The allied forces shifted uneasily and milled around, fingering their weapons nervously.

"I thought they said there would be giants in here?" one of the elves grumbled.

"They be here all right," a dwarf rumbled, and glared around as if daring a giant to come out. "I can still smell 'em."

The elf wrinkled his slender nose. "Is that what that smell is? Here I thought it was you."

The conversation was interrupted as General Adams and his two tanks rolled up through the center and the army parted before him.

"We press on!" General Adams shouted. "Form a circle around me!" he commanded as the tanks rolled onward. "We are going to take that keep!"

The allied forces cheered as they formed up around their commander and began their advance through the sprawling bailey, weaving their way through the sharp spikes.

Mike found himself and Jack in the company of one of the Scadian mercenary companies on the leading edge of the circular formation. Jack's black sword was sheathed on his back and he had his rifle in hand, scanning their surroundings with a critical eye.

The army churned over the rocky ground and picked their way carefully through the large courtyard. Everyone was on alert for any signs of movement, but they trudged on without a hint of life around them. It was as if they were the sole survivors on a scarred, alien world.

Mike smiled at the thought. In some ways that was exactly what they were, assuming of course, that this fortress didn't originate on Earth.

"Where are they?" one of the Scadian mercenaries muttered, and his eyes darted about nervously. "I feel like we are walking into a trap."

Mike couldn't help but laugh. "We probably are," he chuckled, "but maybe they are thinking twice about attacking since we completely owned their ugly little minions!"

"Hells yeah, we did!" Jack hooted and gave Mike a high five.

The mercenary looked at Mike and Jack as if they were both crazy. Mike grinned. Maybe they were.

The allied army eventually reached the center of the bailey, and as they did the wind picked up and began to howl through the spires once again.

Mike noticed that the howl was growing higher in pitch until it sounded unnervingly like screaming. The wind grew stronger and dust began to swirl around them.

"Well, this doesn't look good," Jack quipped, as the unnatural storm grew more intense.

"Ten bucks says something evil is going to show up," Mike shouted over the wind. "Probably through some kind of portal or something."

"Nope," Jack shouted over the howling wind. "This storm is going to get worse until it cuts us to bloody ribbons."

The allies trudged on, pushing through the growing dust storm as the wind screamed through the bladed spires. It seemed that Jack's prediction would be proven right as the flying dirt and stones pelted the beleaguered forces.

Mike kept his shield up to protect his face from the worst of the flying stones. He peeked over the edge so he could still see until a large fragment skipped over the top of the shield and cracked into the top of his head. "Ow!" Mike grunted, and quickly ducked completely behind the shield. He rubbed the sore spot vigorously as Jack laughed.

Jack tapped his black army helmet smartly. "Bet you wish you had a helmet now."

Mike stopped rubbing his head and snorted. "I've got a plan for that."

"Fat lot of good it's doing you now," Jack chuckled as stones pelted them.

The wind picked up even more and the scream became an almost ear-piercing shriek. The dust and stones whizzed dangerously through the air, forcing the army to pack together and to slow to a crawl.

Sounds like ripping cloth and tearing metal suddenly split the air all around them. Flickering points of light appeared all across the bailey and the ripping sound continued, as the points grew ever larger. The swirling debris abruptly changed direction and flew toward the growing points of light and were sucked into the pulsing openings.

Hellish red light throbbed around the frayed edges of the openings while inside was complete and utter blackness. The horrible tearing faded as the rents finally stopped expanding.

The allies froze, clumped together near the center of the bailey, waiting for what would happen next.

They didn't have to wait long.

Roars and howls of delight rang from inside the black fissures. Moments later, the first red-skinned Fomorian leapt from the blackness and landed on the rough ground.

Demons began pouring out of the portals and the Battlemages were the first to react, launching devastating spells in all directions, trying to staunch the flow of Fomorians.

Mike held out his hand and Jack grumbled as he dug around in his pocket before slapping a few bills into Mike's outstretched hand.

"You play too many video games," Jack muttered.

A horribly deformed Fomorian with several arms of different lengths and three legs fell out of the nearest portal. It looked up and saw the humans and grinned. Long fangs filled its too-wide mouth and green saliva dibbled down its chin.

The demon roared in glee and the ground shook with its heavy footfalls. More Fomorians tumbled out of the rift behind it and joined in the charge.

The deformed demon saw Mike and bellowed something in a guttural language that Mike didn't recognize. But Mike knew a challenge when he heard one.

Mike raised his shield and braced himself as the deformed Fomorian threw itself at him.

****

Liz and the other stragglers that had followed the battle tanks into the fortress brought up the rear of the formation. She pushed her way through the tightly packed forces as the wind began to howl, searching for her friends. But when the evil portals began spewing demons, Liz quickly joined the nearest group of soldiers and added her rifle to theirs.

The Fomorians were not fairing any better this time than their brethren before them. Organized volleys of arrows and gunfire decimated the demons as powerful spells took a heavy toll. Those few that actually made it to the front line were quickly dispatched by axe and sword.

Liz loaded another round and was wondering why the demons were even bothering to attack when deep roars that shook the ground echoed from all around the twisted fortress.

"That be no demon," a nearby dwarf spat.

Suddenly from all around the bailey, the huge doors set in the immense towers along the curtain wall burst open and packs of roaring giants charged out.

Dozens of the huge monstrosities carried gigantic boulders in their thick arms. They quickly encircled the allied army and as one, hurled the boulders.

"Incoming!" Shouts of alarm arose from the allied forces as the enormous projectiles soared through the air.

The Fomorians hooted in glee and charged the allies as they continued to pour out of the rifts. With a literal giant distraction, the allied forces' assault had slackened and the demons took full advantage. The beasts charged the lines and were met with only sporadic opposition.

Shields abruptly sprang up all around the army and the boulders struck them with tremendous force. Some of the huge stones rebounded off the glittering shields while others shattered upon impact, raining smaller shards across the bailey.

The giants roared in anger, as their ranged attack was defeated. They then brandished huge weapons and lumbered toward the encircled allies.

When the last boulder came to a rest, the allied army suddenly broke apart and scattered all across the vast bailey, just as the commanders had planned.

The dwarves were experienced battling giants and they knew that tightly packed formations would only make easy targets for the wide swings of the giant weapons. So, when the giants charged in, the allies spread out.

The battle changed in an instant. Where there was once a unified army surrounded by demons, now there was a sprawling, chaotic battlefield made up of countless vicious skirmishes and desperate duels with no discernable lines.

Liz suddenly found herself alone as the battle swirled around her.

A giant stomped through a group of dwarves, trying to crush them beneath its wide feet. The dwarves, however, rolled away and slashed at the giant's legs as it tried desperately to squash its small foes.

Liz raised her pistol and got a bead on the giant's head. The huge creature flinched as the bullet hit it square in the forehead, but continued stomping on the dwarves. Liz fired two more shots into the giant's skull before she realized that her efforts were futile. The giant's skull was just too thick and she was far too close for her sniper rifle to be of much use.

This wasn't the kind of place Liz wanted to be in. Battlefields were for meatheads like Mike and Jack, not people like her. Who in their right mind would *want* to fight hand-to-hand with hundreds of others with even more trying to kill you?

It didn't make sense to her, but she also knew that sometimes there were things worth fighting for. And the survival of her friends and family, and maybe humanity as a whole, was definitely one of them.

Reluctantly, Liz slung her rifle on her back, drew her saber and pistol and waded into the maelstrom of battle in search of her friends.

****

Arrows flew in all directions as the knot of elven spellarchers fired into the churning battlefield all around. Emily was with them, adding her bow to theirs.

The raging Fomorian's still tumbled out of the dark rifts in rising waves. It seemed the longer the rifts were open, the more demons tried to squeeze out. Emily and the spellarchers had tried shooting the black portals, but they had no effect. So instead they concentrated on the howling Fomorians, trying to thin their ever-growing numbers. But for every one they killed, three more seemed to take its place.

Emily and the knot of elves drew the attention of a giant and it lumbered toward them. It was an enormous beast, likely well over fifteen feet tall, with a thick frame and a large bushy beard. Large furs hung about its massive body and it dragged a tree trunk-like club along behind it.

Some of the elves turned to face the new threat and a hail of arrows greeted the giant. It raised a huge hand to protect its face, but otherwise seemed unperturbed by the small shafts that stuck into its thick hide and kept coming.

Various enchantments wreathed the arrows of the spellarchers, but even those did little to harm the giant. Disgusted, Emily lowered her bow and with her free hand, drew her skull-topped scepter.

A bolt of crackling green energy leapt from the scepter and connected with the giant's shoulder. The explosion rocked the huge beast and it roared in pain as the energy residue danced across its skin.

The dwarves had said how the giants were resistant to magic, but Emily had hoped that her scepter, that could kill most creatures with a single shot, would be enough to fell the giant. But her hopes were in vain as the now-angry giant lumbered toward them.

A second bolt exploded on top of the first and this time the giant recoiled from the blast. It shrieked in pain and lowered its hand to cover its wounded shoulder.

The spellarchers saw their opening.

Enchantments danced along the arrows that pounded into the giant's exposed face. One arrow punched through the beast's left eye as several more lodged in the giant's throat. The huge creature dropped its club and clutched at its ruined face and blood ran through its thick fingers.

The giant gurgled as more blood bubbled out of its mouth. It took several labored steps toward Emily and the elves before it fell to its knees and then finally collapsed.

A moment of sadness filled Emily as the giant died. It was a shame to kill such an amazing creature, but she quickly squashed that thought. The giant would have killed her and everyone else if they hadn't stopped it first. *Better it than me*, she decided.

Moral dilemma resolved, Emily returned to the battle at hand.

A lumpy demon charged out of the madness and a green bolt reduced it to a lump of smoking flesh an instant later. Emily put the scepter away and drew another arrow. She still didn't know if her stolen scepter had a limit on the number of shots it had, but she thought it better to save it for the giants than to waste it on demons that her endless arrows could take care of.

The air suddenly shrieked and a black portal abruptly tore itself into existence between Emily and the group of spellarchers. Fomorians spilled out almost immediately and the party scattered as they battled these new foes.

Emily found herself separated and alone, in the center of a swirling battle, facing three large Fomorians. Two of the red-skinned demons were female and the other was male. It was easy to tell since, like many of the goat-headed demons, all three were completely naked.

The male lowered its shaggy head and charged, leading with its large, curly ram horns.

Before Emily could react, a young man with a sword dove into the demon and bore the two of them to the ground. Steel and claws flashed as they struggled in the dirt.

The two female Fomorians moved to help the male, but Emily filled both with arrows before they had gone three steps. The male roared when he saw the females fall and violently pushed himself to his hooved feet.

The demon grabbed the boy's arm and with a vicious twist, tore the limb from its socket. The young man screamed and clutched at the gaping wound. As the boy collapsed the demon howled in victory. The cry ended in a wet gurgle as two arrows buried themselves in the Fomorian's neck.

Emily rushed to the boy's side, but pulled up short when she saw the bleeding had miraculously stopped. As Emily watched, the torn hole in the boy's shoulder began to knit itself back together. Bone grew from the ruined socket and muscles spun around them right before her eyes. Within moments, a new arm had replaced the lost one.

Emily stared in wonder as the young man stood and picked up his fallen sword with his new hand. "That's a neat trick," Emily had to shout over the roar of battle. "How'd you do that?"

The boy shrugged sheepishly.

Several dwarves locked in battle with an enormously fat Fomorian appeared around a nearby spire, and Emily and the boy were quickly swept apart by the tide of combat.

Not knowing where to go, Emily ran for the nearest bladed spire and put her back against it.

Explosions and roars echoed off the surrounding walls as bullets and spells flew across the bailey. Corpses were everywhere, scattered across the courtyard like a child's discarded toys. Bodies of humans, elves, and dwarves lay side by side with demons and giants as the conflict continued to rage around them.

A giant crushed a dwarf to paste under a heavy foot as two elven bade dancers moved in unison through a pack of Fomorians like a swirling tornado of death. A human soldier was surrounded by a pack of demons and torn apart while an elven mage melted the face off a huge armored giant.

Healers and clerics scrambled across the bloody battlefield trying to save everyone they could, but there were far too many. A dwarf priestess, that Emily recognized as Gretta, was skewered by a giant spear as she tried to heal a wounded elf. Nearby, waves of healing light washed over a group of human mercenaries while an elven cleric prayed in their midst.

Emily fired arrows as fast as she could and took down scores of rampaging Fomorians, but the dark portals were still open and more of the goat-headed demons kept pouring out.

A large pack of hideously deformed demons burst from a nearby rift and spotted Emily hiding beside the blade-like pillar. The pack howled gleefully at what they saw as easy prey.

Emily knocked another arrow and was ready to fire when a figure broke through the chaotic battle and drove right into the charging pack of Fomorians. There was a flash of steel and long, dark brown hair that danced through the center of the surprised demons.

Emily lowered her bow, afraid to hit the newcomer. At first, she thought it was an elf, but then Emily saw the leather jacket and pistol. Two demons fell, clutching their throats and giving Emily her first good look at the newcomer. To her surprise, Emily knew the woman that was slaughtering the Fomorians.

Saber in one and pistol in the other, Liz stabbed an ugly female Fomorian in the back and shot two small males before she brutally yanked the blade back out. Another female demon lunged at Liz, but she twisted away, slashing its throat as it went by. Two demons charged her, but Liz slid between them, shooting the one full in the face and jabbed her saber into the throat of the second.

Liz was a beautiful whirlwind of death as she shot and slashed her way through the Fomorians, leaving a trail of goat-headed bodies in her wake.

When the last demon fell, Emily found herself face to face with Liz.

"Where the hell did you learn to do that?" Emily gasped.

Liz shrugged. "I wish I knew." She looked back at the trail of corpses. "It's like something inside just snapped into place… I can't explain it."

"Who cares!" Emily laughed. "Just keep doing it!" A demon suddenly appeared and ran at Liz's exposed back. Emily quickly raised her bow and fired. The demon fell, an arrow lodged in its eye.

"What are you doing here anyways?" Emily asked as if nothing had happened. "I thought you were with the snipers on the hill?"

"I got bored." Liz smiled, but her smile quickly faded. "But we need to keep moving and find the others."

Emily looked around at the chaotic maelstrom of death swirling about them and her heart sank. "Good luck finding anyone in that…"

"I found you," Liz pointed out.

Emily knocked another arrow and together they strode into the killing field.

CHAPTER 27

The giantess' laughter boomed over the battlefield as another spell flared ineffectively off her heavy armor. Ted cursed and dove aside as the giantess' massive double-bladed battle-axe buried into the ground where he had been standing a moment before.

Darts of multi-colored magical energy sprayed from Ted's outstretched hand as the giantess wrenched her axe free in a shower of dirt. The darts pinged harmlessly off the armor like every other incantation Ted had tried.

The huge female was the tallest giant Ted had yet seen. Ted estimated her to be over fifteen feet tall. The armor the giantess wore was made of a dull, dark metal and was formed from heavy, interlocking plates that were covered in sharp projections. The bladed armor resembled the knife-like turrets that jutted up from the ground and the warped shape of the twisted keep itself.

Ted's lab coat hung in tatters around him and a long gouge marred the perfect abs sculpted into his molded breastplate. The giantess moved remarkably fast for such a huge creature and Ted was hard pressed to avoid her next strike.

The huge axe whistled through the air and Ted rolled away, barely avoiding the blow. The giantess roared and stomped after the fleeing

Battlemage as Ted desperately summoned more spells.

Lightning shot from Ted's hand and struck the giantess full in the chest. But the armor absorbed most of the blast and the electricity danced across the metal briefly before dissipating.

The armored giantess laughed again.

Spells were obviously not going to work on whatever type of enchanted armor the giantess wore. Ted suddenly stopped and took a deep breath. It looked like he was going to have to do this the hard way.

"Enough of this nonsense," Ted growled, and smoke started to rise from the poleaxe as it began to glow an angry, cherry red. The heat of the axe head intensified until the blade was white hot and the gem embedded in the end began to glow with a red light of its own.

Ted could see the giantess' wide grin beneath her helm when Ted turned to face her. The battle swirled around them, but the giantess had her sight set on Ted and was eager for the kill.

The huge giantess was caught by surprise when Ted suddenly charged her. The super-heated poleaxe tore a long rent in the armor of the giantess' leg, but it wasn't enough to reach the skin beneath. The giantess roared and spun, hitting Ted with a glancing, backhanded blow that sent him crashing to the ground.

Ted sprang to his feet, but in two long strides the giantess was on him. The huge double-bladed axe was a blur as it descended and Ted threw his heated poleaxe up desperately. The deadly stroke was barely deflected and the force of it knocked Ted back to the ground.

The giantess stood over him, victorious, and raised her axe for the killing blow.

Thunder boomed and the giantess' chest suddenly exploded as she was torn in half.

Ted stared in wonder as bits of giant rained down around him. The colossal axe dropped and stuck in the ground, blade first, followed by the two halves of the giantess that hit the ground with a pair of wet thuds.

The ground trembled as one of the M1A2-Abrams battle tanks rumbled toward him with its main cannon still smoking.

"Hey!" Ted grumbled, as he pulled himself to his feet. "What took you so long?"

The tank didn't stop; instead, it picked up speed as it rumbled by. The machine gunner on top was facing backwards and firing reams of ammunition behind it. It was then that Ted saw the horde of demons and pair of giants following in its wake. And now Ted was right between them.

"Wait for me!" Ted cried as he hiked up his robes, turned, and ran after the fleeing tank. He knew there was no way he could catch up to the tank, but he also knew that facing the demons and giants would be suicide, so on he ran.

The tank slowed as it was forced to weave through the melee around it. Fire and smoke billowed from its main cannon sporadically as it fired at one target or another.

The Abrams grinded to a halt as a wild skirmish engulfed it. The gunner cut down demons all around, but one small Fomorian avoided the hail of bullets and scrambled up the side of the tank unnoticed. The demon snuck behind the gunner and yanked him out.

The soldier and demon struggled until they both fell off the tank and landed hard on the ground. The gunner managed to draw his sidearm and shot the small demon in the chest. But as soon as he had extracted himself from the corpse, more demons converged on him. He unloaded the pistol and dropped several of the beasts, but it wasn't enough. There were too many Fomorians between them and before Ted could get there, three demons pounced on the poor gunner and hacked him apart.

Ted knew he was too late when he finally arrived, but he summoned up another spell anyways. The three Fomorians and the gunner's mutilated body were disintegrated in a brilliant explosion by the liquid fireball that shot from Ted's hand.

With no gunner to keep the demons at bay, Fomorians clawed up the sides of the vulnerable battle tank. Ted reached the surrounded tank and blew the demons off the hatch with a bolt of red energy before pulling himself up its armored hull.

The Abrams cannon fired and Ted was almost knocked back off from the force of the blast. The tank suddenly jerked forward with Ted desperately clinging to the top. The Abrams plowed through a group of demons that was threatening to overwhelm a knot of allies, its heavy treads grinding the demons to paste.

Ted regained his feet and began hurling spells in all directions. From his new vantage point Ted got his first good look at the overall battle. With countless skirmishes spread across the vast bailey, it was hard to judge how the allies were faring, but what Ted saw gave him hope.

The guns and spells of the allies were devastating the Fomorians and there were far less giants running around than Ted could have hoped. There should have been a lot more giants based on the size of the fortress and how many they had glimpsed inside here the other day. The missing giants concerned him, but right now it was working to their advantage.

What was the real threat to the allies was the seemingly endless supply of Fomorians that continued to pour out of their portals. It seemed that for every one killed, three more took its place. The allies were cutting down scores of demons, but the allies were taking losses too, and those they didn't get back.

Near the edge of the battle, Ted spotted a large concentration of demons and giants surrounding a small group of what looked to be Scadians; but what caught his eye was the blue-tinted energy shield that protected part of the formation and the demons that were being flung through the air as if struck by some powerful force.

The tank suddenly jerked as the cannon fired and Ted was nearly knocked off again. In front of the tank a giant was blown apart and a section of the bladed tower behind it exploded.

The tower groaned as it swayed dangerously. A moment later there was a horrible grinding sound and metal shrieked as the tower slowly fell over. The earth shook as dust and debris filled the air as the tower impacted the rocky ground.

The giants and their demon minions recognized the Abrams as the major threat and were working to surround the racing tanks.

The M1A2 picked up speed and swerved between demonic portals that were popping up with increasing frequency. It was all Ted could do to hold on as the driver desperately tried to avoid the rifts and keep from being surrounded at the same time.

The tank careened around a rift, but before the driver could react, another portal suddenly appeared right in front of them. The backside of the tank was sheared off as it passed through the portal and vanished into the blackness.

The M1A2 came to a crashing halt with a large section of the rear simply gone.

Two giants were vaporized as the cannon fired a last shot. Demons howled and cheered at the tank's demise and raced toward it. Ted stood alone atop the ruined tank, knowing that the crew inside would be helpless as they tried to escape.

Goat-headed Fomorians of all sizes swarmed the stricken vehicle and clawed their way up its armored sides.

A towering jet of fire sprayed from Ted's outstretched hand like a flamethrower from Hell as he incinerated the first ranks of demons. The hatch opened and the M1A2 crew began climbing out as Ted continued his assault.

When the last crewmember escaped, and still spraying liquid fire, Ted pointed his glowing poleaxe at the gibbering horde. A lance of crackling red energy erupted from the gem and blew a path through the demons.

"Go!" Ted shouted.

The crew wasted no time and desperately fled the ruined tank and pounded through the cleared path toward the safety of a block of dwarves.

Ted was about to follow when he noticed that his blaze had caught the escaping fuel from the abandoned M1A2 on fire and the flames were licking the exposed ammunition stores inside the tank.

Suddenly, the first shell cooked off and exploded, igniting the entire deposit of 120-mm cannon rounds.

The detonation was extraordinary.

The explosion burned like the sun and scores of demons were instantly vaporized. A column of flame and smoke billowed into the sky and was sucked into the churning maelstrom above.

A smoking body with the remains of a once-white coat soared through the air like a fiery comet and crashed to the ground nearly a hundred feet from the explosion.

****

Liz had just finished healing a wounded dwarf when she saw the thunderous detonation and watched the body land just a few yards away from her. It may have been her imagination, but she could have sworn she saw a faint shimmer of gold around the body before it crashed to the ground.

Liz and Emily rushed to the figure and were shocked to find Ted laying there, face down, with faint wisps of smoke rising off of him. They rolled him over and were even more surprised when he opened his eye. "Ff-fancy meeting you hh-here," he coughed. "I must have died and gone to heaven."

"You aren't dead yet you great oaf, but you sure tried," Liz chided, but she couldn't help but smile back.

Ted tried to sit up, but Liz held him down as Emily with her bow stood guard over them. Liz mouthed a silent prayer and a moment later she was helping a refreshed Ted to his feet.

"Thank you my dear," Ted said, as he dusted himself off with little success before retrieving his poleaxe that had landed nearby. The blade began to glow again as soon as he touched it.

"Have you seen Mike or Jack?" Liz asked, and tried to keep the worry out of her voice.

A tiny little Fomorian leapt from nowhere and landed on Ted's back. He reached behind him and pulled the miniscule demon off disdainfully. The creature struggled in his grasp for a moment and then suddenly it began to convulse as waves of magical energy flowed from Ted into its small body.

Ted tossed the charred husk away. "Actually, yes," he answered, and motioned toward the twisted castle. "I believe they are currently battling near the base of the keep."

Liz ducked as a clawed tentacle tried to grab her. Her saber flashed and a demon howled in agony as its tentacle was cleanly severed. An arrow punched into the tentacled demon's chest and it fell in a writhing heap.

"Good." Liz shot a charging demon point blank in its ugly, goat-like face. "Then that is where we are going."

****

Mike's training with the Guardians and Paladins had prepared him well for battling the demonic Fomorians. However, it had not prepared him for giants. But to be fair, Mike didn't think that there was a way someone could prepare to fight a giant. And yet, he did think that the Scadians were giving a good accounting of themselves against the huge creatures. Years of fighting together had made the humans an effective fighting force and that experience proved invaluable.

Mike was having difficulty maintaining the shields he had set up on the edges of the formation to keep several giants away from the orderly ranks of spearmen that were locked in combat with a horde of deformed Fomorians.

Claws scraped along Mike's shield as he fought several demons at once. A lumpy demon flew backwards with its chest crushed from the ancient impact mace. Mike struck left and right, bludgeoning demons with every stroke.

A few paces away, Jack was a blur as he weaved through the throng, felling Fomorians like some vengeful spirit. Mike thought he heard Jack laughing wildly as he cut his way past him, but Mike knew it must be his imagination.

The demons were pressing in hard from all sides and it was everything the besieged humans could do to keep the formation together. They were completely surrounded, desperately battling for their survival; a knot of humanity lost in a sea of monsters.

A pair of dwarves fought valiantly back-to-back as a growing throng of

Fomorians pressed in around them. Leif and Sven Tarheels cut down countless demons, but their masterful display of martial skill couldn't save them from the unending horde.

Sven died first as a long tentacle wrapped around his ankle and jerked him off his feet only to drag him into an enormous mouthfull of razor-sharp teeth. His brother tried to come to his aid, but Lief got stabbed in the back and watched helplessly as Sven was ripped to shreds before more Fomorians descended on him.

Mike saw the pair fall and was filled with grief. He hadn't known them that well, but they had been kinder than most dwarves.

Mike pushed them from his mind as the Abrams exploded and his heart sank. The tanks were their best chance of beating the giants and without them it would be infinitely harder to find victory. Luckily, General Adams still plowed along in the distance, rallying the allies and dealing death to anything that got in his way. Unfortunately, the final M1A2 inside the bailey was drawing all the giant's attention, and the tank crew was working hard to keep themselves and the general from being overwhelmed.

A long, slimy tongue wrapped around Mike's forearm and tried to pull him off his feet. Instead of fighting the pull, Mike let it take him and he slammed his shield into the demon's open mouth, severing its lower jaw and slicing through its tongue. The ugly beast flailed a moment before a swift blow ended the creature's pain.

The Fomorians surged forward and pressed into the human line, almost breaking through in several places. It was only due to the heroics of a few individuals, including Mike and Jack who rushed in to fill the gaps until the line could be reformed, that kept the formation together.

The push and pull of the struggle continued for several minutes until one of the giants on the left flank discovered there was a limit on how high the summoned shield wall went. The giant reached up and found the edge of the glimmering shield and actually pulled itself over to land with a tremendous crash on the other side.

Thinking fast, Mike jerked the shield wall and it collided with the giants back and knocked it over. The Scadians pounced on the fallen giant and the spearmen made quick work of the helpless creature. There was no time to celebrate though, as the distraction had proven costly. The Fomorians drove in with claws and deformed appendages flailing at the preoccupied humans. The Scadians tried to reform, but the demons were too many.

Fomorians poured into the formation and the organized lines began to break apart. The humans were going to be slaughtered if the demons were not stopped. Mike tried to fight his way to the weak point, but there were just too many demons in the way. For every one Mike knocked away, three more appeared before him.

The battered formation was just about to collapse when a figure in black streaked in and single-handedly filled the gap. Jack twisted and spun like a top, his black blade carving though meat and bone with equal ease. Pieces of armor flew off Jack as the surrounding Fomorians wildly tore at him, but Jack didn't seem to notice, dicing the demons up until the spearmen reformed and pushed the demons back.

A bulky demon suddenly leapt out of the swarm and bore Mike to the ground. Its huge, boney fists pounded him into the ground as Mike struggled to free himself. A powerful blow struck Mike in the face and his head cracked off the ground. His vision swam and he lost control of his protective shields.

The shimmering walls winked out and the giants roared as they waded into the now defenseless humans. "Scatter!" someone shouted, and the Scadians swiftly obeyed. The humans broke into smaller groups and quickly moved away from each other to spread out the giants and lessen their chances of crushing the humans all at once.

The hulking demon had Mike pinned beneath it and pounded away at him with its heavy fists. Mike struggled to get away, but the demon was far too heavy. Thick fists covered in dense bone hammered at Mike's head and chest and it was all he could do to stay conscious as the pounding continued.

Blackness filled his vision and for a moment Mike didn't know where he was. Pain flashed as the Fomorian hit him again and suddenly Mike knew exactly where he was. With no time to waste, Mike twisted with all his considerable might and managed to pull his legs out from under the hulking demon. With a violent kick, Mike pushed the demon off and scrambled shakily to his feet.

Snot flew from the hulking goat-head as it snorted angrily and prepared to charge. Mike raised his shield and swayed unsteadily as he tried to set his feet. The bone-fisted Fomorian took one step and then abruptly stopped. Two holes had appeared in its chest and bright blood gushed out of the wounds. An arrow suddenly whizzed over Mike's shoulder and took the beast in the eye and it died before it hit the ground.

"Hey…" Mike mumbled, and turned to look behind him. "That one was mine…"

Appearing through the chaos of battle and slicing their way through the raging demons toward him was Liz, Emily, and a very battered-looking Ted.

"Boyy am I glad to seee youuu," Mike slurred groggily.

"How very kind," Emily scoffed as they reached him. Mike turned to say something, but his knees gave out and Emily dropped her bow as Mike fell into her. They landed together in a heap with Mike's broad body trapping Emily beneath his armored bulk.

"So, this is what it feels like to have Mike on top of me," Emily grunted. "I imagined it better."

Liz ignored her and put a hand against Mike's rapidly bruising face. She muttered a quick prayer and Mike's bruises vanished. A moment later Mike pulled himself to his feet and retrieved Emily's bow for her.

"Thanks," he muttered sheepishly, as he handed the bow over and turned to Liz. "That's twice now you've saved me. I'm starting to feel like the damsel in distress."

The conversation was cut short as more Fomorians charged in at them from all sides and suddenly everyone was locked in their own personal battles.

"You've got it all wrong," Liz shouted, after she shot an enormously fat demon. "I'm just using you as a meat shield."

A nearby demon nearly blew apart as pieces flew everywhere and a laughing Jack burst through. Liz caught her breath at the sight of him. His armor was battered and blood covered him from head to toe. But what surprised Liz the most were his eyes.

They glittered a brilliant gold.

Before Liz could comment on his appearance, more Fomorians charged in behind Jack and he fell into a rough circle with his friends.

The battle swirled around them as together the Heroes of Awesome fought desperately against a hellish legion at the foot of a twisted castle.

"I thought you said giants didn't have any magic?" Mike shouted over the din of battle.

"They shouldn't," Ted hollered back. "I don't know how they are summoning these demons."

"Well, we need to find out!" Jack yelled, as he beheaded another demon. "Even I can't keep this up forever!"

A large clutch of excessively large Fomorians spilled out of one of the black portals and they barreled directly toward Mike and his friends.

"Wonderful…" Mike muttered, as the huge demons drew closer. They were already hard pressed by the average Fomorians all around them. Add the large ones and Mike wasn't sure they would be able to hold out any longer.

"Do you see that?" Ted suddenly shouted.

"See what?" Mike looked around, but didn't see anything unusual.

The ground rose up around Ted and a wave of earth knocked a score of demons from their feet. "There!" Ted pointed toward the twisted castle.

At first Mike didn't see anything, but then he caught movement along the foot of the nearest warped wall. It was a giant. But this giant was unlike the others as it was completely hidden by a dark, hooded robe and was sneaking along the wall trying not to be seen. Mike was instantly suspicious.

"We should follow it and see where it goes," Ted shouted, as he impaled a demon on his burning poleaxe.

Liz laughed. "Oh, yeah right. Let's just follow the shadowy figure into the evil castle." She stabbed a Fomorian in the neck and shot another. "What could possibly go wrong?"

Emily unleashed a hail of arrows into a crowd of demons that was threatening to overwhelm a small group of dwarves. "I agree with Ted," she shouted. "We can't stay here."

"Well, what are we waiting for?" Jack laughed wildly and charged into the Fomorians between them and the castle, his golden eyes sparkling lustily as he ripped through the demons with his black sword.

Mike cursed at Jack's recklessness, but followed him all the same. The others joined in and soon the entire group was slowly following the bloody path that Jack was leaving in his wake.

"How is he doing that?" Liz asked in awe of Jack's display of skill.

"I dunno," Mike muttered darkly. "It's like he's possessed."

"Fine with me," Emily grunted, as she buried an arrow into a Fomorian's neck. "So long as he stays on our team."

The ranks of demons began to thin the closer to the dark keep they got. This close to the twisted structure Mike realized how immense the keep actually was. The warped walls soared into the sky and were lost in the churning clouds high above. There was no definitive beginning of the keep as the walls were jagged and scattered, almost like the building was some kind of bladed monster that was spilling out into the bailey. The towers twisted and bent around each other and as The Heroes got closer, it was almost like walking into a long, warped tunnel instead of an outer wall. And just like the curtain wall, these walls were decorated with colossal sculptures of people frozen in various poses of violence and lust.

They broke through the last knot of demons and charged toward the twisted keep. A few Fomorians followed, but they were quickly felled by spell and arrow. Jack charged on until Mike grabbed him by the arm and pulled him down behind a large bladed outcropping.

"What's the big idea?" Jack growled. "The giant is getting away!" he snarled, and his golden eyes flashed dangerously.

"Getting away to where?" Mike retorted. "Do you see any doors?"

Jack peeked his head over the stones and looked down the twisted tunnel of a wall. The robed giant snuck along, but there were no doors in sight. Jack snorted, but didn't respond.

"Let's follow and see where it goes, but we need to stay back so it doesn't see us," Liz offered.

"Agreed," Ted nodded. "There is something strange about this."

The friends set off along the wall, sneaking from one twisted section to another. It was almost like walking through some kind of horrible maze where huge statues looked down on you while they committed every kind of wicked deed imaginable. Orgies and battles decorated the dark stone, and sometimes it became impossible to tell where one ended and the other began.

"Interesting décor…" Emily muttered. "I need to get the name of the designer."

They continued along the foot of the twisted keep as the sounds of battle echoed down the cavernous tunnel.

"It stopped." Liz suddenly hissed, and they all dove for cover behind a gigantic foot that protruded from the arching wall.

They peeked over the edge of one colossal toe and watched the robed giant stand along an uninteresting section of wall. It's back was to them, but it was doing something with its hands and Mike thought he heard it saying something.

"What's it doing?" Liz muttered.

"I can't be sure," Ted whispered back. "It's blocking my view."

The friends hid behind the toe for a few moments until there was a soft hissing sound and a faint, dark line appeared along the face of the wall in front of the giant.

The dark line expanded until a colossal doorway had appeared in the twisted wall. The robed giant whispered something and a moment later the doorway began to slide open.

The open door revealed the inside of the keep contained a deeper darkness that the light outside couldn't seem to penetrate.

Mike was glad they had decided to follow the robed giant. If they had tried to find a way inside by themselves they would never have found the entrance.

Before the doors had fully opened, the giant slipped silently inside and vanished into the darkness of the keep.

"Let's go," Jack whispered eagerly.

Before anyone could stop him, Jack slid out from their hiding spot and made for the pitch-black opening. Mike cursed and the others were forced to follow.

They crossed the exposed distance as fast as they could, but they had only gone half way before the hidden door began to slide closed.

Jack reached the shrinking opening first and charged into the blackness followed by Mike, then Liz and Emily. The doors were just about closed when Ted finally snuck between them an instant before they slammed shut.

A complete darkness engulfed them as the doors boomed shut and Mike couldn't help but think it sounded an awful lot like they just got sealed inside a crypt.

CHAPTER 28

Liz's heartbeat pounded in her ears as she searched the darkness but was unable to see anything. Sudden claustrophobia threatened to overwhelm her even though the echo of footsteps gave the impression they were in a large room. Wait…footsteps?

"Who's there?" Liz whispered to the darkness.

"It's just me of course," came Jack's voice from somewhere in front of her. "What are you guys waiting for? The doorway is over here."

"What doorway?" Liz asked at the same time Ted asked. "You can see?"

"Of course, I can see," Jack's voice scoffed. "It's dark in here, but not *that* dark."

"Well, I can't see a thing," Emily muttered from off to Liz's left.

"Me either," Liz agreed.

Liz could hear Jack groan. "You guys are pathetic… just follow my voice. We are alone in a big empty room and there is a giant-sized doorway on this end."

The friends did as they were told and slowly crossed the blackness by following Jack's voice.

"I feel ridiculous," Jack's voice grumbled. "This is like the worst game of Marco Polo ever."

"I can't believe I'm going to say this… but just keep talking," Liz whispered.

Jack's voice chuckled. "It is kinda funny watching you all stumble around like a bunch of blind mice."

Liz could hear Mike's teeth grind in frustration. "That's because we *are* blind, genius."

Jack's laughter echoed off the hidden walls. "Sucks to be you."

"I'm glad you find this funny," Liz chided, "but if somebody shows up we will be helpless. Aren't there any lights or candles or something in here?"

"Nope," came the reply. "But you are almost out of the room now."

Liz could hear the change in the echoing footsteps as they crossed the threshold. They continued on, shuffling along in the darkness with only Jack's annoying ramblings to guide them. The path twisted along, forcing the friends to bump into each other and the walls as they tried to navigate the passage.

Mike stepped in front of her and Liz stopped to avoid running into his back. "Watch it," Liz hissed, and then realized what she had done. "I can see!" she cried without thinking, before clapping her hand over her mouth.

"Me too!" Emily squeaked happily.

The others added their agreement and picked up their pace as the darkness lessened the farther down the passageway they went.

As the light grew, they began to hear muffled voices moaning with pleasure somewhere in the distance.

"At least somebody is having a good time," Emily muttered in the darkness.

The twisting passageway continued to get lighter as the moaning and grunting grew louder. Liz could now make out some detail along the walls and was surprised to see that the walls where lumpy and pooled along the floor almost like they had melted. The warped walls reached high above and were lost in the clinging darkness. Several other smaller passages branched off from the one they were on, but it was decided to stay on the larger path.

They rounded a sharp bend and abruptly found the source of the light.

An immense door stood closed before them with a crack of bright, flickering light shining out from underneath. At least Liz assumed it was a door.

Huge stone and metal bodies were stacked up in a giant pile resembling an enormous orgy of death. The bodies were all nude and so entwined with each other that it was hard to tell what was happening. The lewd door was repulsive and mesmerizing all at once and Liz found herself unable to look away.

The Heroes stopped before the obscene configuration. The moaning and grunting was obviously coming from behind the door and now that they were close, Liz could hear a low, steady chanting as well.

"What now?" Mike asked, as he eyed the door wearily.

Jack sheathed his black sword and gripped his rifle. "We go in."

"And just how do you propose we do that?" Ted pointed to the explicit scene. "I don't see any handles on there and I am *not* about to go poking around looking for one."

"Where is your sense of adventure?" Emily asked dreamily, as she glided up to the colossal door and put her hand on one of the nude figures.

"What are you doing?" Liz hissed in panic. "Don't touch that!"

Emily laughed and stroked the nearest statue. "Do you have any better ideas?" she grinned wickedly. "Besides, there is nothing here that I haven't touched before."

A soft moaning suddenly filled the hallway and Emily jumped back from the door as the metal figures abruptly began to shift and move. The bodies twisted and crawled away from each other allowing light and sound to spill out from the rapidly expanding opening.

Warm air wafted into the hallway, carrying with it the cloying scent of incense and other pungent aromas. The moans and soft cries of pain increased in volume as the door wriggled open and the hallway was filled with the low, droning chant.

"I say we go back," Liz offered hopefully.

"And wander the pitch-black tunnels again?" Mike scoffed. "I didn't come all this way to be scared off by a few horny statues and some stink."

Mike raised his shield and pointed his mace at the opening. "Let's rock this joint!"

"Ooh, Rah!" Jack raised his M4 and the two of them strode into the light.

Liz, Emily, and Ted shared a look before Ted grinned and followed them in. Emily shrugged helplessly, knocked an arrow, and slipped in after the men.

Liz stood alone in the hallway for a moment and shook her head sadly before checking to make sure her rifle was loaded. She only had a few rounds left in her last magazine.

It would have to do.

She took a deep breath and followed her friends inside.

The chamber they entered was enormous. The dark, stone walls looked like melting candle wax near the base and flowed up into sculpted flames that reached several stories above their heads. Titanic humanoid sculptures reached out of the wall of flames high overhead and held up the soaring ceiling.

As magnificent as the structure was, it was not the chamber itself that drew everyone's attention, but the hellish ritual taking place in the center of it.

"I think we know where the demons are coming from…" Ted muttered in awe.

The air thrummed with a primeval power that radiated from a collection of concentric circles carved into the heart of the chamber. Towering flames rose from the rings and burned brightly, giving off the only source of flickering light in the vast chamber. Fiery symbols and demented images were carved into the floor between the rings, making a dizzying pattern that pulsed with dark energies.

Now, Liz knew where the missing giants had gone. They were here, dozens of them, engrossed in a euphoric orgy around the outermost ring, providing a moaning chant that seemed to feed the burning symbols.

None of the naked giants seemed to notice the human's intrusion, so enraptured in their erotic ministrations. But not all the giants were lost in blissful ignorance. Some were scattered across the hard stone floor, pale and unmoving, as if all the life had been siphoned from them.

The outer most wall of flames suddenly dropped, revealing a tall figure standing inside with arms raised. The figure had its back to them and was wearing only a small, black armored skirt and tall, calf-length wrapped sandals, but was obviously a male. His skin was so pale blue it was almost grey and his right arm was encased in a jagged, dark metal gauntlet that was inscribed with burning red symbols. He wasn't as tall as most of the giants, standing at maybe ten feet tall, but from what Liz could see, his body was perfectly sculpted.

"That must be a nephilim," Ted whispered anxiously. "They are said to be masters of the arcane... and completely evil. They spread corruption wherever they go."

"I thought it would be bigger..." Jack grumbled, with a hint of disappointment in his voice.

"That's what she said," Emily mumbled distractedly, never taking her eyes off the magnificent being before them.

Mike raised his shield. "Well, if this thing is summoning the demons then we need to kill it." He took a step forward and Liz reached out and grabbed his arm.

"What are you doing?" he turned around and growled. "We need to kill it while those flames are still low." To emphasize his point, Mike pointed his mace at the outer wall of flames that were slowly growing taller.

Liz held up her rifle and waved it in front of Mike's face. "We brought guns for a reason," she growled back.

Mike stared stupidly at the MK13 for a moment before he chuckled. "Always robbing me of my fun," he grumbled with a grin, and stepped back sheepishly.

Liz and Jack raised their rifles and Liz took careful aim at the back of the nephilim's bald head. The thunderous roar of gunfire filled the cavernous chamber and drowned out all other sounds.

The shots connected, but to Liz's horror the nephilim's skin absorbed the impacts and the bullets fell harmlessly at his sandaled feet.

Liz and Jack unloaded the last of their bullets in a vain attempt to kill the nephilim, but only succeeded in creating a small pile of spent casings on the stone floor.

"Ahhh," a deep voice thundered. "It seems we have company."

Booming laughter echoed throughout the chamber and the unharmed nephilim lowered his arms and slowly turned to face them.

Liz was struck by the sheer beauty of the nephilim. His bare skin was perfectly chiseled muscle and his tiny, armored skirt left little to the imagination. But where his body was perfect, his face was simply breathtaking. With a strong jaw and penetrating eyes, Liz couldn't imagine a more magnificent being. The only thing that Liz thought was strange was the nephilim's elongated skull that swept backwards and had been unnoticeable from behind. But for some reason, Liz found the deformity strangely attractive.

The nephilim saw The Heroes and a sinister smile split his handsome face, revealing a row of large, perfect teeth. His eyes were solid black and seemed to bore into Liz with a startling intensity.

"It has been long since I enjoyed the flesh of the daughters of men," he purred, in a deep, seductively musical voice.

"And you aren't going to today!" Mike boldly shouted back.

The beautiful nephilim laughed. "Oh, how I have missed the defiance of you mortals!" he chuckled darkly. "These wretched Elioud are ideal servants, but sometimes even one such as I, the divine Anak, desires more than mindless devotion."

Liz was having a hard time concentrating on what the beautiful creature was saying. His words flowed like honey and she drank them up eagerly.

"Join me," the silver-tongued nephilim said breathily, "and all of your desires will be fulfilled for all eternity."

Liz desperately wanted to believe this beautiful creature, but something rang hollow. She couldn't quite put her finger on what it was, but a hint of unease began to grow inside her. She glanced at her friends and saw that they too were struggling with the wonderful offer.

Mike's brow was furrowed in concentration while Ted looked confused. Jack growled softly to himself and Emily smiled and nodded along with what the beautiful nephilim was saying.

"Once my father is freed from his prison we will conquer this world," Anak clenched his fists eagerly. "Then we will free the rest of the Fallen and then the Empyrean will finally be ours!"

Liz was confused. She didn't know what he was talking about, but it did sound nice.

Who wouldn't want to rule the world?

Wait… she didn't want to rule anything… did she?

Liz massaged her temples and tried to clear the foggy feeling from her thoughts.

"You will be made lords of this world and pleasure like you have never experienced will be yours," Anak promised passionately. "You have but to submit and pledge your souls to me."

"Never. Gonna. Happen," Jack growled defiantly between clenched teeth.

A look of surprise crossed the nephilim's beautiful face. "You defy me still?" The nephilim suddenly smiled and strode out of the burning symbols and through the wall of flames. Liz gasped, afraid that his perfect body would be burned, but he passed right through them as if the flames were not even there. "All of your darkest desires will be yours in exchange for a simple pledge," he purred. "I see your heart, Jack Treno, and it is black."

Jack's golden eyes flashed angrily, and he growled and bared his teeth like a wild dog. "Your mind tricks will not work on me, demon spawn," he spat. "I will not be controlled!"

Jack suddenly lunged at the nephilim, black sword flashing.

Liz watched numbly, unable to bring herself to move.

Jack drove in hard, a black blur, but the nephilim was quicker. Faster than Liz's eyes could follow, Anak casually stepped away from Jack's strike and disdainfully swatted Jack away with a brutal backhand from his armored gauntlet.

Jack's limp body sailed across the room before crashing to the hard stone floor. When Jack didn't move, the nephilim smiled and turned back to Liz with a lusty grin. "Now where was I?" he purred.

Emily stepped forward eagerly. "You were offering us our every desire," she said dreamily.

"Ah, yessss." Anak sniffed the air. "I see that you are delightfully wicked. You will make an excellent addition to my Pleasure Palace, my sweet Emilia."

Liz shook her head, trying to clear her confusion. *"This isn't right..."* she mumbled to herself. *Why was she so confused?*

"How do you know our names?" Liz asked softly. Speaking was difficult, but with each passing moment her thoughts grew clearer.

The nephilim looked at her and granted Liz a dazzling smile. "What was that, my pet?"

Liz didn't like being called anyone's pet and her anger grew. "I said, how do you know our names?" The anger burned away more of her fogginess and Liz gripped her rifle tightly; feeling it in her hand gave her an anchor to hold on to even if it was out of bullets.

"Why, I know everything," the perfect demigod purred. "I know your deepest, darkest desires." The nephilim shot a glance at Mike. *Was that jealousy that she saw?* "Nothing can stay hidden from me." He sniffed the air and his black eyes widened in surprise.

"My father has sent me a gift," Anak said almost to himself. He sniffed the air again and this time he inhaled deeply as if he smelled some wonderful scent.

"Yessss," he purred blissfully. "You will be perfect."

The nephilim took an eager step toward her.

"Perfect for what?" Liz asked, as she struggled to take a step back from the beautiful being.

"For the completion of the Bore, of course," the nephilim replied, as he slowly advanced on her. "Your little army has forced me to drain some of the power away from the ritual to summon my father's Fomorian minions." The nephilim waved his hand dismissively. "But it is a minor delay. The

Elioud have provided adequate power thus far, but my Anakim are so very far from pure." His black eyes blazed and his gaze froze Liz in place.

"But you are," Anak purred, and took another step toward her. "You are undefiled." He nearly giggled with glee. "Rejoice! Your immaculate soul will be the final sacrifice that will provide more than enough power to finish the Bore and finally release my lord father, Baphomet, from Tartarus!"

Liz dropped her useless rifle and it clattered to the ground. The fog abruptly cleared from her thoughts as the word "sacrifice" sunk in. She quickly drew her saber and pistol, and pointed them at the nephilim that was nearly upon her. "I will not be pledging my soul to you." she snarled angrily. Now that her mind was clear, it swiftly filled with rage at being clouded by such obviously foul thoughts for so long.

The nephilim's laughter boomed throughout the vast chamber and drowned out the moaning of the giants. "Foolish mortal," he laughed darkly. "I do not need your consent for this. I only need your death."

CHAPTER 29

Anak's towering form loomed over Liz and it reached for her with his burning gauntlet. But before she could react, his hand collided with an invisible wall.

A sphere of fire suddenly flew at the nephilim and exploded against his shoulder, spinning him around, but doing little damage to his pristine body.

The demigod roared in anger as Ted stepped forward and launched another fireball that exploded against the beautiful being's bare chest. Anak howled in anger more than pain and retaliated with a bolt of utter blackness that suddenly shot from his unarmed hand.

Mike grabbed Liz's arm and pulled her back as the black bolt struck a glittering golden bubble that sprang up around Ted and exploded. The bubble shattered and Ted was thrown to the ground.

Liz tried to join the fight, but Mike held her back.

"Let me go!" Liz struggled to break free, but Mike's grip was like iron. "I'm going to kill that monster!" she cried angrily, as Ted regained his feet and threw a crackling bolt of lightning at the nephilim.

"Oh, no you don't," Mike replied. "That guy only wants you, so you are going to stay as far away from him as you can get."

A wild howling echoed in the vast chamber and a dark shape rushed toward the nephilim. Jack charged in, black soul sword leading the way.

The nephilim spun away and drew a strange looking whip from his belt that Mike hadn't noticed before. It had a very long handle and the whip appeared to be made of numerous blades that were all linked together.

A beam of golden light shot out from Ted's hand and streaked toward the nephilim, but the beam evaporated before reaching its target. Anak laughed wildly as he cracked his bladed whip at Jack who dove aside at the last moment.

"But I can help," Liz argued. "I'm not some fragile doll that needs protected."

"I know that," Mike said, "but Emily needs your help now."

It was then that Liz realized that Emily wasn't moving. She was standing perfectly still with a dreamy look on her face. Mike finally released Liz and she rushed over to Emily.

Mike waited a moment as he watched Liz try to get Emily's attention and failing that, she holstered her pistol and placed a hand against Emily's head and closed her eyes.

Anak's whip carved a large groove in the floor where it lashed at Jack's dancing figure. His next strike found its mark and drove Jack to his knees. The nephilim raised his bladed whip again, but a glowing cord appeared in the air above him and wrapped around his arm. The nephilim laughed and jerked his arm, shattering the cord in a burst of light.

"A valiant attempt, sorcerer," Anak chuckled, "but you will need to do better than that!"

By now, Jack had regained his feet and slashed at the nephilim's exposed back. But somehow the mighty being anticipated the strike and blocked the black sword by trapping it with his bladed whip without taking his eyes off Ted.

Mike drove in, hoping to take the nephilim unawares. His hopes were in vain as the mighty demigod lashed out with a wave of dark energies that passed through Mike's Aegis Shield and pummeled his senses.

Pain and madness threatened to overwhelm him, but Mike clung to the diamond-hard center of his Will that anchored him to reality. He gritted his teeth and fought the burning madness with a tremendous effort of Will, and slowly pushed it from his mind.

Mike pushed himself to his feet, even though he didn't remember falling, and charged the mighty nephilim.

Jack was caught in a furious duel against the bladed whip that seemed to have a mind of its own, as Ted rapidly traded devastating spells with the laughing nephilim at the same time.

Together the three humans desperately battled the beautiful nephilim in the heart of the twisted fortress as the larger battle raged outside.

****

The sounds of combat were overlaid by Anak's laughter and echoed throughout the vast chamber as Liz closed her eyes and lightly touched Emily's mind.

At first Liz didn't see anything wrong, but delving deeper, she discovered a fine web of spells coating Emily's thoughts. Liz was horrified at how extensive the covering was. The elves called it Compulsion. The healers had shown her how to detect and remove it, but this was taking it to an entirely new level.

Compulsion was a particularly nasty form of mind control that left the victim believing that what they were doing was under their own volition, when in fact they were being guided by the caster of the spell.

The group's slow reaction and Liz's earlier strange feelings for the nephilim suddenly made horrible sense. The nephilim had placed Compulsion on all five of them at once without even Ted noticing. Luckily, she and the others had been able to shake off the spell before it could take total control.

Liz didn't know if she could unravel the amazing fine spell, and even if she could she wasn't sure that she could do it without harming Emily.

Running out of time and without much choice, Liz nervously reached out and experimentally plucked at one of the faint strings. The plucked strand suddenly vanished and some of the connecting webbing faded away with it. Liz breathed a sigh of relief and prayed that her actions weren't damaging Emily in any way.

Liz spied several larger strands that connected a great many lesser webs and she aimed for those. The large cords of Compulsion were made of numerous smaller strands all tightly coiled together. It took several moments, but eventually Liz managed to unravel the large cord and when she did, a large portion of the connecting web vanished.

Bolstered by her success, Liz began the slow work of unraveling the next cord.

****

Mike waded into the melee, but it was as if he was fighting a shadow. To his growing frustration, every swing was either blocked or completely missed the gyrating nephilim. The hellish, bladed whip had scored several long gouges in Mike's armor, but so far he remained unharmed. The same couldn't be said for Jack and Ted.

Sweat ran in torrents down Ted as he hurled spell after spell, but none broke through Anak's powerful defenses. One of Ted's sleeves had been completely burned away, blistering the arm underneath, and the side of his sculpted breastplate was warped and melted.

Blood ran down Jack's face from a long gash above his eye. Both arms were raw and bleeding from the bladed whip, but he fought on ruthlessly, seemingly unaware of his injuries.

The three friends had the nephilim surrounded, but none of them could land a solid blow on this huge, perfect figure. Anak laughed and seemed to be everywhere at once, bladed whip slicing through the air trailing blood, and devastating spells flashing at each of them.

Mike was dismayed at the ease at which the huge creature avoided them while still landing strikes of its own. Mike had the sickening suspicion that the nephilim was toying with them for his own amusement.

A brilliant green bolt of energy suddenly exploded against the nephilim's head. Mike looked back and saw a furious Emily pointing her scepter at the surprised nephilim and fired another green bolt at his head. Mike had seen many creatures killed by a shot from that scepter, but to his dismay the nephilim's pale skin was barely singed.

The second bolt deflected off an invisible shield before reaching Anak and his black eyes narrowed in anger.

"So, you managed to free your little friend," Anak hissed. "No matter. In the end your souls will all feed the Bore."

Liz didn't waste time with a reply and instead fired her pistol at the nephilim's face. The bullets were deflected as well, but the shots distracted the mighty being long enough for Jack to rush in and bring his black sword to bear.

Anak spun away, but not before Jack scored a long cut across the handsome creature's perfect chest. It wasn't a deep cut, but the nephilim hissed in pain as black blood slowly oozed out of the wound.

Emily continued her assault with unrelenting green bolts raining down on the beautiful monster, but each bolt was deflected before reaching his perfect body.

Ted launched a volley of magical darts at the distracted nephilim's exposed back and Anak howled as some of the darts actually found their mark and slammed into him. The mighty creature spun around to face Ted, but not before Liz raised her slender saber and charged in.

Surrounded, Anak wasn't laughing anymore as he found himself hard pressed from five sides. Green bolts and varied spells continued to pound against his shields as he slashed with his bladed whip and danced away from saber, mace, and sword.

Together, the Heroes of Awesome closed in on the mighty nephilim.

The glowing runes on the demigod's gauntlet began to pulse with power. "Enough!" Anak boomed, and suddenly punched the ground at his feet. A wave force radiated out and slammed into the humans, knocking them all to the ground.

"This little dance has been an enjoyable distraction from the task at hand, but now it is time for you to die," Anak jeered. "But first I will take my prize."

With a flick of his wrist, black ropes appeared and quickly wrapped themselves around Emily. "Oh, no you don't!" Emily cried, as she tried to get away, but it was too late. The cords constricted and pinned her hands to her sides. Emily screamed in frustration and struggled against the bindings.

Anak turned his baleful gaze upon Liz. "Come to me my sweet," he purred seductively, and to her horror, Liz found it difficult to resist. She didn't take a step forward, but neither could she get away. Liz was locked in place, struggling to keep the nephilim's Compulsion from settling on her mind.

Mike roared and lunged at the nephilim. Jack appeared at his side and together they rushed the mighty monster. The bladed whip blocked Jack's swing, but Mike found an opening and swung his ancient mace with all his might.

The blessed weapon slammed into the nephilim's side with bone-crushing force. The pale skin charred and blackened where the mace had struck and Anak howled in pain. Where most creatures were blown back by the tremendous force of the impact, the nephilim didn't so much as budge.

Mike was caught by surprise when Anak absorbed the impact and countered with a vicious right hook. The huge armored fist rammed into his chin and the blow sent Mike reeling.

Instead of pursuing, the nephilim abruptly lashed out at Jack with his whip. The blades twisted around Jack's neck and with a vicious jerk, Anak yanked Jack off his feet.

With Mike and Jack struggling to get up, Anak turned its full attention on Ted.

Ted leveled his glowing poleaxe at the mighty creature and a brilliant red beam lanced toward it.

The nephilim's shield absorbed most of the blast, but the beam proved greater and the shield shattered under the onslaught. With Anak reeling from the loss of its shield, Ted pounced on the advantage and summoned up every ounce of power he could hold. He unleashed a tremendous barrage of magical death that completely engulfed the nephilim in fire and light.

When the last explosion ended, Ted wearily lowered his arms and sagged against his poleaxe. A swirling pattern of melted and pulverized stone ringed the prone form at its center.

A form shifted inside the burning crater and to Ted's disbelief, Anak stood, singed in several places, but very much alive.

Tendrils of dark energy gathered around the nephilim and his black eyes blazed with purple fire. "My turn," he hissed.

Between Anak's hands a ball of sparking black and purple energy formed. Power crackled and arced from the sphere, and before Ted could react the orb shot toward him. Ted had just enough time to raise his arm in a futile attempt to ward off the spell.

The black orb shattered Ted's golden shield and detonated in a brilliant explosion.

The force of the blast blew Ted backward and his broken body landed in a heap several yards away, his left arm ending in a charred stump just below the elbow.

Anak's deep laughter echoed throughout the vast chamber.

The shock of seeing Ted's mutilated body gave Liz the strength to force the nephilim's Compulsion off and she rushed to Ted's side.

The nephilim's laughter suddenly cut off. "You are strong of mind," Anak said in surprise, and then grinned wickedly. "You will make a most worthy sacrifice."

"Not today!" Mike had regained his feet and shouted as he drove hard at the mighty demigod.

Nearby Jack howled and also bound toward the nephilim, blood running down his lacerated neck.

Anak lashed out with his whip and Mike caught it with his shield. The whip wrapped around the shield and the blades bit deep. When the nephilim yanked the whip back, it tore the shield from Mike's arm and threw it at Jack.

Jack easily dodged the flying shield, but it was just a distraction. The nephilim summoned a handful of long, glowing shards and launched them as Jack dodged the shield. The shards grew as they flew, until each was several feet in length.

Too late Jack realized the danger. He was caught in mid turn when the long shards rammed into him.

The purple crystal shards pierced Jack's orcish armor as if it were paper and punched through his body. Two of the long shards pierced chest and drove him to the ground, pinning him there.

With Anak concentrating on Jack, Mike saw his opening and took it.

Mike swung the ancient mace at the nephilim's back, but just before it struck, the bladed whip wrapped around Mike's arm and jerked it to a sudden stop.

Anak spun around grinning wickedly and gave the whip a sharp tug. Mike staggered forward as a ghostly dagger of purple mist suddenly took shape in the nephilim's armored fist.

Mike struggled to break free, but the bladed whip had him caught tight.

The huge nephilim towered over Mike and smiled before he rammed the blade home.

"NO!" Liz cried, as the ghostly dagger shattered Mike's barrier and plunged into his chest. The shadowy blade burst out from his back in a shower of blood and Mike sagged in the huge nephilim's grasp.

Blood trickled out of the corner of Mike's mouth as everything went dark.

****

Liz stared in disbelief as Mike's body slid off the ghostly purple dagger and collapsed in a boneless heap at the nephilim's feet. The dagger vanished like smoke as Anak turned to Liz who was still kneeling beside Ted's ruined body.

"A valiant effort," Anak purred. "I found it most arousing." He licked his lips hungrily and strode toward her. "But now the time for play is over.

My father is waiting."

There was no subtle Compulsion this time.

Anak's black eyes blazed as he turned his full power on Liz and hammered her mind with the indomitable force of his Will. The walls around Liz's mind collapsed under the terrible assault and the nephilim bound her to him.

"You see how easy that was," he purred and Liz found herself walking toward him. He eyed her appreciatively and Liz's heart raced as the stunning nephilim inspected her. "Too bad you are needed to finish the Bore. A beauty such as yours seems like such a terrible waste," he sighed. "At least I will have one plaything." He motioned with his armored hand at Emily who was still bound in a tight cocoon.

Emily raged helplessly in her bindings as they magically lifted her off the ground and she floated over to the beckoning nephilim. "There is much fire in that one," he grinned. "She will provide much enjoyment." Only Emily's eyes were visible, but Liz saw the flash of anger there.

The gorgeous demigod turned and strode confidently through the first wall of fire that was once again a tall curtain of dancing purple flames.

Liz followed eagerly, surprised that the flames didn't burn her and delighted to be chosen for such an honor. She hoped that this magnificent being would be proud of her.

Emily thrashed in her wrappings as she floated through the flames, but they didn't harm her either. The second and third rings of flames didn't burn them either and soon they found themselves standing in the center of the elaborate symbol.

Liz was again surprised when she saw that where the floor should have been there was only a wide pit, descending to utter blackness, much like the pit the fortress itself was surrounded by. Its edges were jagged like the stones had been ripped away by some terrible force.

The mighty nephilim gazed into the heart of the darkness and began to speak in a musical tongue that Liz didn't recognize but that she found quite lovely.

A strange wind suddenly kicked up and Anak stopped his chant and looked around in confusion.

The air began to crackle with pent up energy.

The smell of ozone grew strong and then there was a deep, electrical thrum of discharging power. A brilliant flash lit the vast chamber as an arcing sphere of electrical power burst into being just outside the outer wall of flames.

The sphere vanished in a blink, leaving Liz dazed and half blind.

Anak growled deep in his throat and drew his bladed whip as three figures took shape in the smoky haze outside the purple flames.

Liz blinked away the last vestiges of the after burn and stared in wonder at the three shapes that appeared from the brilliant sphere.

One was a stocky dwarf with a great black beard and was covered from head to toe in a dark, glossy plate armor that was engraved with a dizzying array of glowing runes. His helmet was in the shape of a fearsome mask that left only his eyes and beard showing. An immense war hammer was clenched in his gauntleted fist and it, too, pulsed with runic power.

The second was a beautiful elf maiden with long blonde hair that flowed out from under a deep hood. She wore a strange suit of wonderfully elegant, emerald green armor and an ornate spear of extravagant design whose blade seemed to shimmer, rested lightly in her hand. It was not the elf or dwarf that caught Liz's attention, but the towering figure standing behind them.

With wrinkled grey skin, large ears, two long tusks and standing even taller than the mighty nephilim was an enormous elephant-man.

The elephant-man was covered in elaborate silver and gold scale armor that even covered his face and hung the length of his trunk. It was then that Liz noticed the slight swell of the chest, narrower waist and wider hips. Liz was shocked to realize that this was actually an elephant-woman!

She had wicked curved, blade caps on the ends of her ivory tusks and numerous golden hoops dangling from her large ears. Two huge, gem encrusted scimitars of exquisite craftsmanship rested comfortably in her gigantic hands.

The green-armored elf spotted the nephilim and pointed her spear at him. "There it is!" she cried. "Destroy the abomination!"

The three newcomers leapt forward and as one charged through the first wall of purple fire.

The nephilim's black eyes blazed angrily and with a roar, he rushed the newcomers.

The three warriors met the nephilim with a thunderous clash of steel and spell.

Faster than the eye could follow, the four combatants traded blows in a titanic struggle. The nephilim was outnumbered, but was far faster than any of the newcomers and was somehow keeping all three of them at bay with his flashing whip and dark sorcery.

The newcomers were holding their own, however, with every strike from the whip blocked and every dark incantation defeated. The floor shook and the air vibrated with the power of their battle.

The elf and nephilim traded spells while the elephant-woman slashed at the dancing whip with her twin scimitars. The dwarf swung his mighty hammer, but the nephilim twisted away and the floor exploded when the hammer struck.

The deadly dance continued and it soon became obvious that Anak couldn't hold out against the onslaught of these three skilled warriors and he was slowly forced back.

The demigod wrapped his whip around the elephant-woman's wrist but instead of trying to break free, the elephant-woman punched forward and her huge fist drove into the nephilim's temple.

The haze through which Liz had been viewing the battle suddenly fractured and she pounced on the opening. Liz shattered Anak's control and she was suddenly free.

Emily floated a few feet above the ground when her cocoon unexpectedly burst apart. Her shout of joy ended in a groan of pain as she landed hard on her back.

Liz helped her to her feet.

"That sonofabitch is going to pay for that," Emily hissed.

"Come on," Liz urged. "Our weapons are still out there." She motioned outside the fire ring where the bodies of their friends lay.

The combatants continued their titanic struggle as Liz and Emily rushed across the demonic symbol, through the purple fire, and finally reached their discarded weapons.

Anak had been forced back almost to the edge of the pit, but he still fought furiously, making the newcomers earn every step they took.

Liz grasped her pistol angrily and aimed at the struggling warriors, but the huge elephant-woman was blocking her view.

Emily cursed and lowered her scepter. "They are moving too fast. I can't get a shot."

"Me either," Liz snarled in disgust. But then she had an idea. She didn't need a clear shot.

The nephilim moved behind the elephant-woman's wide head again and Liz said a silent prayer as she took careful aim.

Liz pulled the trigger and the bullet sped toward the back of the battling elephant-woman's head. Using the skills learned at the range, Liz willed the bullet to move and it curved around the elephant-woman and slammed into Anak's right eye.

The eye exploded and the nephilim howled in agony. Somehow, he kept the bladed whip rotating and blocked the slashes from the elephant-woman. But the elf lunged forward and plunged her shimmering spear into Anak's chest.

The force of the thrust pushed the stricken nephilim backwards and as he slid off the blade, he tumbled from the ledge and vanished into the bottomless void.

No sooner had Anak vanished into the pit than a horrible wailing echoed out of the pit and the vast chamber began to shake. The colossal stone statues that held up the ceiling writhed in pain and fragments of stone rained down from their tormented movements.

The purple flames flared brilliantly and fountained high into the air as the euphoric giants that had remained engrossed in their blissful orgy throughout the conflict all began to convulse at once. Their eyes rolled back and foam trickled out of their mouths as the horrible wailing grew to a wild crescendo.

The giants suddenly went limp and the wailing abruptly vanished as the flames flared brightly one last time before shriveling up to a small, natural-colored flame around the edges of the symbols carved into the floor.

Darkness fell inside the chamber with most of the arcane fire that had provided the majority of the light going out.

"They did it…" Emily breathed in amazement.

Liz didn't reply, but stared numbly at the bodies of their fallen friends that lay scattered around the darkened chamber. She spotted Mike's body and rushed over to him.

When she reached him, his skin was cold and drained of all color. "No, no, no, nooo…" Liz cradled his limp head in her arms. "You aren't allowed to die on me, you great lump," she sobbed. "I won't allow it."

Golden light welled up around her hands and she forced it into Mike's broken body.

However, the huge wound in his chest didn't heal. Liz prayed and concentrated more than she ever had before, but his broken body stayed the same; cold and lifeless.

"He's gone Liz…" Emily whispered sadly.

But Liz wasn't about to give up. They had been through too much for it to end like this. Desperately Liz plunged herself into Mike's mind, searching for any kind of hope, but she found only blackness. She delved deeper, going farther than she ever had for any healing before. Liz plunged into the blackness.

She sailed through the void for what seemed like an eternity as her hope slowly faded.

There was nothing here but an empty shell.

Then she saw it.

A faint spark… not even a spark, but a ghost of a spark that was fading even as she watched.

Without thinking Liz poured her heart and soul into that spark and filled it with life.

Mike suddenly gasped and sat up.

"How did you do that?" Emily breathed in amazement.

Liz embraced Mike in a tight hug. "I have no idea," she laughed happily as Mike awkwardly returned the embrace.

"Did I miss something?" Mike mumbled wearily.

"Not much," Emily shrugged. "You just died and Liz brought you back."

"Died?" Mike mumbled. "I didn't die... I was lulling the nephilim into a false sense of security... I was just about to make my move."

"Sure, you were..." Emily snorted.

"Oh, my God!" Liz pushed Mike away and scrambled to her feet. "Jack and Ted!"

Emily grabbed her arm and held her back. "Don't worry," she laughed. "They are fine."

"But I have to heal him!" Liz argued. But when she looked to where Jack had been pinned to the floor, she saw him lying there, apparently unharmed although his eyes were still closed as the green-armored elf knelt over him.

Liz turned around and to her vast relief she saw that Ted was actually sitting up, listening to the black-bearded dwarf, but staring at the stump where his left hand had been.

"But how...?" Liz sagged and leaned into Mike, suddenly feeling exhausted and strangely lightheaded. "I was only gone a moment."

"Oh, honey..." Emily shook her head and laughed. "You were gone a lot longer than that."

A huge shape strode out of the darkness and revealed the massive elephant-woman. "While you were saving your human friend here, we were healing the others," she said with a strange accent.

"And just who the hell are you?" Mike asked.

The huge elephant-woman loomed above them. "I am called LuHark," she replied in a deep but strangely feminine voice, "and we are Wardens."

CHAPTER 30

"Wardens?" Mike mumbled as he stood up groggily with Liz's help. "I thought they didn't exist anymore."

The elephant-woman called LuHark smiled. "And so, we would have you believe."

"But why?" Emily asked.

"Because our enemies will not come looking for us if they believe we do not exist," LuHark answered. "Also, not everyone would agree with our methods, thus it is easier to operate in secret where we can do what needs to be done."

"Silence, LuHark," a gruff voice rumbled, and out of the darkness two figures appeared. The speaker was the stocky dwarf with his huge war hammer strapped to his back. Just behind him came Ted who plodded along wearily, leaning heavily on his poleaxe.

"Be at peace, Rodan," LuHark said easily. "I believe these humans can be trusted."

The dwarf called Rodan snorted. "I be glad ter hear that," he grumbled sarcastically. "Why don't ye tell 'em all our secrets while yer at it."

"I haven't told them any secrets," LuHark replied.

"Ye told 'em we be Wardens!" Rodan countered hotly.

LuHark shrugged the accusation off. "There was no point in lying to them Rodan, they would have figured it out eventually."

"I be no sure about that," Rodan rumbled. "Humans are no the sharpest o' creatures."

"Rodan!" the beautiful elf in the green armor reprimanded sharply, as she and Jack strode into the faint light of the burning rings. "Do not insult our new friends," she said as she cautiously eyed Jack.

"Oh, they be our *friends* now, eh?" Rodan growled. "And who made that decision?"

"I did," the elf retorted defiantly, "and unless I am mistaken, these are the Heroes of Awesome, who pass for champions on this world."

"Some champions," Rodan snorted. "Don't look like much ter me."

LuHark scowled down at the dwarf. "I believe Brigit is correct. They held off the nephilim for far longer than we could ever have hoped. If it wasn't for them, The Fallen may have been released and this world would have been consumed by evil."

Rodan crossed his arms over his broad chest, but seemed to relax a little. "Ye may have a point there, Hathi," the dwarf relented, "but that dun make 'em our friends."

"Wait a minute," Liz interrupted. "How do you know who we are?"

The green-armored elf named Brigit smiled. "The Wardens have eyes and ears everywhere."

"Well, if you know so much, what took you so long getting here?" Emily shot back.

"We apologize for the delay," LuHark trumpeted. "We had great difficulty reaching this place. Ever since the Barzakh was torn asunder, it has been increasingly difficult to traverse the eternal Ashvettha."

"Aye," Rodan added. "Yggdrasil's branches heave and sway as if she be caught in some vast cosmic storm."

Ted coughed. "I have a question…"

"Easy there manling," Rodan said gently, as he helped support Ted with surprising tenderness. "Ye been healed, but yer body still be weak and needs ter rest."

"How did you get here?" Ted wheezed and leaned heavily on his poleaxe.

The three Wardens exchanged looks before Rodan threw up his arms in disgust. "Fine. Go ahead n' tell em," he grumbled. "Ye don't listen ter me anyhow."

LuHark towered over them all. "We were teleported here from the Wardencliff Tower on my home world of Nibru," she answered.

"And you are a kefali, yes?" Ted asked weakly.

LuHark nodded. "I am Hathi. Have you met others of my kind?"

"Hathi, no," Liz answered, "but we have meet a few Baribal and Cyno when we fought the minotaur and Felorans."

"Ah, yes..." LuHark sighed. "I forgot the Destroyer and his irksome Isfet had been pulled to this world."

"So, you know this Destroyer?" Liz asked.

"No," the huge Hathi replied, "but as a Peacekeeper in Shambbala I fought Isfet many times before being recruited by the Wardens."

Brigit stepped forward. "You have your answer, now I have a question." She pointed to Jack. "How did this one come to possess Yoma-Ketsueki?"

"Yo-yo what?" Mike mumbled.

"Yoma-Ketsueki," Brigit repeated. "The black Muramasa blade your friend carries."

"I killed the orc that had it and then I kept it," Jack answered defensively. "But I didn't know it had a name. How do you know it?"

"I knew a warrior who carried it long ago..." Brigit looked thoughtful. "Perhaps that is the stain I detected upon your soul during the healing..."

"What do you mean a stain?" Jack growled. "I feel fine!"

"And do all you humans have such strange eyes?" Brigit replied. "Your wounds are healed along with the taint from the nephilim's shards."

"What is wrong with his eyes?" Emily asked.

The green-armored elf shrugged. "I do not know a great deal about you humans, but I do not recall any of them having golden eyes."

"Gold eyes?" LuHark trumpeted in alarm and took a step toward Jack, but Jack quickly raised his black blade threateningly. "Stay away from me," Jack growled. "I appreciate being saved and all, but do not come near me."

"But-" the huge LuHark reached out, but Brigit stepped between them.

"The human has requested he be left alone and we will honor that request," the elf said sternly.

LuHark stared down at Jack, but finally relented and stepped back.

"Can you explain this stain you found?" Liz pressed.

The elf gathered her thoughts before answering. "There is an underlying shadow upon him... something deep that is beyond my skill to heal," Brigit said apologetically. "It could be from prolonged exposure to Yoma-Ketsueki... or it could be something else entirely. I cannot say."

"But he will be fine, right?" Emily asked.

Brigit shrugged helplessly. "I cannot say. As far as I can tell he is perfectly healthy. There is only a hint of a shadow upon him. It is like his body is fighting it somehow, but I cannot determine what it is or how to remove it."

"Well, that's just wonderful..." Jack groaned.

Liz pulled Emily to her comfortingly. "Don't worry," Liz said soothingly. "We will get him out of here and to the healers. He will be fine. You'll see."

"He'd better," Emily growled. "He owes me money."

"I thought I was the one with the shadow on my soul," Jack grumbled at Liz and Emily. "Can I join the group hug?"

"In your dreams," Liz chided, and gave Emily another squeeze before addressing the three Wardens. "So, what happens now?"

"Now," Rodan answered, "yerself and yer companions will leave this corrupted castle and forget that we ever met."

"And what about you?" Liz asked.

"We will remain here," LuHark answered. "We must cleanse this vile place before we can destroy it."

"You three are going to destroy this whole floating island yourselves?" Mike asked dubiously.

"Indeed," Brigit answered confidently. "Once the gravity stones are removed, this whole construct will be swallowed by the pit below us."

"Well, of course." Mike rolled his eyes. "Why wouldn't there be *gravity stones* holding this place up?" he chuckled to himself, as he stumbled over to where his weapons lay. "I suppose you are going down with the ship then?" Mike grunted as he bent down and heaved his shield over his shoulder.

"Mike!" Liz cried. "What do you think you are doing!?"

"Taking my crap and getting out of here," Mike groaned as his legs quivered. "What does it look like?"

Liz put her fists on her hips. "You are in no condition to carry anything anywhere."

"Yes, mom," Mike grinned painfully, but didn't move to put his weapons down. He turned back to the Wardens. "You didn't answer my question."

Liz felt a strange flicker of emotion in the back of her mind, but she was too concerned for Mike to take notice.

"We should have enough time to escape before the island falls," Brigit answered.

"And then back to your world?" Mike groaned.

"No," Lu-Hark said. "Unfortunately, we are stuck here for the foreseeable future. However, there is more than one evil on this world that needs cleansed." The huge Warden looked curiously at Mike. "Why are you so concerned with what will happen to us?"

Mike sagged under the weight of his armor and weapons. "You saved our lives and I am... curious about what you do," Mike gasped. "I... have more... questions."

Brigit looked thoughtful for a moment and then nodded to herself as if she had reached some decision. "Very well." Brigit stepped forward and drew a small silver pendant from a pouch on her belt. She reached out and draped the necklace around Mike's neck. "If we can, we will find you when our duty is complete." The green armored Warden stepped back. "Now, go. All of you require healing and rest. We can take it from here."

"Ye can tell no one o' what ye've seen," Rodan rumbled. "The Order o' Wardens *must* remain a secret."

"We promise," Liz answered solemnly.

LuHark saluted by slamming a huge fist to her chest. "Farewell, humans. You did well here today. Your deeds will be recorded in the Tablet of Destinies."

The weary Heroes of Awesome stepped out into the daylight after what seemed like an eternity wandering through the dark, twisting corridors of the nephilim's castle, unsure of what they would find.

Outside, the storm had subsided, but it was still a gloomy, overcast day. The first thing Liz noticed was the silence. There were no sounds of battle, no gunshots or explosions, no lusty battle roars, nor screams of the dying.

The quiet did not bode well for the allies that Liz and her friends had abandoned in the bailey. Liz's apprehension about what they would find only grew as they made it out of the castle because there was still the warped and winding base of the castle to escape from.

Mike plowed on ahead, seemingly oblivious to the eerie silence that filled the fortress.

Liz was just about to tell Mike to slow down when they rounded another bend, like so many others, and abruptly stepped out into the bailey.

The scene that greeted the weary friends was not at all what Liz had expected.

Spread out before them was the allied army, victorious, amid the ruin and carnage of the battlefield. The huge corpses of the giants littered the ground and the smaller bodies of the demons were little more than decomposing piles of putrid flesh.

The remaining Humvees and armored vehicles had formed a defensive ring around General Adams who was shouting orders from the top of his tank while the clerics moved about the wounded that were laid out inside the circle.

Parties of humans, elves, and dwarves were scouring the ruined bailey for injured as more groups roamed the base of the twisted castle, apparently searching for a way in.

One of the scouts saw them and gave a shout.

Soon a detachment of warriors reached them and escorted the battered friends directly to the general inside the ring of vehicles.

As they made their way through the rows of dead and injured, Liz's heart sank when she spotted the body of Galina laying there in the dust.

What was she doing here? Liz wondered sadly. She had no business being in this battle after just being rescued from the Isfet camp.

Lying beside Galina was the mangled remains of another elf that Liz thought was the red-armored corpse of Darius, but the body was so mutilated that she couldn't be sure.

When The Heroes got there, General Adams was having a discussion with an ugly dwarf lord that Liz didn't recognize and Arch Battlemage Gwydion.

"So, you survived," General Adams smiled when The Heroes reached them. "I take it we have you to thank for this?" He motioned to the slaughter around them.

"What happened here?" Liz asked.

"Well, we were in a bad place there for a while," General Adams replied. "We had more of those cursed demons spilling out of more portals than I could shake a stick at and every time we got a decent force together some giant would break it up." The general looked disgusted. "I've never seen such blind rage and complete lack of self-preservation. Those filthy demons just charged us over and over until we ran out of bullets."

General Adams shook his head, remembering. "We were bogged down and completely surrounded, and I knew we were finished. But then all those portals suddenly vanished and the demons all went mad. They fought anything that was close, including the giants and each other," the general grinned. "With their reinforcements gone, we made quick work of the ugly bastards. And giants didn't stand a chance once their minions were gone. Such big targets are hard to miss."

The general sighed. "Been trying to locate all our wounded and find a way into that ugly castle there ever since. I couldn't figure out what happened, but then you five show up looking like death, so I'm guessing you had something to do with it." General Adams hopped down off his tank. "Care to fill me in?"

So, the friends explained how they had followed a giant through the hidden door and found the chamber inside the dark fortress, where the nephilim was performing a ritual that was allowing him to summon the demons. They told of their battle with Anak, but left out how the Wardens had saved them, instead claiming that they had mortally wounded the mighty being and knocked him into the pit.

"And now we must get off this floating castle at once," Liz finished.

"And why is that?" Gwydion asked politely.

"Well..." Liz muttered.

"Because with the nephilim's death, the powers holding this fortress up will fade, causing it to fall into the pit below," Ted gasped wearily.

"Hmm…" Gwydion stroked his chin thoughtfully. "I have never heard of such a Binding… but then again I have also never encountered one of the legendary nephilim either…" Gwydion turned to the general. "I say we heed their advice and remove ourselves from this vile place."

The dwarf lord snorted. "Bah! We don't know that it will fall," he argued. "I say we blast a hole with these wondrous machines o' yers and search this place fer treasure. I be willin ter bet that there be more than one trinket o' value in such a place."

"That may be," Gwydion agreed, "however, I do not wish to risk all our lives on some possible treasure that may not even exist. I maintain that we leave this place for the safety of solid ground and then wait to see if this construct does, in fact, fall."

The dwarf lord scratched his beard. "I suppose I can agree ter that," he said after some thought. "I'll give it a day, but after that, if it still be floating, me boys n' I'll be back."

"Fair enough." General Adams turned to one of his guards. "Spread the word - we are leaving."

The allied army appeared in better shape than Liz could have hoped for. As the forces gathered up and prepared to move out, Liz guessed that over two thirds of their personnel had survived the battle. The cost of victory had still been high and the loss of life made Liz sad, but she knew it could have been so much worse. Thanks to the quick work of the healers and mages, there were remarkably few casualties due to injury and the last of the wounded were back on their feet as the allied army began its slow march out of the twisted fortress.

Once the entire allied force had crossed the massive drawbridge and was safely on the other side, the majority of the army headed back to the airport while the dwarf lord and his clan remained behind to "watch fer stragglers."

Upon returning to the 911th Air Reserve Station, everyone was quickly loaded back into the troop transports and the convoy made all speed back to the safety of Pittsburgh.

They dropped the last of the dwarves off outside the Varnirborg Gate inside Mt. Washington and no sooner had the convoy returned to the Point and stopped to allow the troops to disembark than an elf scout appeared, eagerly seeking the general.

The scout found General Adams and Arch Battlemage Gwydion listening to the Heroes of Awesome retell their encounter with Anak.

"General!" The scout tried to push passed the human guards. "I have urgent news!"

"Let him through," General Adams ordered.

The scout addressed the general, but never took his eyes off the Arch Battlemage. "Some spies have returned from the west and they bring word about the Destroyer."

"And what have our spies found?" Gwydion asked.

"The Destroyer is searching for something," the scout replied. "The spies could not discover what it is he searches for, but they know that once he finds it he means to attack this city. He has commanded the destruction of the Steel City and the sacrifice of all non-kefali."

"Let us pray that he never finds what he seeks," Gwydion breathed.

"That is the other piece of news, Lord," the scout continued. "It seems that he has discovered the location of what he seeks and is heading for it as we speak."

"Our defenses are not ready for such an assault." The general looked thoughtful. "Perhaps we can distract him."

"What do you have in mind?" Gwydion asked.

"We send some of your mages with a detachment of our tanks and we harass his army and try to distract him from his goal."

"A bold plan," the Arch Battlemage replied. "But I understand that you have few of these mighty 'tanks' remaining... is it wise to risk them when we know they will be needed here?"

"It is a risk I am willing to take," General Adams replied. "If the Abrams can give us the time to finish our defenses then it is worth the risk."

"Will your tanks not be vulnerable on such a mission?" Gwydion asked.

"Yes," General Adams replied. "That is why I would have some of your most skilled Battlemages go with them to keep them hidden and provide protection if needed."

Arch Battlemage Gwydion nodded. "That can be arranged."

While the general and Arch Battlemage discussed their new plans, a strange-looking elf appeared and made his way through the departing volunteers and approached Liz and her friends.

The elf was dressed in fine leather armor and had dark green hair with a pair of small antlers poking out above his ears. As he got closer Liz recognized him as one of Emily's Druid instructors, Rubadub, she thought his name was.

"Thank the Mother I found you!" Rubadub cried, as he approached Emily. He slunk forward and looked uncomfortable being around so many people. "We must leave at once!"

"Leave?" Emily balked. "But I just got back."

"And now you will be going," Rubadub replied. "We have been given a most important mission by the Archmage himself."

"What mission is that?" Emily asked suspiciously.

"Archmage Talsin has instructed us to travel south and discover the identity of this mysterious shadow army that we have been hearing about," Rubadub replied hastily. "Now we must be going. We are already late."

A sudden commotion around the general caused them all to turn.

"The orcs have done what!?" General Adams exclaimed.

"It is true, Lord," the elf scout said. "An orc warband has subjugated several other warbands and has nearly tripled in number. They also have enslaved numerous tribes of goblins and have taken control of some factories several days march east of here."

General Adams ran his hand through his short black hair. "What could they want with a bunch of old factories?"

"Perhaps nothing," said Gwydion. "They may have discovered the factories were supplying us with materials and so they took them."

"Or it is merely a coincidence," Mike offered, although even he didn't really believe it.

General Adams shot Mike a condescending look and Mike shrugged helplessly. "I doubt it, too, but it could be possible," he added.

"I know," the general sighed, "but that was not the news I wanted to hear. We needed those factories for their steel and we cannot afford to send a strike force to take them back now that we know this Destroyer plans to attack us."

Liz didn't like the sound of any of that. "Well, Em, I don't think you should be going-" Liz started to say, but when she turned around she didn't see Emily anywhere. "Emily?" She looked all around, but there was no sign of her or Rubadub.

"They're gone!" Liz cried. "He took her! We have to go after them!"

"And go where exactly?" Mike replied calmly. "Can you walk through trees and talk to birds to find what direction they went?" Before Liz could answer Mike rolled on. "No, you can't. But what we *can* do is get Jack and Ted to the Healers Tent."

"I don't need no stinkin' healers," Jack grumbled, as Ted stared numbly at the stump where his left hand had been.

"But he *took* her," Liz argued, completely ignoring Jack. "And what if the healers can't help Jack?"

"I'm *not* going," Jack growled, but the other two continued to ignore him.

"They will both be fine," Mike grunted, as he heaved his gear into the bed of a waiting truck. "The healers will fix Jack up and those crazy Druid brothers will take care of Emily. And if this Destroyer does come after this city, then Emily may be safer than we are."

Although she hated to admit it, Liz had to agree that Mike did make a good point. But to have Emily snatched away so soon after their battle with the nephilim had left her feeling out of sorts.

Liz finally turned to Jack, but found that he, too, was gone.

She looked around in confusion. "Now, where the hell did he run off to?"

Mike chuckled until he saw the look on Liz's face and he put a comforting arm around her. "Don't worry," he smiled reassuringly. "Everything will turn out fine."

She snuggled into him and let his presence reassure her.

"I know," Liz whispered softly. But deep inside she wasn't so sure.

EPILOGUE

The setting sun painted the sky with brilliant shades of red and orange and the rolling hills were cloaked in shadows as the darkness crept in.

When the last rays of sunlight faded away and the skies grew dark, the shadows in one remote valley began to move.

The shadows shifted and seven hooded figures materialized out of the darkness.

"What is the meaning of this assembly?" one of the figures demanded angrily. "Who dares to summon the Lord of the Nightlands?"

Another of the hooded figures stepped forward and pulled down their hood revealing what had once been a stunningly beautiful elf woman. But now her skin clung to her bones like some starved corpse and her eye sockets glowed with an evil green light.

The other figures recoiled in surprise and the woman's fleshless lips cracked in a cruel smile. "I did," the skeletal elf woman replied softly.

"M-Mistress Sabine!" the cloaked figure that had spoken first stammered. "My apologies, Great Mistress, I was unaware of your presence on this world."

"Now, you are aware," the skeletal Mistress Sabine sneered before addressing the gathering as a whole. "Your pathetic attempt to work together has failed," she hissed. "From now on you will all answer to me."

The hooded figures shifted uneasily, but none made any move to object.

"Good," Sabine hissed. "Now, there will be no more of this mindless wandering. We have a few more... *allies* to gather before we march."

One of the hooded figures finally found the courage to speak. "Great Mistress, we have not been 'mindlessly wandering.' We have discovered that the Blood Rite can be performed on these humans and we have succeeded in creating a great host of risen," the figure said. "What other allies could we possibly need?"

"The Chosen do not make alliances," another of the hooded figures snarled, and other voices were raised in agreement.

"That is so," the skeletal woman's soft voice silenced the others, "but I am above the Chosen and the agreements have already been made."

The hooded figures muttered angrily at this announcement and one of them spoke up. "And what allies are these, Great Mistress? And where are we to march?"

"Ahh," Sabine hissed. "While you have been mindlessly wandering, I have brokered an agreement with those furry zealots and their leader that calls himself the Destroyer, as well as the dull greenskins and their chieftain, some Stormtusk creature."

"Kefali!" one of the figures wailed. "We cannot make common cause with such creatures! They are more treacherous than our blind brethren! And the orcs are little more than mindless beasts." The others sounded their agreement and Sabine let their complaints wash over her.

"All you say is true," Sabine hissed. "However, the prize is worth the indignity of such a temporary alliance."

"What prize could be worth such a thing?" a hooded figure growled.

Sabine looked around at those gathered around her allowing the green light of her eyes to bore into each of them in turn. "I have discovered the location of one of the Seals."

The gathered shadows gasped in surprise.

"Impossible," one of the figures argued. "The Seals are protected by the Druids on Gaea."

Sabine's eyes flashed angrily. "Not this one," she hissed. "To our great fortune, it is located just north of our present location near what my spies call the Steel City."

"The Steel City is protected by not only the humans and their strange weapons, but also by our blind brethren and an army of those mongrel dwarves," one of the figures spat in disgust.

"And that is where the kefali and orcs come in," Sabine grinned wickedly. "We let them do the fighting for us, and while the defenders are distracted, we will find and destroy the Seal." The skeletal elf woman's eyes blazed with power. "Once the Seal is broken, the first of the Eternal Harbingers will finally be released and we will be there, ready to serve Lord Radamanthas upon his coming." The gathered figures muttered eagerly as she spoke. "With one of the Harbingers at our head, we will be unstoppable."

The gathered figures roared their approval, but one of them stepped forward. "A sound plan Mistress," the hooded Lord of the Nightlands nodded, "but these humans are not to be underestimated. My spies tell me that a group of humans from this Steel City just killed one of the Blessed Nephilim."

The skeletal woman was taken aback. "*Humans* killed one of the Blessed? How is that possible?"

"I do not know, Great Mistress," the figure replied. "All I know is that this small band of humans call themselves the Heroes of Awesome."

"This is alarming news... perhaps I have misjudged these humans..." Sabine looked thoughtful. "These... Heroes of Awesome must be eliminated before we strike. We cannot allow anything to keep us from destroying the Seal."

The figure bowed. "I will see it done."

"Good," Sabine's eyes flashed eagerly.

The hooded figure began to move away, but the skeletal woman hissed "But that is not all. There is one more ally that I wish for you to meet and he does not like to be kept waiting." She turned away and motioned with a skeletal hand for the others to follow. The hooded figures silently obeyed and seven shadows moved through the dark forest without a sound.

The skeletal elf flew across the ground like a ghost until she came to rest at the edge of a large clearing. By now, night had fully fallen and the sky was awash with twinkling stars.

Sabine and her six shadows waited in the darkness of the trees.

They didn't have to wait long.

The trees all around them began to rustle as a sudden wind picked up. Above the clearing, stars winked out as something huge blotted out their light. More stars vanished as the black shape drew closer and the air shook with the powerful beat of enormous wings.

All of the stars above the clearing disappeared as a vast blackness filled the sky. The gale grew stronger and the trees swayed wildly as they were buffeted by strong gusts of wind, yet the seven shadows remained untouched by the tempest.

An enormous shape fell from the sky and landed with a tremendous crash in the clearing. The earth shook from the mighty impact as the stars returned to the sky.

The dark shape rose up and dark green scales tipped with red glowed in the moonlight. Massive arms and legs tipped with wicked claws protruded from the long serpentine body and dug long furrows in the soft earth.

Enormous, leathery wings folded up along its back as a long, barbed tail swayed through the air. Huge, golden eyes glittered coldly in the moonlight as they looked down on the gathered shadows.

"A Great Wyrm…" one of the shadows breathed in awe.

"Yes," Sabine's eyes blazed hungrily. "This is mighty Phlebolith, the Blightwing."

The huge dragon bowed his enormous, horned head slightly in acknowledgment. "Greetings, Mistress Sabine," the dragon's deep voice boomed. "I trust these are the Chosen you spoke of?"

"Indeed, Mighty Phlebolith," Sabine answered. "Does our agreement still stand?"

The glittering eyes narrowed as the huge dragon glared at the gathered shadows. After a tense moment, the dragon reached his decision. "It does," Phlebolith thundered.

"Very good," Sabine hissed. "Then I have someone I would like you to meet."

The dragon looked curious as the skeletal elf turned and beckoned to one of the hooded figures behind her. "Come forward Lord Udak."

One of the shadows detached itself and stepped forward. The figure lowered its hood, revealing a handsome, dark-skinned elf male.

"Yes, Mistress?" said Lord Udak.

Sabine's eyes danced wickedly. "You were once considered the greatest Dragon Rider of the Age, were you not?"

"That is so, Mistress," Lord Udak answered stiffly.

The skeletal elf woman's eyes blazed. "How would you like to be so again?"

"I have desired nothing more since my banishment," Lord Udak replied, "but I do not know how this will aid us."

The huge dragon's eyes narrowed dangerously and Lord Udak quickly added. "I mean no disrespect to you, Mighty Phlebolith, but these humans have strange flying machines and powerful weapons that travel great distances. One dragon will be overwhelmed, even one as magnificent as you, Great One."

"Do not fear, Chosen," Phlebolith boomed. "I do not come alone, for I command a Flight of my brethren and together we will aid you in claiming this new world for your own."

The corpse-like Mistress nodded in approval. "Lord Udak, will you lead this Flight in the name of the Shadow?"

Lord Udak smiled, revealing brilliant white teeth with extremely long canines. "It would be my pleasure."

THE END...

About the author

N. J. Colesar enjoys ancient history, mythology,
playing games, and painting miniatures.
Raised in Clearfield, Pennsylvania, N. J. Colesar currently
resides in Pittsburgh with his wife and children.

N.J. COLESAR

BIRTH OF LEGENDS

STEEL CITY SERIES: BOOK 3

STEEL CITY SERIES

THE SHEARING
ORIGINS OF MYTH
BIRTH OF LEGENDS

Keep an eye out for more DarkEnergy novels!

AUTHORS WANTED

Entanglement Interactive is looking for
new and experienced authors to help us expand
the ever-growing DarkEnergy universe!

No experience? No problem!
We love to hear from first time authors.

INTERESTED?
Visit: **www.entanglement-interactive.com/submissions**
OR
Email: **submissions@entanglement-interactive.com**